THE CAVE DWELLER

BETTINA VICTORIA

SBP

SOLITUDE BOOK PUBLISHERS

Also by Bettina Victoria:

The Witch Haunting

CONTENTS

PART ONE

PROLOGUE

It was somewhere deep inside the cave, lived a creature and he dwelled amongst the shadowed stalagmites and stalactites. He echoed nibbling noises and they drifted over the flatworms wriggling in the moistened clumps of green moss coated over the dilapidated stones. He drooled yellow saliva from the corner of his mouth, while he chewed on a long forgotten bone. The Creature nibbled on the marrow and chiselled bits to the ground, beside his large, furry foot. He moved down a tunnel and stood in the hollow entrance at the edge of the cave, staring beyond the precipice and he inhaled the warm summer air and the stench from the swamp, lofting in his direction. The leafy vegetation afar was shrivelled from the heat and the sulphurous, yellow mist looming on the ground amongst the tussock grasses. The Creature glared at the sunlight widening in the clouds and he scampered back into the shadows, despising the faint, golden glow formed on the floor and reflecting from the rugged wall. He leapt into the shadows and disappeared into a fissure. He trudged down the tunnel and caught the scent of something he hadn't discovered before.

It was beneath the shade of the leafy palm trees, Ernst Harford, the speleologist shifted past the shrubs and picked up a twig from the ground. He was thirty five and brunette, wearing a loose brown shirt with a green vest of pocketed tools and pants with beige, laced boots. Ernst shifted past a black snake slivering in the tussock grasses and listening to the chirrups of the birds, he hurried through the archway of the cave into the passage. Ernst smelt the fresh air thinning into crushed dust lingering in-between the walls. He stepped into a deserted cavern with small and long stalagmites and inflamed the twig with a matchstick.

Crinch crunch.

Ernst swiped around and lifted the inflamed stick to the shadowed archway in

9

the rocky wall. The dust and sweat drizzled down his forehead and cheeks.

"I know there's an odd specimen in here," he mumbled, shifting the firelight in the opposite direction.

Crackle.

Ernst shifted to the north and strode towards the passage.

A fleet of bats dropped from the ceiling and soared from the stalactites over him. He swiped the firelight amongst them and hurried around the beige limestone stalagmites.

The bats flew further away into another opening into a passage.

Why were they flying in the opposite direction? wondered Ernst.

Crackle.

Ernst followed the noise to behind the boulders and listened to it fade from behind the flowstone. He approached the dark archway and bowing downward, he lowered the firelight and inspected the tight tunnel.

"Nothing is in here," he said.

Ernst sighed and stood, shifting his back to the arch and looked at the deserted cavern.

The Creature appeared in the arch and opened his picket-toothed mouth and sunk them into the back of his boot. He echoed a yell, dropping the inflamed stick and collided onto the ground and was dragged backward into the tunnel. The leather-bound diary toppled on the mound of dust. He sunk his fingertips into the dirt and rolled the rubble beneath his palms and he yelled. The Creature echoed a loud growl and it soared through the tunnels to the entrance of the cave. The alligators swimming in the swamp all looked up and the growl faded in the daylight.

CHAPTER ONE

ABOARD

I was seventeen when I found the neglected, ochre-walled cave and stepped through the shadowed entrance to follow my urge of exploration. I was unaware of the danger lurking around the limestone stalagmites. It all started in the sweltering hot summer, when the thickets had withered in the plains. Clarence Morley, my brother was sixteen years old and had just completed school to commence his holidays. It was one afternoon, after completing my fishing for the day, I hung the netting over my shoulder and leaked watery driblets onto the footpath and observed the placard near the pier. *The Admiral Baltic* was seeking a rigger and cabin boy to join aboard. I peered back to the moor. Clarence wrapped the dank hawser on the oak post and the boat bobbed on the ocean. He clutched the oak oars and strode across the pier and approaching closer, he looked at the placard.

"Do you want to sail ashore?" I asked.

"Leave?" asked Clarence.

"Yeah," I said.

"What about our mother?" he asked.

"Well, I'm going to be eighteen soon in December," I said.

"She's not going to like it," warned Clarence.

At the evening hour of seven, the drone echoed from the clock throughout the hallway and kitchen. Mrs.Patricia Morley was a fifty-eight-year-old woman. She resembled my brother with dark brown hair and with wrinkles stretched from the corner of her emerald eyes. She wore a light blue, linen dress with beige hosiery and brown, leather shoes. Mrs. Morley washed a few plates beneath the water gushing from the pewter tap and lowered them onto the toiled cloth spread on the sink. Mr. Roger Morley sat on the couch reading the outspread newspaper.

He wore a pair of spectacles with a maroon shirt over a pair of trousers and was intrigued by the article of *The Missing Speleologist*. Clarence and I sat on the table with roast mutton simmering coils of mist and green beans on our plates, with a loaf of sliced bread and dab of yellowy butter on a saucer in front of the ornate candelabra. The tawny-yellow silhouettes flickered on the yellow wainscoting on the walls and the tension drifted in the silence.

"I want to try working on a ship as a rigger," I said. "The vastness of the ocean and being high on the rigging to feel the winds of freedom excite me."

"*Douglas Morley*, you know rigging is dangerous," disapproved Mrs. Morley. "What if you were to topple from the fore-mast because of the ocean winds and the sails?"

"I won't," I said, with a groan.

Mr. Morley lowered the newspaper.

"It's too dangerous," he agreed, rising from the cushioned armchair and sat down at the oak table.

"It's not, I'm sure I'd be trained to fix the rigging and alter the direction of the sails," I argued.

"Douglas, I don't like it and I fear for your safety," she said.

Mr. Morley served himself a spoonful of potatoes from the bowl onto his plate and then cut a piece of mutton.

"Well, it's quite risky," he disapproved, while forking the potato and sliced it in half and after a swallow, he continued, "However, if you're trained well, you shouldn't fall."

"What about being a cabin boy?" asked Clarence. "This is being on the deck."

Mrs. Morley lifted the tablecloth from the sink and folded it with annoyance. She flattened it across her waist and lowered it to the bench. Her discontentment drifted in the silence. Clarence and I exchanged a glance with each other over the candlelight. Mr. Morley caught us and we quickly continued to eat our dinner. Mrs. Morley exhaled and she clamped her lips for a moment, lost within her own indecisiveness. She tread away and looked out of the window to the sea. I leant my shoulders against the chair and tried to calm myself.

"Please?" I continued to argue. "I want to ask the captain for permission to board!"

"Patricia, they're old enough now," said Mr. Morley. "They'll be fine ashore."

"Alright! Go!" exclaimed Mrs. Morley, looking at me. "You better return back here safe from the voyage. If you tumble from the foremast, don't blame me and I attempted to warn you!"

The next day, we trampled back onto the peer and strode up the ramp with our parchment.

Captain Albert Wilshire stood amongst the sailors and inspected the barrels of crimson apples being loaded aboard. He was a brunet man in his late thirties, with a fleet of silvery strands, hidden in his tresses above his ears. I observed he wore a navy coat with golden epaulettes and a white waistcoat overlapping his cotton shirt tucked inside his loose-fitted linen breeches, with a pair of black, leather shoes.

"Hi, sir," I said, feeling nervous. "I'd like to be the rigger, according to the placard and my brother, the cabin boy,"

Captain Albert scrutinized me and he attained our parchments from us.

"Do you have rigging experience?" he asked.

"No, though, I'm willing to learn," I said.

"Me too," added Clarence.

"Welcome aboard," said Captain Albert. "We're voyaging a couple days from now at six thirty in the morning. You best be here earlier before this time to be shown around aboard on the ship."

"Thank you, sir!" I exclaimed, smiling.

Clarence and I shook his hand and we hurried down the pier.

It was at dawn and the early hour of five thirty, on the fifth of July, we dressed into our dark brown and light grey, napped wool caps, a white, linen shirt and a pair of crinkled trousers. It was after lacing our brown-leather shoes, I hadn't packed much in my beige canvas bag, only a hardcover notepad for writing at sea, an ink canister, a pouch of plankton and coiled fishing wire, a calligraphic pen, a piece of bread wrapped in a crinkled cloth and my bronze eyeglass from the hardware store. My silver compass with my initials engraved on the lid with a crimson apple was nestled into my pocket. I strode out of our front, oak door. At six o'clock, my brother and I, carried our bulgy, canvas bags on our shoulders and stepped further onto the peak of the lush slope, looking out to the vastness of the ocean. It was to the west, the white lighthouse arisen on the boulders, shone a mild shaft of light onto the subtle waves and froth for any inbound ships. It was early at this morning hour, the streets were deserted in our city, Half-Moon Bay, California. I strode down the dirt path amongst the wild thickets, swishing in the windy gusts. A few smoky coils drifted from the stout, ash-speckled chimneys of the bakery, where fresh loaves were cooking in the hearth of the ovens. It was further away, the other stores were deserted.

I neared closer to the end of the slope and stopped, pointing to the distance. *"There's the ship!"* I exclaimed.

Clarence stopped beside me and looked opposite the road. *The Admiral Baltic* was anchored nearby the pier at Pillar Point Harbor and fog careened on the stern. It was square-rigged with sturdy masts augmented towards the drifting, grey clouds, with a round foretop and thick, futtock shrouds. I lifted the corner of my mouth into a subtle beam and watched the sails being unfurled from the rigger.

"We're finally leaving!" exclaimed Clarence, side-glancing at me and smiled.

"It has felt like this morning would never come." I confessed.

"Me neither," admitted Clarence, looking further out at the bowsprit poking through a cloud of fog and drenched with trickles of seawater. "Do you think everyone will like us?" He tightened his grip around his taupe pouch on his shoulder and the packed tomato soup cans clinked against his steel, fishing hooks. "I admit, I'm nervous about being the Cabin Boy."

"Don't worry, you'll be fine," I said. "Come on, let's cross over to there."

Clarence and I, descended the last of the slope and I inhaled a whiff of the icy, salty air and soggy seaweed, waiting for my brother. We strode onto the footpath and crossed the road to Pillar Point Harbor, nearing the moored ships. Clarence and I, veered onto the pier, creaking the planks with stubbed, iron nail heads and tread passed the oak posts with slouching, dank ropes. I inhaled the whiffs of the sour and salted ocean air, trying to calm my nerves. I observed the sailors ascending the ramp and carrying cargo onto the deck of the ship. The pale mist lurked from the rippling, deep sapphire ocean and surrounded the stern. The closer I came to the oak ramp to board, the more my nerves twisted in a knot inside my stomach. I subtly beamed following him and tread closer to the ramp and the crowd of sailors. I gazed down at the cargo and the bronze engraving of *Silver Ore 1877*, illumined from the beacon stretched from the lighthouse and it ascended the ramp to the opening of the bulwark and onto the deck. There would be five hundred tons aboard to be delivered to the port of Eastern Europe. I tangled my pocket watch's chain around my finger and strode behind them, listening to the cacophony of their heavy thudding boots and the water plashed to the edge. It was every morning for that past few months, when my brother and I had caught fish, we had never seen ships hauling barrels of silver ore. I suppose *The Admiral Baltic*, the merchant ship also delivering other crates of cargo would be the first one from Half Moon Bay to embark on such a sea route. We waited for a few more men to pass, rolling the barrels up and we tread behind them, through the spacious gap in the bulwark.

"Welcome aboard boys," greeted Captain Albert, shaking our hands. "I'm glad to see you've arrived early."

"Thank you, sir," I said.

I watched another man stride past and he halted beside him.

"This is Quinn Finley. Show them, where they'll be sleeping amongst the seaside," demanded Captain Wilshire.

"Yes, Captain," answered Quinn, nodding and deflected his attention to us. "Come on boys, this way."

We followed him across the deck, where some of the riggers were already adjusting the shrouds on the whipping sails and a few others were steering the oak capstan by clutching the slender oak poles. I noticed a small group were pointing at the bowsprit and skimmed the air with their finger towards the ocean, discussing the intentional sailing route. Quinn stopped at the old, oak hatch with a wrought-iron ringlet and slender plates, stubbed with round, nail-heads. He bowed, hauling it upwards and it bounced onto the deck. Quinn pointed his finger down to the narrow, slanted staircase immersed with silhouettes. Clarence flicked his gaze at me, and it shone with contempt in the dimmed, guttering candle-flame. I knew he was offended, assuming the gesture was insolent, and it suggested we were as bulgy, potato sacks.

"Well?" retorted Quinn. "What are you waiting for now?"

"Yes, sir," I said, quickly.

I conceded to his direction and I stepped onto the creaking, oak plank and inhaled a whiff of the salty ocean air, knowing I was going to regret it. The silhouettes in the storeroom engulfed my shoulders and pouch. I was relieved to hold the slanted railing and loathed the rickety boards beneath every descending footstep. My stomach sunk into a pool of gloom and the buoyancy, as golden sunlight in my chest vanished into deep, grey clouds of disappointment. A rat scurried from the huddled, canvas pouches with potatoes and elm barrels filled with ale and short-stalked, crimson apples packed in oak-wood cartons. I assumed for the scullery there were bottled, tomato sauce in crates. Clarence tread from the last board, hindering behind me and his demeanour reeked of preparing to announce his dispute.

"Oh, seriously…" he trailed, gazing at the rat's tail swaying in mid-air between the pouches and disappearing within them. "*Sir-*," he turned, awkwardly tugging the back of his hat onto his dark-brown locks. "There has to be a mistake."

"Nope," he said, dusting his hands gathered from the railing and rubbed them on the side of his crinkled, linen trousers. "This is where you'll be sleeping for the journey."

"*What?*" disputed Clarence. I shifted my attention away from the pouches and widened my eyes, imploring for him to calm himself, though he didn't, "We *are* a part of the crew," he frowned. "We deserve cabins and beds-I'm going to be the cabin boy-,"

"Precisely," snapped Quinn. "Cleaning the cabins, not sleeping in them."

"But-," argued Clarence.

"*Clarence,*" I hissed, overriding him.

"I want to talk immediately to the captain," demanded Clarence, ignoring me. He glanced back to the pouches with a moth whirling around them. "I refuse to sequester here for the *entire* journey!"

"Clarence, *please*," I urged, becoming embarrassed and annoyed he wasn't carrying not even a remnant of diplomacy, despite we were going to be on the ship for months with the entire crew. Clarence glared at me, astonished I was urging him to behave different and I wasn't arguing with him. I eyed the man, "I apologize for my brother's inconvenience."

"No, I *don't* apologize," stated Clarence, with a scowl. "I want a pillow, blanket and bed every night, after my hard work every day."

Quinn chuckled mockingly. "Well, you're not going to have one. They're for all of the older crew that have assigned themselves earlier, though, we were desperate for a cabin boy and I suppose there isn't room, other than down here for both of you." he said.

"My brother is a rigger, sir!" quarreled Clarence.

"Clarence!" I whispered. "*Stop*."

"Well you could leave the ship, if you want too?" suggested Quinn, treading backward to the staircase. He clutched the railing and ascending the steps, he shifted through the daylight beam onto the deck. "*Too bad, boys*."
We both watched him tread onto the deck.

"Why did you be against me?" asked Clarence, side-glancing at me. He lifted his hat from his ruffled hair and scrunched it in his clasp. "I *refuse* to be mistreated by anyone. We're going to work hard on the ship and just because we're poor, doesn't imply we're potato sacks!"

"*Clarence*," I hissed. "You need to accept sometimes a situation won't be as you want it to be. If they don't respect us, we could pace away from the ship now if we wanted too. However, there wouldn't be point in having prepared and waited to board."

"Fine, we'll stay. *If* they cross the boundary, I refuse to stay quiet. This is already worse enough." believed Clarence.

"It'll be only at night-time, we have to sleep here," I reminded him. "It's unless we're advised of something else," I held his shoulder. "Stop worrying. It's during the day, we'll be doing our assigned duties and it won't be forever, sleeping down here amongst the shadows and surrounded with bulgy potato sacks."

"Fine, Douglas," conceded Clarence, surrendering to my perspective and dropped his bulgy sack to the floor, blowing whirls of dust. He still had his abhorrent demeanour of the situation and he tread to the staircase, grasping the slender railing. "Come on, let's step out of here and back into the fresh air."

I lowered my own pouch to the floor beside his own ransack and followed him back out onto the deck. The ramp was removed, and the sails billowed. Theodore Thurstan, the helmsman held the poking handles and stood in front of the oak wheel. He was a short, blonde-haired man dressed in a loose, soft-beige, linen shirt covered over his green trousers and with a pair of leather, brown boots. We tread past the thick shrouds quivering in the vagrant drafts and inhaled the fresh, salty air and we listened to the waves plashing on the stern. The wrought iron anchor drenched with drizzling seawater and soppy threads of seaweed was lifted by the boatswain, setting *The Admiral Baltic* free to exploration. We halted along the middle of the main deck. I leant my elbows onto the bulwark. I stared afar at Half Moon Bay, the city, I had lived with comfort in for over a decade and my hair tousled onto my ears.

"You're not sad to be leaving, are you?" asked Clarence, noticing I was lost in my own reverie.

"No," I confessed, sliding my elbows backward and clutched the bulwark. "I wouldn't want to stay here, it's much too boring." I strode around the forecastle deck, gazing out to the blue sea. The warm sunlight widened through the rift between the puffy white clouds and twinkling specks appeared on the ripples of the ocean. "I want to wander too places I've never seen before and sail out to sea not knowing what will come." I glanced back to Half Moon Bay and the piers in the far distance. "If I had stayed, I wouldn't see anything and nothing would've changed."

I rolled my sleeves to my elbows.

"That's the way," stated Clarence, slapping my shoulder impressed.

I felt everyone I had known, seemed to be of the shadowed past and a reflection of the crinkled sails. I shifted my back to Half Moon Bay, leaving it far behind in the looming shadow of the ship and stared out at the ocean awaiting me.

CHAPTER TWO
MEETING NORA

It was a few days later on the tenth of July at midday, while I lowered the course rigging ropes, I noticed a girl on the deck. She strode into the shaft of warm, golden sunlight, glistening through the rift in the pale clouds and onto the forecastle deck, peering ashore at the ocean. I unfurled the fore-topsail downward and it swelled in the gusting sea winds. I had swung across on the ropes from the foretop to reach the spar and staring ahead, the bowsprit pioneered across the vastness of the North Pacific Ocean. Somehow, my eyes were fixated to her and an attraction, I had never felt at first sight was irrevocable. Her dark black hair tousled on her shoulders and surprisingly, she wasn't wearing a cotton gown with a hem tousling on her ankles and laced leather, high-heeled shoes. She wore a white, linen shirt with a pair of crinkled trousers with a wrapped fawn-beige belt on her waist and heavy dark-brown boots. She strode past a few sailors bundling the dank netting from the plashes of sea water hurling over-night, from the stormy winds. I was nudged in the arm by another rigger and snapped out of my daze, turning back to him. Leighton Levaire was nineteen with dark-ash blonde curls and they breezed on his forehead and a few strands flicked across his piercing, light blue eyes. He was more experienced at rigging and had been aboard longer, than both of us. He wore a woolen waistcoat over a white cotton shirt and a pair of black breeches with knee-height dark brown, leather boots. The taupe belt wrapped around his waist held a sheathed steel scabbard with a bronze hilt. It was two days earlier, I heard whispers he had Irish descent and been a merchant sailor aboard on a few other ships, previously to this voyage and sailed all-over the North and South Atlantic Ocean and even on a whaling ship, for a candle company seeking more tallow. Yesterday, we had observed a few trevally fishes, swimming beneath the distant ripples of water, though, there wasn't one poking, deep-navy fin anywhere today.

"You should stop day-dreaming, and return back to work," snapped Leighton. "We have to keep to the sailing route of the ship."

"Alright," I conceded. "I'm sorry, I didn't have enough sleep last night."

"Sure, you did." said Leighton, returning me a glare of disbelief and he looked to the girl on the forecastle deck and back to me. He rustled the edge of the sail, feeling uncomfortable. "You're best not to be involved with her."

"Why?" I asked, keen to know more of the girl and the rope knocked into my knee. My bronze compass dangling from a chain, swung forward from my chest and into the buttons of my linen shirt.

"She's the captain's daughter," revealed Leighton, tousling the mainsail and peered up at the augmenting oak mainmast and flicked his glare back to me. "You would be wise to continue *only* with your orders."

"Yes, I will." I said, swallowing and nodded with his warning.

I turned my back to him and looked at her trying to be secretive, not wanting anyone else to notice, while I tugged on the rope and coiled it on my hand. She wouldn't notice me anyway, I was just the rigger boy. I was distracted with my brother treading out of the headquarters, carrying an oak bucket and a toiled cloth draped on his shoulder flapped on his back. Clarence halted a few steps away from the capstan and thumped the bucket onto the deck, spilling runnels of water onto the floorboards. He sighed and dunked the cloth into the soppy water, with floating, white bubbles and froth and he slapped it onto the deck and scrubbed. I swung on the rope and thudded back onto the deck, quivering the board he was cleaning, and he looked up, recognizing my shoes.

"Leave me alone," grumbled Clarence, wiping the mold around the iron nail-head and his curls ruffled in the sea draft. His fingers squeezed into the cloth, leaking trickles of water into the oak floorboards. "I don't want to talk, and we'll be separated anyway."

"Cheer up," I said, looming my shadow over him.

"No," disputed Clarence, stubbornly and looked up. "I don't know what we were thinking to assign ourselves here."

I quickly glanced at the other shouting sailors and knelt the deck, nudging him in the arm and he groaned.

"What?" he asked, stopping his scrubbing of the floorboards. "Don't you understand I have to finish this by the afternoon?"

"Do you know that girl?" I asked, looking at the front of the forecastle. "Have you spoken to her?"

"Who?" he blurted, gaging the sailors and glanced back to me. "I don't see her anywhere."

"She's on the forecastle deck," I whispered into his ear, trying to maintain my secrecy and looked back at Leighton standing on the shrouds, with his back to us. I quickly side-glanced at Nora. "There."

A few sailors moved aside swinging their coarse netting and flicked it on the front of their crumpled, brown linen trousers, revealing her on the forecastle deck.

"*Oh*," gasped Clarence, looking back at her. "Why?"

"I was just curious," I said, smirking.

"Hey!" yelled Leighton, noticing we were talking between ourselves.

"It's alright, I'm coming," I said, turning around and looked back down to my brother. "I'll see you tonight."

Clarence nodded.

For the remainder of the afternoon, I continued rigging and kept wondering of the girl, every day for the week. Our voyage steered in the blustery winds, raging the sides of the ship, as she sailed further and after several days later, the temperature amongst the North Pacific Ocean, became cold. I labored day after day on deck, until my calves ached, and my fingers became calloused. It was amongst the week, I thought of the girl every day and kept searching the deck to notice her. One afternoon, on the fifteenth of July, carrying an oak fishing rod with a baited hook of plankton, I climbed over the bulwark and yearning to be alone, I nestled on the poking, black canon. The ship was sailing at a slowed pace and the rudder was gliding through the water, splashing froth aside. I yawned and leant against the ship, pulling out some bait from my hessian bag, and slid it onto the hook and lowered the wire into the ocean, leaning my head on the boards. The cheese, honey-ham and biscuits were all finished in the tin. Some of the straw-berry jam was still in the glass jar and the crimson apples were always be crunched on in the shadows.

"What are you doing down there?" echoed a feminine voice, from above.

I cringed, not expecting anyone to appear and the spare piece of wire slid out of my fingers, splashing into the ocean. I looked up to see the girl with disheveled, dark curls nestled on her shoulders. She held the bulwark and simpered at my astonished gaze.

"I-was-," I stammered, glancing down at the swinging hook and curled the wire around my fingers and looked back up. "-fishing,"

"Why?" she asked. "Isn't the fish in the scullery enough?"

"I was just bored and wanted to have a break from my chores on deck."

She gestured towards the wire and asked, "Have you caught anything?"

"Uh-," I looked down to the ocean, awkwardly, trying to hide I was blushing. "-no, not yet."

"You know you can be in a lot of trouble, if you stay down there," she said.

"I know," I echoed.

"Why do it?"

"I'm tired and bored," I answered. "You know what's it like after having to alter the rigging all day."

"Aren't your hands sore?" she asked.

"They are," I admitted, nodding.

"Well, why risk falling into the ocean?" she asked, with confusion lifting in her tone.

"You ask a lot of questions," I mumbled, squinting in the sunlight and a few, hazelnut-brown tresses smeared on my brows from the clammy sweat.

"I have a lot I want to know," she said.

"You do?" I asked, slowly.

It was somehow strange, how she even cared to know anything about me. I was flattered.

"What is your name?" she asked.

"I'm Douglas Morley, and yourself?" I introduced, squinting in the sunlight and it warmed onto my cheeks.

"Nora Wilshire," she revealed, leaning over the bulwark with her tousled, dark hair curtaining on her pale cheeks.

"Nice to meet you," I said, grinning.

"You too," said Nora, leaning back and the enormous, white main sail flapped behind her. "I suppose I'll see you around on deck."

"I will," I said, watching her turn and tread away. "Nora."

The wire tugged and snapping my daze away from her back to the ocean, I teetered on the iron canon and lifting the rod, the whiting fish swung in mid-air, flicking driblets from its fins.

Clarence appeared above the bulwark. "Hey Douglas!" he yelled.

"*Clarence*, now I just lost it." I groaned, turning over my shoulder and the fish splashed into the ocean.

I clutched the bulwark and stood on the iron canon.

"You're reckless, aren't you? You could've fallen into the Pacific for sure and be poisoned by a sting-ray." Said Clarence, taking the fishing rod from my clasp.

"You worry too much." I said, swinging back onto the deck and thudded beneath the flapping mainsail.

"When I bought the plankton I meant fishing in the right way," argued Clarence, sinking the rod beside his leather shoe and swung the wire.

"Well, I just felt like it," I admitted.

"Did she talk to you?" asked Clarence.

"Yes," I said, smiling and snatched my fishing rod.

"Is she nice?"

We strode further along the middle of the main deck.

"She was the same as you," I said.

"Well, she has a point," stated Clarence.

"You're both over-reacting," I said.

"Isn't rigging enough for you?" he asked, peering up at the spars of the mainmast. "I would never want to go up there."

"It's the best feeling," I said, smiling. "I feel freedom at its wings."

"I'm already worried, you'd fall away from the spars," said Clarence, shaking his head unimpressed with me. He glanced back to the iron canon. "The current could've changed and you would've drowned. *Don't* do it again."

For the entire night, Nora stayed in my thoughts while the ship swayed in the blustery ocean waves, splattering runnels of froth along the stern. It was in the morning, my rigging position was altered. William Tilley, the boatswain was a few years older than me. He tread onto the deck and paced towards me. He wore a loose cotton shirt with breeches, socks and laced shoes.

"It's under order of Captain Albert from Herlewin, the sailing master, you're now assigned to the foretop." regimented William.

"The foretop?" I astounded, broad-eyed. "What of the rigging?"

"Captain Albert decided he wanted the other sailors with more experience dealing with the mainsail for the moment with the stormy winds." explained William, and he pointed to the round, oak tub around the middle post of the foresail. "This is where you belong now."

"Didn't I lower it properly yesterday?" I argued, pacing behind him and the deck creaked beneath my footsteps.

"Hey, at least it's not down in the scullery, with mice scuttling in the oak cupboards." reminded Clarence, crossing his arms on his chest.

I sighed and flicked a few driblets from the loose puddle with the front of my shoe and they dabbed on the deck. I peered up at the oak tub on the foremast and squinted in the sea breeze gusting into myeyes and they moistened from the light, icy temperature.

"I hate to admit it for your sake, though, you're right." I agreed, glancing at him. "I suppose I'm going to need my spyglass."

"Be careful, when you're up there," said Clarence, glancing at the foretop. "You never know what you might see afar."

"I guess," I said, pacing on the deck. "Captain Albert must have faith and trust in me to ensure we are sailing without any peril."

Somehow, in this moment, I yearned to have a boat of my own and sail from the pier to catch my own fish and not have anyone tell me different to do what I was told. I ventured back beneath the hatch and shuffling my assortment of goods in my old ransack, I found my spyglass and returned back to the deck, wondering, *what would I see?*

"Well, good luck. I'll meet you by the forecastle deck by the evening." said Clarence. "I'll try find some spare bread lying around again."

He walked away, maneuvering amid the seamen and descended into the lower deck to attend to the cushioning of the cabins and change the cotton pillow cases. I ascended the ladder shrouds, feeling a rush of excitement in my chest, being in height again and climbing into the foretop, I smiled at the view of the vastness of the ocean.

CHAPTER THREE

FOG SEEN ON THE FORETOP

It had been several days the ship was burdened in the storm, amongst the South Pacific Ocean and on the seventh, I lay on the foretop, leaning on the dank mast. At eight o'clock in the evening, *The Admiral Baltic* tilted in the frothy waves and rain soared from the melancholic clouds, spattering onto my cheeks. I awoke, dropping my shoulder and the side of my arm onto the floorboards. I clasped the bronze spyglass, rolling into my leg and stood, putting the cold rim to my right eye and closing my other eye, I held the funnel and inspected the distance. My heart pounded. *How could I have been irresponsible enough to have fallen asleep during the early hours of the night watch?* The yellow fog simmered on the periphery of the island and the cragged peak of the dark volcano was above the grove of palm trees with verdant leafage, swaying with the stormy wind. I lowered my spyglass to the huddled wild ferns grown amongst the rustling shrubs spread on the silhouetted land with trundled sticks and sea-blown, cracked shells from the shoreline dotting the grasses.

"*No,*" I whispered, feeling my stomach churn in knots.

I inhaled a whiff of cold, sea-salty air. The rain driblets splattered onto my spyglass and blurred the island. I lowered it away, feeling my heart thud.

"Fog! We're sailing into fog!" I yelled.

All the sailors on the deck hurried in a crowd on the forecastle deck towards the bowstring and panicked, gazing at the fog surrounding the hull. It lurked over the bulwark imbued with sea water and onto the deck, lingering near the drenched mainsail and foresail.

"I've never seen this much fog before!" shouted Leighton , striding from the foresail and along the deck, towards the mainsail's mast.

"*Where did it come from? Look at how deep yellow it is!*" exclaimed William.

The foggy clouds unrolled across and the bowsprit poked through the mists and all the sailors screamed. I echoed one after them, widening my eyes and lowered my spyglass. *Now*, I understood *why* ships had been missing before. Lightning crackled, flashing its lucid shadow onto the deck and accentuated the trickling rain on the whipping, crinkled mainsails and foresails. The raging winds blew forward and lured us in another direction away from our route, as the sea did when the tide elevated, and swimmers would drown unable to yield to the shore. I felt the rain blow in ravenous gusts and drenching my crinkled, linen shirt. The ship slanted and losing balance, my chest rammed into the dank railing of the foretop. I hailed, and my pewter compass dangled in mid-air, as I gazed at the long foremast and the sailor slipping on a puddle. He tangled his leg into the coiled ropes and rolled onto the deck into the bulwark. It was with another wave storming into the rudder, I teetered in the dank rickety floorboards and I was veered over the railing of the foretop. I hollered, descending in mid-air and my spyglass torpedoed in front of me. My drenched, brown locks flicked onto my pale cheeks, jawbone and eyes. I stretched my spread fingers and grasped the handle of the spyglass. The sail of the mainmast whacked onto my arm and the rope tangled around my brawny hand.

"Ah!" I exclaimed, clutching the dank rope and spyglass closely to my chest, and swung backward.

I screamed beneath the flashes of lightning and my eyes watered from the icy draft and my crumpled, linen shirt flapped on my chest and stomach, spreading goosebumps. I soared into the fore-sail and whacked into the shrouds and loosening my clasp of the damp rope, I grunted, thumping onto the deck with my compass clinking nearby my hand. I groaned, sliding the compass beneath my shirt and hindered, recognizing the pair of leather-brown shoes in front of my nose. I slowly looked up to the man looming over me and my heart rapidly palpitated. Herlewin Porter, the sailing master was forty years old and wore a brown tricorn hat on his white-curled wig, with a navy coat covering his white shirt and buttoned silver vest and black trousers with a pair of black boots. The drafts had settled, and the ship was now sailing out into the north-east of the ocean, according to my compass hanging from a chain around my neck and nestled in my grasp. Captain Albert swung open the door and trampled out carrying the sea charts in his grasp. He wobbled, as the ship tilted, and the large dark blue wave soared above the bulwark and drenched the chorded shrouds and dissolved into the deck.

"We're sailing off-course!" yelled Captain Albert.

Herlewin glanced at him and back to me.

"Hello, sir," I mumbled and stood, perceiving the anger burble in his chest, through his clamped lips.

"You *fool*!" seethed Herlewin, grappling my collar and neared his yellowed tooth closer and I gasped. "Why didn't you tell us sooner?" He dragged me upward against the mainsail mast. "*You* have led us into the fog, and we've risked being shipwrecked! We might *never* see daylight again!" His beady grey-blue eyes, flecked with sparkling rage and were red-rimmed from only a few hours of slumber and traces of stale whiskey blew from his parched lips. I swallowed and the disappointment of my own failure to serve orders properly, sunk heavily, more than the iron anchor plunging into the moor.

I heard the approaching footsteps thump on the floorboards and the shout of a familiar voice, "Hey! Leave my brother alone!"

Clarence barged in-between us and he raised the oar, he had found from underneath the store room below the deck and knocked it into his stomach.

"What is the meaning of this?" he blurted, frowning and lifted the oar towards him standing in front of me.

"*Clarence*," I sung, tugging his arm and he didn't move. "Don't worry about it,"

"Don't worry about it!" retorted Herlewin. "*Don't worry about it*- you weren't awake when the ship was nearing the fog!"

"Do calm down!" exclaimed Leighton , standing in-between us and spread out his hands. "This isn't a time to argue between each other!"

I grappled my brother's arms, as I forcefully hauled him away from the sailing master, knowing it wasn't ensured he would lower the oar. Herlewin watched us. Clarence reflected one last menacing glare and permeated his enmity towards him. He shifted around, as we strode from the forecastle deck and glanced back to me.

"I don't like him," he mumbled.

"Me neither, though, you shouldn't have done it to him," I advised, dropping my grasp.

We stopped in the middle of the deck.

"Douglas, they were going to harm you," argued Clarence, lowering the oar and tapped it onto the deck beside his shoe. "Did you want me to just watch?"

"*Clarence*," I sung, clutching his shoulder. "If I'm *ever* in an argument with any of the sailors, don't become involved, otherwise, you'd be dragging yourself into trouble and I wouldn't want you to be potentially harmed."

Clarence tugged his shoulder and I loosened my clasp, perceiving his annoyance.

"Really?" he retorted. "Well," He swung the oar's handle forward. "Can you at least keep an eye out more?"

"It wasn't intentional," I admitted. "I fell asleep, I was tired."

"*Douglas*," said Clarence. "You *know*, you can't do this aboard" he glanced at the fog drifting on the ocean. "I don't even know how we're going to survive this storm."

"Me neither," I agreed, deflecting my glare to the quarter deck and clutching the bulwark, watery driblets flicked onto my spread fingers and my disheveled hair breezed onto my numbed cheeks.

It was further during the night at nine o'clock, a shrieking, gust of icy wind tumbled the dank barrel nearby the piles of coiled ropes. The circular lid rolled away, spilling a mound of dynamite at the front of the staircase, beside the captain's headquarters. I observed a few sailors turned, though, they hurried back to the flapping main-masts and were too concerned the rigging ropes had been altered and we were sailing off-course in the north-east direction. The bronze lantern hanging from the wrought-iron hook creakily swung forward and the handle slowly lifted to the edge, ready to topple to the deck. I felt the rush of nerves flourish in my stomach, as the shriveled, tallow candle guttered the last driblets of melted wax and splattered onto the glass.

"*No,*" I muttered, hurrying across the deck and my shoulders brushed into the surrounding sailors. *I had to prevent the lantern from falling.*

The cacophony of their deep-masculine shouts, the whipping mainsail and their hurrying footsteps rasp the oak boards and the thrown ropes whacking onto the deck, echoed amongst the clashing waves on the bowsprit. I glanced over my shoulder and in the distance, Clarence noticed my presence was gone and frowning, he turned and glared at me.

"What's wrong?" he inquired.

William nearing the boats looked in our direction.

"The lantern!" I yelled back, and turning back around, I glared at the opposite captain's headquarters. I tried to move amongst the sailors being soaked with the rain, though, they held my back and *it was too late.*

The wind hastened in stormy gusts and as the ship slanted, the rusted ringlet of the lantern hurled from the hook. I stopped in the middle of the main deck and swinging my arm in mid-air, I gazed at the sailor striding past nearby the staircase.

"Run!" I yelled.

The lantern clashed onto the deck, shattering the glass and the melted, tallow candle wax drooled onto the drenched boards, and the candle-flame swept onto the dynamite. An enormous, tawny explosion of fire soared into the air, bouncing torn planks, cindered oak shards and iron nail heads. The dying shout of the sailor was engulfed with the wavering flames and the heated haze blew across the billowing sails and swarmed over us, as the ocean waves over the bulwark.

"*No!*" I screamed, widening my eyes.

Clarence and I stood amongst the group of huddled sailors, and we watched the headquarters and quarterdeck exploding into burnt ruins. The bottom corner of the door, with a charred edge revolved in mid-air, and floated a trail of hissing smoke. It splashed into the white dotted froth, drifting on the ripples and sunk underwater. I watched a limp arm fall through the flames and drop to the main-deck with a *thud*. It was with a heartbeat, open-mouthed, and a splash of seawater drenching the golden flames. I turned and the flurry of stormy wind blew a whiff of floating black smoke across the floorboard and revealed the grey hair of the captain.

"*He's dead*," I whispered, striding backward and sinking my fingers into my hair.

I was careless of the sailors trampling past and bumping me. I stared with disbelief and stopped in the middle of the main deck. Lightning flickered and the silhouette of the main mast loomed over me.

"*No!*" I exclaimed.

I heard the droning *crack* above me and snapping out from my horrified reverie, I swiped around and peered up. The hefty shrouds snapped and sprung backward, lashing the air. I bawled with an itch in my throat and the mainmast steered forward, casting a long shadow on the tawny, flickering flames and through the simmering, black smoke. Everyone shouted and screamed, rushing underneath, towards the forecastle and the main mast splashed into the sea, tearing a portion of the bulwark into a cluster of floating shards. William Thurstan, the helmsman hailed and was thrown overboard, and the inflamed wheel revolved on its own, flinging sparks. The floorboards quaked, and the ship convulsed, lifting the rudder and stern. I watched the fire sputter and burn the whipping mainsail, festering heavy, plumes of black smoke into the overcast sky. I felt fright I had never known before and it pounded my heart vastly into my ear drums. I coughed through the black smoke and aggressively trampled through the sailors. The inflamed lower mainsail plummeted straight towards Nora. I stared ahead and bellowed, wrapping my arms around her waist and hurled her out of its shadow. Nora squealed, and we rolled on the puddles and soaked our shirts. The bulwark demolished into flicking shards of oak-wood and the main mast splashed into the ocean, vibrating and slanting the deck. I cried and she squealed, as we slid downward into the mounds of coiled ropes.

"Move off me!" exclaimed Nora, whacking my chest and scowled.

"A thank you, would be good?" I retorted.

"*I didn't need your help*," scoffed Nora, pushing my arms away.

"You almost died-," I argued.

"Well, I could've swam into the ocean," contested Nora, and stood, rolling her sleeves to her elbows.

My bottom lip dropped. She was the *rudest, conceited and overly confident* girl, I had ever met. Or, more egotistical?

"I still can't believe you wouldn't even want to thank me for rescuing you," I answered.

"*Like I said*," argued Nora, lifting the doused rope from the deck and slung it over her shoulder. "I didn't *need* anyone."

I gaped and snapped, "Well *sorry*, I cared enough for your safety."

"You're the foretop boy, aren't you?" asked Nora, prying for more information about me.

"*I am* and a rigger," I confirmed and glancing at my brother, treading slowly with hesitant footsteps towards us. He was unsure if he should be apart of our conversation. "Clarence, my brother is the cabin boy."

"I see," said Nora, folding her arms on my chest and glimpsed at the foresail, flicking driblets onto us. "Where are you from?"

"Half Moon Bay," I exposed.

Clarence appeared, and he looked at both of us, with the burning, tawny flames reflected onto the deck.

"Hello," he greeted.

"This is Nora," I said.

"Hey," greeted Clarence, looking at her and held out his hand. "It's nice to meet you."

Nora narrowed her gaze downward and disapproved his friendly gesture. She shook his hand with diplomacy and she asked, "You must be sixteen?"

"How did you guess?" he asked, smirking.

"I just know," answered Nora.

The rumbling burst of thunder erupted above, and lightening crackled in the sky, flickering a lucid shadow over the deck onto the towering foresail and the remaining portion of the oak main-mast. I heard the tearing noise from the crumpled foremast-sail drift in the burdensome drafts and it fell on all of us. I swallowed the water driblets sinking into my mouth and coughed, loathing the sour-salty taste trickling down my throat and my lips slid on the drenched canvas.

Everyone panicked and the sailors yelled.

I pulled it away from ourselves and noticed the shadow looming on the deck.

"Watch out!" I yelled, looking up and widened my eyes.

We hurried away, as the foremast snapped and surged onto the deck. A couple of sailors snatched my collar and my buttons, pressed onto my neck and stifled my breaths.

"Tie those brothers to the remainder of the mainmast post-now!" yelled one. "They led us to death and now they shall serve the same!!"

"No-," I stammered, gazing at the sailors surrounding us with anger accentuated in their faces. They held ropes stretched between their hands.

They stomped closer.

Clarence side glanced at me and he muttered, "Any ideas?"

"I'll try and think of one," I whispered, inhaling a whiff of icy cold air to swallow down my nerves to the pit of my stomach.

"Try what?" he whispered back.

"I know I made a huge mistake," I announced, ignoring my brother and looking back to the sailors, I strode forward in the rain.

"*What are you doing?*" hissed Clarence, as a feeble echo from behind me.

"This was an inconvenience and I-am-," I could hear my own voice quivering with fear, being inconvincible and stepping on the oak plank. "I'm *very* sorry-," I faltered, as the rope lifted to my chest and the creak echoed from underneath his thumb.

"I bet you are," he answered, challenging me.

Nora's silhouette stretched on the deck. I flicked my glare up and observed, she climbed the shadowed shrouds and stopping midway, her dark hair waved in the floating smoke.

"Leave them alone!" yelled Nora, tugging the rope and coiling it around her leg.

All the sailors looked up and she swung downward on the rope and spreading her boots, she kicked the sailors in their chests and they collided onto the dank floorboards of the deck. Nora grasped the hilt and whipped out a cross-guard, steel two-sided sword and sliced the rope into two pieces and it dropped on the floor. She swung to the opposite shrouds and climbed towards the oaken platform of the foretop. All the sailors trampled across the deck. I felt betrayed as Herlewin clasped Clarence and I, and thudded our shoulders onto the remainder of the mainmast and the sailors coiled dank rope around the front of our chests.

"*Release me!*" I bellowed, with a burst of fury and my cheeks rosined, from the swarming heat blew across the deck and flourished beneath my skin.

Nora leapt from the shrouds and swung forward with the dangling rope, kicking them in the face with her black boots. They yelled, rocking backward. Nora revolved anti-clockwise, kicking the other sailor in the nose and he tumbled onto the deck. Clarence and I, watched as she swung back and her hair breezed in the wind and she leapt down, stamping her boots onto the other two sailors' shoulders and knocked their heads together.

"Who is she again…" trailed Clarence, with awe and not moving his gaze from her, astounded with her ferocity.

"The captain's daughter…" I answered.

We watched Nora leaping from their shoulders and stamping back onto the deck. She wrapped the middle of the rope around their necks and strangled a pair of sailors. Nora heard the stomps of an approaching third sailor and she dodged a fist, releasing a feminine grunt. She kicked him in the groin and his scabbard dropped to the deck, sliding between his two-spread boots. Nora side-stepped and steering the rope, she hurled the two sailors against the capstan and they clanged into the poking, burnt handles. Nora climbed onto a floating, oak crate and swung on the rope towards them. They lifted from the deck, behind the capstan and they broadened their eyes and clashing her boots into their chests, she knocked them over the bulwark. Nora smiled and she peered over her shoulder and noticed Quinn trampling towards her in the shadows of the tawny fire, accentuating the sweat on his ruddy, sun burnt cheeks. Nora swiped the glinting sword in mid-air and fixated her dark-eyed glare at him.

"*You wretch.*" seethed Quinn. "Now, your father is dead, we're obliged to harm you too!"

"No, you're not quite right," muttered Nora, boldly and stamping to the deck, she lifted the rope and hurled it in front of his boots and he tripped, tumbling to the wet deck. She lifted the sword-point to his cheek. "Satisfied now?"

Nora smeared a patch of grease on his cheek from her boot. He shook his head, biting the rope and bulged his eyes up at her and echoed an array of short, deep grunts.

"I thought you would be," she answered, with a condescending tense voice. Nora trampled away, hurrying to us and lowered the sword, cutting the ropes and they loosened from our arms and chests.

"Thank you," said Clarence. "Where did you learn to do all of that?"

"Just observing," she said. "It's natural instinct."

"Oh," he echoed.

Nora reached me.

I lowered the ropes limply hanging on my waist and I said, "Thanks,"

"You're welcome, you rescued me and now, I rescue you," answered Nora, striding on the deck.

The bowsprit swung a strand of seaweed dotted with sand and it rammed into the boulder, tearing the astute point away and it swiveled in the air, plashing into the ocean. *The Admiral Baltic* juddered and stopped in the waves. Clarence, Nora and I, all swayed and clutched the bulwark to avoid toppling over. I glared at the arisen hull nestled into the cragged, limestone boulder protruding from the sea and it was shrouded with a cloud of yellow mist and it drifted onto the ocean, revealing the shadowed island. *What was there?* I wondered, skimming the lush verdure rustle in the squalls of the breeze.

"*No!* They've stolen all the boats!" exclaimed Clarence, glaring away to the East and broadened his eyes.

Nora and I turned, gazing at the sailors nestled in the boats, rowing away at sea and further away from the burning ship.

"We're not going to survive," hushed Clarence, watching the sailors revolve the oars and he glanced at me. "What are we going to do now?"

I coughed and squinted in the floating smoke. The map floated on the water nearby the bobbing crimson apples and the torn pieces of wood. I lifted it and after unrolling it, the water driblets trickled downward over the continents and oceans.

"According, to the sea chart in the captain's cabin, we're near Pitcairn Islands," I revealed.

My thoughts raced with endless possibilities, though, I noticed the floating timber and barrels.

"We're going to row to the island." I decided.

CHAPTER FOUR

THE ISLAND

"How?" asked Clarence, coughing and his emerald eyes watered from the burning smoke. "There aren't any boats and we're going to drown if we stay aboard."

I diverted my glance down to the floating lumber on the ocean and to the dank tangled ropes on the bulwark with a wave undulating over them.

"We'll build one." I decided.

Leighton appeared on the deck, coughing through whiffs of black smoke and strode towards us. He was tall with a pale complexion and icy blue eyes and curly, dark blonde hair. He was dressed in a soppy shirt sagging over his dark brown trousers with a pair of dark brown leather boots.

Crack.

We looked up and hurried aside, as a burning oak spar with the protruding iron hooks and the shrouds collided onto the deck, waving a flurry of smoke. Leighton looked down as a small wave of water splashed onto his legs.

"Where have you been?" stormed Clarence. "I went looking for you and I couldn't find you anywhere!"

Thunder rumbled above the sodden, oak crossbar beneath the fore top-sail. Lightning flickered on the front flying jib and spread our shadows on the flooded deck.

"Well, I was trying to rescue William," he announced, glancing at him.

William was flaxen haired with hazel eyes. He was short with a rotund stomach poking in his linen, white shirt tucked inside of his beige trousers and he wore laced, taupe shoes.

"I'm relieved you both survived," I said, hugging them. "I was worried you had died."

"We thought the same with you," admitted Leighton , rolling his crinkled sleeves to his elbows.

The upper jib was smeared with scattered ashy streaks and the burning cabin built with nail-stubbed oak planks, collapsed into a pile of timber shards. I separated from everyone, splashing across the deck and avoided the piles of spread fire, gleaming their tawny reflections on the shadowed water. I lifted a toppled bucket shrouded with seaweed, scooped some water and dissolved the nearest patch of fire into thick, smoky coils.

"First, we have to stop the fire from spreading any further! *Hurry!*" I exclaimed.

Everyone spread across the deck and all night into the deep hours of the shining moon, we scooped water into our barrels and washed the flames away, leaving behind ashy patches and steam drifted amongst the remains of the fore-mast and main-mast. My eyes stung from the blistering heat, while I tread across the deck and observed the inflamed steering wheel and it revolved around. I climbed the slanted staircase, clutching the remains of the chipped railing and side-stepped around the holes. I reached the quarterdeck and swayed the sodden, oak and iron-bound bucket forward and water splashed onto the wheel. The spinning golden flames dissolved, and whiffs of smoke simmered, as the revulsion slowed in the breeze. I clattered the bucket onto the quarterdeck, and it rolled onto the bulwark. I leapt over the burnt, tilted railing and splashed in the water down in front of the captain's headquarters and found a steel scabbard with a mahogany hilt floating on the deck. I peered up at the foremast and observing the three, square-rigs, I climbed the thick shrouds hanging beneath the foretop and midway, I cut the rope dangling from the poking, iron hooks and it dropped to the foredeck. Clarence noticed and after wiping his forehead with his hand, he hurriedly snatched the dropped rope, before it flew away in the stormy gale. I side-stepped across the damp cordage and squinted in the spattering rain. I stretched out my arm and cut another rope from the soppy rigging.

"*What are you doing?*" asked Nora, appearing on the other side of the fore-mast and squinted up in the rain.

"Well we have to build a raft somehow!" I yelled out, looking down and my voice echoed amongst the storm. "Otherwise, we'll never leave the ship and sink to the bottom of the sea! Here-," I dangled the cut rope in mid-air towards her, "-*catch!*"

I released it. Nora stretched out her hands and she caught it. I looked at the shrouds hanging on the foremast and the last rope dangled from the pro-truding, third iron hook.

"What are you thinking?" yelled out Clarence, cupping his mouth.

I glanced over my shoulder down to the foredeck and I exclaimed, "You never know, we might need these shrouds!"

"How are you going to come down?" asked William.

"Yeah, Douglas!" exclaimed Nora, holding her hip, displeased and clutch-ing the coiled rope in her other hand, it swung beside her thigh. "It's much too dangerous!"

"Staying on this ship is dangerous!" I argued, climbing back to the foretop. I gnashed my teeth, as the rain pelted onto my back, and I cut the shrouds.

"Wait!" yelled out Clarence.

It was too late; the shrouds dropped and they soared into his nose, thud-ding him onto the deck. Clarence bellowed, kicking his legs underneath the shrouds and he rolled the top chords from his mouth onto his chest.

Leighton and William chuckled, and they strode over.

"*Shut it,*" blurted Clarence, annoyed.

They smiled and hauled the shrouds away. Clarence thanked them and deflected his gaze to me.

"Rope!" I yelled back, clutching and leaning over the railing. "Stop worry-ing! Watch!"

I pulled the rope dangling from the foremast and wrapped it around my stomach. I held it tight, slowly descending the foremast and the soggy foresail swept onto the side of my waist. I leapt onto the deck and released my clutch of the rope.

"*Never* do it again," bossed Nora. "Anything could've happened!"

"It had to be done," I declared, puffing a breath and mist blew from my lips. I was relieved to be inhaling the watery sea aroma with only traces of the lingering smoke. "Now for the lumber."

"I'll help you," said Clarence.

We leant over the bulwark and collected scattered pieces of lumber floating in the ocean. After a few hours, the plummeting rain thinned into falling specks and a pale shaft of moonlight shone onto the built raft, as we hammered nails into the lumber. We tied them as quickly as we could with the rope and placed four barrels in-between each of the planks. I tore a few portions of the foresail and threw them inside my hessian sack, remembering the neglected tools in the lower deck. I used to peruse them occasionally, after delivering the potatoes to the galley for dinner to be cooked. William drowsily slept against the remainder of the foremast with his legs spread into a pool of seeping sea water, until Nora nudged him in the shoulder and he awoke.

"Huh?" asked William.

"You need to help me find the food cans," advised Nora. "Hurry, we're running out of time. The ship is half-sunken in the ocean."

"Alright," compromised William, perceiving her demanding demeanour and he didn't argue.

He stood without choice and followed her to the dented opening in the cabin, formerly being the doorway; only the tarnished hinges remained, poking from the oak wall over a pile of charred oak shards. They strode down the slanted, shadowed passage to the galley.

"Done?" inquired Clarence, tying one last knot on the barrel fixed in the lumber and stood, glancing at me.

"Just a few more things," I said.

Everyone returned each other a questioning gaze. They curiously watched and shifted their glare back to me. I wrenched the iron ringlet and the trellis hatch lifted, revealing the staircase flooded with dark sea water.

"Be careful," whispered Nora, behind me above the staircase.

Somehow, she had conceded to my decision, even if she had argued against me. She knew I wouldn't listen.

"I will," I said, over my shoulder.

I inhaled a whiff of icy, watery and salty-scented air and dipped my head underwater. I squinted and swam across to the other side of the store room and pulled the potato sacks from the bottom floor. I found the bulgy pouch nestled beside toppled barrels and spilled tomatoes, floating around a swimming crab and seaweed tendrils. A few bubbles drifted from my nose. I tugged it away underwater and heaved it back to the staircase. I splashed my head above the surface and spluttering a breath, I inhaled the icy air with my stifled throat. I gripped the railing and hauled the pouch above the staircase back onto the deck. My shirt soppily swung on my rumpled trousers. I panted. Leighton curiously eyed the pouch, as I swung it down into the right cornered barrel fixed on the raft.

"What did you find?" he asked.

"An oil-lamp, rope ladders, grappling irons, pickaxes, walking boots and flasks for water-," I said, and paused, then added, "Oh, and I found a Chronometer."

The device was used to measure time and the longitude between the distance at sea. Nora and William appeared beside us. They found aluminum food cans with faded labels of peas, corn, beef-vegetable and tomato soup. They put them into the same barrel.

I rolled my sleeves to my elbows.

"Well, that should do it." I said.

"I hope we make it to the island," said Nora.

"We have too," I said, glaring out to the shadowed island. "It's not far and we're even fortunate enough to be near land. Otherwise, we would've died."

Clarence, Leighton , William and I pushed the raft through a gap in the bulwark into the ocean. One by one, we swung on the dank rope dangling from the foretop and we all climbed inside the barrels on the raft. I used a long plank, as an oar and moved the raft amongst the rippling ocean and through the pale mist hindering on the surface. Clarence, Nora, Leighton and William all stared at the tilted, sunken ship and mast for the last time, until they turned back to stare at the island. We sailed across the ocean and the glow emanating from the oil-lamp guided us on the stormy waves. The raft bobbed and water splashed into our barrels, sinking pools around our shoes. A gust of blowing wind diverted the sailing direction of the raft. I tried directing us North with an oar, though, we rammed into the wet rock beds dotted with dark green seaweed. I tried moving the raft to the side, though, it didn't move.

"We're stuck! We'll just get out here." I announced.

"Alright," agreed Leighton , wriggling in the barrel. His dark blonde curls matted onto his forehead. "I'd do anything, then to sit in these barrels any longer."

"Me too," agreed Clarence, "I think I can feel seaweed floating beneath me."

"I'm sure if I stayed in here one minute more, the raft would sink anyway," said William, peeking down and realized the pool in his barrel had arisen to his calves. "I think there's a hole somewhere!"

"Alright, be careful everyone, the rocks are sharp." I said, feeling certain of my decision and squinted in the spattering rain.

We clutched the brink of the barrels and lifting ourselves, we climbed out of them and swung our soppy, potato sacks over our shoulders and strode onto the serrated, limestone rocks jutting from the ocean. I teetered on the roundest boulder, wobbling my outspread arms and swinging the oil-lamp, I splashed into a puddle near a scuttling, grey crab and with the presence of my foot, it hid beneath a neglected, clam shell. I skimmed the golden glow onto the moist seaweed nestled in the sedimentary rock and after a few more treads, I discovered the clustered mussels and clumps of rock salt. We gathered a pile and threw them inside our pouches with the other food tins from the ship. I hovered my beam of light shining from the oil-lamp onto the waves sinking into the rocks and the floating planks with bent iron nails near the white froth, drifting further towards the shore. I collected and put them into the barrel of the raft.

Clarence noticed and dodged other crab shells and stamped into the puddles.

"What are they for?" he asked.

"Shelter," I said, pulling out the last plank and threw it into the other pile.

"What building a hut or something?" asked Clarence, with a hint of skepticism in his tone and I knew he didn't agree. "*In this weather?*"

"No, not tonight," I said, flicking a glance beneath my damp, hair strands covering my eyes. I brushed them aside with my palm and ascended the rocks. "However, eventually, we'll need some form of shelter. The iron nails on the oak planks will help hold the torn bits of the foresail down into the sand." I lifted the dank rope and heaved the raft around the rock beds. "We're going to have to collect rocks to avoid them from being blown away." I decided, peering up into the melancholic grey clouds. "I fear even using the nails and rocks, won't be enough to sustain our shelter in the storm."

"Well, we can't stay out on the island beneath foresail tents either, *Douglas.*" retorted Clarence, sourly and he strode beside me.

"I never said it," I argued.

"You *were* implying it," he disapproved.

"*Clarence*," I sung. "It's only a temporary solution, until I figure out a better form of shelter."

"Oh, that's just great," he grumbled. "And I thought *the ship's lower deck* was bad."

"We'll explore the island tomorrow," I said. "Maybe, we can build boats and sail out to sea, though, we would most likely die."

"This is the worst suggestion, I have *ever* heard," bickered Clarence, shaking his head. "We would die."

I groaned and said, "*Alright*, let's at least be grateful we *survived* to land."

"Fine." He snapped.

We stamped on the crusty, wet foliage and loose soil in the sand. I dragged the floating raft alongside the rock beds on the shore and further onto the sand. The tide spread on the seaweed mounds and the granulated white, light-grey and beige shells. I observed the lightning flash in the sky, illuminating the palm trees and the lush verdure's swishing boughs, ferns and leaves. Thunder boomed in the dark grey clouds. It was in the distance; I could see the arisen cragged ridge behind the palm tree forest and the neglected dark peak of the volcano. Everyone waited, while I splashed into the shore and pulled the raft further onto the sand. My drenched cotton, pale shirt smeared onto my torso and my rolled beige pants nestled on my knees, soppily clung onto my thighs. I inhaled the salted air and the faint waft of the palm trees. The burdensome flurries of wind lifted the raft high into the air, splattering the murky seawater over me and the gathered planks toppled out of the barrels onto my feet.

"It's flying away!" I yelled, fighting against the gale and squeezed my hand tight around the rope, though, I was dragged forward, leaving a trail sunken in the sand from my shoes. "No! No!"

"Douglas, release it!" yelled Clarence, racing behind me. "Leave it!"

"*We need it!*" I yelled back, panicking, as I was lifted from the sand into the air.

Leighton and William trampled down, blowing clumps of sand from their stamping heels. However, when they reached us, huffing, they were too late. The gale lessened, and I dropped back to the sand, loosening my clutch of the rope and the raft stormed away, being carried back into the ocean. I watched it revolve and bounce on the surface towards the North-East in the distant ocean.

"You have to be kidding me! All for anchoring the raft with stones!" I yelled, curling my fingers into fists and squinting, I loathed the sand blowing into my moistened eyes and mouth. "No!"

"It's better the raft and not you," said Clarence, thumping a hand onto my shoulder.

I huffed a sigh, turning with everyone towards the forest.

"I guess," I said, sighing, and felt disappointed.

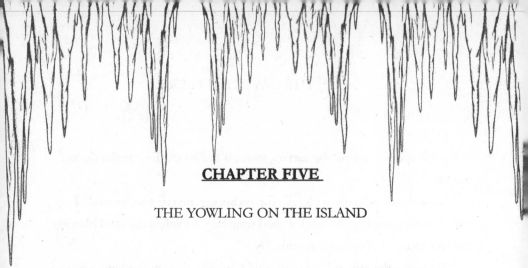

CHAPTER FIVE

THE YOWLING ON THE ISLAND

We walked half a mile into the trees, gathering scattered twigs and brambles from the crusty foliage on the ground, listening to the pythons coiled around the boughs, hissing and writhe. They watched us with their beady yellow eyes and shuffled in the brittle grasses. I felt my compass, jouncing from my stomach and I glanced at the dark-brown monkeys nibbling on the leaves and leaping from each branch. We strode through the flowering shrubs and other dried bushes, moving amongst the palm trees. The hours passed, and the waning moon sunk behind the clouds, with the temperature dropping. It was ten o' clock and the once transparent, looming yellow fog thickened and spread in the forest, making it harder for us to see what lay ahead in the distance. We trudged into the North of the island, deeper into the palm trees and ascended the inclining ground until we reached the summit, into the shadows overcast by the canopies and the sheltering, clustered leaves ahead. We stepped into a small glade, deciding we should stay here for the evening. I dropped the thick, dark brown bough and the ripped, portion of the sail draped over my shoulder, then I knelt to the ground.

"We'll build our shelter here," I decided, untying the rope from the bundled foresail and unrolled it across the sand.

Clarence helped me hold it down and I pulled out a copper nail from the oak plank with a hatchet and hammered it down in the corner, piling of rocks over it. Leighton and William did the same, while Nora whacked a sharp stone into the coconuts, forming holes and after an hour, the sail tents were draped over the slouched, protruding tree branches and they billowed in the wind.

"These won't last long," said Nora, watching me step backwards and inspect them.

"We'll worry about that tomorrow," I said, not knowing the immediate solution. "They'll have to do for the night."

I looked down at the clustered coconuts. "Thank you for opening them." I said.

She smiled, "That's alright."

I felt the thirst drying in my throats and retrieving a coconut, I pressed it to my lips, taking a long swallow. Clarence appeared, clutching the pile of twigs and pressing them against his chin. A thin sweat had appeared on his cheeks and his ruffled, brown hair flared in the breeze. I glanced up with his approach and he dropped them beside my foot, covered with a dingy rag and smeared dirt. I ignored my fatigue and my stinging eyes from the salt water. I lowered the coconut onto the terrain and squatted, sliding a twig through the door of the lamp and cupped the inflamed twig with my fingers. I dropped it into the bundle of sticks.

The fire erupted, flustering into the draft and burned coils of black smoke into the canopy.

"Yes! We have fire!" he exclaimed, smiling and squatting down beside me, until resting a knee to the sand.

William returned with Leighton , carrying a pile of swinging, silver and grey-finned fish speared on the picket sticks.

"I have dinner," he said, proudly and dropped them to the floor.

"Only if we can build the fire," I said, glimpsing at the whiting fish. "Well done."

The storm settled; the thick grey fogs drifted into soft white mists and the raging winds glided into a subtle breeze. We listened to the crackling fire wood, sputtering sparks. I poked the twig into the leaves, pushing them further into the bright golden flames and watched them curl. The light-green feathered birds flapped in the distance, soaring underneath the branches and nestled themselves into their nests for the night. I opened the tin can and poured the crimson tomato soup into the pot. It bubbled. In the slender gaps between the Palm trees, I could see the distant oak barrels drifting in the flowing waves, knocking into our boat nestled beside the limestone rock. At eleven o'clock, after we finished eating, we lay back underneath the rustling sail tents and the summery warmth, blew in heavy gusts as we slept in the sand, I listened to the burning twigs, crackling into my ears and the crickets hidden in the thickets, amongst the stirring draft, whistling in the rustling shrubbery. It was uncomfortable lying in the dirt and sand, with only the shuffled leaves underneath my head for a pillow. The oil-lamp flared its glow onto my tanned arm, while I listened to the swaying leaves. I closed my eyes listening to the hidden insects writhing amongst the shrubbery. It was several hours afterward in a deep slumber, I was roused with the suddenness of a peculiar yowling, burdening the palm trees swishing shrubberies. The distant thump of plunging coconuts bounced onto the barren dirt from the sea breeze. Clarence opened his eyes, still huddled beneath the toiled, weatherworn sailcloth to his chest and shoulder. He passively turned with a broadened glare. The melancholic yowling echoed amongst the distant plashing waves.

"What is that?" he hissed. "I've never heard anything like that before in my life."

"I don't know…" I trailed, becoming apprehensive and I lifted from the sand, glaring afar at the wild verdure.

We both quietened, hearing the drastic shuffling and the crunching footsteps, in-between the leaves. My heart thumped, and I gripped a mound of sand and sunk my fingers deeply, trying to calm my nerves.

Thump, thump. Shuffle. Thump. Shuffle.

I slowly moved towards the edge and my brother stopped me, clasping my arm, though I tugged it away, snatching the picket stick for protection. A footstep thumped, crackling an arid, yellowed leaf and lightning blinked. A strange shadow, with long, pointed ears, extending three-tentacles, with an arched back, appeared on our flapping cover. We both stared at it, petrified and I gripped the picket twig, preparing to attack. The Creature arose its claw and ripped three, long streaks in the crinkled foresail. My heart's pace hastened, as if it would lurch out of my chest. The Creature sniffed the surface, tracing our scent and the winds burdened the verdure and a leafy branch lurched downward. The Creature shrieked, dashing away into the clustered shrubbery and further into the palm tree grove.

I sat up. My brother groaned and squinted. A few sticks from our bundled firewood gusted, stowing in-between the tree trunks and coconuts dropped, from underneath the swishing, slender leaves. I listened to the stormy waves, splashing in the distance, flinging, white spray onto the lonesome, limestone rock arisen from the ocean. I shivered and my eyes stung with weariness. The crumpled foresail flapped dirt and huckleberry leaves, and they glided with the wind's South-Eastern direction, towards the wild thickets. The cacophony of thunder rumbling in the starry-flecked sky, and the soft, crackle of lightning, echoed, as the silvery-white patches illuminated the palm trees. I and Clarence flinched, with goosebumps rushing on our arms and legs from the icy temperature and our damp clothes, flapping on our bodies.

"Now, what do we do!?" he yelled, squinting in the specks of rain falling into our eyes.

"I don't know!" I admitted, as the fore-sail's corner blew sand mounds into the tree boles. I lunged forward and clamped it back to the sand, with a piece bamboo and a few rocks.

I traced my fingers down the ripped, claw-mark.

"What was it?" asked Clarence. "Did you see the shadow of its ears?"

"Yes, I have never seen such a shadow before in my life." I said, glancing at him. "I didn't like the yowling either."

"I hope it doesn't return."

"Me too," I agreed, lying back on the sand and shivered, missing my knit-

ted, navy coverlet back in Half Moon Bay and soot
stained fireplace. "I hope we find a cave, we'll be safer in there, than in the
forest."

At sunrise in the morning, with golden streaks elongating in the blue horizon, I was roused with a penetrating scream. I awoke, sliding my arms in the
snapped twigs, fern foliage and piles of crusty brown and ripe, green leaves,
embedded underneath me in the sand. I panicked, looking at the rippling
ocean and the tilted ship in the distance and the poking bowsprit. A layer
of white froth dotted on the shore, dissolving into the crumbed shells and
scattered pebbles. I crawled on the verdant soil and around the palm trees, inhaling a flurry of summery air. Behind my back, the crinkled foresail billowed
and peering back to the North, I stood, brushing the sand from my knees. A
shaft of sunlight spread behind the clouds, gleaming into my squinting eyes,
through the canopy and the leaves' shadow reflected on the sand.

"Douglas!" yelled Nora. "Come here, *quick!*"

I turned from the sea and trampled towards her tent, slowing my pace into
shuffling footsteps and I asked, "What is it? Is something wrong?"

Nora nodded, dropping the unvarnished copper pan flecked with rust and
she confessed, "I've never seen anything like it before,"

"What's wrong! *What is it!*" yelled Clarence, rushing out of the tent he built
opposite mine earlier at dawn and six o'clock. He crunched vividly on the
twigs. "What have I missed?"

Leighton and William hurried behind him and they all crowded beside
us. Nora eloped a strand of her black hair around her ear and she directed us
around the burning firewood, simmering coils of smoke, from the small copper pot. The handle hung on a twig, between two hoopak sticks sunken into
the sand and the copper pot softly rocked, amongst the undulating breeze.
We shuffled through the sand and she faltered at her fore-sail tent, revealing a
long trail of our food cans, denticulate along the edges, as if picket teeth had
yammered on them. The bits of meat, tuna fish and beans were scattered on

the leaves. A runnel of light-green mucus, trickled on the spilled flaky bits of tuna, beef and the vegetable soup's carrots and celery.

"A *meat* eater…" I announced, observing half of the beef was devoured and only a pool of greasy juice loomed in the aluminum can's corner.

"*Muh-meat*," stammered William, enlarging his blue eyes with terror and he slouched closer. "There's *nothing* left in there, not even a crumb."

"This isn't the worst of it." confided Nora, side-stepping on the furled vegetation.

She lifted the floppy, lush-green leaf revealing a yellow cloud of mist floating into the shrubbery and a three-toed footprint in the soil. William, Leighton and Clarence *gasped*. My heart lurched. I slowly squatted, leaning an elbow onto my knee. I forgot about my hunger lurching in my stomach and having to eat fish for breakfast, after I stared closer.

CHAPTER SIX

FOLLOWING THE
THREE-TOED FOOTPRINTS

The footprints were long and slender, flaring three toes- the middle one was longest and the side ones were short. I raised the crinkled foliage with my stick, revealing the imprint of the heel as a round knob.

"It seems the creature would've had a heavy impact with every striding footstep," I said. "It's been deeply stamped into the ground."

"What kind of animal would have three toes?" blurted Clarence, bending down to the ground, inspecting the footprint closer. He traced his finger along the crusty, muddied edges of the footprint and he glanced back at me, inquiring in silence the possibility of danger.

"I was wondering the same," admitted Nora, enlarging her brown eyes with worry.

"It must've been the same animal we heard yowling last night," I assumed. "I have never seen such a strange shadow appear on my tent." I was distracted with the tuft of dark brown fur, drifting from the curved bacon can and stopping at my shoes. I knelt to the ground, stroking it softly with my thumb, feeling the wiry and thick strands and I decided, "We better be careful, as you've noticed, it prefers meat more than vegetables."

I stood and lifted the verdant clustered leaves, the shade of emerald green, wilting from the orchid bushes and side-stepped onto the brittle wildflowers, clamping them onto the soil. I found another long trail of footprints amongst the yellow mist, hindering on the slope. They curved at the summit and disappeared into the dense shrubbery, overgrown under the jutting branches.

"What are you doing?" asked Nora, nervously.

I already knew she had perceived my decision and I admitted, "I want to investigate them and see where they lead. It's our only way of protecting ourselves if we know exactly where the creature lurks."

"No," she opposed. "You mustn't follow them! It's dangerous! What if The Creature attacks you?"

"I'm curious and if we just stay here, it'll probably come back during the night." I admitted.

"Why don't we just move away and relocate?" suggested Clarence, glancing at the Eastern direction of the island and skimmed the palm trees. He clamped his hand to his forehead, shielding the golden sunlight. "She's right."

"It will follow our scent," I clarified, stepping back near the campfire and retrieved the picket stick slanted on a stone. "We don't want to be avoiding the problem and not solving it."

"*No*, Douglas," he disputed, grabbing my arm. "You don't know what is out here in the forest! We've never seen any footprint like this before!"

I tugged his clasp away.

"Well *maybe*, we can kill it, before it kills us," I declared, glimpsing at all of them and trudged further amongst the bushes and felt the wide leaves brushing around my waist. "Stop worrying, all of you. If I'm cautious, it should be alright."

"No, you mustn't go alone!" exclaimed Nora.

She glanced at Leighton , pleading and urging him to interfere in silence to convince me different. Leighton lifted his hands and took one step backwards, crunching the dry twigs and shook his head.

"I'm not going. If Douglas wants to go, he can. I want to stay out here and collect some more coconuts and fish for dinner." he said.

"*If* we return," grumbled Clarence.

I frowned. "*Clarence.*" I hissed, feeling annoyed.

Clarence strode past and shrugged.

"What? It's true." he muttered.

"You don't know if this would be the outcome," I argued, shifting through the ferns and they slouched around my waist. I glared back at Leighton . "Alright, you keep an eye on the campsite."

Leighton nodded, raising the lush bamboo stick.

"No worries, I'll go catch some more fish for dinner." he decided. Leighton lifted the netted fawn-brown shrouds, dangling the rope coiled on the iron hook and it swung airily, knocking into his knee. He strode past the crinkled foresail and mainsail tents arisen on the sticks, poking from the sands and billowing in the warm gusts of the sea breeze. I watched Leighton become a distant figure, striding on the vastness of the dirt amongst the trees and bushes. He strode on the sand and reaching the shoreline, he splashed his toes in the water, treading in the Eastern direction towards the rock beds.

I looked at William.

"Do you want to come?" I asked.

William glared at the campsite and me. I observed he was indecisive, not knowing whether to stay or leave with us.

Clarence nudged his arm and prompted him to follow. "Come on, come with us. Don't stay here." he said.

William groaned. "Alright, though, make sure I don't regret it." he conceded.

"I'm coming as well," announced Nora, raising the nearest stick and sunk it in the sand. "It'll be too hard just waiting here to know the outcome."

I beamed, feeling surprised and impressed with her decision. Everyone discerned their fear and walked around the footprints sunken in the soil, listening to the chirrups of the parrots. They flapped their light-green feathered wings, swooping underneath the leaves blossomed on the branches.

"*I don't want to follow the footprints…I don't want to follow the footprints.*" trailed Clarence, fixating his glare to them.

The ground elevated into a slope and the scents of the salty water, distant marsh tracts, budded wild-flowers and sour seaweed drifted in the air.

"If we're doomed, I'll blame you," commented Clarence, staring at the clustered iris shrubs. "What if the creature leaps out from the bushes and trees?"

"I doubt it," I said, trying to calm him. "If it did, we *wouldn't* survive. You know what scares me more? Snakes."

"What about lions and tigers?" asked Clarence, staring afar into the distant thickets. "They're worse than snakes. However, it's interesting, we haven't noticed not one tiger or lion footprint. Maybe, there aren't any around. However, it had three toes. How do we know if it's more dangerous or not? I think it would be."

"I suppose, this is risky and there isn't really any choice." I said.

"There is always a choice," snapped Clarence, feeling annoyed and he frowned. "Why can't we just turn back around?"

"Well, sometimes there's an influence of a choice and we're not really in control of what we're doing from a feeling," I explained.

He gazed at the canopy sheltering above us and wiped the moist perspiration drizzling on his cheek. A coconut dropped from the tree, rustling the leaves and he winced, as it thumped to the ground. The Ringtail Monkey scurried on the branch, with his brown tail, curled behind his legs. He carried pawpaw in his fanged mouth and leapt onto another branch, disappearing into a hollow at the top of the nearest tree trunk. Clarence tossed a coconut in his hand, flinging loose brittle, brown coir from the round shell and it spread to the ground.

"I guess we'll need this later, I'm already thirsty." he said.

"Definitely," I agreed, pulling out my own coconut from my pouch and unpinned the slender, bamboo piece and pressed the coconut to my parched lips, swallowing the last remnant of coconut water, quenching my thirst. "We're going to have to collect more for the afternoon. I don't know how much fish Leighton will catch for dinner later."

I slid my coconut back inside my hessian pouch, deciding if I was desperate, I'd eat it later.

"Those fish were hard to catch, yesterday, especially while I was hungry," said Clarence, stamping on a pile of foliage. "With one move of our shadows, they dash away. Maybe, we should just catch crabs instead and try to find more mussels?"

"We ate all of the mussels," I said. "I don't think there's any left on the rock bed we explored."

"What about on the other end of the island, towards the West and South?" he asked. "We still haven't explored it, maybe, we might discover some oysters."

"I suppose we could explore the other rock beds afterward."

We trudged on the shriveled leafage and the white wild-flowers drooping in the soil. The trail of footprints curved in the dirt furthering underneath the thickets near the fern bushes. Nora neared closer to me. I felt like taking the lead and exploring the unknown courageously, as I was adjusted to the possibilities of danger, however, I felt more frightened of her presence, than the three-toed footprints. I couldn't control the irrevocable emotion flourishing in my chest, every time she stood beside me. I felt my flustered cheeks weren't too comforting either and they had remained beneath the summer sunlight for hours. I wanted to hide behind the nearest tree trunk and stay far away from her to avoid having these feelings. I couldn't control them overpowering me. Nora's ruddy lips were softly moist, beneath the sunbeams flaring through the canopy. Every-time I flicked a gaze to them, the temptation to kiss them was inescapable. Her hand swung near mine and my fingers tingled. I wanted to hold her hand, though, it was much too soon and even if we had been alone together. I hadn't known her for long and there was the possibility of an awkward refusal. I exhaled, trying to calm my racing pulse and smelt her stale rose fragrance drifting from her moist collarbone. There was something about her presence I liked, the other girls didn't have. She seemed to be a wandering leaf, being blown with the windy flurries of freedom. Nora had a hidden yearn for exploration, as I did and ever since the fire burned the masts, her entrapment on the ship was freed and she could pioneer into her own independence. She had been an anchor fastened to the chains swindled on the windlass; fixed to her family's expectations not to wander elsewhere. I yearned secretly for us to be alone and continue wandering in the palm tree forest together, stepping in any direction with such an impulsiveness in the spur of the moment. I felt my shoe nudge into something solid and almost tripping, I snapped out of my contemplation. I glared down to the shards of green cane, leaves and torn twigs, confused and sliding them aside with my shoe, I revealed the soaked oak wood flecked with mildew.

"What's wrong?" asked Clarence, stopping on the spread coconut coir on the shuffled verdures and brushwood. "What is it?"

"I'm not too sure," I confessed, lifting the piece of rotting wood from the mud and wiped the leaking driblets, uncovering the remainder of the engraved letters.

Everyone crowded around and leaning on their crooked sticks, they skimmed the signage with awe,

Danger!
Don't enter the cave.
Turn back, while you're still alive.

I could perceive their lingering trepidation, accentuated silently with exchanging worried glances.

"Ah, alright. *Turn back*," announced Clarence, nodding and trying to sound cogent with his decision. He turned, preparing to stride back to the coast of the island.

I held his shoulder.

"We're not going anywhere," I assured, stepping further in the narrow, dirt tunnel in-between the clustered verdure with the rocking of the leaves from the palm trees.

"If there's a cave around here, I want to see it." I echoed, in the tense silence lingering with our dispute.

"Douglas, *no*," he hissed, hesitating to move beyond the signage. "*Somebody* put the sign there purposely."

"Stop worrying," I insisted, rolling my eyes and pointed at the signage with my lifted stick. "This signage is old. Can't you see the mildew festering in the corners?"

"It doesn't matter," disagreed Clarence. "I've changed my mind. Don't you ever question things, before you impulsively decide to do it?"

"Nope." I confessed.

"I hate to admit it, but Clarence has a point," added William. "Can't we just return back to the campsite and not follow onwards?"

"I'm curious," I admitted, pointing to the distance with my stick. "I want to see what we'll find," I lifted it higher and skimmed it airily, between two, tree trunks and the rugged rock precipice in the far distance. "Besides, I think we're close and it's the rooftop of the cave."

"Alright," said Nora. "We'll just have a look, though if we can see any form of danger, do you promise we'll turn around?"

"If all of you want to turn back to the campsite, I won't stand in your way." I said.

The gale blew and sprinkled the mucilage onto the shrubbery. We tread on the spread leafage. Nora walked closer to me. We approached a lime-skinned python coiled on a thick, curved branch hanging above us.

"Stay calm," I murmured, glancing at the python and it watched us with its slit pupils widened in its sharp, yellow eyes.

"I've never liked pythons," confessed Nora, revealing her palpable discomfort. She waved her hand at a buzzing fly and it circled beside her shoulder. She heard hissing in the bushes. "Or, *snakes.*"

"Me neither," I said, feeling my stomach lurch and not bearing to look at the python any longer. I glanced back to the tall bushes and leant my stick against them, searching the ground.

I saw a slender black tail, sliver underneath the shrub.

"I suppose speaking of snakes, be careful, there's more around here. There's more water and sunlight in these bushes." I warned.

The shrubs brushed against my legs. I observed half of the creature's footprint was hidden underneath the covering dried brown and lush-green leaves. I pushed more foliage aside and revealed the slimy, watered swamp floating a yellow miasma. The deep whistle of the crickets sung in the long, wild grasses and brown moths buzzed, whirling around the mire.

"*Pwoah*," exclaimed Clarence, loathing the malodor and covered his nose with his thumb and finger. "That smell," he eyed the swamp, "Now, we know where it comes from."

"Yeah," echoed William. "I thought rotting seaweed was bad."

Nora waved her hand around her nose. "Oh, it's terrible." she complained. Clarence, Nora and William huddled closer and peeked from behind my shoulders, standing in-between the bushes.

The clouds of yellow fog simmered from the moist dark-green surface of the swamp.

I pointed upward.

"*There's the cave!*" I exclaimed.

CHAPTER SEVEN

THE VOLCANO'S CAVE

I heard a trickle of water dripping from the ochre stalactite, splatting onto the ground. It sung in the silence amongst the distant echo of the rippling swamp water and waddling of the alligator's tails. The interior of the cave was rugged beige limestone rock and the walls were two feet wide. A dewy stench drifted from the swamp, churning with the stale, rocky aroma. I felt the soft gust of warm air blow across my cheeks, from the lancet archway in the walls. I stepped out of the warm, golden sunlight on the craggy floor and crunched a footstep further into the shadow, feeling it was forbidden.

Clarence peeked on the side of the entrance, blocking the daylight and it gleamed around his shoulders.

"Have you changed your mind yet?" He asked, glimpsing at the ceiling of russet dripstones uneasily and winced, as a granulate of crumbed rock fell onto the floor.

William and Nora appeared at the entrance, peering inside the cavern.

"Yeah, Douglas?" echoed William, with terror lingering in his tone. "Aren't the footprints enough in the ground to prove to you the possibility of danger?"

"No," I answered, stepping closer to the archway.

I lifted the lantern, flaring the golden light into the dark tunnel. I waved my hand, beckoning them to come inside the cave. "Come on! Don't you want to see what's inside?" I exclaimed.

Nora exhaled and crossed her arms on her chest.

"Please just come out now." she echoed.

"Why?" I argued, over my shoulder. "To stay with the alligators?"

"No, but surely there's another part of the island we can find to stay and rest for the evening," pressed Nora.

"Well, we can't necessarily climb back down either," I declared.

Nora and Clarence exchanged glances and stepped inside the cave, huddling closely and flashed their golden lantern glows along the walls.

Thwip! Thwip!

They looked to the archway in the corner of the cavern.

"Hello?" I called out, flashing my light beam from the oil-lamp through the archway and skimmed the glow across the crowd of stalagmites with mist levitating on the ground.

I heard a dashing movement from behind the smallest pair of light beige stalagmites grown in the shadows and diverted my lamp light to them. I stepped further through the archway. I grew closer and my heart thumped in my chest.

"*Douglas, stop!*" hissed Nora.

Clarence hindered near the front half of the cavern, standing in the shaft of daylight, too frightened to come beside me.

"*Douglas,*" he warned.

I ignored him, approaching the short stalagmites and peeked over them. A crowd of bats flapped past and I bellowed, rising my arms over my cheeks and dropped my lantern. They ascended to the ceiling, grappling the pointed limestone dents with their talons and hung upside down, wrapping their wings around their black furred bodies.

Clarence trampled through the archway and lifted the lantern.

"See?" he said, returning the lantern back to me and the iron handle was warm. "Can we just leave here?"

I exhaled, flattening my shirt and brushed the dirt dust on my trousers.

"No." I said.

"Why?" whispered Nora, bowing beneath the arch and lifting her lantern light, she skimmed the glow onto the bats. "I don't want to sleep with them tonight."

"It looks like you will," I teased, sniggering. "They'll be nestled right beside you. *All night.*" I chuckled, treading further in the dark tunnel and flashed my lamp light on the stalagmites.

Nora scoffed a gasp, lowering her glow from the ceiling to the rugged ground and followed behind me.

"Where will you be sleeping, Douglas? Perhaps, near the bat droppings?" she answered.

Clarence looked to me.

I chuckled, "No, you're with the bats remember? It's going to be you."

Clarence looked back to Nora.

"Douglas, I'm being serious now, we need to not step further in the cave. We don't know what's dwelling in here." She whispered.

I stopped, knowing she was right. What if The Creature was dangerous? How would we survive? Clarence glanced back through the archway. William hindered at the entrance of the cave.

"What are you doing?" asked Clarence.

"Staying out here," he answered.

"Why?" I asked, with my voice echoing down the tunnel. "Stop being frightened of the unknown," I looked at my brother and William, "*Both of you.*"

"Douglas, stop denying it," urged Clarence, clutching the cragged edge of the archway and peered back down the tunnel. "Come back now. We'll find a way back over to the other side of the swamp and away from the alligators. Don't you want to see a way out of this island and back to Half-Moon Bay?"

"Yeah," I said, reaching the end of the dark tunnel and observed the decline in the ground. "However, I'm not listening to you. If you want, you can stay, but I'm going further inside."

Clarence groaned and glanced back to the front of the cave. "I guess, I'll see you later in the afternoon, William. Unfortunately, I have to my follow my brother."

"Same with me," echoed Nora. "I suppose I don't know what to do, if I were to go back outside of the cave. If I were to follow down the side of the cliff, I'd meet with the alligators and perhaps if I were to hurry into the trees, there's probably more snakes in the grasses of the forest. I don't want to leave either of you, as well."

"I'm flattered," I echoed, with a sarcastic tone.

"I suppose you should be," she echoed, stepping further into the dark tunnel. "Bye, William."

William waved. "I'll wait out here. Bye!" he echoed back.

We moved further onwards, bowing in the second archway. I felt an adrenalin rush of venturing somewhere, I had never been before and wondered what nature awaited me. I presumed The Creature was small by the size of the archway and one head shorter than us. I shone my round luminance from my lamp onto the jagged floor and observed another long trail of the pointed, three-toed footprints with a round heel sunken in the ground. He must've had an unusual strength, observing the mud wasn't moistened for the footprints to have been formed in the solid rock.

"*Douglas*," hissed Clarence, taking a few cautious and timid steps into the cave. "*Stop*. You know this is wrong, why are you doing it?"

He avoided the dent in the floor and side-stepped around it. He nudged into a pile of crumbed rock debris. He dodged underneath a bat flapping above him and he broadened his eyes.

"I hate those things," mumbled Clarence, watching the bat flap away in the distance.

I turned and tip-toed into the dark slowly, clutching the wall for support to avoid slipping and breaking my lantern.

~

Meanwhile, The Creature twitched his long, light-beige ear, listening to the vibration moving in the walls and our resounding, distant voices, he couldn't recognize. *Who were we?* He scratched his earlobe with a finger of his curved claw and flicked his lucid yellow eyes to the shadowed archway. The Creature lifted the bone from the ground and yammered on the round bumps, slavering green saliva driblets on the chiseled mortar sinking in his bright red tongue and after a mouthful, he dropped it to the rubble. He pursued the echo of shifting debris and our footsteps stamping through the caverns, sheltered with jagged helictites and totem poles arisen to the ceiling. He strode through the winding tunnel into another chamber with a broad splattermite and he stopped in front of the large rock huddled near the opposite wall. It slid across, revealing a long shadowed tunnel and the top points of his ears and horns skimmed past the wilting, frail gossamer on the ceiling, crunching and flattening the crawling scorpions, squirting juice from their crushed, black shells. The Creature arrived at the end of the shaft and squirming through a hollow fissure, he chafed stone bits with his hind claws in the dirt and crawled out into the passage. He quickened his pace and he stopped at the end of the tunnel, peeking his moist bright yellow eye, from the side of the rugged wall. He observed our silhouettes elongated on the floor and his nose swelled, inhaling our slender grey threads of our sweaty scents.

He neared closer.

CHAPTER EIGHT

ROCKFALL

I shifted around and glimpsed a pair of light beige ears and partitioned, dark brown tufts of conical hair, gliding across the clustered, limestone stalagmites. I gasped and my heart lurched in my chest. *What else was in the cavern?* I raised the golden light from my lamp onto the cragged peaks of the stalagmites.

"I *just* saw a pair of ears behind the stalagmites!" I announced.

"*Yeah right,*" doubted Clarence, striding beside me.

He clutched one serrate peak and spread his fingers on the rock, inspecting them for himself and he searched the rugged floor.

"There's *nothing* there." said Clarence.

"But, I *swear-,*" I blurted, glancing for myself and my heart sunk into a pool of disappointment within my chest, feeling embarrassed of not having seen the creature. "It was there, whatever it was,"

I sighed and expelled one short breath.

Clarence thumped a hand onto my shoulder. "The dark is playing tricks with your eyes." he said.

I stared one moment longer at the floor and hovered my iridescent beam closer, observing the rugged floor was chafed with slender, frail claw marks and proving him wrong, I pointed at them, "No, something was here," I deflected my glance to him and back to the floor. "*See?*"

Clarence squatted, lowering the luminance of his lantern downward and traced the dusty points of the claw marks in the rocky ground.

"Douglas, why did you want to come in here again?" he asked.

Nora appeared, peeking over the stalagmites, scrutinizing them for her own justification and she confessed, "I don't like what I'm seeing," she glanced back to me. "This can only mean danger for all of us."

Crackle

"What was the noise?" whispered Clarence, turning and looking at the tunnel.

"It sounds like something is hiding nearby," whispered Nora.

I flashed my glow shining from my lamp into the archway.

"I want to find out," I said, glancing over my shoulder. "Come on, let's see."

"No, Douglas," murmured Nora, tugging my arm. "What if we're killed?"

I was shocked with the touch of her fingertips and tried not to feel overwhelmed with the immediacy of attraction and my cheeks lightly burned. I tore my arm away from her clasp and we walked in the direction of the sound, holding the wall for support, gripping onto the curvature of protruding rocks to avoid toppling onto the sloping ground. The bits of crumbed debris were nudged from our shoes and rolled downward, being engulfed into the dark. I feared stepping into a dent in the ground and dropping my lantern, as the black handle felt slippery in my clammy hand and it would be difficult to determine what was coming from behind us. I followed into a round tunnel. We discovered a small cavern. I stopped and dodged my light in-between two, shadowed archways and observed one was short, than, the other.

Crackle!

I turned to the left archway and tread towards it.

"Douglas," hissed Clarence, following behind me. "Can you just stop?"

"I know I can hear it," I whispered over my shoulder, emerging into the dark and somehow, the exploration of this cave had become more intriguing.

Clarence and Nora continued following behind me, with hesitant footsteps, looking at the walls and the ceiling, with lightly, broadened eyes reeking with trepidity. I thought for a moment, we were trapped in the chamber and I drastically strode around the walls, flashing the light from my lamp amongst them. I panicked and felt the sudden rush of terror soaring from my stomach, quivering my shoulders and my heart thudded.

Crickle! Crackle!

I pursued the noise, following it to the North East corner of the chamber and the light from my lamp swished over the point of a narrow cleft in the wall. I crawled inside into the other chamber with my palms and knees sliding on the floor and stamped on the stone fragments. Clarence and Nora crawled behind me and reached the opposite end. We stood and all looked up at the ceiling. I stiffened and listened to the crack penetrate into the deserted silence of the cavern. I lifted the radiance from the lamp and revealed the wobbling large boulders.

"Oh no!" I cried out. "They're going to *fall!*"

"Watch out!" exclaimed Clarence, yanking my arm.

One rock fell above my head and clashed into a pile of pieces spreading onto the ground. They continued dropping, while the floor shook and stone bits rained onto us. The rocks rolled from above the cliff.

I swung around, holding my lamp light.

"Quick! *Run!*" I exclaimed.

Clarence, Nora and I trampled down the adjoining passage, while the rocks continued dropping and colliding onto the floor. The clouds of beige dust soared into the air and spread into crumbed pieces. I swayed my hand amongst the hovering dust motes and coughed. My foot caught into a dent and tripping, I toppled to the floor and squinting, I watched my brother reach the end of the passage and dodge the rocks. I stretched my quivering hand, eager for savior, feeling the small rocks hurling to the floor and rolling into my legs. A large boulder wobbled its shadow onto my shoulder and I held my breath, feeling the blood oozing and trickling from my knee in beads into the floor's indentation. They reached the impenetrable opening at the end of the passage.

Clarence stopped, clutching the brink of the wall, looking around and realized my absence.

"*Douglas?*" he puffed, looking at the front narrow tunnel, eyeing me lying on the floor. He lowered his hand and stepped forward.

I raised a weak hand.

"*No.*" I murmured.

"Are you kidding?" he retorted. "I'm not leaving you there!"

"You'll die!" echoed Nora.

The boulder teetered closer to the threshold. Clarence ran back, dodging the other falling rocks with a side-step and by the fourth one, he skidded on a sheet of dust wobbling his arms and collided into the wall. The rock soared behind his back and collapsed into a dusty white mound on the floor.

Clarence panted and exclaimed, "Phew," He bounced his eyebrows and slouched on the wall. "That was a close one."

I tapped his arm and smiled. "Never do anything like this again."

Crack

We both looked up, as the large boulder rolled downward. Clarence rapidly dived into my torso and I surged against the wall with a grunt. I scraped scratches on my knees and reddened welts on my shoulders. The boulder clashed to the floor, partitioning into three, dusty chunks. Clarence lost balance and bowing forward, he scraped his left hand on the sharp, miniature rock formations on the wall and calloused his palm. He panted and his dusty, dark brown locks matted his reddened, sweaty cheeks. The last group of rocks plummeted onto the other debris, piling into a wall and he disappeared from sight. I was neglected, *alone*, behind the wall of rocks with whirling pale dust, drifting on the floor in front of my shoes. It was behind me in the cavern, I heard the sharp claws chafing on the rugged ground and turning, a pair of moist golden eyes blistered in the dark, fixating on my chest.

CHAPTER NINE

WHAT ELSE IS IN THE CAVE?

A bat with furled black wings, soared from the light brown dripstones and screeched.

I shuddered back into the sharp beige speleothems.

"Ah!" I echoed, watching the bat flap through the dust. I panted against the rugged wall, and looked back down to the boulders. The glowering, golden eyes with crimson veins were gone. What had been watching me a moment ago?

The claws scrawled on the rocky wall from the nearest archway, increasing the pace of my heartbeat. I listened to them sinking into the rough dents. I swallowed and tread forward, leaning on the front of my shoes and the silhouette of the claws elongated on the beige stalagmites. The Creature dashed in the distance of the tunnel's end. I swiped around, glimpsing a shadow on the floor and shifting into the cragged wall's edge. The feeble echo of hastened, pitter-pattering shrunk further in the tunnel.

"Hello?" I called out, lifting the quivering match stick and flame through the round entrance.

Nothing answered, except my footsteps and shaky breaths. I swallowed, feeling my heart beat and echo in the silence. I bowed into the shadowed archway and strode through a tight, shadowed tunnel infested with stringy-netted web, the threads slivered on my ears and through my brown tresses.

"Maybe not," I whispered, shifting slowly through the floating, yellow mists on the floor.

I stepped into a cavern of ochre stalagmites and stalactites drooping from the ceiling, infested with floating yellow smoke. A lucid yellow lava seethed in a canal on the rugged wall, flooding through the shadowed opening into an adjoining ante-chamber. I strode inside with awe, gazing at the surrounding stalagmites. Turning, I heard the crackling echo and felt the tension lurking behind my shoulders.

I side-glanced at the shadowed crevice.

An array of shiny, picket teeth deep-set in the widening jaw, lifted in the shadows.

I swallowed, lifting the dimmed glow from the lantern, accentuating their sharp contours lathered with a moist layer of green saliva.

I screamed and revolved the oil lamp around, flashing the beam on the array of stalactites and it clattered to the floor, smashing a portion of the glass into a shattered mound. The flame blew out, hissing smoky tendrils from the warm oil pooling on the ground. I heard a moist, beige nose snuffling my scent. I looked back to the crevice, as my eyes adjusted to the dark and watched the teeth clamp together and shrink backwards into the shadows. My heart hammered and I watched a few pieces of debris rolling out of the crevice, bouncing in front of my laces, dangling on my shoes. I panted and I tread backwards and swallowed. I had been right, we weren't alone in the shadowed tunnels and something unusual was roaming amongst the speleothems. What was in the cave with us? What was I alone with in here? I ignited a match onto the rough limestone and flared the flame, revealing a trail of ants crawling onto a slender trail of green mucus, I hadn't seen before.

Crackle.

The cacophony of my pounding heat, my nerves tingling and the subtle moaning breeze in the round crevices, lurked into the chamber. I slowly squatted and pulled out the withered candle from my pouch and a packet of matches. I struck a match along the rocky wall and inflamed the burnt candlewick and deflected my amber glow to the archway, observing a peculiar whirl of yellow mist lofting out of the passage onto the rubble. I strode through the strange mist and bowing beneath the archway's low edge, I ventured through the tunnel.

Crackle.

I stopped midway, watching the rocks roll across the opposite end.

My heart thumped faster and broad-eyed, I tread closer having an argument with myself, between my curiosity and urge to flee in the opposite direction. The three-toed footprints and the picket teeth haunted me. What did The Creature look like?

My heart thumped, as I reached the end and lifting my soft yellow candle-light, I cringed and screamed.

"Watch it!" exclaimed Clarence.

I panted and lowered the candlelight, looking at him and puffed, "*It's only you.*" I deeply exhaled, feeling relieved.

"Who else would you think it would be?" asked Clarence, bewildered.

"You mean, what else?" I corrected, trying to calm myself and listened to the beating of my heart.

"You saw it?" echoed Clarence.

"Just it's teeth," I whispered. "-enough to frighten me for a lifetime."

Nora rushed through the inter-joining crevice and her dark hair bounced a few bits of stone onto the floor, as she neared us. "What happened to you?" she blurted.

I lowered my tone and whispered, "We must be cautious of the cave dwell-er."

"The cave dweller?" asked Clarence.

Nora shrieked at the sight of my bloodied patch stained in my trousers. "You're hurt!" she exclaimed.

Nora lowered the pouch from her shoulder and unfastened the thick rope around my waist. She pulled out a coiled linen bandage and unwrapped it, while we moved further into the overshadowed cavern. My brother carefully lowered his lantern to the floor, flaring the dimmed golden illuminance on the floor. I looked back down the tunnel, shrouded with rock remnants and the piled boulders, blocking the far entrance. My stomach churned at the thought of being isolated in the cave forever in never-ending darkness. I flicked my glance back down to the candlelight and knew the packet of matches wouldn't last for long.

"Had enough?" asked Clarence, with a daring anger prowling in his tone. He sat opposite me, watching me roll my trousers on my left leg and the tight fabric, peeled on the sticky, bloodied gauze and it stung. I clenched the side of my mouth, quirking my upper lip, despising the burn.

I glanced at him and said, "Don't give me that, I didn't expect any of this to happen. I thought I'd step in for a moment and then go back outside." I trailed away, knowing if I elaborated I'd be lying and it'd be obvious. Nora covered my gauze with the linen band and I echoed, "*Urgh*,"

"Well, thanks to you, we are now trapped in the cave," snapped Clarence, with fury trembling in his tone and it echoed in the neglected silence. "Who knows, what will happen with William and Leighton still outside near the shore," he frowned. "Hopefully, they won't come following us."

"Well, I guess they wouldn't be able too," I answered, deviating my glare back to Nora shifting closer, with the unwrapped band spread in-between her pale fingertips. I held the bottom end to stop it from falling and looked at her, "It's alright, I'll do it."

"No, it's okay," she argued, looking into my eyes and her own softened. "I want to do it."

"You do…" echoed Clarence, suspiciously and fixated his glare onto her fingers leaning closer to my knee with enmity, as a buzzing insect.

"Of course," she said, wrapping the bandage on my knee and beamed. "There we are," she knelt backwards and stood. "Let's keep going, hopefully we can find a chamber for the evening to rest, with nothing else happening." She shifted around and leant against the wall. "I'm already tired."

"Yeah, staying down here, isn't good," agreed Clarence. "I can barely breathe

from the rock's dust. A campfire would be good and cooking some of the tomato soup we have brought with us. It's the least we can do to help ourselves
survive inside of here. I'm hungry and I hate wandering around with an empty
stomach."

"If we set up a campfire, we're going to attract unnecessary attention," I
disputed. "Have some coconut water and fruit for the moment?"

"No," he exclaimed, indignantly. "I can't survive on *just* fruit!"

"Well at least let us find a chamber with a mild draft floating inside the
tunnels to guide the smoke from the campfire out," I suggested, trying to
calm his growing annoyance at being controlled. "Otherwise, the smoke will
suffocate us."

Clarence tilted his head on the wall, huffing a breath and softened his tone.
"Alright, I guess you're right. I wouldn't want it to happen."

I clutched a protruding piece of rock and slowly stood, wincing and bit my
teeth, with the prickling in my wound. The long slivers of blood drenched my
right leg. I lowered my hand, offering it to my brother and he held it, slowly
standing and moaned, putting a hand to his back.

"Are you alright?" I asked.

"No," he said, slowly rubbing and straightening his back. He limped down
the tunnel, bouncing his hand onto the wall for support. "I hope it will be
better tomorrow."

"Wait-," I said.

He halted, watching me rip a piece of my shirt's sleeve away and rub it on
my lower calve.

"Blood has a strong scent," I said, tossing it into my pouch. I was relieved I
had wiped the majority of the blood away and only faint rivulets were stained
on my right leg.

I tread further amongst the chain of impenetrable tunnels and an eddy of
wind blew from the opposite end, shrinking my candlelight. Turning over my
shoulder, I hadn't noticed the absence of my brother and flashed my candle-

light onto the narrow passage. My heart raced, thrumming in my chest.

"Clarence?" I asked, glancing in the cloudy, white fog from the dropped pile of boulders. "*He's not here. I can't see him anywhere.*"

Where was he?

Nora looked for herself.

"I don't see him either. We have to find him! He can't be this far, he was with us only one moment ago. He must've gone his own way?" she asked.

I exhaled through my nose, clamping my parched lips and exclaimed, "I can't believe he would do this to us!"

"Sh!" shushed Nora, tapping my arm. "Don't be too loud!" She poured a driblet of kerosene into the oil lamp and brightened the dimmed glow into a flickering, golden radiance, shining the shaft into the tunnel.

We both inspected the floor, ensuring there weren't any unexpected holes or curved dents to cause a swollen and bruised ankle.

"*Let's explore this way,*" I decided, treading down the Northern tunnel. "This brother of mine!"

CHAPTER TEN

WILLIAM SEEKS HELP

At the hour of two o'clock in the afternoon, the golden summer rays shone onto the lush verdure, swaying ferns and the arid, fig trees, with shriveling branches, sinking onto the furrowed exterior of the cave. The cragged precipice slanted a shadow onto the swamp. William, with reddened cheeks and sweat coating beneath his shirt and trousers rolled to his knees, strolled indecisively in front of the cave's limestone archway. A few light ash-blonde locks smeared onto his forehead and he wiped them aside, treading into the hot sunlight and he gazed afar. The miniature oak bowsprit lifted on the ocean's surface with the slanted sail-cloth and ripped burnt threads, flapping in the sea breeze. He observed the burnt lumber floating on the ripples of water and patches of white froth, undulating onto the scattered shells, poking coral bits and damp seaweed. He turned from the palm trees and distant light green bamboo thickets towards the East, staring back to the denticulate ochre wall.

"I don't know what to do," puffed William, tapping a long stick onto the dusty floor. *Should he lie to Leighton when he arrives back to the campsite? Should he be honest? No, he had to be honest, even if he was going to appear as a coward. Their lives depended on it.* He stopped at the cliff's periphery, glimpsing at the alligators down below.

Their beady crimson eyes fixated on him and opening their ravenous jaws, they swallowed slimy water, as they waited for him to near the swamp. William moved from the edge, following the descending land of rock intersecting with the forest's soil and shuffled through the tangled dried weeds, brushing onto his ankles. He stopped at the front of the spring, jumping onto the trail of wet stones and bowed underneath the waterfall pouring over him. Driblets tapped onto his cheek. He could see the slender coils of smoke drifting above the palm trees canopy, swaying their leaves.

"Help," he mumbled, glaring at the golden flames drifting heavy whiffs of smoke and crackling sticks and shriveled leafage. "*Help.*"

William moaned, brushing through the thick foliage and verdant ferns, with their slender leaves brushing onto his torso, waist and calves. The ocean's fresh and salty draft blew in heavy gusts, as the coconut grove thinned, and the shore and their campsite appeared through the towering trunks. William descended the slope and brushed through the last of the dried verdure with crusty leafage snapping beneath his shoes and he stepped onto the sand. William panted and he stopped, and a wave of sand glided from his shoes and bowing, he clutched his knees. After a long exhale, he sat onto the log with bark peeling a few strands into the sand, nestling in front of the campfire. A trail of ants crawled towards his leg and he brushed them away, flicking them onto the sand. Leighton appeared around the South-East outskirts of the island and vegetation, carrying a bundle of silver-scaled, barracuda fish swinging beside his leg and a piece of blue coral drenched in sea water in his other hand. The sand blew from his shuffling footsteps. He dropped them into the barrel, sodden from the last tropical rainfall showered one hour before and sunk the picket stick into the sand.

"What's wrong?" he asked, lifting the barrel and dropped it closer to the campfire. The burning twigs crackled and streams of black smoke drifted into the sky. He poked the picket stick beneath a few loose shriveled leafage dotting on the sand and hurled them into the fire, watching them curl and dissolve into ash. "You seem distressed," he flicked his gaze to him. "Where's Douglas, Clarence and Nora?"

"It's no use," murmured William, shaking his head.

The cacophony of the waves splashing along the shoreline and hiss of the warm winds echoed. Leighton silenced, waiting for him to elaborate, though he didn't and wiped the trickling beads of sweat from his forehead, with his crinkled sleeve rolled loosely underneath his elbow. He tread closer towards him and dusted the sand from his hands, by rubbing them on his waist. He sat down beside him on the log, hurling the stick into the camp-fire and clapped his shoulder.

"What is it?" he asked.

William stared numbly into the flames, avoiding his gaze.

"William, *tell me*." He insisted, flicking his gaze from the sand to him. "It was like the time, a few months ago, when the shrouds weren't latched properly on the iron hooks and you were frightened of telling me, because I would tell the captain? And the other time, when I pointed over the bulwark and the humpback whale was in view, and you refused to tell me the capstan, wasn't revolving properly?"

William slowly, shook his head. "It's worse than the humpback whale, capstan and the iron hooks for the shrouds."

"Well, whatever it is-," began Leighton , though paused, as he abruptly blurted, "I can't believe, I didn't step inside the cave- I could've been there with them!"

He watched the black crab dawdling across the sand, avoiding the warmth from the flickering flames. Somehow, he could feel his fears, becoming as deep as the South Pacific Ocean and being engulfed by the wretched, sea urchins into infinite dread. He wanted to be like the scuttling crab and hide back into the reefs and rock-beds, soaked in froth and sea-water; to venture back into the ship's cabin and pretend nothing ever happened.

Leighton snatched the nearby picket stick and speared it, lifting the crab in mid-air, watching the revolving, miniature legs and lowered it beside his shoe.

"What cave?" he asked.

"Well-well-," stammered William, moving his attention to the crab and avoided his gaze. He inhaled a whiff of air and he looked back to him. "The footprint led somewhere dangerous-," he paused, shifting his back to him and felt shameful for his cowardliness.

"Dangerous? *A cave?*" asked Leighton , impatiently and squinted in the blistering summer sunlight, illuminating his pale complexion. "How dangerous?" He stood from the log and moved into the canopy's shade, shuffling the sand. "Are they injured?"

"I don't know!" exclaimed William. "Rocks fell in the tunnel! I heard them and I didn't want to go further inside." He broadened his hazel eyes, twinkling with terror. "I don't think they have a chance of surviving what lives inside the cave."

"*You left them?*" inquired Leighton , speculating over the situation and pulled out fishing wire from his loose pocket. He spun a coil around his calloused fingers. "You didn't even *intend* to try and help, or haul the rocks down?" He frowned and his tone pierced with disdain. "How *could you* do this William? It's very selfish!"

"Well, they're too heavy!" exploited William, awkwardly, "Even the alligators- *predators*- swam away from the growl. They fear themselves, what lives there."

"What *growl?* Alligators? What lives in there? What are you talking about?" asked Leighton , exhaling his frustration. "This isn't going to be easy." He scowled, raising a twig. "*How could they have been this foolish?*"

"It's not my fault!" he argued. "It was Douglas who led the way inside!"

"I *know* it wasn't Clarence or Nora! It was Douglas. He always pioneers like he's onboard the ship and using the wheel to guide the stern!" he blurted, shaking his head and tossed the stick.

It flew into the nearest brush and a mound of arid tawny leaves, furled inward burnt from the sunlight.

"He's never been afraid to follow what feels right to him," agreed William.

"I thought they would only *follow and not be foolish.*" he breathed out. "Now we have no choice, though, to find a way inside and help them out."

'No!" exploited William. "You don't understand. I think there's a *creature* living in there! The footprints led to the cave, though, I'm unsure!"

"Precisely," answered Leighton , glimpsing out to the sea at the sunken ship's oak bowstring, jutting from the waves, towards the sky in a shaft of golden sunlight. His blue eyes glistened with an emotionless shield, as he contemplated his decision. "If we don't rescue them, who will? They won't survive. We don't know what we're fighting against."

"No, we don't." said William.

Leighton overrode him, "If they were foolish enough to follow their curiosity into the unknown, with the possibility of danger, then can you imagine what they will do once inside of the cave?" He shook his head, treading back into the tent formed by the torn piece of the sail. He lunged and retrieved the hessian sacks and holding one, he threw the other to him and it skidded on the sand in front of his boots.

"What's that for?" he asked, pulling out a dingy rope and a coconut shell.

"Climbing," responded Leighton , striding along the sand and further into the flock of palm trees. "Come, we don't have one minute to lose."

"But-but-," fumbled William, petrified, following behind him, while he tread through the bushes with a firm pressed mouth. "What if-" he stopped, as he swiped around and flicked a whirling fly with a wave of his hand.

"Yes?" asked Leighton .

"*The creature tries to attack us?*" breathed out William.

"Stop worrying," snapped Leighton , shifting back around, and he stomped through the bushes.

William followed, still yearning to stay on the sandy shore for the remainder of the day until the arrival of nightfall. He listened to the shuffling leaves and the whistling crickets singing in the silence of the palm trees, swaying in the humidity. A thin sweat lathered his freckled, pale cheeks and his dark blonde fringe smeared to his forehead.

"There isn't a way inside!" argued William, trying to persuade him different to his decision and hurrying his pace, he brushed his legs against the long verdant, green leaves. "There isn't another entrance."

Leighton stopped his strides, leaning his stick into the damp soil.

"I want to see for myself, *then* I will make a decision. Perhaps, there's *another* entrance elsewhere we haven't found?" He admitted, turning back and continuing to trudge through the wet mud, they reached the swamp. He hid behind the bushes, gazing up at the cave's rugged rooftop protruding from the cliff. "Is this it?"

"Yes," puffed William, feeling complied to follow and concede beneath his patronizing consent.

Leighton glanced at the swarm of alligators resting on the cornered edge of the swamp and snapping occasionally at the buzzing flies and mosquitos with their long jaws.

"We'll sneak to the East, moving around the swamp, to avoid them noticing us." said Leighton, looking at the forest's periphery. "This way." He released the leaf from the bushes and shifted their direction to the North-East, further into the palm trees towards the opposite side of the swamp. They emerged underneath the waterfall, stepping onto the wet sleek stones jutting in the pool of water, being careful not to slip.

"I don't know about this," echoed William. "Are you sure going into a cave we know nothing about is a good decision?"

"There's not much of a choice." said Leighton.

They climbed the slanted path, treading onto the precipice and stopped at the cave's shadowed opening. The alligators noticed them and crowded around the cliff's base, hoping they would fall. Leighton stepped underneath the denticulate roof of the jutting rock and shifted his brass lantern's glow along the short stalagmites arisen near the walls. He ventured further through the opening of the tunnel. William followed behind him and with a few more tunnels, they discovered the wall of boulders. Leighton stamped his hands on them, attempting to heave and revolve the boulders forward. He clamped his lips and pressed his shoulders against them and puffing a breath, he concluded, "It's not going to open," he leant away from them. "We definitely, can't continue onward." He glanced at him. "Alright, now I understand, why you didn't bother to try this way into the cave."

They hurried back through the tunnels and his light flashed along the rocky wall, as they stepped out of the cave.

"We need to find another entrance." said Leighton , observing the prickly bush and slanted foothill alongside the cave's wall. "Let's try going this way." He retrieved the green, sugar cane from the floor and leant it against the prickly bush, brushing the leafage aside and allowed them to pass. "Be careful, it's steep here."

"Are you sure, we should go in this direction?" asked William, anxiously, tracing the wall with his bouncing fingers. He gazed down at the alligators stirring their tails, within the grimy, viridescent water and positioning themselves at the bottom of the foothill and the drifting miasma. "They're following us."

"Let them," said Leighton , over his shoulder and unexpectedly, his left foot sunk into a hole in the soil, between two, tangled bundles of brittle, yellow weeds and wild grass. He bellowed, the sugar cane snapped and he lost balance, sliding on the slope and teetering at the brink, he dangled his shoes in mid-air. The dirt sprinkled into the sour yellow miasma festering on the swamp's fringe. Leighton gripped the solid light-green cane protruding from the soil and the salient lime-stone. An alligator lifted from the swamp, padding his claws at the bottom of the cliff and opened his jaw. Leighton 's fingers reddened and stung from his clasp of the cane. He yelled, clutching another rock incision and panting, he pulled himself back onto the slope, coating his linen shirt with arid soil.

William hauled him further behind the nearest palm tree's bole.

"Are you alright?" he asked.

"Just," said Leighton , nodding and lay on the overgrown thickets, puffing a breath relieved. His head throbbed with a mild dizziness, as he gazed into the golden sunlight, flaring behind the floating puffy clouds. "Let's keep moving."

They strode through the grasses near the cave's exterior and followed the long beige rocky wall until they reached the South.

Leighton stopped and pointed, "There! Do you see it?" he asked.

William gazed over his shoulder, with a partially opened-mouth to the round fissure in the bottom of the rocky wall, almost covered from the bush's long leaves.

Leighton trudged closer towards the edge of the slope and squatted near the dark opening and tossed a rock. They heard the distant *crackle,* as it collided onto the ground. He flicked his glare to him.

"Only the sound of the falling rock, can determine how deep the cave entrance is to be." He exclaimed, dropping his sack and pulled out the rope, once hanging around the ship's masts and billowing mainsail. He coiled it on the nearest tree bole and wrapped it around his waist. He tugged it, ensuring it was fastened and would hold. "It should be alright."

"Leighton , are you sure about this?" asked William. "What if it's the wrong way inside?"

"Stop panicking," he insisted, stepping forwards and rolled dirt into the opening of the cave.

Leighton shifted, putting his back to the entrance and passively stepped backwards, holding onto the rope and descended into the magma funnel. His figure and clothes were covered in shadow, until he disappeared into the dark. William pressed his hands into the grass and peered down into the hole, until he heard his shoes thud to the ground.

"You can come down now!" his voice echoed, hearing the soft whip of the thick, beige rope being untied.

"Coming!" exclaimed William, loathing he was putting himself in a vulnerable situation.

He pulled the rope upward and tied it around his paunch, before he changed his mind and tied one knot. The dark reflecting from the jagged wall in the magma funnel engulfed him. He stamped his dirt-smeared shoes onto the rocky craters and he slowly descended further into the cave. It was three-quarters of the way down, William observed the leaves from the shrubbery were miniature and poked in the distance along the round brink of the funnel.

Leighton peeked over his shoulder, striding in the shadows and cupped the sides of his mouth.

"Steady." he echoed.

"I am," reverberated back, Leighton .

William dropped his shoes from the solidified magma and dangling adrift in mid-air, he softly descended onto the rugged limestone ground inside of the cave and exhaled, relieved. He untied the rope, "What if we need it?"

"Well done," said Leighton , clapping him on the shoulder and decided, "Don't worry, just leave it, I have another one."

William peered up at the long rope hanging on the magma funnel and a sense of sorrow overwhelmed him, watching the clouds drifting to the west. His heart sunk, knowing he wouldn't see them for a while.

Leighton dragged one match on the rocky wall and inflamed it, revealing the chamber's curved walls and stepped closer towards the arched crevice.

"This way, come on." he said, bowing and avoided his head bumping on the low crust and walked into the shadowed tunnel.

William hesitated, before inhaling a whiff of the rocky aroma to calm his nerves and followed inside.

"I hope we find them soon." He echoed, wincing at his own voice drifting to the shadowed end of the funnel.

"Me too." agreed Leighton , lifting his unvarnished, bronze lantern and the withered tallow candle's flame, shone on the opposite archway. "Don't worry, we'll find them."

Somehow both of them knew, it would be tough amongst the dark tunnels.

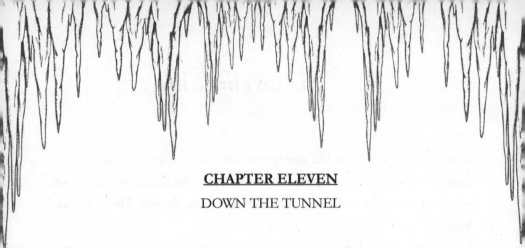

CHAPTER ELEVEN
DOWN THE TUNNEL

I bowed beneath a jagged lime-green stalactite drooping from the ceiling and a whiff of yellow smoke drifted across my nose. I ducked beneath the cluster of speleothems, touching the rocky wall and strode on the crushed piles of calcium carbonate scattered on the ground. I heard the brass oil lamp clatter inside of my ransack, after I had decided to retain the oil in the vial for darker tunnels and use a tallow candle to guide us.

"Must you always disagree with me?" I asked. "First, you didn't want to come into the cave and now you don't want to go down here."

I frowned and thought, *Just stop bickering with me.* Somehow, every time she looked at me, I felt my cheeks lightly burn with warmth.

"Always," she admitted, pointing in the opposite tunnel. "Now, this way."

"No," I disputed, deviating my dimmed, golden lamplight in the opposite arch. "I think I can hear trickling water down here."

"We want to be avoiding water. We could slip and fall." argued Nora.

"No, we need water," I blurted. "To fill our coconut shells."

"Alright!" exclaimed Nora, annoyed, following behind me. "You know, I'm tempted to go my own way in here."

"Well, maybe, you should." I said, flustered in the cheeks.

"You're cold-hearted," scoffed Nora.

"Cold hearted?" I echoed, bowing beneath the dripstones and winced as a driblet tapped onto my ear, slivering down my earlobe to my neck. "Come on, give me a break." I slid my fingers on the cragged dents of the wall. "If you want, leave, but I guarantee you'll become lost without me."

Nora gaped and shoved me in the shoulder. "You arrogant-," she paused, as a bat flapped past, swishing her hair onto her shoulder. "-bat."

"I am not," I snapped, looking over my shoulder. "I was just being honest."

"Honest?" she echoed. "No way, you underestimate me."

"Oh, really now?" I asked, pausing midway down the tunnel and held a round rock poking from the wall and she abruptly stopped in front of my chest. I looked at her and a silence drifted in the passage. "What makes you think this Nora? Who was the one on the ship, who had to be rescued from the falling mast?"

"Don't undermine me," snapped Nora, with a temper rising in her tone and shoved me in the shoulder. "You're annoying."

"Likewise," I stated, following behind her into the pitch-darkness and watched the contour of her tousling, black hair on her back.

A silence drifted momentarily, before we began crackling the stone debris in the tunnel. The air was stagnant and heavy, carrying a repugnant stench and it didn't willingly move, as the tunnel became impermeable. My chest tightened, and I inhaled as much as I could, trying to calm my growing dizziness.

"Hold my hand," I offered.

"What?" asked Nora, shocked with my gesture.

"Just in case, we become lost," I said.

Nora looked down at my fingers and exhaling, she held my hand. The immediacy of her touch, flustered my cheeks with heat and a rush of emotion ruptured through my chest. I observed her palm was clammy, like my own. A sense of comfort overwhelmed me. I wondered if she could detect, I was using the shadows as an excuse and I avoided looking over my shoulder to unveil the smirk growing on my lips, with every footstep, crackling the stone bits. I felt a little guilty, admitting to myself, I was glad Clarence wasn't here in this moment to see us, holding hands in the tunnel.

"Clarence!" yelled Nora. "Can you hear me?"

"Don't yell," I urged.

"Why?"

"You know why."

"Oh, really?" she retorted.

"Yes, *really*," I stated.

Nora side-glanced at me, annoyed and opening her mouth, I released the clutch of her fingers and covered my hand onto her lips, stopping her from yelling. Her large, brown eyes glistened in the dark, searching my demeanour to suppose if I liked touching her lips.

"It's for everyone's safety," I said, looking at her.

Nora's black brows dropped, and she lowered my hand away from her lips. The silence reeking of our entranced attraction exchanged between us, shattered away,

"*Don't* ever do that again." implored Nora, lifting her oil lamp's glow onto my chest. "We *do* have to find him."

"I know yelling can be dangerous," I whispered.

"I think following you and your decisions are more dangerous, Douglas," she retorted.

"They're not," I argued.

"Well, they are," she claimed. "Obviously."

I was about to argue more, until we heard a *crackle*.

Nora and I turned, and we looked to the wide, silhouetted arc of the cavern.

"Clarence, must be down there," assumed Nora. "I hear footsteps."

"No," I urged, following behind her and bowing underneath the crusted rocky edge of the arc in-between the walls. "This is a bad idea."

We descended the slope and walked into the shadows spread in-between the confines of rock. I lifted my lamplight and discovered the tunnel ended in a fork way of two openings in the cave. Nora and I stopped, indecisive of which passage we should take, and I swayed the wavering, golden illumination of my candle onto both, revealing the walls were curved.

"Well?" she asked, hoping I could decide.

"I don't know..." I trailed, side stepping into the right tunnel, leading eastward. "The temperature is about the same in each of them, I can't tell which one could possibly lead to a colder chamber."

Nora rubbed her cheek, feeling frustrated and groped onto the brink of the wall, inspecting them for herself and sniffed the air in the left tunnel and supplied her own judgement, "The stench is floating from this direction, we should avoid it."

I knelt down to the floor, swiping my candle airily, allowing the coils of smoke to drift from the burning matchstick and nestled it in a crevice, between the two tunnels.

"The smoke will lead us in the North-East direction. Air moves smoke." I explained, inspecting the smoke closely.

We watched it drift from the matchstick and linger to the east tunnel. I stood, stamping on the match and decided, "*North East*, it is."

"How do you know for sure, your brother could be around there?" asked Nora, smiling.

"I don't know, though, I'm suspecting he would follow in the same direction as the wind, because he's against us being led in the cave from the beginning-," I admitted, turning to look at her. "He'd want to find the first possible way out of here."

We strode down the tunnel, through the Helictite Chamber and we didn't find him in there and searched the Speleothem Chamber. The ceiling was covered with clustered, jagged, light-beige speleothems, however, we couldn't find him anywhere amongst the other rock columns.

Pitter- Patter.

Pitter-Patter.

I swiped around, dashing the glow of my candle onto the wide, serrate cleft in the opposite wall.

"*Something is coming,*" I whispered, catching a whiff of her stale, floral perfume drifting from her neck.

I panicked and heard the echo of *pit-pattering*, grow louder down the tunnel. I broadened my eyes and stood in front of Nora and protectively swayed an arm over her waist. We both intently stared into the tunnel, waiting and listened to the pitter-pattering drastically stop, into a faint crackle. *Why did I come in here?* I thought. *What if I never find my brother? What if whatever comes out...kills us...*

I snapped out of my thoughts, seeing a figure dressed in a shirt and pair of vague, beige trousers emerging out of the shadows and the pitter-pattering shifted into stamping footsteps. Clarence squinted in the candlelight , emphasizing the crumbed debris sprinkled in his disheveled, dark brown tresses and his fringe covered his eyes. He raised his hand, attempting to block it away.

"Drop it, will you?" asked Clarence.

"Phew," I said, lowering the radiance onto the floor and relieved to see my brother stepping under the low wall, to avoid bumping his head. "I'm glad it's only you."

I wrapped an arm over his shoulder. Nora hugged his stomach. I leant away and thumped a hand on his back.

"I was beginning to worry, I'd never see you again," I admitted. "Or, something else was coming down the tunnel."

"Well, nothing ever did." smirked Clarence, ruffling his brown hair and shaking the stone bits onto the floor. He flicked his fringe away from his eyes and suggested, "I think we should light firewood for the evening. It seems like we're going to be in here for a while."

"Good idea," agreed Nora. "I think we're all feeling tired and should eat some dinner. I saw some sticks scattered around in the Speleothem Chamber before," she turned, glancing down the other tunnel. "It's in the North-East. "

We walked into the tunnel and continued through a few more, passing into small, round caverns, until we reached back to the Speleothem Chamber.

"I see a few over there," observed Clarence, pointing to the floor in-between a boulder and column.

"I'll search at the back of the chamber," indicated Nora, treading to the far corner and began collecting the fronds of moss and short twigs.

I climbed onto the sloped beige, flowstone and bowed underneath the tiny, soda straws grown from the ceiling and leapt over the rim stone dam onto another slope. I curiously touched the sharp bottom of the speleothems with awe and perused the chamber, noticing a few twigs beside a distant, bunch of stalagmites in the corner of the cavern, nearby Nora. I jumped down onto the floor and my hessian pouch thumped on my back. It was with the impact of my shoes, a few bats swooped from the ceiling and screeched, flapping further away into a gloomy, cluster of stalactites. I strode past the slender totem pole, collecting the twigs and tore away a thread of grown vine, coiling around a rock. It was the only desiccated greenery, I had observed, since stepping foot into the cave. I stopped, feeling mesmerized with fright and fascination at the grown stalagmite. It was different from the other surrounding stalagmites and rock formations. I observed it steamed a plume of green mist from the astute, rugged peak.

"You should come and look at this." I called out.

Nora and Clarence held a bundle of twigs and stones in their crossed arms and gathered beside me, inspecting the stalagmite.

"*Look*," I said, lingering my pointed finger on the layer of green mucus, drenched on the peak and lathered in thick, diluted, light green streams, down to the rotund, bulging base of the stalagmite.

"What do you think it is?" asked Clarence, lowering his bundle to the floor.

"Pass me a stick," I asked, holding out my hand.

Clarence nodded, and he retrieved one, giving it to me. I poked the gooey layer of the stalagmite and the twig erupted into flames, simmering coils of squealing, green smoke and the peak dissolved into ash onto the floor. I cringed and glanced at the pile, then to Nora and Clarence.

"There's *acid* inside the substance," I said, dropping the twig quickly and it rolled, knocking into the half-remains of the stalagmite and bounced onto the smaller stalagmite. "I knew it was dangerous."

"Where did it come from?" asked Nora. "Stalactites don't drip such strong forms of acid, with a thick and green appearance. Only, carbonate acid from fallen rainwater."

I became distressed and worried, knowing exactly where it had come from; a flush of goosebumps dotted on my skin at the thought of the three-toed footprint.

"I don't know if it's a good idea to be lighting a fire anymore in here. It might attract the wrong attention and it's best we avoid it." I probed, glancing at them.

"*There's nothing in here*," insisted Clarence. "Stop thinking there is! You probably hallucinated in the dark you thought you saw picket teeth, but it was something else."

"I don't agree," I retorted. "Why is it the footprints led to the cave from the beginning? This acid substance didn't just appear on the stalagmite and where did the picket teeth come from? You saw the footprints for yourself!"

"Stop it," intervened Nora. "You're starting to scare me."

"*Alright*," I said, groaning and changed the topic. "We'll set up camp in the Helictite chamber? What do you think?"

"No," said Clarence. "Let's just stay here, I'm tired."

"I wouldn't feel comfortable in here." I said, glancing back over my shoulder, "What about the small cavern back there?"

"Alright," said Clarence, looking at Nora. "You alright with it?"

"As long as we aren't sleeping beside the strange stalagmite, I'll be fine." said Nora.

We all tread out of the Speleothem Chamber and back into the adjoining tunnel and stepped into a deserted round cavern with only a few rocks spread apart along the wall. I gathered all of the twigs and we unrolled the ripped, crinkled pieces from the foresail onto the ground. Clarence rolled the rocks

across the floor and put them around the campfire. He scavenged through his
sack and pulled out the last beef tin he had hidden inside of his tent.

"Do you have to eat it in here?" I asked, glaring at the tin.

"Where else, would I?" retorted Clarence, pulling the lid backward and revealed the slimy, brown bits of meat and he poured it inside of the pan. "We
haven't stopped all day, I'm hungry."

"Clarence, but-," I pressed, anxiously, watching him nestle it comfortably
on the twigs and strike a match, crackling an orange, bouncing spark and he
inflamed the mound of twigs. "I don't think we should be cooking meat inside
of here."

"Stop worrying, we just had this discussion one minute ago, must we have
it again?" retorted Clarence. "There isn't a creature in here. Worst case, the
bats will attack us."

"This still won't be pleasant," said Nora, overhearing us and eyed the pan,
burbling the greasy, brown liquid and levitating steam.

I sniffed the aroma of cooking meat and my stomach twisted with hunger.
Clarence lifted the handle and tilted the pan, pouring a portion into his oak
bowl and he ate it with his pewter fork.

He swallowed and offered the pan towards me and to Nora, "Have some."

I was a contradiction, as I was starved from wandering in the caverns.
Nora and I listened and ate our own portions. After we had finished eating,
we all lay down and covered ourselves with the torn, crinkled pieces from
the mainsails. I peered from the side of the tallest stalagmite and watched my
brother wrap his arm over her shoulders in the fire-light, as she trembled, and
he chuckled, poking a stick in the burning shards, twigs, leaves and rubble.
Envy, that was what I felt. *Annoyance.* The longer I stared, the more the jealousy prickled in my chest and I shifted my back to them, ignoring his buoyant,
flirtatious chuckle echoing over the flames. The rocky floor lightly prickled my
back and shifting onto my shoulder, I revolved the poking, bronze knob, and
dimmed the tawny radiance. I heard only the feeble noise of the bat wings,

flapping in the distance and echo in the silence. Hours passed, and the twirls of steam hovered from the burning twigs and drifted into the hollow tunnels. The wood crackled, and the fire's glow shrunk. I was restless, and I awoke at ten-thirty, watching the blaze and the blurring, streams of warmth and puffs of smoke, floating to the stalactites in the ceiling. I had been frightened without a draught, we would suffocate with the smoke lingering in the walls and watching the smoke slowly disappear, I presumed there was a hidden crack, somewhere in the ceiling, I couldn't see.

The Creature roamed his furred feet on the quaking floor and amongst the stalagmites. He stood watching us sleep in the passage, and his claw scoped around the rocky ledge, breathing heavily through his partially opened jaw of sharp teeth.

It was during the late midnight hour, I awoke, and almost turned onto my shoulder to sleep again, until I heard a crunching footstep nearby and I stared numbly at the stalagmite and glanced at the archway opposite us.

The Creature inhaled the aroma of cooked beef with a side wriggle of his nose. A voracious hunger swelled in his jaws and he followed it through the chamber, thumping around the totem pole, flowstone and into the jagged, silhouettes reflected from the speleothems. The Creature reached the miniature stalagmites poking on the sides of the hollow, lancet tunnel and he stepped inside, with a rivulet of saliva trickling from the corner of his mouth. He came out and emerged into the opposite hole, wiping it with his claw and quickened his pace.

I heard the scurrying footsteps and felt petrified to follow their direction.

CHAPTER TWELVE

FOLLOWING THE SCURRYING FOOTSTEPS

I swallowed, pushing the torn piece of the sail away used as a blanket the night before and crawled across the floor, twisting the knob of the oil lamp, flaring the glow. I caressed the handle and stood, quietly stepping around my brother, while he snored and leant on the side of his arm, sinking against the cragged floor. He nestled his cheek into the crinkled, ripped bundle of the foresail.

Crinch, crunch.

I heard echoing from the archway and pacing into the squashed passage, I checked one last time over my shoulder to ensure neither of them were awake. I turned back, and slowly tread into the patch of shadows. My palms began sweating and my pulse raced, while I pursued the noises crackling at the end of the passage. I ventured back into the speleothem chamber, wondering why nobody else could hear the noise as I did.

The silence loomed in the chamber. I listened, hearing only the tension burdening the ambiance of the chamber, with only the whiffs of mist levitating around the stalagmites.

Crinch, crunch.

I swiped around, biting my bottom lip and flashed the round glow from my oil lamp onto the rugged wall and the opening of another passage. I hurried past the stalagmites and crackling the loose, scattered rubble, I wanted to say something, though a feeling inside of my chest warned me not too. I listened, staying quiet and clamped my lips, hearing only my footsteps cracking the stone bits on the floor. I stepped into another chamber, with thousands of clustered helictites above me and I observed a round, black pool, with slime drenching the surface. I tread around the brink and reaching the other side, I stepped in-between slender, short stalagmites, and lifted my lamp light and discovered a curved, pitch-black arc, hidden behind a group of thick, white helictites. The speckled, ochre crystals glinted in my glow. I stopped, hearing the nudged rubble inside from the scurrying footsteps. I felt gloom plunder in the bottom of my stomach, and I squatted and bowed beneath the helictites, being careful their sharp, jagged points didn't chafe on my neck. I stood in the verge of the shadow and only the dimmed light from the prior cavern shone on my shoes. My eyes adjusted to the dark and my perception became more concise, while I traced my illumination across the totem poles scudded on the rocky foothill. The Creature dashed across the left row of limestone columns. I swiped around, listening to the rapid rush of rolling and crackling debris. I wasn't quick enough to see what had disappeared, though, I switched my oil lamp to the opposite wall of the cavern. It was with a few more footsteps, my golden lamp light shone onto a narrow crevice and clutching the wall, I shone the glow inside, searching the tight tunnel and shadows.

Nothing was in there.

I squeezed myself through and stepped in the interior, discovering a wounding staircase, hewn in the rock. I carefully descended each of the jutting stairs with the beam of light moving and revealing each one. I was cautious of any dissolution allowing sudden pitfalls to occur. When I reached the bottom, I scrunched my nose and lifted the corner of my upper lip. A rotting fetid lingered through the crevice. I blocked my nose with my covering palm and coughed, avoiding to inhale the air. My chest stifled, as I ventured further into the lightless cavern. I found the three claw marks engraved in the rock and scrawled from sharp-pointed claws. I stepped backward and nudged my back into a serrated, jutting piece in the wall. I gasped and turned around, flashing the beam of light from my oil lamp onto the wall, relieved it wasn't the claw. I didn't know the thick-furred, three-toed feet stood hidden behind the bottom of the stalagmites and they crunched away, moving to the other side of the chamber.

My heart bounced in my chest as I heard the fast echo of *crickle-crackle*. I swiped around and inspected my lamp light across the stalagmites and stopped on the middle one, trembling my hand.

"Hello?" I asked.

No noise answered from behind the stalagmite, only the presence of something sinister nearby and the air tightened with tension.

"Hello?" I repeated again, and slowly swallowed, pressing my lips together.

I held my breath and slowly emerged closer to the stalagmites. My heart's pace quickened, drumming into my ears. Suddenly, a thick rat, with oily black fur and a long, sallow tail dashed out from behind the stalagmite and scuttled underneath my widened legs. I felt the whacking tail sliver on my ankle. I bellowed and clattered the oil lamp to the floor and a portion of the bulbous side smashed, bouncing shattered glass pieces and the light blew out, enclosing me in the dark. I heard the rat scampering behind me. I turned and wondered, *why was the rat running away?*

Goosebumps flecked on my skin at the thought.

I heard in the dark, *crinch...crunch...crinch...crunch...*

I slowly turned and gazed at the stalagmites, just in time to see a pair of short, beige horns dashing behind them. I screamed, clasping the handle of the lamp and dashed back out of the chamber, tripping on a dead bat and the wing caught onto my shoelace.

"Ah! *Ah*," I panted, lifting my shoe and shook it, trying to swing it away and it thumped onto the ground. In the distance of the chamber, behind my back, a pair of gleaming, golden eyes shone in the shadows amongst the stalagmites.

A light growl echoed.

I swiped around over my shoulder, clutching the protrusion of the sharp rock in the wall and the gleaming eyes dashed away, sinking back into the darkness. I rushed up the hewn staircase and the poking bumps in the rocky walls, skimmed vastly in the shadows beneath my ascending shoes. I didn't think twice of the collapsing rocks and reaching the summit, I knocked my leg into a totem pole and tripped, falling onto the ground. My palms scraped on the sharp points, forming reddened gashes. My cheeks flushed with heat, my throat itched from thirst and after I lifted myself from the floor, I heard the footsteps climbing up the stairs. I panicked, not knowing, whichever way I turned, seemed to be a blur of darkness without the guidance of my oil lamp. My heart thudded rapidly, and I heard the pitter-pattering come from the staircase. I couldn't think, which way was it again?

I clawed my hands into my hair, frustrated.

Left? No, I thought. *It would lead into a wall.*

Right? I strode in this direction and bumped my knee into another totem pole and splashed into a black puddle.

I stopped, swishing my foot and flicked driblets in the air. *No, this isn't the way and in the proper direction.*

Straight?

I swayed around and looked ahead, spotting the opening and trampled towards it while my mind swindled. The pitter-pattering resounded behind me. I didn't want to look back to risk slowing my footsteps. The fear rushed inside of me, racing my adrenalin. I sounded a cry, trampling into the other shadowed chamber. There were stalagmites everywhere and I tried to recognize one of them- the chipped, green one, with a disintegrated peak or even the shorter stalagmites, though, they were a clustered blur, all appearing the same. I furrowed, gnashing my teeth while I strode around each of them.

I'm done for tonight, I thought. *The Creature, whatever is lurking down there with the horns is going to appear any moment and I'm going to die. I'm never going to see my brother again. I'm never going to see my mother or-*, my heart leapt a beat, *Nora again.*

Pitter-patter.

I snapped out of my thoughts and turned around, following the direction of the noise and movement hidden in the shadows. I inhaled the stale air with the rocky scent and exhaled short breaths with the rise of trepidity. My fears of the worst situation to occur, now seemed to arrive. It was now, a matter of life or death and I hurried behind the nearest stalagmite, trying to calm myself. I leant my head against the wall, with my heart hammering and my chest fluctuating upward and downward. I pulled out the box of matches from my pocket and after inflaming a matchstick, I ignited the tallow candle inside the lamp. I grappled the rubble and felt the cold, frail sliver of sweat trickling from my forehead onto my temple and cheekbone. It glistened sleekly in the luminance and clung to my jawbone.

I covered my mouth and heard the loud, *crinch, crunch!*

It's here, I thought, staring numbly at the rugged wall opposite me and listened to the roaming footsteps, *crinch, crunch!*

If I stayed here, The Creature would surely find me…

I inhaled another whiff of air, mustering courage and peeking from the side of the cragged stalagmite, I spotted the impassable pointed archway opposite me. It was only in this moment, I became aware of I was *lost*, alone and a growl echoed through the nearest hole.

CHAPTER THIRTEEN

CRINCH-CRUNCH

An array of *picket teeth* lifted in the shadows, snuffling the air from a light-beige, moist nose behind my ear. I swiped around, and glided my lamp light over them, accentuating their picket contours lathered with a shiny, moist layer of green saliva. I screamed, revolving the oil lamp and flashed the wavering, feeble candle flame on the fleet of stalactites. The Creature had scrunched skin along the bridge of his nose, sagging onto the nostrils and his partially opened jaw lifted into clamped teeth. I watched it dash back into the shadowed crevice. My heart rapidly palpitated in my chest. A few pieces of debris rolled from the edge of the rocky ledge, plunging in front of my shoes.

I panted and tread backwards and swallowed.

My heart pounded, nerves tingled in my chest and the subtle moaning breeze loomed in the pointed openings and into the cavern. The Creature hastened past the tunnel. I swiped around, broad-eyed and reaching the archway, I stopped.

Crinch, crunch!

Crinch, crunch!

"No," I gasped.

The pace in my heart hastened, as if it would lurch out of my chest. I dropped my lower lip and the air gathered inside of my lungs, climbed and grew inside of my throat, as a scream. I lifted the sharpest rock and quivering, I felt another stream of sweat drenched my back.

It's coming. It's going to kill me.

It found me. It tricked me.

I'm gone.

I'm dead.

I snapped out of my panic and heard Nora's blurting voice echo in the tunnel.

"Nora!" I exclaimed.

Nora sung a penetrating squeal in the dark, eyeing the arisen sharp rock in my hand above her head and the glow from her oil-lamp swished over my nose and dropped to the floor.

"Ah!" I bellowed, dropping the rock relieved. "Nora! You scared me!"

"Douglas!" she retorted, emerging out of the passage and putting a hand to her hip, unimpressed. "I was looking everywhere for you! What are you doing? You were missing from the campsite! I was worried about you!"

"I-I-," I stammered, not knowing how to immediately answer her. *"Nora-look-."*

"Don't you Nora, me," she snapped and frowned. *"Don't go wandering off like the way you did!"*

"I had too!" I blurted, realizing I sounded ridiculous, as compared to her logical response. "It was necessary!"

"No, it wasn't!" she disputed. "What if I couldn't find you?"

"I heard something okay?" I argued. "It was important to follow!"

"Without us?" she asked, shaking her head. "No, *wrong.*"

"Look, just because it's your opinion, doesn't mean you're right!" I said.

"I am right," said Nora. "You're just not admitting it and this cave is humungous and unrecognizable in the dark, you should've known better."

I groaned, loathing how logical she sounded, and I couldn't argue against her anymore, even as much as I denied it and knew she was right. I stayed silent and released my frustration through an exhale and leant back against the wall. I felt a headache stretched across my forehead. What had I seen tonight? What did those horns belong too?

The flash of memory of the short horns raced past the stalagmites.

"We have to get out of this vicinity now!" I blurted, snatching her hand with the thought of them.

I tugged her abruptly forward and we trampled down the passage.

"Douglas! Wait!" exclaimed Nora. "What's going on? Don't take the oil lamp without my permission!"

Suddenly, Clarence appeared at the front of the passage, with his bronze lantern, shining the golden luminance onto us. We both squinted, and it dodged between the walls.

"*Where were you?*" blurted Clarence.

"Calm down," urged Nora.

I could perceive he was angry with me, with the movement of his vast strides. We stopped at the front of the passage and he lowered his bronze lantern, flaring the light onto our chests.

"Why did you go wandering on your own in here?" asked Clarence.

"I heard footsteps," I explained, "And I was worried, it was one of the sailors finding their way in here and they were spying on us, or-," I paused, knowing he had doubted me before. Should I tell him the truth? I conceded to being fearless and I didn't care anymore what he thought, or, about his skeptical perspective and it gushed out of me, as water undulating on the shoreline, "*The Creature.*"

"What Creature?" he asked.

"Yeah, Douglas?" echoed Nora, returning me a worried glare.

Her eyes were slightly widened and moistened, with a glinting shine.

"I saw it," I said. "It has *horns.*"

Clarence and Nora hushed quiet, listening intently about my observation.

"They were short and light beige," I added. They exchanged a glance with one another, doubting what I had seen. "It was hiding behind the stalagmites."

"C'mon, Douglas," said Clarence, "*Really?*"

"Yes, *really,*" I insisted. "I saw it with my own eyes, it was there rising from behind the boulder and then they dashed in-between two stalagmites, but they were shadowed, and I couldn't see them closely enough."

"This is why, you should stop being curious all the time and want to know about things, you shouldn't!" exclaimed

Clarence, grappling my shoulder and frowned. "If it's none of your concern, then don't worry about it."

I shrugged and tread past him, hearing the crackle echo from beneath my footsteps on the ground.

"I was trying to protect us!" I implored.

"Well, you're not good at it," snapped Clarence, "What if you were killed? We went looking for you and then we found ourselves more trapped and lost in this cave! Do you ever stop to *think!*"

I glowered at him, with an irrevocable anger swelling inside of me. Did he ever appreciate anything I was trying to do for him and Nora, or, the courage I had to even investigate what I had heard?

"Stop," intervened Nora, stretching out her arms and leant her fingertips against our stomachs to avoid us from arguing anymore. "*That is enough between both of you,*" she looked at me and then back to him.

We both quietened and a long, growl echoed from the end of the tunnel and we all looked down in the same direction.

"Let's return back to the campsite." suggested Clarence. "I think we all need some rest."

We hurried out of the passage and began treading into the large cavern with the multiple archways. I was relieved to be back in here and Clarence guided us into two large, round, widened archways.

"It's quite obvious," I echoed down the tunnel. "We should never cook inside of here again or light a campfire, otherwise, The Creature wouldn't have come in our direction from the first place."

I stepped back into the small cavern and the distress I had before, dissolved into relief. I beamed and lifted the corner of my lips, eyeing the mound of burnt embers, twigs and burnt leaves clustered in the middle of the cavern around the crumpled foresail pieces.

"I know," bickered Clarence. "However, if we're to survive we have to eat, especially if neither of us intended on being stuck in here."

He sat down on the boulder near his lumpy, potato sack and scavenged through it, pulling out a coconut. He began hitting it against a sharp rock, trying to form a cracked splintered line. I heard the sound of the enclosed water, swishing inside of the shell, and my dried throat and mouth quenched with thirst. Clarence opened a crack inside the coconut and he brought it to his mouth, sipping on the water and after a long swallow, he noticed Nora was watching him and he offered it to her to drink. Nora thanked him, and swallowed a short sip, knowing she was being polite by not taking a larger one and returned it back to him. I sat down in my bundled sail and wiped my palm across my forehead drenched in rivulets of perspiration, clearing it away and rubbed it onto my pocket. *What had I seen? Who was The Creature? What did it entirely look like? Was The Creature the reason, causing the strange substance to dissolve the stalagmite's peak?* I bit on a piece of stale bread and chewed it slowly and pulled the top away from the flask and sipped the stream water, which was half full. I didn't take a long swallow, because I wanted to save some for tomorrow. I was beginning to worry about finding water to survive inside of the cave, until we found a way out. Somehow, I knew it was going to be longer than a few days and this worried me. We had to find water soon, otherwise, we'd perish in here and the thought of becoming a rotten skeleton lying on the floor amongst the stalagmites and drooping stalactites, frightened me. I put the bottle top back on the flask and back into my potato sack. I lay down, listening to Nora and Clarence muttering between themselves. I felt neglected and pulled the crumpled piece of the sail over my shoulder. Their voices turned into muffling and my eyesight blurred, until I fell asleep. The long hours passed and I dreamt of the island with the waves splashing onto the shore and the froth sinking into the swirled pearl and beige shells, dissolving into the dank twigs in the marshland on the eastern tract.

In the morning on the second day, I awoke with a yawn and the smell of crackling bacon being turned on sticks in the smoke. I broadened my eyes and waved my hands through the smoke simmering from the sticks.

"Did you listen to anything I told you?" I blurted. "Stop!"

"We were hungry!" argued Clarence.

I snatched the stick away from him and flustered the smoke away with the whipping sail, moving in the air. Clarence and Nora coughed, dropping their burnt twigs into the campfire. I was pleased they separated from each other, and sniggered behind the flapping, crumpled sail. I dropped it to the floor and folded it, tying the rope around and swooped a thick, bound knot.

"We can't stay here now," I said, "Start packing."

"C'mon, Douglas," sung Clarence, sourly, "You're not seriously considering the existence of that creature again, are you?"

"Did you not hear the growl?" I retorted. "You were there last night."

"Maybe, it was an animal," he suggested. "If you're going to argue about the weird stalagmite again, it might've been from the ceiling or something else, we're ignorant about of this cave."

"Oh stop, with your skeptical perspective!" I exclaimed. "Stop denying, what is in here!" I stood, swinging the rolled sail over my shoulder and it bounced on my back. "Is it because you're frightened of accepting the truth and the dangerous possibilities we could encounter?"

Clarence silenced, clamping his lips together and returned me a vile, sharpened glare of enmity, while he began packing the last tins away into his potato sack. He echoed his compressed, silent anger with the clang of his pan dipping on the cans and into his hessian ransack.

"We haven't seen it, Douglas," added Nora.

I loathed she was siding with him.

"Well, if you keep cooking meat in here, I assure you, *you will*," I stated. "There wasn't bones in the cavern for nothing."

Clarence slowed the stuffing of his ransack and rolling of his sail and looked at me.

"Which is *why*," he said, "If you're right, you're utterly stupid for leading us in here. We could've been on the island now instead and cooking and eating as much as we liked."

I irrevocably fumed through my nose.

"Clarence, *stop* with the attitude," I seethed, over engaging with his narrow disposition and perspectives.

"Why?" he retorted. "Does the truth bother you?"

I scowled and although, he was my brother, he was really starting to annoy me.

"Do you want to go our separate ways?" I asked. "I'm not afraid of exploring the tunnels in this cave alone?"

"*No*," disputed Nora, permeating her overpowering demeanour and she stood between us, swinging her pouch over her shoulder and stomped towards me. "You will *die* if you go alone and you're *definitely* staying with us."

"*Fine, but he better remain quiet.*" I complied, unable to resist her demand.

"Yeah, because you're 'always right', aren't you?" retorted Clarence.

"Clarence!" I exclaimed.

"Whatever," he said, with a hot-tempered tone. "Are we going or not?"

I nodded and we stepped out of the cavern. I was silently unsure, which way to explore for water and I wondered what Nora and Clarence thought to see if they knew anything more than me.

"I've been thinking," I announced, "We need water first to survive in here and at the same time, see if we can smell air in any of the tunnel, particularly, if it's salty. This will definitely lead us towards the island."

"For once, I agree," said Clarence. "I can't live off coconut water the next few days. I could drink one an hour and I only have three left inside of my pouch."

"Well, I noticed last night, while searching for you, the mud became slightly moist in the Dripstone Tunnel," said Nora, "When I reached the Splattermite Chamber, some of the mud was soggy and I became annoyed, because it clung to the bottom of my shoe and only removed, when I wiped it on the edge of a boulder."

"Which arch was this one?" I asked, while we walked down the tunnel and into the cavern archways. "I can't remember."

"The second one on the right," said Nora, and we walked inside, eyeing the ceiling of brown, dripstones, which were different to the jagged, shawls of helictites I had encountered last night.

These were small and hung as stature droplets, white and light beige from the calcium carbonate deposits in the limestone rock. They weren't long, though, very short, just at the verge of becoming soda straws and eventual, thick stalactites. We strode into the ginormous chamber, with the thick, splattermites grown as towers amongst the unlevelled floor. One stood near the sedimentary rock precipice of the cliff and small, clustered stalactites hung from the ceiling.

"It was over here," directed Nora, pointing ahead.

We walked amongst the gigantic, splattermites, passing a thick, tall and slender totem pole nearby, which was still forming into its surrounding rock formations. We passed underneath the shadow of the cliff and I felt the size of an ant, while walking in this chamber and with every word spoken, it echoed and bounced in the vacuity of air. I began to feel the hardened rock and karst terrain, under my shoe soles changing into moist mud and eventually, when I climbed the inclined floor, it became soggier. Nora hovered the radiance of her oil lamp onto the muddy trail and she was disappointed when it stopped in front of large, round boulder.

"Aw," sung Clarence, annoyed and whacked the uneven surface of the cliff and bits of rock flicked from his fingertips. "A dead end."

Nora touched the boulder and bowed her forehead onto the surface.

"Sorry," she said, turning her back and leant her shoulders against the wall "Now, what are we going to do?"

The boulder jostled.

"Watch out!" I panicked.

I pulled her arm and slid my fingers down her wrist. Our hands touched, releasing a pool of warm emotion inside of my chest and I quickly dropped her hand, not knowing whether I should allow myself to feel this way. I think she had felt something too, as she eyed my hand and glanced at me with twinkling, softened affection in her eyes. We both looked back to the wall by the shifting boulder and it rolled across, revealing a long tunnel and strands of moss dangled down from the ceiling.

"Woah," gasped Clarence, broadening his eyes and he glanced at me. "Did you *see* it?"

He looked back and lifted his radiance onto the boulder and he touched it, peeking into the front of the tunnel and the end wasn't discernible, as it was engulfed with shadows.

"I wonder where this leads too," probed Clarence, slowly and glanced back at me, searching for approval whether we should be exploring or not.

"The trail continues on in here," I noticed, inspecting the floor and fluidity amongst the soluble rock. I tread inside, lightly touching the wall.

Later at nightfall, we found a secluded antechamber intersecting with the doline cavern.

"Has your brother always been attracted to danger?" asked Nora.

"Always," confessed Clarence. "He's risky and never remains on the safe side and he's careless about himself."

"I hate this about him," disapproved Nora. "He needs to take care of himself more." She leant her elbows on her knees. "I always worry if he's going to seriously injure himself from his own carelessness and not applying logic properly." She sighed. "He becomes angry, every time I tell him to be careful."

"That's him," agreed Clarence, hurling a piece of stone in the air and caught it in his palm, with the sound of the crackling fire. "Never tell him what to do, he doesn't like it and he's stubborn."

"Is he with someone?" she asked.

"With someone?"

"Yes, as in, does he have a girlfriend?"

I quietened and realised she was asking, because she liked me? Or, because she was just curious? Why would she care?

"Yeah, Douglas, likes another girl," bluffed Clarence. "He's really sad he had to leave her behind. I'm sorry. He's really not over her at all." He lounged backward onto the boulder, twisting his finger around a strand of her black hair and playfully flicked it.

I gritted my teeth, feeling my cheeks infuriated. *He was telling her lies.*

"Oh," said Nora, echoing her disappointment. "How odd, it seemed he held my hand and showed much affection for me."

I leant my forehead into the wall.

Did I hear disappointment in her voice? I supposed if she was disappointed, she was interested and liked me. She had liked my affection. A spider crawled out of the hole onto my neck. I gasped, feeling it beneath my shirt and spread my fingers everywhere on the front of my buttons. I hurried to the end of the corridor, tangling myself in the silvery stretched spider webs clinging and thatched onto the furrowed walls. *She did suspect something from a guy like myself.* I thought, exhaling a breath from my lips. I calmed myself and tread back into the cavern.

"Oh, Douglas!" exclaimed Nora, peering up at me, as I walked around them. "We were just discussing-,"

"The direction we should embark on towards in the cave." intervened Clarence.

I yawned and sat down on the floor, unrolling the sail.

"Sure," I said, echoing with sarcasm in my tone. *"There's a map drawn in the dirt too."* I wrapped in the piece of the sail over my shoulder and shifted my back to them. "Good night!" I closed my eyes and could feel Nora staring at me.

In the morning, we packed our bags early. Nora and Clarence cautiously followed behind me, past the towering splattermites through a hollow round crevice into the passage. I arrived at the middle of the cavern and I stopped and overheard, *crickle crackle*. Nora shrieked and pointed to the floor.

"There it is again!" she cried.

Clarence and I looked down at the sunken, three-toed footprint and the terror seeping from within us, began to flood the silence.

"Quick, back to the chamber!" announced Clarence. "I don't care about finding water in this direction of the cave! I'll thirst!"

The boulder rolled across the opening and enclosed us in the dark, with only the golden dimmed radiance shining from our oil lamps.

"Oh no!" cried Nora.

"Great," he grumbled. "Now we're stuck!" He paced in front of me and slouching his back, he examined the floor and found the trail of three-toed footprints with his lamplight, stamped towards the wall. "Well, this is just really good, isn't it?"

"Everyone stay close," I said, catching up to him. "We don't want to become lost."

We all huddled closely together and lifting my golden candlelight onto the left wall at the end of the passage, Nora shrieked, Clarence cringed and I gasped. The Creature's shadow of his furred body loomed on the rugged, limestone wall and it slivered aside and disappeared in the shadows.

CHAPTER FOURTEEN

CARBONITE ACID IN THE LIME CHAMBER

In the morning at ten o'clock, I thought I heard a stone scrawling on the wall, though when I turned, it was *a claw* with thick, fawn-brown fur and sharp, black fingernails. Slowly, it descended on the rocky wall shifting into the dark. I wobbled the bronze oil lamp to the side, gliding the radiant, golden beam onto the round archway, revealing a mound of dilapidated white marrow, wending with a soft warm gusting breeze. The funnel passage's curvature was revealed, with porous sedimentary rock. We glimpsed a rotund heel, covered in thick brown strands, moving behind the bend in the wall.

Crickle, Crackle. Crickle, Crackle.

"Let's just stay here," whispered Clarence, glancing at me and he grabbed the end of my shirt-I swiped around, annoyed and pulled it away. "Stop, I have to see."

"Don't," he hissed, through gritted teeth and tried to deter me, by pulling on my arm. "No, *you* stop!"

I continued swaying my arm in the air, furrowing my eyebrows and I tugged it away. "Enough," I demanded, treading through the arc into the passage.

"Douglas, *no!*" cried Nora, following behind me.

I stepped into a cavern and The Creature was nowhere to be seen, while I flashed my light around. "It has to be in here somewhere," I muttered, determined to find the hidden specimen.

"Douglas," hissed Clarence, frightened and lingering at the entrance. "*You actually want to find it?*"

"Before it finds us, *yes*," I answered, "Otherwise, we're doomed."

"The air is moist," I observed, sniffing a whiff of the wet-rock aroma drifting through the tunnel, "We'll go in this direction,"

"It smells like rotting eggs," echoed Clarence, annoyed and blocked his nose, "Are you sure we should go this way? What if it leads somewhere else?"

We tread into another cavern and the gigantic stalactites of thirty meters hanging from the ceiling, trickled rivulets of sleek water and were surrounded with clustered long, soda straws. There were piles of disintegrated rock on the floor, tumbled from the smallest stalactite's peak and the air drifted a wet stone aroma.

"Look at those," gasped Clarence, tilting his head and raising his oil lamp, he flashed his beam of light onto the soda streams and silver specks twinkled.

"They're formed from acid water seeping through the rock," I informed, gazing with an incessant terror at the ground. "Wait a minute, acid water…." I trailed, turning to him and Nora. "We must be careful in here."

"Why?" he asked. "What's wrong?"

"I think I know why."muttered Nora.

I broadened my eyes, swaying my oil lamp's glow on the long, thin and wide rifts splintered in the rugged floor and I murmured, "We have to get out of here, *now*."

Nora groaned, very annoyed at my sudden and impulsive changed perspective and she said, "You change your mind quickly!

Why are you always bringing us to a dangerous situation?"

"Danger?" repeated Clarence.

"Carbonate acid water, dissolves in limestone-," I blurted, and my heart began to palpitate and a feverish tingle warmed my palms and I swallowed, before muttering, "and *crumbles rock*." I side-glanced at Nora. "Do you have rope?"

"Yes," said Nora, scavenging through her ransack and pulled out the rope. She unrolled it to the floor. "I hope this is long enough."

"It's not, but it'll have to do," I said.

I tied my rope around the nearest stalagmite and my waist. Nora and Clarence observed and did the same.

"This is only for protection," I said, pulling on the rope and ensuring it was tight enough. "Be cautious, stepping over every crack you can see. There's a huge difference between *water* on limestone and *carbonate acid water*."

I huffed, slowly taking one step forwards and crumbled a small rock beneath my shoe. My eyes broadened, as I lowered my oil lamp and shone the wavering candleflame onto the grouped fissures. I wondered if I could discover another way around them.

I found a portion in the ground and lunged a long step, avoiding pressing on the cracks with my heel. "If we step on just one crack, we'll never come out of here alive, I assure you."

"Oh, now you tell us," said Clarence, annoyed, side-stepping over every crack she could, and his voice dropped to a sarcastic notch. "This is just *great*, *Douglas*."

"Hey, I didn't know this chamber had them, okay?" I retorted, stepping on a serrated portion. "*Until now.*" I glanced back at the floor and awkwardly dodged another crack. "How was I supposed to know of the permeability in the floor?"

"If the air was moist and you already knew of carbonate acid water, then perhaps you could've presumed of the precarious consequence?" she argued.

"Do you *always* have to argue with me?" I blurted. "I thought maybe it would lead to a stream! Or a waterfall or a dam! Which would lead us back out to the island!"

"You could've thought of the possibility!" she argued.

"Well, I *didn't*," I snapped, frowning and wondered how I could even consider having an attraction towards her at this moment in between our bickering. *How could she even possibly think, I would lead all of us purposely into a dangerous situation? After, especially I had rescued her from the python and the alligators!*

"Both of you, please!" urged Clarence, shaking his head and broadened his eyes. "Just be quiet, we're going to reach the other side, it's *alright*."

Nora partially-opened her lips and inhaled a whiff of air. We exchanged a glare, knowing he was right and we looked away from each other. I suddenly, felt awkward in her presence and yearned for us, *not* to argue, even though I really disagreed with her viewpoint. She was beautiful and feisty, always causing a rupture of annoyance.

I was distracted with a gust of wind blowing across my oil lamp and it sunk through the fissure in the bulbous glass. The inflamed candlewick, diminished into a coil of smoke, leaving us vulnerable to our surroundings. I shifted my hand to my pocket, unable to find the packet of matches and realized, they must've fallen out. I stepped forwards with my hand stretched out, bouncing my fingers onto the walls and squinted, trying to adjust my eyesight to the suddenness of the shadows and heard the crack drifting from the floor. I stamped another footstep forward and it echoed louder.

"Douglas, I don't like the sound of it-," began Clarence, wincing and he stopped far behind me. "Don't move."

"I'll just try and move away," I said, stepping backwards and my leg nudged into a small stalagmite. I startled a cry, teetering backwards and swung my arms in the air.

The porosity dilapidated the rock beneath my shoes.

I wailed, falling with a mound of crumbled debris.

CHAPTER FIFTEEN

WANDERING IN THE HYPOGEAN LAIR

"Ahh!" I hollered, soaring down in the round wide funnel of darkness.

The rope loosened around the totem pole, slivering on the dusty rubble and descended over the curved edge of the doline. My heart thrummed wildly. *Was I going to die?* I stretched out my hand to the above rope, though my fingers only scoped through air and a piece of falling stone. I glanced over my shoulder, observing the shadowed ground with cracks and the huddled sharp stalagmites, becoming more discernable.

I panicked, broadening my eyes and screamed, "*No!*"

I was relieved, as the knotted rope caught into a poking limestone hook on the funnel's wall and the rope bounced, faltering my descent. I bellowed, squeezing my eyes shut and felt the rope coiled around my stomach tighten. I halted, swinging above the tallest stalagmite's piercing peak and it brushed over my stomach, tickling my terror and with the slender touch of the cold rock, goosebumps flecked on my body. I inhaled the air and was relieved, I hadn't fallen on any of them.

"*Douglas! Douglas!*" yelled out Clarence, appearing on the side of the doline and gripped the edge. His dark brown tresses fell around his cheeks. "Can you hear me? Are you alright? Are you alive?"

Nora appeared beside him. "Can you hear us?" She exclaimed, lowering the oil-lamp and skimmed the glow on the curved walls and shrieked, noticing, I dangled on the rope. "Douglas!"

"Yes, I can!" I answered, with a cracked ache in my throat and warned, "Stay back! Don't move any closer! Be careful! The rocks could crumble beneath you, as well!"

I was disappointed in myself to have formed a doline, though I tried to comfort myself; I couldn't control the amount of porosity in the bedrocks. A wretched, crooked noise sung in the silence and feeling myself drop, I clutched onto two of the stalagmite peaks, protecting myself from falling on them and the rope lowered me to the floor. A plume of dust soared beneath my body and shifting on the ground, my cheek rubbed into the dark beige debris. I moaned, leaning my palms into the dissolved pieces of limestone rock and my legs ached from the hastened impact of the plummeting fall. I slid my hand into my pocket and pulled out my pocketknife and cut the rope away from my ankle, dropping myself to the rubble. I rolled onto my back, laying there momentarily with a hand on my stomach, trying to soften the ebbing pain. I knew I'd have a purplish bruise swell on my shoulders tomorrow. I listened to my brother's footsteps, becoming vaguer, as he tread away from the doline's jagged periphery.

"Douglas, I don't have any other rope!" he called.

I watched him scavenge his pockets and shuffling through his bulging sack.

"Me neither!" echoed Nora, shuffling through her own hessian pouch and she reappeared at the doline's edge. "Oh, Douglas! What are you going to do now?"

"Don't worry," I wailed, unable to gather the last remnant of my voice to make it resound louder. "Stay there."

"I can't leave you down there all by yourself!" yelled back Clarence, annoyed at my perspective and panicking.

He strode around the doline, avoiding the cracks and his dimmed tawny glow shining from his tallow candle skimmed on the curved edge.

"I'm going to try and find a way down there. Maybe, there's another tunnel somewhere?" rambled Clarence, with a determined disposition and puffed a breath, frustrated. He turned frontward to the doline. "There has to be a way down there."

"Clarence," I pleaded, deciding to raise myself from the floor; otherwise, I'd be tempted to lay there the whole evening.

I felt my fingertips brush a circular object and glimpsing down at my compass with a cracked glass surface, I observed a small fragment was missing.

"No," I gasped, dragging the silver chain in the debris and held it in my palm.

I tapped the compass and brought it closer to my eyes. My perception adjusted to the dark. I observed the contour of the slender, black needle lingering on the S and shook it beside my ear, hearing a *clink*.

Clarence lowered the oil lamp, shining the golden flare of light into the hollow doline.

"Do you still have the thermometer by any chance?" he echoed.

"Yeah," I confirmed, rummaging through my hessian sack and pulled out the thermometer. The mercury had arisen an inch. "It's now at twenty degrees. I think my compass might still work, though, I'm not too sure."

"I wouldn't rely on it," he echoed back, bouncing and whirling his voice between the round walls. "It could lead you wrongly somewhere."

"I have to find a way back up," I decided, glaring with fright at the impenetrable shadows in the tall, broad opening in-between the walls. "This is the most dangerous part of the cave. It's the hypogean vicinity."

"Hypogean," hushed Nora, glancing at my brother and she looked down at me. "Douglas, please be very careful! Now, I feel even more worried for you. Do you have any more matchsticks to light your candle?"

"I do," I said. "Please don't worry, I'm sure I can survive."

I tried to be convincing, though I could perceive she was perturbed by biting the corner of her bottom lip.

"Hypogean?" asked Clarence.

"In Speleology, it means there isn't any form of light in the caverns. I'm at the lowest level possible." I explained, keeping the remainder of the information to myself, having a hunch I would frighten him again and it would worry them. *Only where Troglobites dwell, there's lack of air. I doubt to find the waterfall I had found before,* I thought. *Scorpions, spiders, beetles...*

I stared into the dark cleaved archway of the hypogean lair and stepping through it into the round passage, I hindered in the silhouettes reflecting from the ceiling and the soft illumination spread on the floor, from the doline's rotund periphery.

"Where are you going?" called out Clarence and warned, "Don't go in there!"

"Stay where you are!" demanded Nora, scowling. "Don't you ever realize following your curiosity is going to lead you somewhere you shouldn't be in?"

"It's the only way out!" I argued, side-stepping around the scattered, miniature craters in the floor and the scorpions crawled onto my shoe.

I stopped, lifting my shoe into the air and shook them away. I struck a matchstick against the wall, flaring a small flame and the glow swelled in the dark, shining onto the large pile of scorpions scuttling on the ochre ground. The situation seemed to feel more detrimental, revealing them. A chill slivered down my back and it crawled on my spine. I whacked the nearest tarantula onto the ground, and it scuttled amongst the cockroaches, disappearing into the miniature hole in the wall. Some of the scorpions were climbing onto my looped shoelaces and ankle, towards my left leg's bloodied lesion. I became worried, they would lower their tails and sting me. I shook my leg and the majority dropped off, though, one remained and nipped my leg. I cried, feeling the pinching sensation in my calve.

"Ah!" I exclaimed, limping to the nearest boulder and clutching it, I supported myself to avoid toppling to the ground.

"What's wrong?" reverberated Clarence's voice.

"Nuh-nothing-," I lied, brushing the other maggots as quickly as I could away from my leg and clenched my teeth.

"C'mon, Douglas," he returned, not believing me.

"Scorpion bit me!" I answered, clutching my leg and limped further down towards the arc in the wall. I stopped, ripping a piece of linen from my crinkled sleeve and wrapped it around my leg above the poisoned bite, to stop the venom travelling further in my veins.

"Don't move," he demanded. "I have something I can throw down to you." He untied the rope and pulled out a bottle from his pouch. "Do you want to try and catch it? It's a tonic- but it's in a glass bottle."

"You keep it," I murmured. "What if something happens to you?"

"No," he said.

I moved out of the shadows. He threw the bottle down. I stepped forward, catching it and held it close to my chest, slouching against the wall. I swiveled the cap, pouring a dollop into my palm and smeared it onto my reddened wound. It prickled and I gritted my teeth, loathing the sensation and put the tonic back into my pouch.

"Are you better?" he asked.

"Kinda'," I breathed out. "Don't wait on me."

"Can't you just wait there, until I try and find a way down?" he inquired.

"I could..." I answered slowly, contemplating the possibility. "We'd have more of a chance of not losing each other."

"Alright, I think I'll try heading Southwards and see where it leads me."

"I agree," said Nora. "We should *definitely* try to find him down there and not leave him for too long alone. Make sure you don't move."

"I won't," I echoed back. "Be cautious," I flicked a glance at my brother. "*Both* of you."

"Yep," he nodded.

Clarence waved and both of them, stepped backwards and disappeared. I nestled my tallow candle into the small crater within the rock and waited for hours, seated on the ground and stared glumly at the wall. I wondered of the atmospheric circumstance had occurred to form the cragged curves in the limestone and loosely tilted my head, beginning to feel drowsy. My eyes burned from the long, enduring hours of lost sleep. I closed them, dreaming of Leighton and William, pondering what they were doing this very moment and it was only after hearing a bouncing pebble, I awoke from my slumber.

I jerked my head, startled and asked, "Nora? Clarence?"

I skimmed the doline's chamber with blurred eyesight, realizing they weren't anywhere. I lifted from the ground and clasped my warm candle from the curvature in the rock and stepped into the shadows. I couldn't remember how long I had been there or what day it was in the week. My head dizzied and throbbed, as I moved into the impenetrable darkness, stepping beneath the draperies of silvery-white spiderwebs and further into the tunnel.

Could it be Clarence? How did he find me quick? I wondered, awing at the walls. I discovered the lava flooded long ago, was smoldered in reddened magma streams in the round ceiling and walls. The ground inclined and it became difficult proceeding further. My breaths shortened in the airless tunnel amongst the lingering mustiness and heat in the atmosphere. I smelt the faint whiff of inflammable gases, lurking near and felt the sweat inside of my shoes rubbing on my heels, forming reddened blisters with every footfall on the uneven ground. A rush of heat flustered in my cheeks and panting a breath from exhaustion, I climbed the last step and reached the summit of the slope. I clutched the wall, embracing my dizziness which tempted to teeter me backwards. The draperies of crusted lava lined on the surrounding walls, were porous and peculiar with a hidden radiance from the opaque, crystallized specks. I observed the ecologies didn't survive on sunlight as the other troglofauna did in the upper levels of the cave. They were surviving on the minerals of the dark-green bacteria, growing on the floor and feeding on the chemical vitality from the lime-stone debris.

I stopped, sitting on a rock and rested against the wall.

It was after observing the ants crawling on the rocky ground, I heard the distant *splash* of a liquid from the corbeled arch in the distance. The *crackle* of falling rubble echoed and I knew it wasn't from a gust of wind, seeping through a hole in the ceiling. I turned and the gleam of orange light shone on the ground. The silhouette of the paired conical fur, pointed-horns, long ears and a lanky body loomed on the crimson stalagmites.

CHAPTER SIXTEEN
THE FIRST ENCOUNTER WITH THE CREATURE

A mauled foot and ankle bone lurched from the precipice, through the lime-stone stalactites. I turned and recoiled and bellowed into the flowstone. It *thumped* onto the ground in front of my brown leather shoes amongst the impenetrable cavern and the shaft of dimmed light from my wavering, golden flame. I observed the green mucus drenched the round white knob and the dark-brown laces.

"*Ah!*" I screamed, with my chest rising and lowering, between my distressed breaths.

Vomit swiveled in my throat. I dashed quickly as possible towards the entrance into a soda-straw ante-chamber and black, dead scorpions dangled from spider-webs onto my forehead and cheeks.

"*I have to get out of here.*" I whispered.

The cold legs from the dead scorpions, slid on the nape of my neck, chilling my spine. My fingers brushed on all the rocky curves in the walls and hurrying through to the end, I shuddered, as a flock of bats flew past, whip-ping their membranous wings onto my face.

"AAH! AAH!" I bellowed, squinting and not bearing the terror built in my chest.

I panted in the silence and heard the familiar rapidity of the debris crunch-ing and being rolled from the distant tunnel.

"No," I whispered.

My bellow, had invited The Creature in my direction.

No, I was going to die and become like the-the-I looked down to my shoe-The Foot- my own would be gone. Someone, get me out of here. I felt gooseflesh crawling on my skin as if the maggots were coating my shoulders and back. I ran around the saw-toothed stalagmites, with yellow mists drifting over my waist and trampling through a passage, I squished the crowd of millipedes and yellowy-white slush, smeared into the cragged floor.

"Disgusting," I whispered, side-stepping into a vacant patch of rugged rock without insects. "*Disgusting-* this *whole* place."

What was the green mucus?

The feeble echo of hastened, pitter-pattering shrunk further into the distant tunnel.

"Hello?" I called out, treading down further into the dark. "Anyone there?"

Nothing answered, except the lonesome pacing of my footsteps. I swallowed, feeling my thumping heartbeat echo in the silence.

"*Maybe, not,*" I whispered, treading slowly through the floating, yellow mists on the floor.

I stepped into a cavern, awing at the lime-rock stalagmites and stalactites drooping from the ceiling, infested with floating, yellow smoke. A lucid, yellow lava seethed in a canal on the rugged wall, flooding through the shadowed opening into an adjoining antechamber.

A *growl* curled through the pitch-black hole.

I shifted around and observed a pair of lucid, yellow eyes shining with malevolence and the nose of scrounged, rotund layers of skin, inhaling my scent. I panted and dropped the withered candle into the rubble and tallow driblets oozed beneath the burnt wick. The Creature clamped his picket teeth and dashed backward into the shadowed tunnel, scrawling his black claws and dropped a fountain of debris to the floor. I exhaled and tread back, crackling the rubble and left the flame to flicker an illumined silhouette on the ochre wall. I turned and hurried through the nearest passage. Web tangled and slid on my disheveled, brown hair, swishing on my light-golden tanned cheeks. I reached the end, striding into another chamber with jagged stalactites hanging from the ceiling. The cacophony of my beating heart, the nerves tingling in my chest and the subtle moaning breeze from the hollow chinks echoed. I swiped around, short of breath and looked down at the stone debris rolling down a rocky slope and stopping in the middle of the cavern.

The clouds of fog around the stalactites seemed to revolve in a slow passage of time.

I was neglected. *Alone, in the dark with him.*

He was here. In the back corner.

I expelled another breath and swallowing, I bounced my hand onto the wall. *And I was going to die.*

His pair of conical dark-brown fur poking from his head, lurked across the speleothems and disappeared in the dark.

One minute passed.

I exhaled.

The Creature's curved black claws slowly slid up the stalagmites and groped the jagged peaks, sinking into the dents.

My heart hammered rapidly, I couldn't feel one trace of thought.

The thick brown fur, resembling the shade of an oak tree's trunk was camouflaged in the shadows. I swallowed, stepping slowly backwards, shuddering into the sharp curves of rock in the wall and chafed slender ashy-white scratches on my arm. I regretted everything I had decided; to follow into the unknown with curiosity and probe what lived in the dark.

Oh, you've found it, Douglas, I thought. *It's alive. There is something dwelling in the cave and any minute now-*I rammed my shoulders into the wall and stopped.

The Creature lifted behind the misty stalagmites.

My heart thumped, and panicking at the sight of The Creature, I crouched behind the large boulder, eyeing the dimples in the ground. I recognized them to be in the slender contours of his black claws. The Creature sniffed the air, flaring his nostrils and lowered further to the edge and sipped the lava globules with his tongue. I peeked from the boulder's edge covered with the tawny

light reflecting from the flowing lava river. I had never seen such a strange
specimen, before in my entire life. I blinked twice, trying to understand it did
exist. He had a pair of conical brown tufts of fur poking from his head and
thick furred brows, arching over his bright golden eyes with slit pupils. His
ears were long and wide, with large round earlobes and he had a beard of fur
resembling jagged speleothems drooping from his angular jawbone. He had
a wide, furry chest and a slender pale waist and legs, though large three-toed
feet with slender, black nails. A set of three tentacles were coiled and poking
from his ears. They were the most intriguing and I became lost in awe. The
Creature dipped a crustacean anthropoid and a wriggling worm coiled in ivy,
dangling from a strand into the lava and they steamed, crisping dry. I flinched,
and he lifted them with his singular finger and thumb, swinging them amongst
the whirling orange fog. He sniffed them, leaning forwards and recoiled,
curling his three lime tentacles. They rolled inwards, and he growled, dropping
them to the ground and nudged them with a finger. He hissed and snarled,
widening his bright yellow eyes, with black round pupils.

I gasped.

He stopped, twitching his right ear and swung around, gazing in my direction. The Creature straightened his arched back, as he leant his elbow onto his
knee. My heart hammered faster in my chest and I thought it would lurch out,
though, calming myself, I slid my hand into my pocket touching the pocketknife's handle. The lime tentacles unrolled, as he sniffed my scent and poked
his light-beige nose into the air and side-stepped with his right foot, quaking
the floor. I winced at the reverberation and clumsily lost balance stamping
on the dust, echoing a thin crusty noise. The Creature dropped behind the
stalagmites and echoed a high- notched, curling noise from his throat, calling
me to come out from my hiding. I knew I wouldn't survive and glancing at
the opposite small boulder and if I didn't move there, he would surely find
me here any moment. I listened to the thumping footsteps emerging closer,
rolling a small rock near my shoe and clasping it, I waited for them to become

louder. I peeked at The Creature shifting closer towards the boulder, tracing my clammy palm's scent. I crawled vividly across the ground and slid to the nearby rock, pressing my shoulders against the serrations in the wall and hugged my knees close to my chest. I didn't want The Creature glimpsing my dirt-smeared shoe. I heard the crackling rubble and his grinding fingernails on the limestone ground. He sniffed and his nostrils wriggled, as he inhaled the yellow mist steamed from the popping bubbles and the burbling lava lake. His fluffy foot stepped in the silhouette hibernating between the rocky wall and boulder.

Don't breathe. I thought. *Stay calm.*

I glimpsed at the middle, long toe sliding closer. I knew now, I had to make a quick decision- I either stayed here and assume The Creature didn't only rely on smell, though movement as well. Only to prove to himself as evidence another life form was in fact lurking in his lava-lake chamber. I didn't know if I could crawl, as I suspected, as any immediate shifting movement would cause The Creature to detect my presence in my chosen direction. The torrents of the orange fog levitating from the lava river, continued to gust in my route and beads of sweat slowly trickled on my forehead and the heat began to feel unbearable. His inhale drifted from behind the large rock and I knew he could smell my perspiration drizzling down my cheeks. The Creature glanced sideways and his picket teeth appeared in the shadows, slivering saliva from the corner of his mouth, onto his beige skin. His dark-brown jagged beard of fur leant on the stalagmite.

Run, I urged myself. *Run. What are you doing just sitting here? Run. You fool.*

I was indecisive one moment longer, until I couldn't handle the tension stifling in the silence any longer. The anguish squirming in my chest, prickled for me to move- I shifted across to the tawny stalagmite, becoming nervous with my shadow reflecting on the ground. My right knee dragged onto the debris and the thin sheet of red dust. The Creature's long ears and paired conical tufts of dark-brown fur, skimmed the summit of the opposite sarsen. He turned and gazed in my direction, listening to the echoing noise. Thirst itched in my throat. I had the temptation to lower my ransack from my shoulder and pull out a coconut.

How was I going to escape The Creature? I wondered. *How would I see daylight again?*

The Creature jumped onto the sarsen and stalagmite's peak, chafing his claws into the limestone and bits trundled, bouncing onto my head. I flinched and my thoughts of escape and swallowing fresh remnants of water vanished.

I double-blinked.

He bowed downward, drifting a whiff of warm foul breath over my forehead and cheek. I side-glimpsed at an up-close of his dangling, dark-brown furred beard and his rack of picket teeth, moist from the slimy saliva. I was unable to stay quiet any longer, with the surge of terror soaring from my torso, throat and mouth. I bellowed and crawled backward, sliding my fingers and legs into the rough floor with my bulgy, hessian pouch bouncing on my shoulder and back. The Creature leant downward, arching his back and his three-toes spread on the stalagmite, supporting his posture and balance. He dropped his bottom jaw and released a hiss, feeling displeased at his discovery and my presence in his chamber. I panted and stopped at the bottom of the wall, with my right leg stretched beside the edge of the lava lake. The unbearable plumes of warmth eddied onto my body and smeared my dappled, linen shirt to my sweaty chest, stomach and arms. My tresses moistened on my forehead from the beads of sweat and they curtained loosely onto my brows. I wiped my sleeve over them. I watched The Creature rising from his squatted position and preparing to leap from the peak of the stalagmite.

"Don't-don't come any closer!" I yelled, raising a stone in my wobbling hand. "I'll- I'll-," I stopped and with doubt asked myself. *You'll do what? He's the one with the fangs, claws and sharp teeth.*

I gulped and dropped the rock, feeling helpless.

The Creature inhaled my scent and staring at the limestone stalactites, he yawped and curled his claws inward to his palms.

I trembled and dashed from the wall, and half-crawled on the ground. I arose from teetering footsteps and trampled around the beige stalagmites with tawny mists, floating over my trousers. The Creature leapt to the ground and strode amongst the stalagmites, chasing me. I felt short of breath from the heat and I stopped on the eastern outskirt, leaning against the bulging embodiment of the largest stalagmite. The miniature crystals twinkled in the rosined luminance from the lava river. The Creature side-stomped in-between another two stalagmites. I yelled, while he pursued me. I ran around the chamber, until I stopped at the opposite rock, facing him. The Creature halted, emerging out of the stalagmites and stood in front of them. He curiously blinked and gazed at me with his bright, yellow-green eyes, until he hid behind the nearest rock. I was bewildered with his sudden urge to hide from me. I presumed he was only chasing me out of being territorially invaded. It seemed, although, he was curious of me, as I was of him, he was frightened. My pulse was racing wildly, rushing the blood in my veins and carrying my terror. I calmed myself, while my cheeks burned.

After I had caught my breath, I attempted to communicate with him.

"Whu-what are you?" I stammered, glaring at The Creature and his eyes blinked above the craggy boulder, clutching the edges with his claws. "Can you understand me?"

I didn't know what would happen and he continued to hide behind the two stalagmites and the rock in-between them. His two separated tufts of dark brown hair and large pointed ears poked from the rock and his slit-eyes brightened yellow, as he lifted his nose and sniffed the air.

"Mrouw," he hailed, scrawling his claws down the short, limestone pillar. He brashly lowered and disappeared behind the stalagmite. The lime silhouette of his tentacles shone on the ground. I waited for another moment, ponderously staring at his shadow and he didn't answer me.

The Creature's growling noises echoed in the cavern and he looked back to me.

"Do you have a name?" I asked, trying again to communicate with The Creature. He tilted his head, listening to the sound of my voice. I patted a hand to my chest. "See, my name is-is-Doug-Douglas." I tread backward and swallowed, "I'm guessing you don't-," My shoulder hit into the gigantic boulder. "-understand anything I'm saying to you."

I watched him, embrace a long-stride closer towards me. The three-toed, furred foot imprinted the outline into the rugged floor, matching the trail I had found on the island and inside the tunnel.

"Ghar-," growled The Creature. "-Koll,"

"Gharkoll," I repeated.

"Drolk," said The Creature, crunching his furred, three toed foot onto the rubble.

"Gharkoll Drr-," I stammered, stepping backward away from him. "Drolk." I nodded. "I understand. Gharkoll Drolk."

"Grr," curled The Creature, from his mouth.

I swallowed and took another step away from him, trying to ignore the rapid beats of my heart in my chest. The Creature paused, intently gazing at me with his luminous, yellow eyes and leant forward, wriggling his nose and inhaled my aroma, observing it was unfamiliar and distinct to him from the cave surroundings. I became nervous, wondering what he was thinking when he smelt me from afar.

"Well, okay," I swallowed, feeling uncomfortable and slowly, stepped sideways, as I skimmed my back and fingers against the rock. "Nuh-nice-meeting you-," I slid my fingers through my ruffled hair and fumbled, "I'll-jus-just-be-going now-,"

The Creature scratched his long, dark brown ear with a singular, sharp black fingernail and tilted his head, watching me step back from the rock and away from him. He dropped his hand sluggishly beside his bent leg and responded with a curling wail, asking, why I was leaving him. I stopped at the hewn stairs in the rock and stamped my shoe onto the bottom step.

"Bye...now..." I trailed, skimming my fingers along the curved wall and lifted my other boot.

The Creature deeply growled and tread forward, softly quivering the cragged ground, crunching the disseminated bedrock.

I turned around and hurriedly descended the steps, feeling my pace quicken. The Creature wailed, urging for me to stop, though, I continued descending the stairs and he halted at the summit, watching me slip and stop for a moment, until I reached the bottom. I panted and looked at him. The Creature emerged further in the shadows beneath the flowstone curtains and he hissed, poking out his slender, dark-green tongue and snarled.

"Go- go back-," I stammered, pacing back further into the dark and I flicked my hand forward, motioning for him to return back to the stalagmite chamber.

The Creature deeply growled-it was a masculine sound and choir of rumbling, baritone tones. He glowered at me and he stepped down the stairs, jumping two at a time and the impact of his colliding feet, formed miniature craters and frail cracks, underneath his curved claws. I bellowed, feeling threatened of his rapidity and I hastened my pace, ducking underneath the longer, sloped flowstone and felt the wispy, fronds of moss gliding onto my neck. My hands balled into fists and I trampled into a corbeled fissure, and I changed my mind.

"Stay away from me!" I exclaimed.

How naive could I have been to be curious of such an animal? One without proper, scientific consensus and identification of its existence? The wide tunnel midway became tighter and I felt the bulging rock, lightly tap on my arms and gliding across my pouch.

Thump!

Thump!

Thump! I heard behind me, echoing unevenly in the tunnel and the gruff, inhaling whiffs of air gliding through The Creature's mouth and snuffling through his nose. The roar whorled through his warm breath, exhaling from his mouth, fangs and racks of picket, stained teeth. I didn't notice a rock on the floor ahead and tripped. My pace slowed, and The Creature sunk his picket teeth into my ankle, trickling blood onto my crinkled sock. I rocked my head back and screamed, hearing the crackle of my splintering ankle bone. The bottom of my trousers pooled with blood and his sticky, green saliva, dribbled onto my looped shoelaces. I bowed, grappling a debris mound, and clashed them onto his thick dark-brown fur cones.

The Creature flinched, releasing his bite of my ankle.

I slid on the beige dust and rolled onto my arm with agony and clutching the curvature in the rock, I attempted to crawl forward, though his silhouette of long-ears and lime tentacles', and pointed cones of fur, loomed on me. I glanced over my shoulder, screaming as the jaw of picket teeth enlarged in front of my nose and engulfed my collar. I listened to the rapid biting of the moist teeth and tongue jerking on my collar and warm saliva slivering onto my ear and a speckle flew onto my cheek. I bellowed, swinging my shoes on the floor and horror, I had never known before swallowed my entire being. The Creature dragged me forward and my shoulders brushed on the rough walls, scraping light scratches and slender beige streaks onto my crumpled sleeves. He growled, and blistering gusts of warm breath eddied into my ear and his yellow eyes darkened to the shade of gold and flashed in the dark. The venom burned on my skin and my back was dragged on the stone floor, sliding my shoes onto the edge of the walls. The dripstones blurred, and the echo of thick, thumping footsteps crunched on the debris and disintegrated into crumbed dust. I would probably never see daylight again. His short, light fawn horns scraped onto the low rugged ceiling and chiseled bits rained onto my forehead, bouncing onto my cheeks and his serrate beard brushed onto my chin. The smell of rotting fish levitated from the end of the tunnel and he stepped backward, dragging me into the small cavern. The Creature slid his picket teeth out of my ankle, leaving a trail of small round wounds in my skin. He arose and blew a gust of warm, sour fish breath from his opened jaws over my cheeks and lingered his bloodied teeth near my nose. His picket teeth slid across my arm, shoulder, ear and forehead, inhaling my fearful and sweaty waft with his nostrils. He stepped backward, squelching and stretched a slender thread of saliva. I screamed, side-stepping around the ochre, limestone stalagmite, as his claw swiped through the air and I staggered past the stalagmite batch, with my legs swishing through the yellow mists. He swiped his claw onto my shoulder, piercing bloody scratches and ripped my linen shirt, dangling a few loose threads. I screamed again, whacking my hand over them. I reached the end of the passage and turning into another, I clutched the wall for support, and I squinted in the dark, though ahead of me, I panicked and slowed my footsteps.

Only a rocky wall stood in the distance.

CHAPTER SEVENTEEN

THE GLOWORM CAVERN
AND THE CHEMICAL COMBUSTION

I deflected my gaze to the cloud of yellow fog, looming across the right wall and revealed a pitch-black archway. It was with fear, relief and curiosity, I limped down the neglected tight passage and my fingers slid down the cragged dents in the wall. I felt blood leak on my scrounged sock covering my ankle and lathering my leather shoe and a trail was left on the floor. Gharkoll pursued me, sinking his curved, black claws into the crumbled debris. My cheeks flustered with a layer of sweat and bowing through the round archway, the moss tendrils slivered over my neck and disheveled brown hair. I strode around the stalagmites and their cragged peaks skimmed beneath my dashing fingers and breaths puffed from my lips. Gharkoll soared through the curved archway, sliding his conical horns and tufts of fur across the rock, flinging debris in front of his three-toed claws. His front teeth shone slimy in the dark, as his furry, three-toed claws stormed through the heap of steamy rubble and they collided into the walls.

Crunch, crunch.

I panted short of breath in the heat looming in the curved tunnel of reddened magma, my shoe sunk into a deep dent and I screamed, with pain intensifying in my ankle, as an iron poker scrawling through my veins. I teetered in the middle of the passage and the short, jagged speleothems in the ceiling blurred, as I lowered, and my clasp loosened from the poking rocks.

Gharkoll emerged closer, quivering the floor. I snatched a piece of rubble and hurled it at his wrinkled nose and his three, lime tentacles expelled a hissing noise and they demolished into a pile of dusty ash, coating his furry legs. A paralytic effect came over my bloody ankle and my foot numbed, spreading a tingly sensation to my toes and with one last footstep, I toppled to the floor, sinking my palms to the sharp dents. Gharkoll 's claw whacked onto my shoulder. I bellowed, rolling onto my back and crawled behind the stalagmites. His three-toed, furry feet appeared at the opposite end. I halted, peering up and recoiled. Gharkoll opened his jaws and saliva dripped from his picket teeth.

"Ah!" I shouted, clutching the jagged peaks and stood, bouncing my hand on the wall.

I limped into another tunnel. Gharkoll screeched and followed, through the hindering yellow fog. I cringed beneath a screeching bat, flapping his ebony, membranous wings and sliding his curved talons on my disheveled, brown hair. I hurried through into a wide cavern with a black lake. I kept wondering where Nora and Clarence were in the cave and *if* I would ever see them again. It was deep in the other caverns, treading through the tunnels and past the shawls of flowstone, I could feel they were nearby. I listened to the overshadowed water ripple and I jumped on each of the rocks, amongst the slender stalagmites that had lanceolate peaks, twinkling with crystalized specks. Gharkoll stopped at the rocky periphery and wailed, disappointed, I was escaping him. I reached the other side and hurried amongst the slender speleothems and beneath the ochre shawls, clinging to the stalactites. I peeked over my shoulder and I watched him shift around and stride back through the archway.

"He doesn't like water," I whispered, frowning and watched the last of his poking tentacles shift across the tunnel's wall and sink into the silhouettes.

I turned and hurriedly, tread amongst the forest of round stalagmites, both ochre, beige with white patches from the crystals twinkling in the dark. Seemingly, it was apparent Gharkoll has some form of intelligence, comparable to the other troglophiles', such as the bats in the cave. He wanted to communicate and know more about me and what I was. Somehow, it scared me. What was *Grogoch*? What was he trying to explain? Had he been here in the cave, his entire existence? It seemed to be his species name. I crunched on a few pebbles scatted on the brink. I avoided nudging into the light green stalagmites, noticing the unusual viridescent dots shrouding around the bulbous knobs, as if they had been consumed with I suspected, something from Gharkoll. A poison or that odd acidic substance, we had found earlier before. Meanwhile, I heard footsteps and followed them, through a broad, round archway.

"Clarence?" I whispered.

~

"I always become annoyed at my brother," admitted Clarence, treading through the curved tunnel and slowed his footsteps, as the walls narrowed. His moist hand bounced on the protruding, silhouetted taupe rocks. "He doesn't understand how I feel about exploring, like for instance, I didn't want to come in here. I wanted to stay out on the island and just catch fish and collect the coconuts to keep an eye out for possible ships sailing out in the distance."

"I know," said Nora. "I didn't want to come in here either,"

She teetered and stamped in an incision formed in the floor.

"Be careful," advised Clarence, seizing her hand.

Nora returned him a scrutinizing glare with his touch, and he pulled his hand away.

"It's like *now*, he has brought himself into more trouble and I'm worried. What if I never find him again? Or, he becomes lost?" continued Clarence.

"Don't worry," said Nora, trying to comfort him and bowed beneath the conulites in the ceiling, sweeping through her dark hair. "I know we can find him. He'd be somewhere in the lower level down here."

"Yeah," said Clarence, unconvinced. "I hope he isn't too injured from the fall and he's still there at the bottom of the hole."

"Me too," agreed Nora. "It would be terrible if he continued wandering in the cave on his own."

They ventured into a wide, long chamber and he stopped, gaping at the speleothems in the ceiling and the turquoise glows shining in the dark navy rock.

Clarence gasped and pointed upward.

"Glow-worms," he said.

Nora side-stepped beside him and her eyes twinkled, with their luminescent reflection. He continued perusing them, until he saw a dingy, burgundy bag nestled beside the stalagmite and a curved niche in the wall.

"Hey, what is this?" he exclaimed, flashing the candlelight in the creaky lantern down onto the bag. He squatted and pulled on the torn strap, dragging it across the depresses and lifted the flap back.

Nora knelt to the floor beside him, curious, while he scavenged through the burgundy bag. Clarence pulled out a black bottle, smeared with streaks of dirt and oily fingerprints dabbed long ago. He revolved it beneath the dimmed, guttering yellow candle-flame, reading the label and he announced, "Chloride," He looked up at her, oozing the liquid along the black stalk and one driblet leaked through the bottle-top onto the floor. "I remember this chemical being spoken about from another voyage. It's used to put animals too sleep."

"Really?" she asked, interested. "Why would someone be carrying such a substance around in this cave?" Her eyes deviated to the rugged denticulations in the floor and she distanced into a short reverie, before glancing back to him. "Clarence...I don't think Douglas ever lied to us. Whoever was here before us, knew that something dangerous was lurking around in the caverns. Or, he knew possibly, he'd encounter other cave dwelling specimens and it'd interrupt his analysis of the rocks."

Clarence leant the bottle onto the hessian pouch and he looked up at her, speculating over her observation and he said, "If this is the case," He put the three Chloride bottles into the pouch. "We must hurry."

"Yes, we shouldn't stop," she agreed, looking at the shadowed archway. "Douglas, might be in a precarious situation."

Clarence frowned at the sound of concern in her face. He felt a sting of jealousy inside of his chest, while he rolled out the other clinking bottles and they nudged into his shoes.

Clarence lifted his lantern from the ground and he stood.

"Let's see if we can find Douglas," he said, flashing his luminance to the nearest, cornered opening and it elongated onto the floor, revealing it declined and it was steep. "I think this is the right way,"

"What makes you certain?" asked Nora, "Just because the floor is descending, doesn't mean it's in the right direction," She pointed to the opposite archway and treading towards it, she leant her hand onto the wall and peeked inside. "The floor is declining here, as well," she smelt the air. "This tunnel has a watery scent amongst the mustiness of the rock, meaning it's most likely to lead us to the dilapidated rock from the carbonate acid water and the bottom of the doline."

"I would never have thought of this direction. Alright, we'll try this tunnel and see if it leads us to him." said Clarence, with a smirk.

They strode into the archway and were submerged with the shadows inside of the passage.

"*Douglas*!" yelled Clarence, stepping out of the shadowed opening and emerged closer into the weak light shining from the round, jagged outskirts of the doline into the trundled, salient rocks surrounding the ground. "*Douglas!*"

"Douglas, where are you?" echoed Nora, with her hands cupped around her ruddy mouth.

Clarence breathed out and frowned. He cracked onto the limestone bits. "*Douglas, can you hear me?*" he blurted.

He vividly searched the circular ground, skimming his radiance flared from his lantern onto the rocks and crumbled fragments.

"*Why* hadn't he just stayed here, like I had told him? He's gone wandering again!" exclaimed Clarence.

"There'd have to be a reason," suggested Nora, putting a strand around her ear. "Otherwise, he would've stayed here to not complicate the situation."

She drastically shone her round, golden lantern light onto the jagged floor and became disappointed to not find my shoe sole's mark.

"*No,*" said Clarence, scowling. "He's done this purposely again," He lifted the glow of his lantern, revealing the gigantic, broad opening and followed down the dark tunnel. He spotted my shoe's imprint sunken in the moist mud and his anger stung inside of his chest and his voice reverberated in the walls, "Why couldn't he have just stayed and made it easier?" His tone lifted a notch. "*But, oh no,* he had to leave, *didn't he!*"

Nora fearfully glanced at the tunnel and followed him, swinging the oil lamp, crackling the rubble with her vivid and hastened footsteps and she warned, "Wait, Clarence, we don't know if we should going be this way! It's too dark down here."

"Yeah, that's *why* he came down here!" echoed Clarence, stopping midway in the tunnel.

"What is it?" she asked.

"*Oh no,*" he groaned and looked away from the ground, rubbing his forehead with his dirt-smudged fingers.

Nora lowered her lantern light to the ground and shrieked, revealing the trail of three-toed footprints recessed beside my own.

Clarence glanced to the ground.

"*Well, this is just great,*" he grumbled, striding forward in the clammy mud and followed both the footprint trails and he held his swinging, lantern outward. "*Gharkoll has followed him.*"

He raised the pace of his strides and reaching the end of the tunnel, he scrutinized over my footprint covered with a splotch of blood. Clarence stopped, observing it had dried and deciphered it had been longer than one hour, I had been there.

"I hope he's not dead," said Nora, "It's quite dry the blood."

Clarence side glanced at her. "I hope so too." He said, angrily shaking his head and he hurried to the left passage and the bottles of Chloride clattered in his hessian sack, swaying on his back. "He's *always* wandering where he shouldn't be and never listening and always doing what he wants!" He exhaled through his nose. "*Never* considering the consequences!"

"Calm down," replied Nora, touching and bouncing her fingertips on the shawls of light beige flowstone on the walls. "If we're to find him, we must concentrate."

"I can't be relaxed," he confessed, glimpsing at her. "He's *my brother*, what if I never see him again?"

Clarence and Nora climbed the hewn steps and reached the stalagmite chamber with the burbling lava river, reflecting a rosined glow on the limestone granulates. He found the footprint in the magma tunnel ahead beside the two separated, three-toed footprints. Clarence followed them and his thirst intensified and itched in his throat, though, he didn't stop his movement to drink the coconut water and dissolve the uncomfortable feeling away. They ascended the steep floor, avoiding the uneven ditches and dents. Clarence felt a dizziness churn in his head and he stopped, clutching the poking rock piece in the wall and he inhaled a whiff of the still unmoving air. His dry mouth watered at the sound of the splashing water ahead and he tip-toed cautiously, through the round arch into another spacious chamber. The rush of flurrying warm air breezed over him. It was a waterfall of scorching lava, plunging from the precipice of rock into the pool and splattering driblets onto the scrawny stalagmites.

"No," groaned Clarence, panting a breath and wiped a bead of sweat with his sleeve. He dropped his hessian sack to the floor and conceding to his thirst, he pulled out his coconut, swallowing the last sweet remnant of coconut water. He lowered it back inside of his hessian sack, "I have no idea, how we're going to survive without water."

"Don't worry, I'm sure we'll find a stream somewhere," said Nora, mesmerized with the tawny smoke levitating from the rippling surface of lava.

They both realized the further they proceeded closer to the splashing lava waterfall, that the cave bio-speleology had changed; the millipedes and black beetles crawling on the floor, fed on the clumps of moist bat guano. They scuttled through the warm, scudded lava puddles enveloping in the gouges near the pool. There wasn't light or evaporation. Clarence knelt to the brink of the pool and he could see the anthropoids swimming in the lava. He was shocked, as these hadn't been alive for millions of years and they had swum in water, not lava.

"Impossible," he muttered. "How can it be?"

Nora bowed beside him and lingered her oil lamp's flared radiance onto them.

"I'm not sure." she gasped.

A wail echoed from above. Clarence glimpsed at the ceiling and observed the enormous crowd of bats hanging upside down amongst the stalactites. They heard the abrupt splash on the opposite end of the pool behind the boulder and it startled them. Nora tip- toed nearby the brink of the lava pool and after poking her head from the large boulder, she gasped and trampled back. She hushed with a whisper, petrified and she tugged his shoulder, "*The Creature.*"

Clarence took one longer swallow from the coconut shell and tipped the remnant onto a small, crater curved in the floor and put it silently back into his sack.

"Where?" he whispered.

"Opposite us," she said.

Clarence glared to the left, observing another large rock and he said, "We'll head over there,"

He lifted his sack from the floor and avoided making any rattle from the clinking bottles and the cans. He held it with both hands and they swiftly tread in the dank, sticky, mud along the edge. They hid behind the rock and spying on Gharkoll , they saw him dipping his long, lime tentacles from both of his ears into the rippling pool and swallowed long gulps of water. His eyes were slit and bright yellow, contrasting in the shadows with a sharper vision to see in the dark. Nora gaped and covered her mouth with her hand, astonished at what she could see.

"It seems to be *how* he drinks," whispered Clarence.

Gharkoll endured one more, long swallow through his lime tentacles and a
trace of mist simmered from the rippling

surface, he withdrew them out of the water and they shrunk, as they neared
closer to his large brown, pointed ears. The tentacles weren't curved, and they
straightened back to their ordinary appearance, radiant as his eyes. Gharkoll
scooped a bundle of millipedes with his claw and he crunched them into his
mouth and the green juice drizzled in thin streams from his sharp teeth and
onto the conical tufts of fur hanging from his jaw. Gharkoll gulped one last
swallow and wiped his claw on his mouth. He lurked into the round archway,
adjoining to the cavern. My distant yell and the deep baritone growl from Gharkoll, echoed in the passage.

Clarence swiped around in panic, listening to us both.

"Nobody touches my brother," he muttered, defiantly and he pulled out the
bottle from his sack, clutching it tight in his hand.

Clarence stood from behind the large rock and tread around the pool in
pursuit to rescue me.

"Wait! Clarence! It could be too dangerous!" exclaimed Nora, trampling
behind him.

Clarence ignored her, too fervent to find me and he bowed underneath the
low edge, stepping through the archway.

"Douglas!" he yelled, passing a gallery of slender, crimson stalagmites.
"Douglas! Can you hear me!"

"Clarence?" I exclaimed, hearing him vaguely from the distance.

Clarence followed the sound of my voice and passed into another cavern, with sharp, clustered speleothems and haloclines on the ceiling. The red
smoke revolved around his ankles and he cautiously emerged into the shadowed chamber, surrounded with short, broad knobby stalagmites, scattered on
the floor.

"Douglas?" he called out, inquiringly, and wiped his nose coated in sweat with a finger.

"Don't...come..." I responded, and my voice echoed in the narrow tunnel.

I didn't want him to be injured.

Clarence ignored my plead and slowed his footsteps into another passage, with red and tawny light flickering from the stretched, inflamed lava pools and the shadows from the stalactites loomed on the walls, and slanted on the floor. He stopped at the entrance, fixating a glare at Gharkoll prowling around the thick column formed from the growth of the stalagmite, searching for me. I dragged my shoe and blood-stained ankle behind another boulder. Clarence unplugged the cork from the Chloride bottle, sliding it into his pocket. He tread behind the broadest stalagmites.

Nora hurried beside him. "What are you going to do?" she asked, eyeing the Chloride bottle and flicked her glare back to him. "Don't do it, we know nothing of this creature."

"He's going to kill my brother," said Clarence, frowning. "I have to do something, otherwise, he'll die."

"Do you think one bottle would put the creature asleep?" she asked. "Maybe, two, might be better?"

"I'll try one first and if that doesn't work, we'll try another." he said.

Clarence diverted his attention back to Gharkoll leaping from the floor onto the rock and the stalactite, scrawling his claws down the peak, chiseling granules to the floor. I hurried behind the stalagmites and boulder in the middle of the cavern, though, observed Gharkoll's shadow looming on the ground. I peered upward and cringed into the wall and yelled. Gharkoll collided onto the boulder and raised his claw above my cheek.

Clarence charged from behind the stalagmite, bellowing and tossed the Chloride bottle.

It bounced once on the floor, spilling the liquid onto his torso and clashed in-between Gharkoll's three-toed, furry feet and shattered into a mound of crackled glass. The thick plumes of smoke erupted around his skinny, beige legs and body. I bellowed, not expecting the thrown bottle and coughed, loathing the aroma. I shifted backward to the nearest cluster of stalagmites and turned to see who had thrown the bottle, though, my confusion deepened at the sight of the empty arch. A hand grappled my shoulder. I recoiled, turning around.

"It *was* you! Where did you find the bottle from?" I exclaimed.

"Stay back!" yelled Clarence, pulling my arm and dragged me further into the dark tunnel. "Hide!"

I felt a relieved smile loosen across my lips and I hugged him. "You found me!" My smile broadened, when I found Nora's arms wrapping around my waist. I grinned, hugging her back.

"I'm glad you're alive," said Nora, squeezing me tight.

I thought I would stop breathing for a moment and she loosened her clutch around my stomach.

"Me too," I said.

Clarence tried pushing me further into the tunnel, though, I tugged my arm away.

"No!" I yelled. "There's something I have to tell you about the creature!"

"Like?" he asked.

I glanced down at the cluttered bottles in the hessian sack dropped to the floor and I yelled, "What did you throw at him?"

Clarence was shocked with my sudden infuriation and we both turned back to the chamber, distracted with the curling screech.

It was too late.

CHAPTER EIGHTEEN

METAMORPHOSIS INTO A MUTANT

I stood at the entrance of the tunnel with my palm leaning against the gouged wall and watched the writhing creature. A couple of short light-beige horns sprouted on the crown of his dark brown tufts of fur. A crowd of round bumps swelled on his wrinkled forehead and a larger one appeared between his thick-haired eyebrows. Gharkoll echoed a deep loud growl, slouching in the mists and raising his claw, his fingernails sprouted. I quivered, treading backwards in the cragged stalagmites and broadened my eyes, glaring at the horned silhouette looming on the wall. My breaths became shaky, the sweat trickled on the nape of my neck and beneath my linen shirt. I wiped the beads of sweat drizzling on my forehead and flustered cheeks with my crinkled sleeve. Gharkoll tilted his head back and echoed a loud growl, as the soft lime light from the flowstone and glinting on his picket teeth sprouting like the stalactites. He closed his golden-eyes and after re-opening them, the rosined glow swelled around his slit black pupils and he echoed a deep moan. Clarence tugged my arm, furthering me inside of the tunnel and he released his grasp.

"Why did you do this to him?" I hissed. "Now look at what you've done!"

"He *was* going to attack you!" argued Clarence, glancing back to Gharkoll. He recoiled and looked down at the clustered bottles inside of the hessian sack, leaning against the wall. "You should be thanking me, more than anything, not yelling at me!"

"No, he wasn't! He was just frightened," I disagreed, glancing at the bottles and squatted near the hessian pouch, shifting one bottle around. "*Chloride?*"

"*Yeah,*" he blurted, bowing and lifted the hessian sack, shifting it over his shoulder. "Don't worry about it! We have-too-," he spluttered a cough, from the drifting cloud of tawny smoke. "We have to get out of here!"

"You're killing him, he's worthy to survive!" I yelled back, and frowned. "You've hurt an innocent animal!"

"He's *not* an animal!" he refuted, immediately and glimpsed at Gharkoll struggle and stomp though the mist with a crouched back and curling his claws into his beige palms. "I don't know what he is…" he glanced back to me. "I don't care." I noticed his small nose was smeared with a thin line of sweat. "All I *do* care about is escaping out of here alive. Now come with me."

"We know nothing of this creature," I snapped, frowning and feeling agitated. "He was curious of me, when I found him and tried to communicate with me." A surge of heat flushed my cheeks and prickled my eyes and struggling to breathe, I tread forward.

"Communicate?" retorted Clarence, while we strode down the crimson rock tunnel. "Why would it try to do it with us? Douglas, it seemed like it was going to attack you and it was only tricking you into being 'friendly'."

"I don't believe you," I said, glancing at Nora's beige boots striding on the stone ground, crackling the granules into ash. She had remained quiet, not wanting to become between us. I stopped at the end of the tunnel. "It was the way he was trying to communicate to me, with a high-notched noise."

I glanced back down the tunnel, observing Gharkoll loathed the smell of the chemical floating in the air and he swiped his claws, agitated at the intoxicating aroma and attempted to make it disappear.

He released a bloodcurdling screech, penetrating the silence and the stalactites trembled with his agony. Gharkoll 's furred claws curled into fists and he arched his back, protruding his dark beige fur and his luminous, lime tentacles rolled inward to his ears. The thick, green globules slithered down the stalactites and splattered onto him, releasing puffs of steam from his beige fur and he teetered a side-step, rumbling the ground. He knocked into a boulder, disturbed from the sharp pain spreading in his body and he stomped his left foot, dilapidating another rock into a pile of rubble. The heated, yellow and green fog simmered from the ground, festering in thick clouds around him and in-between the rocks, stinging his eyes. Gharkoll became dizzy and it swindled inside of his head and he thumped to the ground, swinging his three-toed, fluffy feet into the air. He rocked his head and his short horns scraped into the rugged, ochre stalagmite, forming thin, white ashy lines and he yowled, suffocating in the yellow fog, levitating around his jawbone. I sighed and yearned to help him, though, I knew I couldn't and if I did, I would never step out of the cavern alive. Gharkoll inhaled and stretched his ruddy, upper lip across his slimy, red gums and hollered a guttural growl. He spread his jaws apart and his rack of small picket teeth grew longer and the two, prominent front teeth sprouted half an-inch into fangs. His beige fur camouflaged with the limestone walls, deepened to oak-brown and the three, lime tentacles unrolled from his pointed, wide ears and swelled miniature holes. An array of small bumps augmented on his forehead, above his thick, dark-brown hairy eyebrows.

"What's happening to him…" I trailed, watching the thick green globs falling from the stalactites and spreading onto his fur and he screeched, wiping his claws into the sticky liquid.

"I don't know." muttered Clarence, slowly, and refrained from shifting his horrified glare from Gharkoll.

"Whatever it is, I don't like it," murmured Nora, frightened. "I have a bad feeling about this moment."

"Me too," I said, and swallowed. "What is the liquid? It wouldn't be carbonate acid alone."

"There'd *have* to be carbonate acid," agreed Nora. "Haven't you noticed the crumbed bits on the floor and some of the stalactites peaks are chipped?"

"Yes, the driblets of Chloride must be mixing with it."

We watched Gharkoll writhing in the pool of sticky liquid, engulfing him and he lifted his knees to his stomach, bending his legs. The disintegrated rubble trundled across into the dark-green fluid, gathering around him. He tilted his head forward and inhaled his last breath, as the last green globs splattered on his face. Gharkoll wrapped himself, as a ball and the globs dripped from his fur and onto the rubble, sprouting around him and covered his horns and formed into a slimy, green stalagmite with yellow patches and brown streaks. He faintly, wailed inside of the slimy stalagmite and released his sorrow from being trapped and revolved his claws, nudging the interior and formed bumps on the surface. They disappeared, as he slid them away and the yellow patches gleamed brighter in the shadows. Gharkoll burst one last screech, until it decreased into a curving sing and nothing could be heard, except for the feeble, burbling lava river and the bubbles popped in the distance. The whiffs of fog lurked from the hollow chinks in the rocky ground.

"Okay, he's dead," said Clarence, nudging my arm and he snapped me out of my daze. "Now, let's go."

I turned from the lime stalagmite.

"I wouldn't be certain, though, we have just learnt something." I said.

"What is it?" asked Clarence.

"Gharkoll is sensitive to any other chemical outside of the cave. He can't survive out of the cave and its atmospheric surroundings." I realized. "This is why he didn't stay out the night, when we first arrived at the island and only discovered claw marks on the tent."

"Does it really matter?" asked Clarence. "He's already died inside of his stalagmite,"

"You don't know it," I said.

"*He is* admit it," bickered Clarence. "You heard the last growl."

"Honestly, you two," said Nora, frowning, and she glanced at both of them. "I think we need to concentrate on what truly matters-*finding a way out*. This is giving us the perfect opportunity to escape, without feeling threatened from Gharkoll, which is such a relief."

I sighed and we stepped down another tunnel, winding to the North- East, according to my compass.

"We're heading slightly off course, though, it's alright for the moment, as long as we stay towards the Northern direction. I'm sure we'll find a passage with some air and it will guide us out of here." I directed.

"It sounds promising," said Nora, beaming and tapped me on the shoulder.

We disappeared into the shadowed archway. It was back in the cavern, Gharkoll squirmed inside of the unordinary stalagmite and it trembled. He lifted his claws and they scraped through the peak of the stalagmite and it tore open, puffing a cloud of yellow smoke.

A small growl echoed.

His small, conical fawn-brown horns lifted through the slimy, dark green liquid, stretching an array of stringy threads and his pointed ears poked in the smoke. He screeched, and his picket teeth and jaws stretched against the slimy, inner walls of the green stalactite. It was with another scrape of his claw, the slimy stalagmite tore apart and revealed his furry brown legs, surrounded with mist, sinking into the floor. Gharkoll hissed, poking out his long, dark viridescent tongue and growled, resonating a feeble vibration in his throat. He climbed onto the tallest stalagmite and his fore and hind claws sunk onto the limestone knobs rolling chiseled bits of stone with each ascending stride. The red glow shone from the lava river, reflected onto his wide, curious eyes and they shifted from lucid yellow to tawny orange to crimson, with a ferocious and sinister intensity. The rotund, poking lumps on his forehead lifted the wrinkled lids and opened into a crowd of eyes. Gharkoll tilted his head and short horns backward, echoing a burdened screech from his opened jaw and clutched the peak of the stalagmite with his overlapping claws.

~

It was hours later at seven-thirty and ignorant of such a mutation, I stepped further in the silhouetted caverns and knelt to the floor, shoving the sailcloth into my hessian pouch, with the chord dangling loosely on the ground. I peered up at Nora.

"Are you acquainted with anyone?" I asked.

"No," she said. "Why?"

I couldn't tell her the truth about how I felt about her, yet, it was too soon; I was treading amongst heavy, warm waters.

"I think my brother likes you." I whispered, flicking my gaze past the speleothems at Clarence opposite us, unrolling his blanket on the floor with much disappointment, there wasn't a pillow.

"What makes you say it?" she asked.

"He lied to you Nora," I said, bluntly, tightening the rope around my pouch.

"He did?"

"Yes," I said, rising one leg. "I don't have any interest in anyone from my home at Half-Moon Bay."

Nora gasped, broad-mouthed and slowly stood, watching me walk away and sit onto the rock.

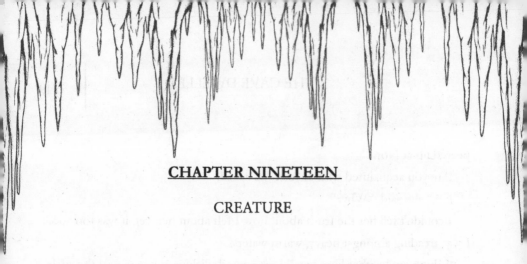

CHAPTER NINETEEN

CREATURE

Gharkoll Drolk, The Creature had changed; he could feel it in his grown, curved claws and the sprouted picket teeth in his mouth. His vision had enhanced and he could hasten it through the stalagmites, past the fog drifting through the tunnels. He hadn't liked the substance hurled at him- his fur was still aching from the driblets sinking through into his brawny torso. The brown strands were still prickling, especially after he strode past the acidic lime stalagmites, puffing fog from their jagged peaks. The horns protruding from his head, which he saw in the pool's reflection were strange. He wasn't used to them on the front of his crown. He could smell the rush of adrenalin and the fear in sweat, trickling on bare skin from one of the humans in the distance. He could hear the gurgling rush of crimson blood and sniff it inside of a bat's veins. Even the scuttle from the scorpions, hibernating in the narrow, winding tunnels intersected with the caverns and antechambers, surrounded the short stalagmites. He could hear the acid in the rocks, seeping from the rain driblets and drizzling through the ceiling on the walls and every ant crawling in a long trail on the rubble into the smallest fissures. He snatched a bat with his spreading, crimson tongue and the membranous black wing, flapped from his mouth. Blood drizzled into picket teeth and gums, though the sour taste dissolving in his mouth was disgusting. He dropped it to the floor, smearing his three-toed foot onto the bat's torso and it flattened, with a bent wing. It was worst of all, the taste of bat's blood wasn't enough for him anymore. He needed something stronger to crackle in his mouth and to crumble into splinters in his picket teeth; to dissolve them into mound of ashy marrow. He didn't want to swallow Troglobites either, anymore. Those soft, moist glowing worms huddled in the walls. They would be like a snack, more than anything and his stomach, would still churn with hunger the entire night and endless hours in the caverns. He needed something *filling*. A swindling itch in his throat, elevated into his mouth; it was a sibilate triumvirate of noises. He lowered his jaw and echoing a sound; it peaked into a penetrating deep growl, swindling through the opposite pointed archway, with a flickering tawny glow on the brown wall. Gharkoll strode forwards down the cavern, feeling the newly-born crowd of eyes, seeing in the far distance, through the opposite cavern, even before he reached the end of the tunnel's round archway. His ears didn't hear a subtle noise from two miles, though his hearing had intensified; the sound of a foreign voice and rubble, lurched in the silhouettes, as stormy waves clashing on the shore. Someone was coming into the cave, something, he knew he could sink his picket teeth into and suckle the crimson blood. He remembered the two boys and girl, with the clashing glass fragments and half of the CHLORIDE label, with a chiseled brink, now was, CHLORI dilapidated beneath his three-toed foot.

PART TWO

CHAPTER TWENTY

STALAGMITE SULPHIDES

It was during Monday and Tuesday, throughout dawn to dusk, an ignorance prevailed over all of us. Gharkoll 's vision sharpened, and his slit pupils swelled, shifting from lucid yellow to the shade of crimson and the writhing of the ants in the soggy moss lathered in his venom, intensified in his eardrums. Gharkoll chafed his claws onto the stalagmite, snuffling with a growl and approaching the tunnel's entrance, his sight swept through the shadows into the distant cavern, hearing the drifting voices float from the funnel's hole. He strode down, inhaling the aroma of verdant leaves and the salty ocean seeping into the cavern. The voices chattered into his long brown ears and the hunger *swarmed* his mouth, watering for warm, juicy blood and flesh. His lime tentacles tingled the closer he came to the winding tunnel and he followed the descent into the cavern, with the burbling Sulphur pools. He inhaled the mist with his wrinkled nose and suckled remnants of the Sulphur mist with his lime tentacles, leaving a long trail of three-toed footprints. He hunched at the brink and swallowed a mouthful of the Sulphur pool water. Gharkoll slid his gleaming eyes to the stalagmite, observing the yellowed shade in the ochre rock and feeling the hunger in his tentacles, he bent them to the jagged peak and suckled the sulphides. The thick puffs of revolving yellow fog hindered around his ears and the yellow patches shriveled, shifting the rock to ash and the stalagmite steamed- the peak slouched and dilapidated into piles of rock on the ground. He waited for the tingling to disappear and he shrunk his tentacles into their ordinary shortened poise from his ears. The crowd of flapping bats with spread membranous black wings amongst the stalactites dropped one by one from the ceiling in the warm mist and fell to the floor in a scattered trail. Gharkoll pinned his claw into the bat's stomach and bloody juice slithered down to the floor and he growled, kicking it into the debris. He disappeared into another winding passage and heard the footsteps striding on the arid thickets, drying in the hot summer sunlight outside and drifting through the hole of the magma funnel.

The hunger churned in his stomach- he was *famished*.

Gharkoll heard the distant dropping pebble *plink* on the floor. He turned around and his hastened vision swept past the dark walls and the netted, stringy gossamer hanging from the wall to the small round cavern with two pointed archways and a hole in the ceiling. He strode past a batch of crawling spiders and unrolled his forked tongue, snatching a hairy tarantula. Meanwhile, Leighton , William and Henrietta stopped near the precipice, overlooking the sea and looked down the hole of the magma funnel. They were unaware Gharkoll slowed his pace out of the fissure and lurked in the dark at the edge of the golden daylight beam. He peered up, tilting his light-beige horns and dark brown fur cones, blinking the radiance away on his tentacles, and he listened,

"We should go down here." directed Leighton , pointing down the magma funnel into the dark. "It leads into the cave."

"Alright," agreed William.

Gharkoll sniffed their scents and hissed, dropping his bottom jaw, revealing his two, sharp glinting fangs and blew heavy, warm breaths. His mouth watered and lifting his nose, he could smell the fresh sweat drizzling on their necks. He crunched his three-toed claw on the skull, with a hidden scorpion inside and it diminished into a dust pile. The orange mist lingered across his furry, thin legs and he skimmed the cavern, following the scents to the bottom of the magma funnel.

Gharkoll peeked upward and heard William's voice, "Are you sure, we should go down there? I think I just saw something…"

Gharkoll brashly shifted away.

Leighton appeared at the summit of the funnel and clutching the rocky edge, he looked for himself.

"I don't see anything," he said, glancing back at William. "Are you sure, you saw something?"

William nodded and he looked back down to the silhouetted terrain.

"I have a hunch we should go another way." He insisted.

Leighton shook his head, sinking his hand inside of the brown, hessian pouch and pulled out a coiled rope. He tied one end to a totem pole and he unrolled and dropped it in the lava funnel, and it dangled in mid-air in the dark. Gharkoll 's crimson eyes gleamed in the dark and he poked his nose at the edge of the slanted shadows and sniffed the rope, wondering what it was. He looked up, twitching his right ear with his lime antennas glowing in the dark and he listened to them.

"It won't take that long, and I doubt Clarence, Douglas and Nora stayed at the front of the cave. They would've found a tunnel down below by now. It's been *hours*." said Leighton .

"I *know*," said William, sighing, and he clutched the rope. "I'm just not too comfortable with climbing down."

"Just take, one baby step at a time," he said, holding the rope. "I'll go down first?"

"Alright, you first, then I'll go." said William, with a nod.

Leighton lowered his leg into the hole and clasping the rope, he descended the funnel. Gharkoll listened to their reverberating footsteps stamp against the curved, jagged wall. Leighton reached the ground and tugging the rope, he released it and it swung against the wall. He glared up, unaware of Gharkoll standing behind the shadowed boulder and stalagmites, fixating his crimson eyes, onto his back.

"You can come down now." echoed Leighton .

William nodded, and he descended very slowly in the funnel.

Leighton became impatient and clutched his hips. Gharkoll lowered behind the boulder. He heard the rapidity of a chafing claw in the ground and he turned, feeling suspicious.

William landed on the ground and unconfined the rope, leaving it to dangle in mid-air and treading beside him.

"What's wrong?" he asked, following the direction of his engrossed gaze to the boulder.

Gharkoll had arched his back to hide and mimic the round shape of the boulder. He looked at the fissure in the distance, wondering if he could crawl through it, unsure, whether he could defeat these humans or not at the same time.

Leighton inflamed a stick and stepped slowly towards the boulder. He heard Gharkoll's breaths, exhaling through his picket teeth and causing tension in the silence. Gharkoll rolled his tentacles inwards and he scampered away behind the wall of rocks and disappeared into the fissure, flicking stones from his claws. Leighton drastically swished his firelight over the rocks, observing the trail of three-toed footprints and undefined, claw marks in the rocky ash. He followed the crackling noise of Gharkoll suddenly stopping inside the fissure. Leighton bowed and peeked inside.

Gharkoll's claw jutted out and swiped the flame.,

Leighton cringed and gasped, "*Argh!*" He watched the claw disappearing inside of the shadows.

"What's wrong?" echoed William, behind him.

Leighton huffed, widening his light-blue eyes, shiny with terror. William began to squat to have a closer inspection.

"*No, don't,*" declared Leighton , crossing his arm over his chest.

"Why?" asked William, bewildered.

Leighton looked away from the small fissure.

"There's something crawling in here. I'm not too sure what it was, and we should head in the opposite direction to avoid it."
he guided.

"I agree," said William.

They found the entrance to a small, tight tunnel and the sound of watery drips echoed in the silence.

Leighton flashed his golden glow from the lantern around the brink of the crusted rock, illuminating the uphill tunnel.

"Watch your step in here. There's water everywhere on the rocks and it's going to be slippery." he said.

"Right," said William, rolling up his sleeves to his elbows to avoid them being scratched with gashes from the sharp, limestone, beige curves in the rocky floor. "I'll go first," He bowed under the rounded edge.

Leighton followed after him. They crawled through the tight tunnel, covering themselves with water rivulets leaking from the slender cracks in the ceiling and their shoulders brushed against the serrate, curved walls, as they pressed their shoes on the rugged ground. William couldn't see what was ahead of him and squinting in the shadows, he unexpectedly, found himself falling through the hole.

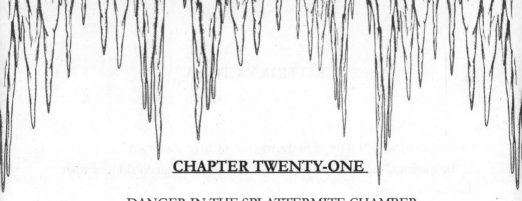

CHAPTER TWENTY-ONE

DANGER IN THE SPLATTERMITE CHAMBER

William grabbed the viridescent, fern fronds dangling in mid-air above him. He quivered with terror, peeking over his shoulder and gasped. A pair of beige, pointed horns, dark-brown furred cones and three, straight lime tentacles, poking from fawn-brown ears, glided beneath his leather shoes in the dark. He hailed with his heart palpitating rapidly in his chest. William puffed a breath, and he widened his moist eyes at the furred claw appearing beneath his dusty shoelaces.

"William?" asked Leighton , vividly crawling forward and looked down the hole. "Can you hear me?"

"Yeah!" he echoed back, panicking and distressed, as the ferns snapped and the tearing noise resounded in the dark.

William screamed, splashing into a murky puddle and bounced a wave of water onto the walls, surrounded with dusty rubble. He groaned and stood, squeezing the water saturated in his shirt and driblets tapped onto the terrain.

"*William! William!*" yelled Leighton , flashing the glow from his lantern down the hole and the faint shaft of light, swished back and forth along the remaining, fern fronds. "Are you alright?"

Gharkoll squatted inside of the shadowed crevice, drooling a driblet of green saliva from the corner of his mouth and it trickled in beads along his dark brown, serrate tufts of fur. He glowered at William with an adamant vigor to pursue him.

"Yes," echoed William, looking at Leighton at the top of the hole, with his worried expression illumined with the oil lamp's candle, guttering streaks of

159

warm, melted wax. "I'll try to find a way out of here, *don't worry*."

"Be cautious," he said, clutching the crusty edge. "I still don't know what the claw belonged too."

"Please, don't say anymore," answered William. "You're making me nervous."

He heard scampering footsteps and turned, looking suspiciously at the empty crevice in the wall and into the impenetrable chamber ahead.

William looked away.

"What's wrong?" asked Leighton .

"Nothing," said William, disregarding the noise. "I thought I heard something, though it was probably mice or bats."

"Make sure, you're alert," said Leighton . "I'll wait for you on the other side of the tunnel. Make sure you find your way westward, as I'm sure that is in the same direction of the tunnel. Then, we'll begin to move North-West and eventually the North, to where Clarence, Douglas and Nora might be."

"I will," said William. "It sounds like a good idea."

"Alright, I'll see you soon," said Leighton , using the luminance from his lantern and he moved around and shifted his back against the wall and tiny, stone bits fell to the ground.

William watched him disappear. It was meanwhile, Gharkoll strode onto the rocky precipice jutting over the lake with thick steam simmering from the surface. He sighed, looking away and felt annoyed with himself. When crawling through the tunnel, he hadn't been more attentive and he didn't expect to hear the sudden splash from the lake, flicking, grimy water into the air. He looked at the isolated rock in the steam bewildered.

Why did he feel something was looming around here, though he could never glimpse it? Or maybe, he was imagining things?

William tread further away from the crevice and on the wet rubble around the fringe of the pool, following the *splash* on the opposite side. He stopped, noticing the patches of water on the stones, surrounding the three-toed footprints and glanced around at the dolomite stalagmites.

Nothing is there, he thought.

Crick

Crack

William hesitated to move for one moment and intently listened, before deciding to investigate what caused the noise. An ominous silence lurked amongst the huddled stalagmites surrounded with lurking mist. His hitched breath echoed, as he shone the golden lantern light on them and gasped at the sight of the torn, dark-green stalagmite, augmenting over the short pair spele-othems. He swallowed, lowering the light onto the trail of footprints and the claws marks scrawled in the gooey interior of the stalagmite, dangling moist threads of slime. The pair of short-conical horns swept across the opposite wall of speleothems in front of him.

William gasped, swinging the firelight around and skimmed the huddled speleothems. His heart thudded and he whispered,

"Who's there?"

He strode on the scattered debris and closer to the slope of flowstone. His grey eyes moistened with horror, as he looked over the jagged speleothems drizzled with the drooled rivulets of lime-green saliva, drifting with a vagrant odor.

William winced.

A troglobite hurled out of the shadows, brushing onto his shoulder and he screamed. It echoed down the dark lancet, shrouded with a lingering, whiff of yellow mist. He looked at the millipede writhing on the floor and crawling into the miniature crevice of the wall.

"I hate this place." he whispered.

Scuffle. Scuffle.

He looked back to the opposite, South-East archway.

Scuffle. Scuffle.

"Douglas?" he asked, with his heart hammering louder. "Clarence?"

William tread around the side speleothems, drenched with scuttling ants attracted from the moist aroma of the saliva and he ventured closer to the archway.

"Nora?" he whispered.

He flashed his inflamed stick into the tunnel.

Crackle.

The chafing of claws on the rocky wall echoed.

His heart thudded, watching the pebbles roll to the front of his dark-brown leather shoes smeared with dust.

"Hello?" he whispered, staring into the pitch-black passage.

Nobody responded to him. William was distracted with the crawling, shiny-black scorpions on the rugged wall and he was ignorant of the shadowed furry clawed foot, stepping backwards in the far distance.

A stone was nudged.

William looked back down, lifting his flames higher into the dark and the shaft of golden-tawny light slivered further to the end of the tunnel, revealing the lonesome pebble. A bead of sweat slowly drizzled on his forehead and onto the side of his eyebrow. He held his breath and glancing over his shoulder at the round, green stalagmite cavern, he didn't observe another opening anywhere else. William tread inside the tunnel and he skimmed his luminance onto the denticulate floor. He observed the slender, uneven claw-marks and the odd splotches of gooey light-green saliva patterned everywhere. Leighton 's warning echoed in his ear, as a feeble whisper, chilling his shoulders and back. He couldn't head in the opposite direction? Somehow, he knew something was wrong and yet, he ignored the prickling tension drifting from beyond in the impenetrable tunnel. The fire sputtered, engulfing the top portion of the stick and the radiance dimmed. His hitched breaths echoed, as more rubble rolled from his shoes and he stopped midway, hearing the movement in the distance. He looked down, nervously and clamped his lips, trying to hush his breaths.

Leighton's breath felt forbidden- he waited, unsure if he should continue or not. The warning in his chest swelled, urging him to shift back down through the opening, though, he double blinked- he *couldn't*.

There wasn't another way out. He was stuck here. In the tunnel. Lonesome. He had *no choice*, but to discover what was on the other end, even if he did or *didn't* like what he found. William swallowed and wobbling the stick, the crackle reverberated with his subtle footsteps. The beads of sweat drizzled from his frumpy, dark blonde hair matted to his forehead onto his eyebrows, from the muggy warmth drifting at the end of the tunnel.

'*It's probably some innocent animal or a flock of bats,*' He thought, trying to calm his nerves and he anxiously tightened his clasp around the stick, until his knuckles were sallow.

The closer he came to the end, the more his nerves intensified, and gooseflesh spread onto his shoulders. He stopped at the round opening and lowering his light, he discovered a hewn, limestone steep staircase. Even if he were to turn around now, he'd be *trapped inside of the cavern* and *rot* into a skeleton. His bones would be engulfed with the sticky, green substance. Ants would slowly nibble the mortar away with time. *He flinched at his own thought.* William held onto the rock poking from the wall and descended the stairs, rolling a few more loose pebbles. An aroma of stale blood and marrow drifted from the bottom of the staircase and swallowing his nausea back down his throat, he bowed beneath a group of huddled sharp stalactites, stepping into a deserted, round cavern with enormous walls. His isolated footsteps reverberated vulnerably amongst the group of dark beige splattermites, resembling poles of rock scattered over the slope. William puffed a breath, descending the last remnant of his radiance onto the floor. Bones. Skulls. Everywhere. They were speckled with dried, crimson blood and stained dirt, festering with pallid-yellow smoke. His stomach revolved. The gush of queasiness swiveled back into his throat. He glared at the splinters of crumbled bone and nibbled, rotund knobs spread everywhere. William loathed the aroma and he rubbed his nose onto his sleeve and swallowing a whiff of stale air, he crunched onto them. He shuddered, as scorpions, millipedes and ants crawled from underneath onto the bones and his shoes.

"What-what…eats…humans…" he murmured to himself, passing the middle splattermites and gazed at the gigantic stalactites.

William found them intimidating, as if they would fall any moment and suffocate him to his death. The crushed, white marrow smeared as patches onto his shoes and stepping out of the pile of bones, towards the end of the cavern, beside the boulders, he wiped his sole on the widest splattermite, disgusted.

Crick Crack

William swiped around in the direction of the noise, glaring back at the Southern splattermites and stepped backward. *What was making that noise?* He wondered.

"Douglas?" he asked, rising his firelight in the shadowed splattermites and bit his bottom lip. "This isn't funny. Come out, if it's you."

The silence loomed ahead, and the uncomfortable shifting of his stomach returned.

Crick Crack, reverberated from the flowstone and the second middle splattermite nestled diagonally opposite him

"Hello?" he asked, moving closer and held his breath.

William reached the flowstone and he traced the limestone shawls and crackled the tumbled debris. A thick, dark grey rat scurried in between his legs. William bellowed and recoiling, he hurled his firelight onto the splattermite and it bounced onto the floor. He panted and watched the flames smoldering the stones and smoky coils drifted onto the moss, elongated on the bottom of the splattermite.

His neglected breaths echoed in the silence.

It was behind him, Gharkoll lifted in the yellow mist simmering from the batch of rocks and he clamped his claws onto the cragged dents, watching him with blazing eyes. William felt the prickling sensation on his shoulders and a thin trail of sweat passively trickled from the nape of his neck and down his spine, drenching his shirt. *The same kind of felling from the passage and the boulder, with Leighton . He couldn't push it away, no matter how much he tried.*

William turned and his heart rapidly thrummed in his chest. He was going to see it, whatever hungered for warm, *bloody* flesh. Gharkoll dropped behind the rocks and the dark-brown point of his right furred cone behind his horn, camouflaged with the nearby, short stalagmite peaks and the hindering yellow mist. William suspiciously looked at them. He wiped the clammy sweat with his sleeve from his forehead. He stared one moment longer and he looked away, dismissing the built tension and fear inside of his chest. *I'm being ridiculous.* He thought. *Nothing was there.*

Gharkoll lifted his gleaming, red eye in the narrow gap between the stalagmite and rock, arching his claws on the ground, expelling a hot breath from his jaws.

William frowned.

Gharkoll moved back behind the rock.

William glanced back, striding passively towards the stalagmites and rocks. His heart lurched in his chest, as he looked down to the ground. The eddies of yellow mist drifted and revealed the three toed footprints. *Whatever had three toes, was watching him and had moved...*

The wide-eared, pointed horns and furry cones silhouette lurked over him and the last flicker of the flames shriveled into the stick, floating a coil of mist.

William looked upward, and he screamed. Gharkoll jumped from the top of the splattermite and collided his claws into his shoulders. William swayed backward, echoing a blood-chilling bellow and treading on the sticks, he clashed into the wall.

Gharkoll engulfed a portion of his arm and splattered blood onto the flowstone.

William screamed one notch louder, "AAAH!"

Gharkoll continued to feed on him and lightly squirmed.

"Move off me!" he screamed, clashing Gharkoll on the wall several times and despised the feeling of his tongue, sinking into his warm blood.

Gharkoll lifted his bloodied jaws and screeched in front of him, stretching a slender, string of pale, light-green saliva in-between his picket teeth. William squinted, as speckles of spit smattered onto his horn-rimmed glasses and freckled cheeks. He hurled a whiff of warm breath from his jaw and fogged his glasses. William stumbled backward, passing the curtains of flowstone and whacked Gharkoll into the nearest sarsen.

Gharkoll wailed, scrawling his claws into his shirt and ripped long holes and bloodied gashes.

William yelled, tilting his head and clamped his fingers onto his right arm. It was with a few footsteps, he limped away and deflected his hand onto the serrated wall. The blood pooled on his shirt, smearing onto his shoulder and he became short of breath. He looked over his shoulder and he slowed his pace, astonished.

Gharkoll crawled onto the boulder and screeching, his three, green tentacles unrolled from his ears.

William bellowed, hastening his pace and followed into the narrow tunnel, with stringy web and sprigs slivering over his forehead and flustered cheeks. William stopped in the middle of the cavern. He was short of breath and thirsty, with a throbbing headache and flecks of arid blood splattered onto his collarbone; he thought he would faint. He leant his shoulder onto the limestone pillar. Gharkoll stepped through the opposite opening and the crackle augmented in the hollow cavern. William panicked and he leant his shoulder away and looked back, wondering where Gharkoll had hidden.

A piece of rubble collided onto his head. William wobbled his lower lip and peered upward.

Gharkoll hung from the astute point of the stalactite, with his black claws sunken into the curvature of the limestone.

William stepped backward and screamed.

Gharkoll released thick, slimy, green globules from his tentacles. William bellowed, as they splattered all over his hair and slobbered stickily onto his cheeks, down onto his shoulders and back. His perception blurred, and his eyes stung from the poison, releasing light-green steam from his head and body. Gharkoll hurled another two, sticky beryl-green threads from his tentacles and climbed the stalactite towards the shadowed ceiling. William lifted into the air, screaming and kicking and loathed the burning poison prickle on his ears, neck and shoulders and he couldn't see anymore. His fingertips sunk and dragged downward into the poisonous, beryl-green threads, trying to snap them away, though they only poked as pale, round bone knobs smeared with slime. William was shifted higher and he dangled in-between the crowd of stalagmites, and he screamed a notch louder, despising he couldn't move. Gharkoll crawled down the thickest stalactite and engulfed his head with his broadened mouth. His sharp teeth sunk into his neck and rivulets of blood drizzled and drenched onto his dingy, cotton shirt and his collarbone. Gharkoll tore away his head and leapt onto the other stalactite, chafing thin, white ashy streaks with his claws.

CHAPTER TWENTY-TWO

BLOOD ON THE STALAGMITE
AND ONE MOMENT
WITH NORA ALONE

It was one hour later, following the scent of ocean gusts and crushed marrow seeping through the hollow chinks, our inner fears were provoked. We tread deeper into the hypogean lair, in the eighth cavern's antechamber and through a lucid orange picket archway. I lifted my candlelight onto a stalagmite, drenched in spattered blood and swallowed. The walls embellished with curtains of flowstone, had shifted from light ochre to deep fawn-brown and were drenched in trickles of crimson blood along the cragged edges.

"Whose blood does it belong too?" I asked, eyeing them.

"It's *fresh and wet*," whispered Clarence, paling in the cheeks and bowed closer, squinting in the wavering, yellow flame. He gulped, glancing at us. "And it's drizzling…" He flashed his guttering candle's flame onto the rotund base of the stalagmite, scrutinizing the trickles of blood on the beige dents in the floor. They pooled onto a trail of scuttling ants. "Who's in the cave apart from us?"

"You don't think Leighton and William came into the cave, do you?" I retorted, lowering my candlelight and revealed the crimson blood shining on the dusty-beige floor, leading into a tall, pointed fissure. "Come on, this way."

"No," whispered Nora, deviating her glare from the bloody stalagmite to the floor, tracing the driblets and paced beside me. "We are *not* following a blood trail." She stopped in front of the fissure, and her voice became demanding, "This is the perfect way to get ourselves killed."

"What if someone is in trouble and they need our help?" I blurted. "What if one of them did come in the cave looking for us?"

"That's *just great* Douglas," retorted Clarence, scowling and tread beneath the huddled, jagged short stalactites, closer to me. The deep, golden luminance flared from his bronze-paneled oil-lamp, slanted onto his pale cheeks and accented the sharp twinkle of disapproval in his deep emerald eyes. "If they followed us in here and one of them is injured or dead, *I blame you.*"
I gnashed my teeth. "I was always trying to protect us, Clarence. You know it."

"Along with your curiosity," he snapped, fuming and he shoved past my arm, bowing through the fissure and crackled on the splinters of bone. "It's not you've risked our lives, though, you've killed somebody now."

"I have not," I disputed, following behind him through the dark and crunched on something on the floor. I heard the traces of scuttling in the passage. My stomach revolved, as I lifted my light onto the large, black-shelled scorpions crawling in the long, narrow tunnel. The slouches of gossamer with spiders hung from thin strands and slivered above us. Nora hitched a disgusted exhale, lifting her lamp's glow onto the wall.

Clarence stopped midway and turning, his oil-lamp swung beside his leg and held out his hand, "Here, Nora,"

I felt his competitive and caring disposition in the dark. Nora clutched his hand and she recoiled with the spider-web slinking on her neck.

"Wait," I murmured, stopping midway, feeling my shoulders crawling with tingling gooseflesh and eyeing the ground. A few scorpions were smeared on the dents, flattened with light-green mucus on the three-toed footprint. "Gharkoll has definitely gone in this direction. Maybe, Nora is right."

"We'll glimpse quickly." decided Clarence, taking the lead and strode confidently past me. His luminance shriveled into a small, stretched shaft of light on the ground and lifted the nearby stick.

Clarence lugged out the short-withered candle from the oil-lamp and tearing a piece of linen from his toiled, dirt-streaked sleeve, he wrapped it around the loose stick, and inflamed it. A large, black scorpion scuttled onto his dark-brown, leather shoe crusted with dried mire and he kicked it to the wall, poking the yellowy, golden flames at each of them. *"Move,"*

He poked a few more, crackling a spark and they separated from the pathway's ground, crawling to the side of the walls and he led us further to the impenetrable province of the cave. It was with each footstep, I became nervous as the scorpion's arisen, curved tail lurked near my ankle and recoiled, with a few slouching, spider-webs brushing on my forehead and cheeks. Clarence descended the flames, unveiling a hidden, slanted fissure in the rocky wall. He slid his fingers across the dark-green, tendrils of moss hanging as a curtain over the entrance. He pushed them across and revealed a shadowed chamber. Our footsteps echoed in the silence and with a few more treads, our shoes shifted to a sticky, liquid lathered on the fissures. We lowered our inflamed candles and sticks and found a long rivulet of dark-yellowy fluid with frail crimson-blood, winding around the stalagmites grown with chiseled fragments of rock.

"What is it?" I asked, bewildered and lightly turned my head, with the warm golden light reflecting onto my thick, chestnut brown eyebrows and squatted, inspecting it more intently. "There's blood with a fluid from Gharkoll . It doesn't seem to have come from a stream."

"Whatever it is, don't touch it," warned Clarence. "It reminds me of the green slime we saw on the stalagmite the first time we entered in the upper story caverns." He lifted his firelight to the opposite, wide opening in the wall. "Let's keep exploring this way."

Nora awkwardly peered down at it.

"Do you want to taste it?" I joked.

She scowled and shoved my arm. "That's *not* funny."

I snickered and broadly grinned. "You know I was only kidding right?"

Nora shook her head and rolled her eyes. We ascended the soft slope of beige rubble, venturing through the wide opening and bowed our heads beneath the crust of rock and she echoed, *"Obviously."*

We stopped on the summit, marveling at the enormity of the hall and the augmenting, splattermites far-stretching to the opposite end, amongst the thick, totem poles. Nora, Clarence and I, moved further amongst them and reaching the opposite end, we tread through another four more passages. My thirst was irrevocable and sipping on the last driblets of our coconuts, the lack of water became life-threatening.

After three more miles, descending the sloping floor beneath the drip-stones, we didn't find another trace of either Leighton and William to know certainly if it had been their blood. It was with the approach of the late after-noon hour at five o' clock, it was bewildering, despite the icy winds blew from further in the caverns and warm remnants and subtle yellow coils of smoke, drifted amongst the stalagmites. I could smell the combination of ocean water and hidden traces of burbling magma.

"Wait," I said, gazing at the tunnels ahead, with a bright, red light flickering through the round holes and fork-way. "Have you noticed the further we head south, the more-warm it becomes in the cave?"

"You don't think the volcano is preparing to erupt, do you?" asked Clarence, nervously.

"I think it is," I said.

"How much longer would we have in the cave?" asked Clarence.

"It would be a few more days," intervened Nora, timidly.

"A few more days to find a way out of here?" he blurted, and he shook his head, unimpressed and strode further to the end of the tunnel. "We won't make it."

"*We can try,*" I argued.

The following day at nightfall on the twelfth day in the cave, not knowing whether Leighton was alive or not, it still disturbed me. The stormy, ocean winds blew, and the enormous, grey wave soared upward, hanging in mid-air and loomed a silhouette onto the dotted, white froth and the sands. The gathered firewood trundled across into the arid foliage, beneath the slouching, fern trees and the plumes of dirt, scattered into the abrupt, swaying ferns. The silvery-scaled, trevally fishes with their dead black and yellow-rimmed eyes and opened mouths, swung on the wire from the hoopak sticks beneath the flashes of lightning. It was with a thunderous, iridescent white flash, Leighton lay on the floor with his parched mouth partially-opened on the limestone and his brown eyes, staring stiffly to the floor, vacant and gone. I abruptly awoke, staring at the shadowed, round stalactites and their sharp peaks, softly illuminated with the tawny glow from the crackling firewood.

Nora's legs suddenly blocked them.

I gasped, recoiling and whispered, "*You scared me*," I wiped my fingers and thumb over my forehead and down my cheeks, trying to dissolve the visions from the nightmare away.

"Come with me," she urged, tugging my shoulder and bewildered with her urgency, I stood from the rock.

Clarence was asleep, and she hauled me through the archway.

"Is it Gharkoll ?" I whispered.

"No," she said, sliding her clasp from my wrist to my hand. Her sudden touch was like she sparked a candle-flame through me.

"Where are we heading?" I asked.

"You'll see," she said, leading me through an archway in the passage.

I tried apprehending she was holding my hand and with each stride, I wondered if she was leading us to a newly-discovered cavern. After wandering through the shadowed passages together, it felt like a surreal dream exploring them with our two lonesome shadows drifting on the walls. I was trying to remain calm being alone with the one girl I liked and accepting the fact, she was interested in me too. I was just a poor, cabin and rigger boy, who had sat on the foretop to gaze at the seas. It was somehow, bewildering she wasn't interested in Leighton , who had been more favorable with her father on *The Admiral Baltic*.

We tread through the archway, and I awed at the twinkling, turquoise soda streams drooping from the dark ceiling, with luminescent, dotted glow-worms in the curved hollows.

"Do you like it?" asked Nora, peering up at them.

"Yeah," I answered, feeling the ground sloping downward and shifted my attention away to our entwined fingers. My olive tanned complexion from the sun shining on the island was distinct against her pale fingers. We halted, moving along the beige path, with the iridescent aqua waterfall flooding into a pool. "I'm surprised...." She neared the water and the soft glow, flickered on our clothes, accentuating the beige marks on our sleeves and buttons. "You're holding my hand, after we argued?"

"Well..." trailed Nora, striding from the edge of the water towards the opening and I held onto every moment in the silence, with agony. I noticed her cheeks were becoming lightly scarlet, as we walked through a small passage. "...I always wanted too..."

"You did?" I asked, impressed.

Nora nodded coyly and with the sound of our crackling and shuffling footsteps in the tunnel, my stomach tightened from nerves. Should I tell her the truth?

I pondered my gaze along the scudded debris and I decided to confess, "Me too." I slid my clammy fingers into her own and held her hand. "I just never knew if I should tell you."

"As for me," said Nora, glancing into my eyes. "I didn't want to tell you, how I felt in fear you'd hurt me."

"I thought you liked my brother," I said.

"What?" asked Nora, astounded and broadened her eyes. "No, what gave you this impression?"

"Well, when he was around you and he gave you his attention, you'd stick around with him." I explained, becoming more confused with every tread.

"He's friendly and nice to talk too, though, it doesn't mean I like him." she answered, eyeing me. "I like someone else."

I beamed, tugging the side of my lips and we stopped into the cavern's entrance, gazing at each other and leant against the wall. It was nice to be alone with her and not have my brother around- he couldn't interrupt us now in the dark. We could be together, explore where we hadn't before and finally, express ourselves. She softly stroked my arms, reeking with her silent adoration for only me.

"Douglas!" echoed Clarence's voice and the sound of his footsteps hurried down the passage.

Nora quickly leant away from me, stepping backwards and crackled a stone. Clarence hurried through the entrance and he looked at us, trying to figure if something intimate had happened without his presence.

"What are you two doing in here?" he asked.

"We were just exploring," I said. "She awoke, and I did, as well," I slapped him on the shoulder. "There isn't any need to worry. We'll be coming back soon."

Clarence side-glanced at me, knowing what I was implying, and he shoved his shoulder, bouncing my hand away.

"Alright." He said, looking at Nora and me, with tension in his voice. "Don't do it again. I could've gone looking for you and never come back alive. Or, become lost in the caverns. It's very selfish of both of you, not to consider me." He fumed through his nose and turned his back to us, treading through the archway and with the heavy pace of his footsteps, I could feel the annoyance and anger in his disposition.

I awkwardly looked back to Nora, sliding my fingers through my tousling, brown hair and tread closer back to her.

"He'll be alright." I said.

Nora's black eyelashes flicked, as our noses hindered closely together.

"I'm sure he will be." she echoed, feebly from her pout.

Our lips lingered closely apart and soft affection reflected into both of our eyes, as we neared closer to each other in the turquoise glow shining from the ceiling. My cheeks burned, more than the lava in the canal. I wanted to embrace her, feel every remnant of her warmth through her chest and skin. It was uncertain whether we were going to live or die in the cave, and if I didn't kiss her now, when would I? Probably *never.* Every-time I had gazed at her on the ship, every imaginary thought of wanting to hold her in my arms could now be true…I deflected my eyes to the floor, seeing the three-tentacle silhouette shifting on the spread rubble. I swallowed, clamping my hand onto her lips and she broadened her eyes. The thumping of the clawed feet trembled the debris on the curved dents in the ground, around the slender, stalagmites along the walls. An echoing growl, gliding whiffs of air through his picket teeth traced our scents in the shadowed cavern. I nodded at Nora, sliding my clammy fingers from her pout and stepped away from behind the boulder. We softly side-stepped, shifting around the other rocks and panicking, we surveyed the cavern. I and Nora, crouched behind the bend in the wall, moving out of sight into the tunnel, as he lurked into the cavern. My eyes burned from ignoring the urge to fall asleep. Gharkoll didn't impede lingering in the opposite tunnel and with a crackle of a bone poking on the side of his bloodied mouth, it collided onto the floor. I feared our heartbeats thumping in our chests were too loud for Gharkoll to hear them. I heard his thick black claw sinking into the dropped bone and the *crackle* echoed in the cavern, across the slender, iridescent turquoise soda straws.

We peeked from the side of the wall, with the silhouettes from the ceiling reflected onto our faces. Nora crossed her arm over my stomach and loosely hung on the front of my waist.

I looked at her.

Nora mouthed, *"We should leave-,"*

I mouthed back, *"Wait a moment."*

I looked back to the cavern and she tugged on my arm in the dark tunnel. Gharkoll 's pair of eyes, beneath his thick, furry beige brows flicked over the stalagmites and his crowd of red eyes glistened on his wrinkled forehead and they flicked upward to the huddled stalactites. I was fascinated with his lime

tentacles, glowing iridescent from his enormous, light beige ears. The closer
he shifted, the more I observed they were lightly moist with his predatory gait.
I gazed from the silhouettes on the jagged stalagmites and sharp peaks and
I noticed the swelling miniature holes, drizzling moist, yellow acidic driblets.
One spattered on the front of his dark brown furred claw. My heart thumped.
Nora's hand clenched around my arm and her fingers spread an array of
crinkles on my toiled linen sleeve, urging for us to leave. I turned, and her
brown eyes, usually light hazel were now dark brown and shiny with fright.
She nocked her head backward, bouncing her messy, black hair strands on her
chest and shoulders. I turned from him and nudged her in the arm, insisting
we move quickly. Her clutch loosened, and we side-stepped further into the
tunnel, shifting in the dark. Gharkoll's footsteps grew louder, dilapidating the
stone bits. We shifted into another cavern. I inhaled the musty stone lofting
from the stalagmites and the dust clinging to the flowstone shawls and the
sour fetid. We moved behind the stalagmites, though hindering at the last
one in a row, I stepped too vastly into the ground, echoing a knocked pebble. I flinched, biting my lip. Gharkoll swiped around, sniveling and his lime
antennas brightened. Nora trundled through the netted web, screaming, and
through the yellow mist and the spiders crawled through her disheveled hair.
She turned the corner and the notch of her scream, emanated louder. Nora
spotted the bloodied foot in the middle of the corridor. I trampled around the
wall and bellowed, recoiling and dropped the candle to the floor, observing
the poking knob of bone and the flesh.

We trampled back to the campsite. I gaped, wide-eyed in the entrance.

"Clarence!" I exclaimed, striding around our pouches. "He's gone!"

CHAPTER TWENTY-THREE

SOMETHING IS FOLLOWING US

The following morning, on the twenty-third of July at ten o'clock in the North-West province of the cave, Gharkoll stopped at the rim-stone dam of burbling, crimson and iridescent yellow lava. He dipped his foot inside, cleaning the squashed flatworms, with a flick of his curved toenail and they splashed back inside of the trickling canal. He twitched his long ear with his sharp hearing and listened to the distant echo of a footstep, soaring down the tunnel. Gharkoll hurried into the hollow lancet, following its direction and after a few swift turns, he slowed his pace, reaching the loudest notch of the footstep and exhaling human breath. He crouched behind the stalagmite, rock and dolostone column, with his claw clasped on the protruding dent on the floor. Gharkoll scrawled his thick curved, black claws downward and the crumbed stone bits surrounded his furred three-toed feet and the longest, yellowed toenail. He peeked with his pair of golden eyes from the rugged edge, blazing with a ferocious intensity. He eyed Leighton stepping into the chamber and skimming his firelight onto the wall of beige speleogens and lingering, whiffs of clouded mist, shrouding around the stalactites. Leighton emerged to the round, pool of green sea water floating white froth and trickling from a distant passage. He stopped near a mound of flowstone and in-between two stalagmites. Leighton lowered the firelight on his stick to the sarsen and a girl, with dust smeared on her cheeks and tousled, mahogany hair. She lifted from the ground.

Leighton bellowed and panted, softly dropping the firelight from her squinting eyes.

"Oh, Henrietta, it's only you." he muttered.

Henrietta stood, wearing a toiled pale-white shirt, overlapping a pair of khaki trousers and a pair of leather-brown boots.

"Sorry, I frightened you." she said.

"That's alright," said Leighton , shaking his head. "How did you find your way in here?"

"I escaped the sailors and their boats, swimming to the island. They were harassing me and pinching my breasts." explained Henrietta. "After the storm came, I wandered through the palm trees on the island and found the southern-entrance of the cave."

"Ah, I see…" trailed Leighton , feeling uncomfortable and he thumped her on the shoulder. "I apologize, they did that to you."

"*Don't*," she said, exhaling and rolled her eyes. "However, I *do* want to leave the cave and head back to the island."

"You can come back to our camp-site, after I've found William, Douglas, Clarence and Nora." He offered. "I've caught fish too, hopefully, we won't spend another three nights here in the cave." He paused. "Have you seen a claw in here?"

"A claw?" asked Henrietta.

Leighton nodded, sternly and frowned.

"Yes, I've seen one, yesterday…" he said.

He turned, lifting his golden firelight to the opposite wide, tunnel and calcium carbonate rubble scattered along the wall of speleogens. "I think, we're not alone in here."

"I have smelt a strange odor," admitted Henrietta.

"Where?"

She pointed down the impenetrable end of the karst tunnel. "It was in this direction."

"What sort?" asked Leighton .

"It was of rotting blood, bones and rock." echoed Henrietta.

A short silence drifted with their indecisiveness, whether they should venture towards the odor, or in the opposite arc.

Gharkoll lifted from his hiding, eyeing their bare necks and he envisioned his picket teeth, sinking into their skin and tasting their bloody juice and tearing a portion of their flesh away. He sensed Leighton knew he was being inspected and he couldn't stay longer, and he softly scampered in the silhouettes falling from the opposite wall of speleogens in the distance into the arc. His short, beige horns and long dark-brown furred cones, protruding from his tresses immersed into the dark.

Leighton halted and swiped around. "*What was that?*" he whispered.

Henrietta stopped behind him, stamping in the soggy dirt imbued with the puddles, surrounding the pool.

"I don't know," she whispered, with her tone hitched with growing fright.

Henrietta hesitated to move another step and fear glinted in her broadened eyes, from the reflected moonlight seeping through the clefts in the walls, chipped from the falling granules on the cragged floor. A thin layer of clammy sweat from the humidity in the cavern, covered her cheeks and forehead. A few dark-golden, wispy strands from her disheveled, hair smeared across her jawbone, while she contemplated on whether they should continue trudging into the same direction of the noise or not.

Henrietta glanced back to him.

"I don't think we should go down there," she decided.

"I want to see," said Leighton , pulling out the pistol from the sack and swinging it back over his shoulder, it wobbled on his shoulder. He stamped through the puddles, splattering the driblets onto the variety of miniature, slender, wide and tall, misty stalagmites.

Henrietta trampled behind him to the arch.

"*Wait*," she urged, tugging his arm, as he bowed and ventured inside the arc. "Can't we head in another direction?"

"No," said Leighton . "I'm curious to look and if it is Gharkoll with the claw, I would like to inflame and kill him,"

"*Don't you dare*," whispered back Henrietta. "That's dangerous," she held his shoulder, though, with stubbornness he shrugged it away and felt fixed on his decision.

Leighton ruminated the radiance from the firelight into the shadowed tunnel. He frowned, trying to catch a glimpse of the creature, though he couldn't see him anywhere.

"What if it was a bat or another animal?" asked Henrietta.

Leighton side-glanced at her, warningly, communicating for her to stay quiet and he lifted his pewter pistol, clamping his finger on the trigger and echoed a *click*. He observed a pair of shiny, jagged picket teeth at the far end of the tunnel and he cringed, expelling a bullet in the distance. A plume of beige dust blew on the ground. Henrietta squealed. Leighton blocked her waist, waiting for another sign of Gharkoll , though the beige dust settled to the terrain and he didn't appear.

"Don't do it again," she said, distressed. "Nothing was there."

Leighton eyed the dark and he glimpsed back to her. "*There was.*"

Leighton tread slowly further, with both the firelight and pistol in front of him. His heart thrummed in his chest. Henrietta followed behind him and wincing, at every movement, even at the shadow slivering on the jagged wall with the reflection of the flickering, tawny-golden fire. They stepped through a small cavern. Leighton inspected the pair of archways of which way to follow. He gasped, lowering his firelight to the ground and discovered the dropped chronometer.

"I recognize this device." said Leighton . "Douglas packed it the night we abandoned the ship." He looked back to Henrietta, "We must head towards the North."

They stepped into the round-tunnel. Gharkoll camouflaged with the rock in the ceiling and his horns and furred cones hung as miniature stalactites. He tilted his head and a droplet of gooey, green saliva slobbered along the corner of his dark-beige mouth and splattered on the floor. Henrietta heard the feeble, wet sound and stopped behind the wavering, golden shadow skimming on the wall, as it disappeared further into the tunnel. She turned and looked down to the floor, observing the saliva droplet, saturating the rock with thin coils of smoke and she looked up confused at the ceiling-*nothing was there*. She disregarded her suspicion, and hastened her pace, striding further down the tunnel. Gharkoll glanced one blistering, lucid, crimson eye, near his furred shoulder to their heads disappearing into the dark. He flared his nostrils and inhaled her clammy-sweat and sea-salt scent, and he crawled across the ceiling, sinking his claws into the ochre-dents, showering dust to the ground, behind them. His dimmed tentacles blinked to their softest, lime luminance and guided him in the dark tunnel. He followed the bend in the wall, and reaching the end to the smaller archway, he dropped to the floor.

"No, *wait*," warned Henrietta, stopping in the passage of columned, stalagmites. Gharkoll hurried behind the slope of flowstone and peeked in-between the array of soda straws on the wall, in the far corner. "*I know* I heard something, this time."

Leighton stopped midway down the passage and probed the twinkling, crystallized specks in the ceiling. He swung around, still, partially under his daze and he asked, "Uh-where?"

"It was the sound of crunching rubble," she hushed, skimming the inflamed stick back to the arc and along the floor, discovering the round, toe marks in the ground. She followed them towards the cornered flowstone and dangling soda-straws.

"*Henrietta*," he called out, moving further down the passage. "*Come on, there's nothing there!*"

Henrietta moved closer to the flowstone, ignoring him and too intrigued of the heavy, breathing from behind the flowstone to justify her horror. Gharkoll's eyes glinted behind the crust of the flowstone and the batch of silhouetted, soda-straw points, seeing her legs approaching closer.

Henrietta stopped in front of the small rock beside the flowstone. She flicked her burning twig down from the wall and skimmed it across his camouflaged fur leaning against the wall, and she lowered her lip. A hand clutched her shoulder and she hailed, swiping around.

"*Don't do this to me!*" she blurted.

"*Come on,*" sung Leighton , pulling her arm and away from the flowstone.

Henrietta's footsteps slightly partitioned on the floor, while she indecisively looked back to the silhouetted corner and waited for Gharkoll to come out.

"There was *fur*, against the wall," whispered Henrietta, turning back around. "It matched the rock, exactly and if I didn't look closely, I wouldn't have noticed it to be different."

Leighton stopped one meter ahead of her. Gharkoll shifted across the soda-straws, pacing across the opposite boulder, nearby the arch and slouched his back, disguising himself.

Leighton turned."What?" he asked.

Henrietta pointed to the shadowed corner. "*Something* is hiding behind the flowstone." she whispered.

Leighton flicked his glance back to her and the flowstone and lifted the two-sided, steel scabbard. "Are you sure?" he asked.

"I'm sure," said Henrietta, nodding.

"*Stay here,*" said Leighton , moving back cautiously to the flowstone and maintained his distance. He emerged close, skimming his flames over the flowstone and he announced, "There's nothing here,"

"*What?*" exclaimed Henrietta, shocked and striding backward, she looked for herself and frowned, crossing her arms. "This is strange. I really believe, I heard the sound of the breaths coming from behind there."

Leighton tapped her on the shoulder and he said, "It's alright, let's keep moving further into the cave."

They turned and continued down the tunnel. Gharkoll waited behind the boulder, watching them venture into the other tunnel and followed them. He tread past the archway and echoed crackling noises.

Henrietta and Leighton swiped around, finding the creature wasn't in sight. Leighton strode to the end. *"Who's there?"* he asked.

A couple of bats flapped past, dropping rubble from the wall, echoing a *crackle* on the floor. The sudden rush of fright tightened his chest and loosened.

Leighton shifted, and shook his head.

"Just *bats*," he commented, with annoyance.

They continued walking to the end of the tunnel. Gharkoll unrolled his tongue and coiled it around a flapping bat and sunk his picket teeth into round, furry stomach, splintering the membrane and lower bones in his wing. The blood driblets leaked into his mouth and he climbed onto the wall, amongst the ceiling and he crawled with a swift pace above them. It was midway, he slid his picket-teeth out from the bat and it dropped from his mouth. The bat's flabby, membranous wings whipped in the silhouettes. Leighton and Henrietta abruptly stopped and bellowed at the suddenness of the dead bat dropping in front of their shoes. The blood on its torso, juicy and drizzling from the round wounds, pooled across the poking, small knobs of bone and the terrain, covering a small piece of debris.

Henrietta huffed, whacked her chest with her hand. *"That scared me,"* she whispered.

She slid her hand away and puffing, she looked down at the bat and green saliva dissolving into smoke. A few holes flecked on the wings and the miniature, skeletal bones. Henrietta stepped back and shrieked, squeezing her clutch on Leighton's arm. He looked up at the ceiling, bewildered, and inspected the round, furred ball camouflaged as the upper formation of a huddled stalactite, then down at the bat.

"I wonder what caused the wings to dissolve," he said.

"Me too," she confessed. "I've never seen anything like it before," she glanced back to the tunnel, "Let's keep going,"

Leighton suspiciously looked at the ceiling, trying to find where the substance would be trickling from and after not finding anything, they tread further into another chamber. He said, "It's weird, there wasn't even one speckle of a liquid on the ceiling anywhere."

"Maybe, the bat had flown from another chamber and it was only now, it began to feel the effects of the liquid?" suggested Henrietta.

"Probably," his voice echoed.

Gharkoll's flicked fur, disguised as the conulites, stretched, as he shifted his claws forward and lowering his head in mid-air, he watched them disappear into the cavern. He followed to the end, hearing the vivid, scorching flames wend into his long, beige-pointed ears from the hollow-opening. Leighton looked around at the towering, columned splattermites and the endless array of totem poles, spreading down the slope to the distant opening in the far rocky wall. Together they paced along the beige slopes on the decimated debris and further to the end. Henrietta stepped into a crevice and suddenly, the entire cavern quivered. The rubble soared down from the precipice, piling in front of her and lathered white dust onto her shoulders and she squealed. Leighton stopped looking at the splattermite and he trampled towards her.

"Henrietta!" he yelled, shining his fire-light at the piled rubble. "Are you alright?"

Henrietta's tight breaths echoed in-between the rubble and she echoed, "*I am*,"

Leighton heavily sighed. "I don't know what to do." he said.

Gharkoll peeked one blistering, red eye onto Leighton's dark, ash-blonde tresses. He side-stepped his large, three-toed foot around the base of the stalagmite and he tip-toed behind the opposite splattermite. Leighton stiffened his back, hearing the footsteps and felt the harmful, demeanour reeking over him, as the silhouettes engulfed the stalagmite peaks. He looked suspiciously at the empty gap between both of the speleothems, unable to push away the feeling, *the creature was there.*

CHAPTER TWENTY-FOUR

DREAD

Leighton lifted his inflamed stick from the boulder and he shone the flickering, golden radiance onto the vacuity between the two rock formations, unable to release his discomfort and suspicion of the tension lingering in the atmosphere. His heart thumped; *thud, thud, thud* in his chest. Leighton moved closer, skimming the firelight on the ground and he glanced behind the stalagmite, observing the three-toed footprint on the ground. He frowned, touching the pointed toe contours with his fingertips. Gharkoll poked his head from the side of the splattermite. Leighton glimpsed the broad-eared and tentacle' silhouette on the rugged floor and he turned, slowly rising from his squatted position. He strode nearer and the beating of his heart intensified, the closer he came to the splattermite. He inhaled a whiff of air nervously and his heart jolted in his chest, reaching the epitome of leaping heartbeats and fear. *He's behind there*, he thought, stepping to the side and he looked to the ground behind the splattermite. Leighton recoiled, as a black, shiny-shelled scorpion with an arisen, curved tail scurried across the floor. Gharkoll wasn't there. Leighton relaxed his stiffened chest and he slouched his shoulders against the splattermite. *It was just your fear, creating the imitation of sensory to believe something was there.* He glimpsed back to the three-toed footprint. He uneasily, sunk his fingertips into his wavy tresses. *Wait, though, how fresh was the footprint?*

Gharkoll stood on the *opposite* side of the splattermite and he lifted his upper lip across his pointed fangs and the ravenous hunger burdened his warm mouth, as he looked down to Leighton 's shoe. He lifted his foot and climbed to the

summit of the splattermite, tracing the scents of carbonite acid and clutching
the edges with his claws, he gazed down at him. His tentacles softly glowed,
oozing a miniature driblet of yellow, acidic poison and it dropped in mid-air,
half an inch away from the splattermite. It missed Leighton 's shoulder and
dabbed the floor.

Leighton heard the frail echo of the tapping noise and looking down,
he was confused, observing it dissolved into thick, yellow mist and a crater
formed in the rock.

He frowned. *"How did it happen?"* he muttered.

Leighton squatted, watching the mist thin pellucid and fade in the air.
Crack

A shower of bits tapped on the ground, surrounding the miniature crater.
He looked up, watching a crowd of bats flapping in the ceiling of stalactites
and observed the neglected summit on the splattermite.

Leighton looked away.

It was far in the dark distance of the clustered splattermites and behind his
back, Gharkoll crawled around the lower half of the stalactite and clinging
to the point, he lowered his legs and they dangled in mid-air. He dropped to
the ground, echoing a *thump*. Leighton swiped around brashly, with his mouth
ajar. He perused the splattermites, searching for the reason behind the noise
and after nothing appeared, he began treading towards it.

"Douglas?" he inquired, with terror in his voice, echoing in the cavern.

Leighton followed the descent in the slope and discovered a portion of
a steaming, stalactite toppled on the ground, surrounded with rubble and
although, he wondered, *how* it had happened, he ignored it and continued
towards the darkest splattermites. He glanced up, observing the broad, jagged
peak hanging from the ceiling and when he shifted his gaze back down to the
floor, Gharkoll 's silhouette appeared in his firelight.

"Ah!!" bellowed Leighton . *"There it is again!"*

He followed the direction of the slanted shadow to the top of the splattermite and it was empty.

"What the..." trailed Leighton slowly, and circled around it with a frown. "...he should be up there..."

Leighton stopped, tilting his head and looked at the peak.

It was behind his back, Gharkoll side-stepped out of hiding from the bottom of the adjacent splattermite. His lime-green tentacles gleamed a bright radiance.

Leighton heard the echoing *crunch* of the dissipating rock and the heavy, exhaling breaths. A nervousness overwhelmed him, and goosebumps flecked on his shoulders, while he slowly, turned around.

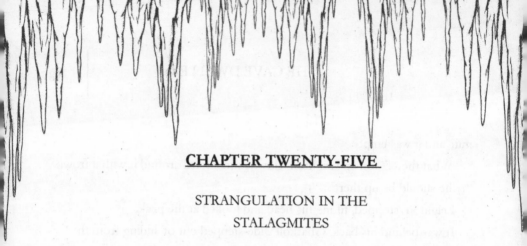

CHAPTER TWENTY-FIVE

STRANGULATION IN THE
STALAGMITES

Leighton heard his own one heart-beat thump and his tight breath echoed in the silence. A *crackle* of debris rolled in front of him. He bellowed, astonished and realized Gharkoll *wasn't* there.

Leighton huffed a breath, easing the tension in his chest and he chuckled, rolling his eyes.

"*I'm scaring myself,*" he muttered.

He stiffened his shoulders and although, it was hot in the cavern, goose bumps flourished beneath his shirt onto his shoulders. He heard a moistened noise floating from behind him in the dark. Gharkoll's dimmed, green tentacles slurped around the ochre, spikey peaks of the paired stalagmites and whipped on his shoulders, wrapping around his neck and burned reddened welts on his skin. Leighton echoed a harried, guttural scream. The yellow mist simmered from the miniature holes, over his parched lips and nose, as trickles of yellow poison slivered on his chin and neck, drenching his collar. Gharkoll's small beige horns and the tall, dark-brown tufts of furred cones lifted behind his back and his crimson, glistening eye shone on the side of his neck. Leighton choked with stifled breaths and he teetered on the small calcite conulites. He lost his balance and falling to the side, they scraped across his ankles and the bottom of his trousers. His blue eyes watered, and he wriggled in the blistering, clouds of yellow mist, floating around him and he collapsed onto the ground. Gharkoll wailed with triumph, as he sunk his fangs and rack of picket teeth into his leg, drizzling beads of blood and dragged him over

the sharp stalagmite peaks, scrawling slender holes onto his crinkled trousers.
Leighton slid on the rocks, smearing a sheet of white-beige dust on the front
of his linen shirt and the warm, long tentacles wrapped around his waist and
he was lifted higher into the air. He screamed with agony and squirming,
he clutched the tentacles and screamed louder at the sight of the red eyes
and enormous picket teeth lunging over him and inhaled a whiff of his foul
breath.

Gharkoll engulfed his ear, sinking his shiny, picket teeth through his skin
and a splutter of blood oozed down from the corner of his mouth, drenching
his fur. Leighton screamed at the tinging pain in his ear and he side-glanced
upward, as the blood and green saliva trickled in a long rivulet on his neck,
shiny with a layer of perspiration. He bellowed, stretching out his hand and
grabbing a rock, he collided it into Gharkoll 's crowd of red eyes on his forehead.

Gharkoll recoiled away and his moist picket teeth and mouth left a moist
layer of saliva on where his ear had used to be, as he echoed a piercing
screech. Leighton held his left ear for a moment and crawled on the floor, as
the tentacles writhed in mid-air above him. He grappled a poking curvature
of limestone from the wall and stood and limping forward, with the last of
his strength, he rammed Gharkoll into the enormous boulder. He yawped
at the sharp rock dabbing his back and his tentacles loosened, as he dropped
to the floor and a gash swelled on his dark, brown fur. The dark-green beads
of blood leaked onto his fur and some thick strands became sticky. Leighton
cried, sliding his fingers back over his ear and blood drenched over it, leaking
onto his knuckles and wrist. He maneuvered around the airy gaps between
the splattermites and stalagmites, running on the stones. Gharkoll pursued
after him, striding with speed, that Leighton 's footsteps resembled the pace
of the scorpions crawling in the corners of the cavern, festering with algae.
Leighton glanced over his shoulder, still in the state of shock that his ear had
been torn away and the blood stickily oozed onto his shirt's collar. He became

short of breath, as he reached the short, slender totem-pole at the edge of the slope and he leant against the solidified, strings of trickled carbonic acid and limestone.

Leighton broadened his eyes, gasping, horrified.

Gharkoll scampered closer onto the rock and a rotund ball swelled amongst the crowd of crimson eyes in the middle of his beige forehead. The lid lifted, dragging the scrawny wrinkles, revealing a larger eye infested with dark-green veins.

Leighton quivered, expelling a guttural scream and his throat scratched.

Gharkoll surged an atomic beam of light from his large eye and it plunged into his shoulder. Leighton hailed, falling backward and the tendrils of fog erupted from the disintegrating patch in his crumpled, pale-linen shirt, revealing a crimson bloodied abrasion.

Gharkoll hunched closer, crunching a footstep on the stones and they dissolved beneath the impact of his falling, three-toed foot, into a mound of white dust. He hissed and fixating his large, round eye onto him, it gleamed a bright tawny radiance and another atomic beam was emitted into his torso. Leighton screamed, spreading his arms and he swung backward against the broad, limestone totem pole, with his shoulders brashly sliding down the jutting, sharp edge. He tumbled to the floor and quivering, with his shoulder festering mist, the atomic wave spread across his crinkled linen shirt, staining black-ashy streaks, until his buttons burned. One by one, they dropped to the floor. Gharkoll's large eye in the middle of his forehead sung a monotonous, hum, penetrating into his eardrums and the sound of his cry, lifted a notch with hitched agony.

Leighton jerked on the floor, releasing splatters of frothy, white saliva from his bottom lip.

Gharkoll's shadow manifested from the lime-light reflecting from his tentacles onto the nearest towering stalagmites, loomed over him. He thumped his three- toed foot onto his stomach, sinking it as deeply as he could. Leighton echoed stifled breaths from suffocation. Gharkoll gnashed his picket teeth and lowering his bottom jaw, he stretched a string of green saliva in between his gums, shining in the dark. His tentacles stretched from his ears and wound down into his chest.

Leighton squirmed on the floor and bellowed, as flicking, yellowed and bloodied driblets smattered onto the stalagmite and the totem pole, oozing to their rugged bases until they trickled to the ground.

~

Gharkoll drunk the fluids of his body and they slivered inside of his tentacles, as thick globules. Leighton 's skin withered and became arid, until only the contour of his skeleton was visible beneath the layer of his skin. He slivered his lime tentacles away from his stomach, leaving two, round holes and they shrunk back to their ordinary poise from his ears. Gharkoll tilted his head, releasing a high-notched screech and it echoed inside the chamber, quivering the green stalactites. The thick yellow fog lurked around Gharkoll 's fawn-brown furred legs and he strode down the slope into the shadowed splattermites and stopped at the wall. He lifted the lid of his eye and the beam of green light discharged out onto the rock and it slid across, revealing a cleaved stairwell. He stepped inside, and the rock slid back, shielding the entrance. Gharkoll paced down the stairs with a predatory gait, quivering them with every falling impact of his feet. He arrived to the bottom of the rocky staircase and inhaled a sweet, moist sweat and *dread* racing through the feminine adrenaline. He heard her thrumming heart, from the distress of being neglected. Gharkoll peeked from the edge and he eyed Henrietta's shoulder, yearning to sink his picket teeth into her bloody tendons and bones, and tear a portion away.

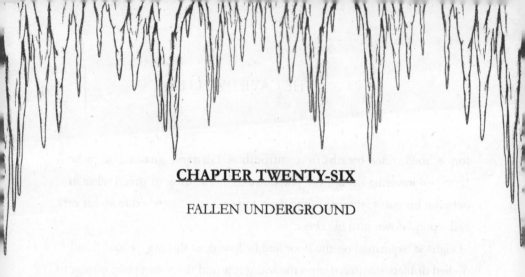

CHAPTER TWENTY-SIX

FALLEN UNDERGROUND

It was heading to the South-East, we flashed our dimmed, golden lantern and lamplight onto the ceiling and felt disappointed. The traces of air we had followed, weren't leading into a hollow opening on elevated ground. It was on the twenty-fourth of July and after leaving the white, crystallized soda-straw cavern earlier in dawn, to venture through the winding tunnels, ascending around the flowstone chamber, the wind gusts of salt and watery froth, lurked stronger and taunted us. Every footfall had become tiresome, our limbs pained with every stride and our toiled clothes smeared with the soft-beige dirt on our sleeves, were uncomfortable. It was by noon, we inhaled the thickened plumes of the ocean scented air blustering in the widest cavern, we had encountered after four miles. My stomach sunk into a pitch-black pit of gloom, lifting the last of my flickering, golden flame from the small, tallow candle, shrinking into a cascade of runnels into pools to the oil lamp's rotund base. The ceiling had a wide crevice and the soft, golden sunlight gleams reflected onto the crusted brink, dangling loose vine, tangled weeds and grasses. I tightened my clasp around the ringlet of the oil lamp, until my knuckles became sallow, despite speckled with beige dust after being swished on the dank stalagmite's peak. I kicked a rock, hurling it into the opposite dark brown boulder. *Death,* that was all I could perceive on the stalagmites. *Us,* dying and as a pile of bones, all because of my buoyancy. Gharkoll would hurt us, and the skeletal rib-cages, decaying on the silhouettes amongst the black-shelled maggots and scuttling scorpions, permeated our own inevitable calamity. Nora and Clarence trundled through on the chipped rubble, pivoting a couple from the front of their shoes and peered up, disappointed.

"*No*," cried Nora, bitterly and swung the side of her lip.

I was unable to cease my attraction towards her, even amongst her annoyance- her mouth managed to stay the lightest ruddy shade, the one of a rose paling in summer heat and drifting a soft floral scent. Clarence caught me looking at her lips and I glanced away, pretending to stare at the slender stalactite hanging behind my shoulder. Nora strode further into the middle of the cavern, glaring at the ceiling and her silhouette elongated on the floor. She turned away and tread past us. Clarence watched her moving to the opposite archway.

Nora leant her palm and fingers on the rocky edge of the wall and peered over her shoulder.

"There's a strange odor in this tunnel, and I'm unsure if we should follow down there." she echoed.

"There isn't choice," echoed Clarence. He exhaled, nudging the rubble and the silver cutlery inside his pouch shuffled onto the thermometer with his extra pair of crinkled shirts, echoing a clattering noise. "There has to be another way out of here," His moistened cheeks were lightly reddened from frustration and a few dark brown tresses smeared onto his forehead, overlapping his thick, masculine eyebrows. "How is it we've walked for hours and not found anything?" He deflected his gaze from the ceiling to me. "*Are you sure* this would be the only entrance revealing the wind? What if there's another one?"

"I doubt it," I said, unable to deign to optimism in fear I would fool all of us again. "We need to keep heading in the Southern direction and not waste one more minute here," I pulled out my compass from underneath my shirt. It was despite the havoc of the stormy waves, the showering icy rain on the foretop and the fires burning shards of wood from the deck, it still was able to guide me. "If we're to find a way out of here, that is the only way we are going to do it."

I pointed to the archway, holding out my silver compass, softly glistening in the dark and watched the needle, slide in-between the E and S. "We're still not completely in the South caverns, we'll have to continue right."

We stopped, when we came out of the passage, glaring at the peculiarity in the wall and the stained, crimson blood driblets flecked on the sharp cavities. My heart sunk into a silhouetted pit of gloom, horror and shock, recognizing the dark ash-blonde locks. They were disheveled and musty, curtained with rocky dust and nestled inside the fissure splintered in the sharp rocky wall. His freckled cheeks were *emaciated*-it seemed he had been here for a few days, without one beam of golden, summery sunlight widening through a rift in partitioning, puffy clouds onto his complexion. I inhaled a vagrant stench and it pinched my nose. It was with one more step closer, my heartbeats became harried, as I observed the lathered, dried pool of blood inside the shadowed fissure within the curved wall. The trail of ants crawled along the smeared, dark beige streaks on his nostril.

"*William?*" I asked. "What…are…you…" I stopped, observing it was *very* unordinary for him to even be squished inside such a narrow fissure and I trembled. My breaths tightened, and I gulped, nudging his ear with a twig. Nora and Clarence, standing beside me, *cringed*. I felt goosebumps flourish on my arms from becoming repulsed. A heavy feeling thudded passively inside of my chest, warning me to stay away from his head, though, I couldn't control my curiosity. "*William?*"

The mauled head rolled out of the wall. I recoiled, startled and screamed, treading backward and saw the sudden rush of the crowded beetles crawling towards it. I screamed, eyeing his partially opened, parched mouth and the pair of his pale eyes and pupils, elongated with frail veins. A snake crawled out from his lower lip.

I winced, screaming a notch louder.

"*Disgusting,*" I muttered, stepping further away from the head and his dark blonde hair.

I paced into the ensuing cavern, feeling like I shouldn't be in there. My skin crawled with slivering streams of fear. William's slouched body was tangled with dark green sticky strands formed from a substance and he wilted in-between the rugged peaks of the stalactites. I screamed, lowering the dimmed glow flared from my oil lamp and stepped back into the boulder, feeling petrified. I broadened my eyes and gaped. There were ashy covered bones scattered around the scudded stalagmites with yellow, ionized mist, eddying from the hollow chinks on the floor and buzzing mosquitos. After one cloud blew across, a pile of dead bats were revealed on the floor and some were bloodied with their wings torn. I shuddered and yearned to vomit, gazing longer with disbelief at my headless friend's body hanging amongst the stalactites. I screamed again and tripped over the rolling bundle of bones underneath my shoes. Gharkoll appeared amongst him, clutching the stalactite and he squirted a globule of the thick-green poison onto the other stalactite and drizzled into thick, long, rivulets over the denticulate, protrusions in the rock. He scurried across, chafing the rock with his claws and his dark brown fur, contrasted against the light-beige limestone.

I hid and shivered, behind the nearest rock.

Gharkoll *was* still alive.

He had never died in the green stalagmite and he was different, from what I had seen and met before. His eyes lacked the soft shine of curiosity and friendlessness, though, now sharply glinted with a ferocious, incessant hatred and hunger. Gharkoll wrapped the opposite peak, with his three- lime tentacles sprouted from his ears, and he side-stepped onto the other stalactite. He lifted them, and they slivered backward in mid-air, jutting shortened from his ears and back to their ordinary appearance. I was shocked at the crowd of glowering, crimson eyes on his forehead and the short, sharp beige horns grown in front of the dark-brown furred cones and he disappeared inside a fissure in the ceiling.

"Let's run *outta'* here," murmured Clarence, gawking at the stalactites and

William's wilting body. He stepped backward and he hurried away into the passage.

"*Clarence!*" I called out, running after him with Nora close to me. "*Wait!*"

We arrived into a cavern of two, lancet archways and I didn't know which way he went. I was frightened to expose my voice, after what we had just found.

I stepped to the left archway.

"*Clarence?* Are you down here?" I whispered.

"Yeah," he echoed.

We followed the direction of his echoing voice into a small ante-chamber, with another hole in the wall, leading into another passage.

I scowled at him.

"Don't go running like you just did," I demanded.

"Well," he began, dropping his sack to the floor. "It was the most frightening circumstance, I've ever seen in my life."

"*Me too,*" I admitted. "It's along with Gharkoll , turning into a stalagmite before." I frowned at him, "*You* altered him into a dangerous *mutant!*"

"What are you talking about?" he exclaimed.

"You should never have thrown the chloride!" I yelled. "You shifted his genes! He now won't just consume the bats in the cave, though, us too!"

Nora barged inside the chamber and hurled her pouch to the ground.

"It's done now. Don't worry about it. We must rest to avoid acquiring hypothermia." she announced.

Clarence and I exchanged a vile glare with each other and conceding, I knelt to the ground and widened my pouch, pulling out the crinkled piece of the fore-sail and kept the remainder of my infuriation to myself.

~

It was during the night, my thoughts plagued me, with blurred visions of William's mauled, bloodied head and his sallow eyes flung back in their sockets. I

restlessly rolled onto my shoulder and glared at Nora tucked beneath the potato sack and sleeping beside me. A scorpion crawled close to her spread, black
hair and I tapped it with a stick, nudging it away and it scuttled along the edge
of the wall around the stones. I closed my eyes, trying to fall into a deep slumber when I heard a distant, frail scream lurking from the shadowed tunnel.

My eyes reopened.

I glared glumly at the stalactites, listening intently to the last of the frail
scream dissolve into the cavern's silence. An ant crawled on my arm and I
didn't wipe it away immediately, still sitting within the terror overwhelming
me. I couldn't ignore it. Who was inside of the cave, apart from us? I slid away
the potato sack from my body and I quietly lifted the oil-lamp, trying not to
awaken Clarence and Nora. I slowly stood and tip-toed around the boulders
and her spread, dark hair, avoiding the granules. I was about to sneak into
the fissure, when I saw a shifting shadow in the oil lamp's light and heard the
rolling potato sack. I swiped around, seeing Nora missing and I turned to the
side and winced, bouncing to the edge of the wall.

"*Where* are you going?" snapped Nora, shining the lantern's light into my
cheeks and I squinted. "You're not going somewhere, you shouldn't be again,
are you?"

I clamped my hand on the lamplight and lowered it down, with the gleam
shining in-between my spread fingers.

"I heard something," I whispered. "Stay here."

"*No*," said Nora, standing in front of me and she blocked the entrance of
the tunnel. "I won't allow you to go. I don't want to see you become hurt."

"Do you have to be bossy all the time?" I retorted, becoming annoyed.
"Just let me be."

"You're making a stupid decision," disputed Nora. "I have to tell you to
protect you."

"I don't need to be protected," I argued, with a vast whisper. "I've looked
after myself my whole life aboard the ship," I anticipated a step around her

and she blocked me.

"I don't care," insisted Nora. "You mustn't continue in the cave on your own. Can you use your logic for once?"

"Something is wrong and I have to see it," I said. "Stay here with my brother."

Clarence groaned, sliding his arm away from his forehead and he lifted from the floor. His legs were still covered with the potato sack.

"What are you arguing about? Can't you see I'm *trying* to sleep?" he asked.

"He wants to leave and go wandering again," said Nora, fiercely. She scowled and didn't move the lantern. "I don't want him to go."

"Douglas, really?" he blurted, with disbelief. "Aren't you tired?"

"I am," I said. "I can't sleep anyway."

Clarence stood. "There's no way, you're going on your own. What's wrong?" he asked.

"Didn't any of you hear the scream?" I asked.

"No," said Nora.

I became distracted at Nora's lips lingering close to mine and I couldn't stop the temptation and the yearn to kiss her again. I tried to concentrate and ignore my feelings, and the closer she came to me, the harder it became to figure which way was the correct direction. I had to think twice, before making a final decision. Only because I had heat flushes every time she neared closely to me.

"Well, I wasn't hearing things," I said. "There's other people in the cave and I need to know who it is." I put the compass to the tunnel, where I had heard the feeble scream. "North," I glanced up from the compass. "That's weird, it's in the same direction we were heading towards in the cave."

"What do you think they came in from another entrance?" asked Clarence.

"*I think, yes,*" I nodded. "Otherwise, it doesn't make any sense. The front entrance is closed and it's in the opposite direction."

I waited for them to pack their sacks and swing them over their shoul-

ders, before guiding them down the tunnel. I stopped in-between five archways, unaware which was the correct direction I should walk down. I flicked
a match and held it in the right tunnel, double checking the direction of the
wind and found the flame flickering to the side. I blew it out and dropped the
steaming, burnt match to the ground. I glanced at the compass and observed
we were heading Northwards and I was relieved. We continued onwards and
after treading through a few more passages, we stopped at the end of one,
feeling petrified. The blood oozed in the callused ground and spread in a pool
beneath the speleothems, covered in slivers of carbonate water. My heart beat
loudly in my ears and my pulse raced with every footstep, as I skimmed my
flared, golden glow on the long streak of blood trickling from the pool into a
cleft in the wall.

I shivered and trembled my oil-lamp.

"Come over here!" I called out over my shoulder.

Nora shrieked, covering her mouth and she closed her eyes, glancing away
from the blood. Clarence gasped and leant against the speleothems unable to
look any longer.

"...the question is..." I said slowly, following alongside the blood. "Where
did the blood come from?"

My stomach churned with every footstep. I thought of William, then of
Leighton. Could they both have come inside the cave? Maybe, I had been
wrong the whole time? It wasn't just William that had died. Now, I *had* to
know. I began following the stream of blood trickling into the tight, narrow
passage and I wiped away the wispy spider web clinging to the ceiling, with my
fingers and onto the side of my trousers.

"Douglas!" hissed Clarence.

I stopped midway down the tunnel and beneath a slanted ceiling. "Yeah?"
I asked.

"What are you doing?" he asked. "Return back here! The worst to do is to
follow the blood!"

Nora peeked from behind his shoulder and echoed behind him, "He's right."

"I want to know who is dead," I whispered. "I just hope it's not Leighton ."

"Leighton is on the island," said Clarence.

"We don't know that," I said, turning briefly over my shoulder and felt too stubborn to consider their perspective.

I strode down the tunnel, bowing beneath the ceiling and leapt my hand on the wall.

Nora groaned, and she echoed, "If you get us into trouble again…"

"Well, keep your distance," I blurted.

They followed cautiously behind me and when I reached the end of the tunnel, the trail of blood thickened and widened towards an opening, with a spread crimson pool. I recoiled and followed into a small cavern and observed the trail had dried on the ground and wound to the left into another archway.

Clarence quickened his pace and caught up beside me.

"That's a lot of blood." he muttered.

He moved further in front of me towards the archway.

I waited for Nora to reach me. "Are you alright?" she asked.

"*No*," she admitted. "I feel uncomfortable doing this and want to go in the opposite direction. Can we just stay here?"

"You can, if you want too," I murmured, rubbing her arm.

"Alright," said Nora, with a nod.

I beamed and sliding my fingers away from her arm, I tread into the wide, round archway. I wiped beads of sweat from my forehead and my brother panicked, swaying an arm in front of my stomach. I stopped, swinging my foot airily before having to put it back down to the ground.

"What is it?" I whispered, unsure even if I should be uttering a word. I was tempted to sip from the water flask in my ransack, hearing the sound of it clink into the chronometer and the last tomato soup can.

We strode into another deserted cavern. Clarence explored the other tunnels. I tread further and tripped on a vine thread stretched on the floor. I bellowed and teetering on the edge of the pool I splashed inside of the luminescent, yellow water, flicking driblets to the periphery. I coughed, spluttering breaths in the heavy plumes of yellow smoke, and the slimy water lathered my cheeks. A windy force beneath, swindled around my legs, and floated bubbles in the green froth around my shirt and descended me beneath the surface. I choked on the water, gurgling, with bubbles floating from my partially-opened mouth and the heat burned my throat, while my arms sunk down below. The air began vanishing from my lungs, my vision blurred of the rippling water with a swivel of frothy white bubbles. I was drowning, and with the bubbles swindling around my shoes, I was dragged downward into the pool.

CHAPTER TWENTY-SEVEN

EATING HUMAN FLESH

I screamed and plunged onto a sordid moss cushion, beneath the water's flickering, turquoise light on my soggy, linen shirt. I puffed, glaring at the surrounding walls and the shawls of pale flowstone hanging from the slanted ceiling. A dreary shadow lurked amongst them, as if it was infinitely enclosed without daylight and the shriveled foliage hunkering on the skeleton's fingers in the corner were etiolated. I was in an underground parallel dimension, interconnected with the cave and green moss festered on the walls, coating the rock. It wasn't limestone and there wasn't any magma in sight. It was obsidian with lime-green flecks gathered in a few dimples and covered with a strange curtain of threaded bacteria. I suspected it was from his mutant metamorphosis. I peered through the round archway and the dangling curtain of slinky, moss strands billowed with a gust of warm wind, hurling a whiff of feeble yellow mist and it breezed over my trousers and shoes. I wiped my hand through my dank, disheveled hair, flicking a few driblets onto the black walls and snapping the elongated debris, I nervously strode closer. I pushed them aside, revealing the endless, silhouetted tunnel and drips of carbonite acid water tapped onto the floor. I assumed this entire province was in the North- East section of the cave and beneath the Do-line Chamber. A yellow light flickered at the end of the tunnel and swallowing, I tread inside the cavern. The stalactites weren't knobby or with porous contours, though were serrate and slender, arisen in the green luminance flickering on the wall. They reminded me of Gharkoll 's picket teeth. I thought carbonite-acid water trickled onto my ear, though, peering at my collar, it was *fresh* crimson blood. A pallid arm and fingers with a thin layer of green slime, drooped from the crevice in the wall, amongst the whirling, yellow mist and it floated from the ochre speleothems. I panted and stepped away, recognizing the crumpled, light-blue cotton shirt, infested with a swarm of crawling maggots and the shadowed, still light-blue eye.

"*Leighton* ..." I whispered, disgusted and watched his arm being hauled backward into the crevice.

My heart pounded, eyeing a few green driblets fleck on the ceiling and flick in mid-air and dab onto the drizzled crimson blood on the stalactite. I recoiled, and the beads slivered on the sharp point and tapped to the cragged floor. A hissing noise, echoed from behind the nearest boulder. I panicked and watched it glide across and reveal Gharkoll standing in the opening's shadowed tunnel. He held Leighton 's lower-half of his leg in his picket teeth and blood drizzled on the corner of his mouth. The One Eye was lucid and crimson and shrunk the pale-gleam and it dimmed, revealing only the illumined green veins. I was veiled behind the fog and I hurried into an obsidian cavern, with more viridescent mosses and white lichen, flecked on the dimples. I felt nausea swindle in my throat, as I remembered Leighton 's boots standing on the main-mast's third, square-rig and his front-leg leaning on the beige shrouds of the ship. The vomit undulated, like the ocean's white froth along the shoreline. I kept swallowing it down, with remnants of the sour water from the pool- *there wasn't time to vomit now*. I hitched a breath, swiping around and paced towards the lancet opening in the wall, though I saw Gharkoll stride across the winding tunnel. I stopped and luckily, made it in time, behind the sarsens and medium-sized stalagmites. He turned and disregarded my noise, watching a fleet of myriapoda-millipedes and centipedes nudge the obsidian fragments and rotting exoskeletons. The lime-tentacles moistened with the gathering, yellow poison and flashed a glow on the rugged edges of the ceiling and revealed the dark-brown dripstones and the debris. My heart beats echoed loudly, as if they could be heard reverberating in the chamber. I

tread through the slender crevice. The spiders dangled from the ceiling and a
few dropped onto my neck and my collar.

"*Ah*," I bellowed, wincing and stepped backward, crunching a piece of
rubble and the dead, brown-shelled crayfish with remaining arid and speckled
moist-black bacteria.

Gharkoll 's movement drifted from the opposite tunnel and his pacing
echoed louder through the distant caverns. I hurried through a round fissure
into a chamber.

Crick, crack

Crick, crack

I knew I didn't have enough time to hurry towards the crevice for him not
to catch me and I hid behind the flowstone shawls and peeked from the edge.
Gharkoll appeared, and I observed his venom trickling from the miniature
holes in his tentacles had shifted- the shade of watery, light green had become
sticky, dark-green like the mosses and bacteria. It wasn't neurotoxin, inflicting
only paralysis, fever and nausea, though with one driblet tapping beside his
dark-brown furred foot, the debris shattered into ash. It was hemo-toxin, con-
taining also dangerous acid and it slivered a chill on my back. He was immune
to his own venom. I waited for him to shift around and trace my scent in
the archway I had run through a few minutes ago and watched him turn left,
tracking me to my hiding place. I swallowed, and knew I had to risk trampling
from the flowstone shawls. I clasped dark rubble with my heart beating and
sweat trickling behind my ear, I lifted from the obsidian flowstone behind
Gharkoll . My clammy fingers quivered, as I eyed his slender, fawn-beige short
horns and dark brown furred cones and hurled it across the chamber.

The piece of rubble revolved in mid-air.

Gharkoll twitched his crimson eyes, watching it plummet to the floor,
bounce along the distant ground. He strode towards it and I hurried out of
hiding, dashing in the opposite direction, and passage.

Gharkoll growled, hearing the vast swipe of air, and he turned in my direction.

"*Dammit*," I whispered.

I heard his movement nearing closer and just as I stepped out of the passage into the adjoined cavern, the malevolent footsteps intensified. I panted and swallowed, with my cheeks sweltering with warmth and I squashed myself into the wall's hollow, disguising myself as Gharkoll strode through the cavern. I felt sweat drenched on my cheeks, smeared with patches of beige rock and grime. He sniffed the air, prying where I was with his luminescent red and hungry eyes. I watched his horns shifting past the stalagmites and his claws shifting through the mist, following the scent of my ripped piece of linen drenched in blood on the tunnel's floor. I leant out of the crevice and slowly, lifting my foot in the air, I clamped it softly to the ground. Gharkoll stopped, twitching his ear backwards and I trampled quickly into the nearest archway. He followed me and stamping in the cavern, I tried to hush my exhales. I peeked from the edge of the wall at the end of the tunnel. My heart began hammering at the sight of Gharkoll hunched over Henrietta. The rivulets of wet blood oozed down her neck and dabbed onto her collarbone from Gharkoll's slender fangs.

I swallowed.

Gharkoll devoured a portion of her shoulder and tore it away, leaving only the bloodied knobs. I flinched and looked away, not believing what I had just seen, and I slowly glimpsed back. Gharkoll sunk his tentacles into her flesh and withdrew her fluid and her body quivered on the floor, as splatters of slimy, green liquid and blood smeared and trickled down the wall. I gasped and closed my eyes, looking away.

Gharkoll's broad-eared shadow, along with Henrietta's quivering body shadow moved on the wall and another flow of slimy, green blood oozed on the floor, trickling into the tunnel. I side stepped and trembled, slouching my arm against the wall. Gharkoll tore another portion of her shoulder away and with a *crunch*, of her splintering bones, he swallowed the mouthful. His nose lifted, and his ear twitched in my direction, listening intently to the movement of my head. Gharkoll licked the corners of his lips with his slimy, green tongue and he shifted around, stamping *towards me.*

I moved away and hid behind the opposite, clustered black, slender and wide totem poles. Gharkoll stopped at the boulders and sniffed them, tracing my scent and he growled, disappointed, I wasn't there. He turned, gazing at the stalagmite and prowled towards me. I writhed further behind them, with my shoulder gliding past the obsidian speleogens and lathered my hair, ears, cheeks and linen trousers in thick, moist mire hoping my scent would be disguised with the foul aroma. Gharkoll ventured closer, sniffing the air and shrieked, narrowing his crowd of crimson, moist eyes at my chest, listening to my palpitating heartbeats beneath the clumps of mud. His picket teeth lathered with saliva drizzled onto the floor, burning the side of my shoe and lunging, he traced his nose across my crinkled shirt, blowing whiffs of air from his wrinkled nose across my buttons. His crowd of eyes lingered above my chest with the protruding pair of horns and augmenting cones above my cheeks, nose and forehead, provoked such a fear I had never felt before. The scream, I yearned to release from the bottom of my stomach and soul, hindered in my throat and tickled my gums, as he sunk his nose to my heart, gliding his moist nose and the points of his picket teeth above the crinkles, higher to my collar. *Don't scream. Don't scream Douglas. Don't twitch your mouth.* The ants crawled from the outskirts of the mire onto my shoulder and neck, tracing the thin, drying patch along to my jawbone and earlobe.

They tickled slowly...

I needed a rock, a piece of stone or the thermometer from my pouch. *Any-thing.* I couldn't twitch a finger and if my heartbeat was the last movement, at least I had tried to survive against him. Gharkoll 's nose hindered on my heart and widening his jaw, he spread his picket teeth and pierced my skin with their points. His warm, moist end of his slimy, red tongue lathered the crumples in my shirt. The lime tentacles shining on the mud smeared to my cheeks, prickled my ears and with one last inhale, he lifted from my chest and thumped his claw onto the stalagmite's peak, chiseling a few pieces of stone onto my stomach. He screeched and with a disappointed demeanour, his ear tentacles dimmed to a light shade of lime and slowly shifted back to their dimmed appearance of dark- green. The slivering, yellow driblets shrunk back into the holes and slowly closed, as he strode through the pitch-black round archway. I puffed a breath, relieved and waited for his crinch-crunching to shrink in the tunnel's end and I sat up from the mire, wiping the ants away from my neck, though they smeared onto my palm and fingers. I swallowed, eager to find a waterfall and I stood clutching the jagged peak, where his claws had been. I tread around the stalagmites in the opposite direction. The tunnel was more narrow and uncomfortable with dangling moss-green roots and stepping into the cavern, my heart lurched-he appeared in the opposite archway. I hid behind the enormous, turquoise-splattermite column, with drizzled beige, limestone driblets and sinking my head against them, I looked to the side. Gharkoll lurked inside the chamber and squatting softly, I snatched a pebble and hid in the cleft within the wall, trying to disguise myself with the rock. He ventured further, following the rapidity of the shifting air, as it twisted into his long, beige pointed ears and the lime tentacles, flickered iridescent again. Gharkoll shifted closer, brushing his tentacles onto my shoulder, burning a shaft of yellow poison and my linen shirt and mud dissolved, blowing ten-drils of smoke. I hurled the stone to the opposite side of the cavern and the descending crackle on the debris, echoed in the black, rocky walls. Gharkoll swiped around, immediately and watched the stone bouncing across the debris and it collided into the short stalagmite. He became curious of what had caused the noise and he followed it across the cavern and waiting for him to reach the opposite side, he inspected the side of the stalagmite. I felt relieved and I stepped out of the cleft and hurrying through the tunnel, I thought I escaped him.

CHAPTER TWENTY-EIGHT

THE DROPPING STALACTITE IN THE URANIUM CAVERN

It was with the approach of sunset, Gharkoll arched his beige-furred claw on the serrated rock.

Crack.

Henrietta stopped beside the flowstone and speleothems, listening, and he slid his claw away, dropping stone bits into the dark. She turned, looking with broadened eyes, flecked with shining fright and skimmed her lantern's glow on the ground. A frail, plume of wind blew through the end of the tunnel, rolling the loose rubble and she inhaled the crushed stone aroma. Henrietta wiped her sleeve over her flustered cheek and she disregarded her suspicion of being followed and tread down the passage. Gharkoll leant forward and wriggling the side of his light-beige nose, he inhaled her clammy sweat breeding down her neck in a slender rivulet. His breaths became heavier and a droplet of saliva trickled from the corner of his mouth, tapping to the floor in-between his long, middle toe. He dimmed his lime tentacles and they faded to an un-illuminated appearance, jutting into the dark, while he softly followed behind her. His mouth swelled with leaking saliva and the voracious hunger lingered in his warmth teeth. The yearn to have sweltering blood in his mouth taunted him with each step and inhaling her clammy sweat drizzling from her hair, poison blistered in his tentacles' as rivulets of lava oozing in the canals. Henrietta strode down the neglected passage, nervously, glaring at the golden glow flicker onto the bending, rugged wall. She held her breath and stepped into the cavern with the yellow Sulphur pools, simmering coils of smoke withheld in the curved craters. Gharkoll blurred in the clouds of sulphurous fog, behind her and extending his tentacles from his ears, he lifted into the stalactites. Henrietta swiped around, watching the whiffs of mist lurking higher into the ceiling and dissolve into the dark. She moved through the rotund opening into another passage, venturing into a cavern with uranium ores shining in the sedimentary rock. Gharkoll prowled in the silhouettes behind her, with a vicious gait and puffed warm breaths through his short, slender fangs. A bead of saliva drizzled from the corner of his mouth. He watched her, peruse the uranium cores with her glowing, lantern-beam. He shifted behind the broad, totem-column, sinking his claws into the hard rock.

A few more chiseled bits trundled to the floor.

Henrietta turned and swallowed, lifting her flickering, candle flame's light in the lantern to the neglected archway and the flood of yellow mist breeding on the floor to the totem pole. She could hear a swipe of air, wending around the base. *Why was it twice now bits of rock had suddenly tumbled, without even a quiver from the ground?*

Henrietta frowned. "How will I ever find Leighton now?" she muttered.

She turned. Gharkoll absorbed the grey clusters of uranium rock and liquefied them with globules of spitting lime acid, swallowing the remnants with his tentacles and The Eye shriveled, revolving backwards in it's socket. Henrietta screamed, listening to the moist noises puckering in the silence, with the distant echo of the rippling Sulphur pools. The yellow gleam flickered onto the side of Gharkoll 's cheek and The One Eye fixated back to her. Gharkoll squelched, bending his long claws and they glinted in her lantern's glow. Henrietta screamed and hurried across the cavern, stopping beside a boulder. She watched Gharkoll fixate his One Eye to the ceiling and the stalactite wobbled, raining debris from the ceiling. Henrietta peered up and dashed out of its long shadow, rushing to the tunnel. The stalactite stormed down from the ceiling and clashed to the floor, blocking the entrance of the tunnel, gusting a plume of white smoke and hurled a flood of revolving rubble down the slope. Henrietta screamed, clattering the lantern to the ground and coughed, covering her nose and mouth with her palm. She nudged the dropped portion of the stalactite and tried to push it forward, though it didn't move. The sound of heavy breathing echoed behind her. Henrietta struck a match and shifting around, she lifted the pale glow onto the wet nostrils and a warm whiff of breath blew from the rack of picket teeth and gusted onto her wrist. She *screamed*, looking at the pair of crimson eyes near the flame and a small growl curled through his serrate, shiny teeth. Henrietta dropped the flame and screamed a notch louder, swinging her loose strands of hair onto her flustered cheeks, as the furred claw stomped on the match and coils of smoke drifted in-between his hairy toes.

Snap.

The match splintered into two pieces and rolled beneath the arched claws into the edge of the wall. Henrietta cried and the creature lurched forward, crunching his picket teeth into her shoe and sunk them into her laces. She screamed until her throat itched, feeling the front of her shoe sinking into the froth and saliva drooling from the corner of his ruddy mouth, drizzling beads of blood. Her cheeks drenched in sweat, as her fingers dragged on the floor, rolling the limestone debris and crushed dust. Gharkoll crunched her toe bones and they dissolved into splinters and mounds of marrow in his wet mouth. Henrietta tilted her wavy, dark ash-blonde locks on her shoulders and screamed with agony. He chafed his claws backwards, brushing his fur on the narrow tunnel and rocky walls. The blood drenched onto her ankle, spattering onto the bottom of her trousers and wrinkled white socks. She screamed a notch louder and her fingers slid backwards onto the lime-glow flaring onto the ground. Her disheveled hair flopped onto the floor, covering her forehead and flustered cheeks, skimming over the bits of rubble. Gharkoll lifted his picket-toothed mouth and her stomach swindled, as she plummeted the declining, rocky floor in the tunnel. She panted, with watery tears swollen in her eyes and reddened welts on her cheeks and smeared, beige-dust gashes.

Henrietta lifted her shoe and screamed-the front portion was missing. Her chest lifted and lowered, staring at the thick, layered blood on the hole and whimpered, realizing she would *never* have toes again.

Gharkoll spat out the scrounged leather and it rolled in front of her.

Henrietta cried, and she rolled on the floor, crawling into the dank dirt, smudging the mud onto her trousers and shirt. The creature prowled behind her in the shadows and screeched, curling his fingers. He lurked a ferocious, predatory gait with each stride, leaving behind a trail of holes from his sinking brawny, black claws. His forked, viridescent tongue slithered between his bottom picket-teeth. She dragged herself in the mud, with her elbows and glancing over her shoulder, with a wispy strand of hair dangling over her nose, she rolled her thigh on the mud and sunk deeper into the silhouettes. Gharkoll 's One Eye opened amongst the crowd of eyes on his forehead and expanded a beam of piercing radiation over her. Henrietta squealed and she teetered and her fingers quivered. A light-green patch swelled on her neck, chest and shoulder. Henrietta swung backward, sliding her shoulders on the sharp protrusions in the floor and scraped welts on her skin. She screamed, as coils of mist puffed from her watery-blue eyes and stretched crimson veins. They stung, reddening around the rims and she toppled onto the slope of flowstone, rolling to the floor. Gharkoll loomed closer through the toothed, slender batch of stalagmites, dodging each of them and brushed his furred shoulder onto their astute peaks. He reached her and squatting, he slouched his back and bit into her torso, tearing a piece of bloodied flesh and blood drenched the miniature craters opposite his three-toed foot.

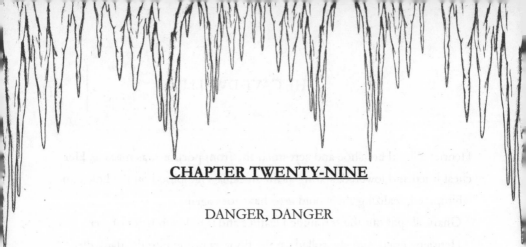

CHAPTER TWENTY-NINE

DANGER, DANGER

I felt danger lurked in the silent cavern and my heart leapt frantic beats in my chest, with each passive footstep around the serrate speleothems and through, a few lancet openings. I skimmed the last remnant of my flickering candlelight beneath the clustered stalactites. The blood drenched the floor, shrouding the round stalagmite bases and the yellow mists lurked on my ankles and looped shoelaces, sagging on my leather shoes. I strode further in the curved dents and faltered in the middle of the chamber, flashing my lamp light onto the torn stalagmite and the threads of light green goo, elongated on the exterior moist, viridescent skins. The warm, yellow puffs hurled from the torn crevice and blew onto the bottom of my rolled trousers. The brittle-dark green vines adorned on the limestone walls, bloomed a flower specimen I had never seen before and I assumed it was a Lilly, though its petals were patterned with loose, black lines. The shortened, withered tallow candle, dripping melted rivulets speckled on the hollows beside my brown-leather shoe, with each cautious footstep. I was worried about Nora and Clarence. I had the compass, and they would be lost in the cave without me and endangered the longer, I was separated from them. I felt protective. They still would be venturing in the South-West caverns and inter-joined limestone stalactite antechambers. After observing how my brother sometimes peered at her with a hidden attraction, which he wasn't willing to admit to me, and them being alone together now, also worried me. It was eventually, it would be either him or me to confess how we felt first and only if we could find the right direction again, drifting with the island's winds, seeping

in the hollow chinks somewhere, vagrant with the foliage. However, seemingly, not able to push away the sense of danger reeking in these hypogean and
pitch-black chambers, with scorpions scuttling on the floors, past the curtains
of stringy gossamer on the walls and lower floors, it would be me with something mauled soon, not them. I tried to calm myself by considering, everything
I thought to be sensing was only a falsity from the fear racing with every swift
movement, though, I knew I was wrong. I lifted my quivering golden flame on
the nearing batch of stalactites and blood was splattered on their peaks.

"*Disgusting*," I whispered, swallowing and despite the lingering warmth,
gooseflesh flourished on my shoulders from the rupture of fright.

I clenched the ringlet of the lamp and my knuckles whitened. Gharkoll had
torn through the stalagmite and wasn't dead. Where was he? I heard a scream
drifting from the end of the passage and clamping my lips, I slowly turned to
the sharp opening, leading into the distant winding passage.

Crick Crack

All of my living fears; the cacophony of my shaky hitched breaths, my
beating heart and racing blood intensified in the silence and even slowly
attempting to turn, seemed to strengthen my vulnerability in the silhouetted
cavern. The soft ticking of my compass's needle swindled and gnashing my
teeth, I clutched it, trying to hush the noise.

Crick Crack

My swallow echoed, as if it was a cascade of water plashing into a pool
of floating white froth. *It was the scrawling of the claws, dissolving in the curved and
augmenting denticulations.* I tread backward, sweeping the last of my candle-light
on the floor and spotted a bloodied finger amongst the rubble and recoiled
into the towering column, with solidified limestone and acid water. I expelled
a loud breath and sliding my calloused, sweaty fingers onto the beige contours, I heard the growl echoing from the far-end of the cavern. I felt my
body numbing with terror. I didn't have a choice, though to continue onward
and the other passage was still blocked with dilapidated rubble and filled to

the lime-speleothems. The last remnants of hemo-toxin poison were still lightly influencing my vision from a pounding headache. I double-blinked, hitching a breath and tread closer into the broad passage. I pried from behind the stalagmites and it made my hairs on my arms *prickle*. There were glow-worms nestled in the dark walls and leaping my hand over them, I trudged on the dank mud, dizzily swaying with each footstep. Gharkoll stalked my footsteps and his crowd of glistening red eyes, deflected away from me to the wall, distracted. I was astonished he had a sudden fascination with the spread glow-worms. He stopped beneath the luminescent, turquoise and slender soda straws, reflecting their glow onto his pair of dark-brown conical fur and beige horns. I rushed to the nearest mound of boulders, with sweat soaking on my heated skin and cheeks. My fingers lathered with dried, crusty wax driblets sunk into the floor. I watched through the airy gap, Gharkoll bending his tentacles to the wall, suckling the turquoise glow and engulfing the worms. I panted, disgusted and watched the shriveled glow worms slide upward in his tentacles and they brightened, from dimmed-green to a lime radiance. I screamed, dreading the closeness of the lime glow skimming on the silhouetted walls and the trembling floor, behind my shoes. I panted and stumbled backward into another cavern with a moist waft of wet rock and hid behind the sloped flowstone, the rocks and stalagmites, leaving a trail of blood driblets. I peeked from the edge, as Gharkoll strode with hunched shoulders, snarling and drizzling saliva onto the ground. My ankle ached, and massaging it with my thumb, I anxiously glanced back to him. He seemed to be distract-ed, tracing a particular scent along the wall. Gharkoll wriggled his beige nose and he sniffed the wet carbonite acid drizzling on the limestone wall and his eyes glimmered with a hungry intensity. Gharkoll surged his tentacles into the carbonite acid streams, leaking on the walls and suckled them, soaring as globules into his ears. The two pouches swelled beneath his dark brown, jagged hair, at the back of his neck and elongated slender, green veins. A slurping noise echoed in the cavern. I watched, panting. All the water shriveled and the rocky wall was left arid and the carbonate acid churned inside of his swollen pouches, beneath his serrate, dark-brown fur overlapping his slender, beige neck. I recoiled, glancing at the crimson blood patch on the speleothem. Gharkoll dropped his gaze to the trail on the floor, dilating his wrinkled beige nostrils and inhaled the salty aroma, pursuing me.

"*No*," I gasped, shaking my head and forcing myself to move, I crawled around the speleothems behind the rock.

I stood, attempting to escape with sibilate footsteps and looked over my shoulder. Gharkoll was gone and turning in front of me, he dropped from the ceiling, with an opened jaw and his jagged teeth and prominent fangs neared my nose. The driblets of dark-green acid slivered down his tentacles and tapped onto the clefts, disintegrating the rubble into spread ash. A swarm of yellowy-green poison augmented in his slimy, tongue and splurged into my eyes.

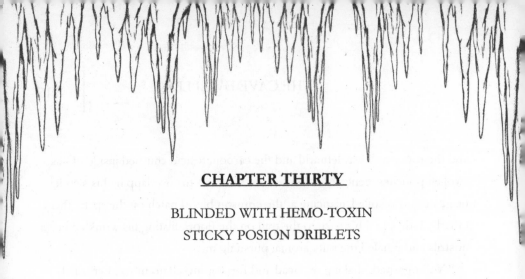

CHAPTER THIRTY

BLINDED WITH HEMO-TOXIN
STICKY POSION DRIBLETS

The cavern was impenetrable, my vision was gone and I knew I could die in
less than one minute. I could hear him coming closer, and the flames scorching from the distant golden-yellow pools. A vague, blurred glimpse of the last
distant stalagmite appeared at the far end of the passage. It was from memory,
he stood opposite me. I rolled my arm onto the debris, crackling a few bits
into my shoulder. Gharkoll 's claw clashed down beside my other arm, scraping the debris and they hurled into the wall. It was with this sudden movement
wending into my ear, I knew he would come striding from the left, through a
gap between the two stalagmites. My fingers swayed everywhere, touching the
stalagmite peaks and the sharp points on the wall and crystallized specks in
the slender, icicles. I noticed heavy puffs of yellow smoke flourished from the
floor and blowing onto my legs. I kicked rubble from the front of my shoes
and abruptly knocked into the round bases of the stalagmites. I felt some of
the sordid, light green bacteria stretched on the floor and it slid beneath my
fingers. I panted heavily, and crawled on the rock bits, rolling them from my
knees into the curved hollows in the floor. My subtle moans reverberated in
the cavern's warmth, with fresh blood drizzling from my wounds to my arms
and elbows. The burning pain in them intensified and swinging into the nearest
stalagmite, I felt too human to sustain the last remnant of my strength hauling
in my veins. I hailed and stopped amongst the last remnants of my strength to
ensure my survival and sinking into the pain, I knew I was risking failure of my

entire determination to escape the pitch-black cave. If I stopped to dwell here incessantly in the darkness of the cavern, every hour and minute seeking the right entrance out towards the South, would've been a waste of time. I didn't have a candle or any form of light and had to find it inside of myself instead. It was continuing in the last notch of my pain, I would've expired my strength completely and I would've collapsed forever. I was needing this last one breath to sustain my strength and for at least another hour, it was important. My ankle was still swollen and seemingly, the inner tendons were twisted from his heavy, sliding picket teeth. The miniature round holes were still crustily bloodied and traced with yellow venom threads. I waited for the intensity of the poison in my eyes to soften and the tinging in my ankle to thin. I inhaled a whiff of the sour water on the obsidian wall, gathering the last remnants of my adrenalin to make the next step and I slid my fingers upward onto the sharp peak of the stalagmite and stood. It was amongst this pain with every stride, I concentrated on shift-ing my fingers around in the dark, swaying them everywhere and occasionally moaned from the stinging poison in my eyes. It felt impossible with each step to defeat Gharkoll - he had taken me to the worst of my being in the caverns. Whether or not, the combustion of chloride and carbonic acid could weaken him, I wouldn't be weakened by him. I was still curious, even if every crunch of debris was closer to my death. If I continued to believe I would die in this moment, I would- whatever I believed in this pitch-black cavern, now at my weakest point, would happen; I was vulnerable. If I thought the opposite of *how* to survive him, despite being close to plummeting, maybe, I might survive to prevent dying forever-I needed *water* to try and wash the poison away clinging to my eyes. *Think, Douglas*, I thought. *Where is there water? You're in the underground, you fell beneath the lower story in the eastern cavern and you found a pool in the North-East. You came through the underground tunnel into a few caverns, and you must be still in the East.* I had to tread through a right tunnel and when Gharkoll had hurled poison to my eyes, he had done it, as I stood opposite the left archway, leading to the South-East and closer to escape the cavern entirely. My heart sunk, knowing I'd be temporarily detoured amongst this adversity and gnashing my teeth, I became more determined, striding through the darkness and swishing my fingers through a cloud of green smoke, they brushed on the slender, limestone totem pole and my shoe brushed on the round boulder. I held it, trembling and hearing Gharkoll near closer behind me, dilapidating the rubble beneath his heavy feet. I stretched my fingers and they brushed down the thick fur strands, sliding to the middle of his torso. I panted and quivering, I felt the lower points of his spikey beard to his parched lip and sleek, sharp teeth. I dropped my fingers, feeling the mucus and poison on them. I screamed, stepping backward into the jagged wall. My fingertips prickled and my skin reddened. I slid my hands on the wall and swaying them out, I tried to see in the dark and my eyes burned as scorching fire. I screamed, forcing them open to see a remnant of the large totem pole, pioneering over me. Tears moistened in my stinging eyes and down my cheeks. I needed water and quickly, otherwise, perhaps, I would never see again. Or maybe, I would never find the water in less than half- an hour to falter the consequences from his poison, as each driblet dwelled and dissolved inside of my pupils. Gharkoll wasn't worried, he hurled another mound of poison from his moist, lime tentacles and they splattered onto my shoulder, back and waist leaking driblets.

CHAPTER THIRTY-ONE

SUCKLED IN
THE SULPHUR POOLS CAVERN

I staggered through a wide arch beneath the lime stalactites, holding my injured arm with a reddened welt and scratch. The blood oozed on my sleeve, as it flapped loosely on my arm. I trampled around the curved periphery of the yellow, acidic pool and it was luminescent amongst the shadowed, obsidian walls. An earthquake shook in the ground and the stalactites trembled above me, hurling a mound of dilapidated debris and showered them onto my shoulders. I observed the temperature in the air lifted a notch warmer and after the tremor stopped, the crumbled stone bits lurched into the curved dents in the floor. I swallowed, realizing the earthquakes weren't from the island, though, the volcano- it was going to *erupt*. My skin flecked with goosebumps. I listened to Gharkoll veering down the passage.

How much longer did we have to survive in the cave before it did explode?

The heat had intensified, meaning the gases would too soon and breathing would be harder in the caverns. I could barely inhale a few whiffs of air, as it was with the lurking yellow and green mists in the caverns. I panicked with each footstep around the stalagmites and I watched, astonished as the front pair drastically shifted from ochre to dark beige to lime, with ash-speckled curves in the rock and porous globules. It was in less than a few days, more carbon dioxide would linger in the caverns. I suspected if I was still underground in this dimension, finding a way out before the volcano did explode lava, would mean, I die. The two people I loved most, would never see sunlight again. I felt stress pain my chest- there wasn't one minute of relaxation, ever since I had stepped in here. My body was weak and every footfall was with agony. I could collapse on the boulders any minute. The reddened welts on my skin burned, the scratches on my fingers stung, and my eyes still prickled from the remnants of poison. I dashed around the corner, hiding beside the precipice's flowstone. When I turned, Gharkoll dropped in front of me, sinking his claws into the floor. I reached for a rock and hurled it into his stomach, dilapidating it into crumbled beige ash. He screeched. I bellowed with the pain in my arm and I ran around the base of the denticulate cliff. I ran into a taut passage with moss dangling onto my hair and it slivered over my ears. I arrived to the opposite end into an enormous cavern. A rotten egg aroma lurked through the slanted crevice in the black, rocky wall. I groaned and found it hard to breathe. I ran into a cavern with a mineral spring. I followed the scent to The Sulphur Pools, festering smoke from the surface and the hydrogen sulfide tendrils breezed into my nose and my breaths stifled. I became under awe. I heard a *crack* above me. I looked up and one fragment of rock fell from the ceiling. I bowed just as it clashed to the floor, smashing into several pieces behind my shoes. I dodged a few more towering, stalagmites and a round, thick totem pole. I dashed into the arch and down a tunnel, bowing my head beneath the low, rocky ceiling. Gharkoll bellowed with a rush of heated infuriation, annoyed I was ahead of him and the growling notch, deepened in his throat.

I rushed out the opposite end and ran over a small, arched bridge of limestone grown over the Sulphur Stream. The other-side was a batch of round-peaked stalagmites and the terrain was a combination of viridescent rock and limestone. The stalactites and shawls were the opposite. I bowed beneath them, feeling their points scrawling onto my tresses and they smeared onto my cheeks. Gharkoll screeched. I halted amongst them. He was standing at the front of the arched limestone bridge. He fixated his crimson eyes onto me and he pervaded he was *inescapable*, as soon as he crossed over to the other side. I broadened my eyes and turning, I hurried away and side-stepped each of the stalagmites. *How could I have been naïve in the beginning to believe he was innocent? He was just a kind, friendly animal curious of me too?* I thought.

I frowned and annoyed with myself, I trampled on the rubble and down the slope of dolomite rock. I heard the hastened pace of Gharkoll and the momentum in his strides hastened, as he leapt onto the middle, paired and sharp stalagmites. I teetered down the slope with dust and crushed rock, rolling from the front of my shoes. I stretched my arms and wobbled. I panted and reaching the end, I lost balance and swung my arm downward, near the Sulphur Stream. The heat and horrid egg waft breezed over my flustered cheeks and nose. I coughed and observed a rock, the size of my palm. I lifted it from the ground and hurled it with such anger at Gharkoll's torso. I felt wrinkles forming in my forehead from the distress and fury, he had ruptured.

"There!" I exclaimed, with my locks tumbling over my thick, brown brows. *"Take that!"*

I knew it would infuriate him more and it did. Gharkoll's tentacles illumined a brighter shade of lime, as if they were going to shift into yellow. I somehow, felt exhausted with his burdensome tenaciousness. I didn't care- *he had asked for a reaction from me.* Gharkoll rushed down the slope and I dashed around the curving brink along the rust of the rock to the west. All of my tendons were pained and my legs ached from each pace and footfall. My throat itched from thirst and short of breath. I suddenly reached the opposite side and I realized Gharkoll had stopped and his footsteps weren't behind me. I stared at the curved brink of the Sulphur Stream and the opposite dark opening in the wall. *If only I could make it there, I could escape.* I thought. Gharkoll appeared behind me and poked his short horns, brown furred cones. He wriggled globules of poison down his lime tentacles protruding from his ears and they surged out, splattering onto my back. He lifted his thick, black claws and from a curling growl, it arose into a screech.

"AH!" I hailed, swinging backward and leant onto my heels.

The poison saturated my shirt, burning the linen and swindled coils of mist along the nape of my neck and my back. I stepped forward and hurried along the brink of the Sulphur Stream without hesitation, risking the possibility the Sulphur water would have a worst reaction with the poison, if I splashed a handful onto my back. I smeared my fingers into the lathered green globules and they oozed down my spine. I rummaged and plashed the handful of water onto my back. I screamed, as another whiff of smoke drifted from the reddened welt and it darkened to crimson. I knew I would have a scar there now forever. I yelled, weakly trampling along the brink of the Sulphur Stream and panted and moaned with each footstep. I heard his pace ascending louder behind me. I reached the front of the pool and I leapt onto the boulder amongst the festering mist, sliding my shoe into the water and driblets spluttered onto my calve. I inhaled a whiff of air and feeling dizzy, I jumped to the other side of the stream. The archway ahead of me swayed in my vision.

Gharkoll jumped onto the boulder and the opposite side, trampling after me. His tentacle grappled my arm.I bellowed, fighting against his grasp and my fingers lathered on the poison oozing from the miniature holes. I yelled, feeling them sting and rubbed them onto the front of my trousers, smearing long dashes. Gharkoll 's three tentacles stretched from his ears and wrapped around my arms. I felt they were cold and damp on my skin. I echoed a loud scream and listened to my own agony echo in the vastness of the hollow cavern and it diminished lost in the shadows. I squeezed my eyes closed and lifted my lip above my gritted teeth. *I was tired of evil and everything he had endured upon me in the cave. It was I whom wanted to squeeze his tentacles and squirt his own poison back to him to taste what he lurched out from his own self. What was I to him? His victim to be condemned in his dark cave; he yearned for me to hurt. He liked the idea of me to be hurt. There was some part of me that was tired of suffering from his monstrous self and the hidden fury inside of me grew like the green bacteria on the rocks. I was going to become a monster too, because he was an odd specimen first. I didn't want his tentacles.* Gharkoll hauled me backward in the air across the festering mist and he whipped me around to face him. I bellowed at my highest notch, until I lost my voice and gazed at the crowd of moist, red, gleaming eyes on his crinkled forehead. Gharkoll 's actual pair of eyes beneath his furry, brown eyebrows, glistened with satisfaction he had finally caught me. He dragged me upward. I screamed, dangling in the mists and he screeched with victory.

I kicked in the air.

"Help! Help! *Help!*" I yelled, gazing over my shoulder at the upper precipice. "Anybody!"

Gharkoll lurched me against the wall, descending rubble from my shoulders and they rolled in a swarm beneath my uplifted shoes, hanging in mid-air.

"No! No! No!" I screamed.

Gharkoll 's middle tentacle of the three in his right ear, loosened its clasp and hindering in front of my right arm, it sunk into my skin and suckled my fluid. I bellowed and squirmed on the wall in his lime luminance reflecting onto my cheeks and chin. Gharkoll 's hemotoxin venom drizzled from his picket teeth and flecked onto my arms. I screamed and watched my skin shifting from a sallow complexion to light viridescent. My sockets yellowed and my lips parched. I shifted my gaze to the fleet of flowstone and they blurred, descending onto the opposite limestone and totem poles. It seemed remnants of the venom had also been dissolved in my blood and immediately, swelling occurred. A dark-purplish bruise surrounded the wound, where the tentacle had suckled. I quivered against the stalagmite with sweat drenching my forehead and cheeks. I watched Gharkoll screech and crawled through the tunnel, as I thought he was going to kill me.

I heard Nora's voice echo in the dark, "*Stay away from him!*"

CHAPTER THIRTY-TWO

RESCUED

The coarse beige rope ladder unrolled from the jagged precipice, bouncing on the wall and dangled in the lurking tawny smoke and it whacked on the ground. Nora appeared out of the dark hindering on the upper, towering boulders and she clutched them. Her black hair disheveled around her flustered cheeks from her hastened pace in the tunnels.

"*Hurry, Douglas!* Quick!" yelled Nora.

I barely breathed, as I trundled across the cavern, covering my fingers on my bloodied arm and felt the driblets sinking into them. My palm was still calloused and it ached from the burning grazes and scratches on them. I tripped midway, slipping my boot into a dip in the ground. I yelled and swung forward onto the ground. Gharkoll reached closer and swiping his claw across my calve, he scrawled bloodied scratches in my skin and blood swelled on my trousers. I tilted my head, screaming, and he scratched my back. The linen tore with warm wind blowing across my skin. I trampled to the other side, holding the rope ladder. Nora gritted her teeth and slowly hauled the rope backward, with a few hair strands smearing to her forehead. Gharkoll hastened his pace and bit the corner of my trousers, drizzling light-green mucus onto his lips on the small, peeling flakes. I screamed, clenching the rope, as tightly as possible and felt a driblet of sweat drizzling on the side of my forehead and cheek. I searched the wall, and I clutched the protruding, round limestone rock and heaved myself upward. Gharkoll 's picket teeth sunk into my trousers, and he hauled my leg back downward.

"Ah!" I bellowed, feeling my chest and the front of my stomach, sliding down along the jagged dents in the ground. Nora squealed, being dragged forwards on the floor of the cliff and her leather, taupe shoes clamped with mud poked from the precipice of the cliff. I peered over my shoulder and gritted my teeth. I lifted my leg and a portion of my trousers tore from my ankle. Gharkoll thundered to the ground. I looked back up to Nora and she hauled the rope backward again, dragging me up to the cliff. .

"Hold on!" she yelled, offering her hand.

I felt short of breath with dry lips and aching from thirst, I held her clammy hand and was dragged upward to the ground. I lowered my shoulder onto her lap. I heavily panted, as I gazed into her eyes. Gharkoll was outraged. He hailed and stepped backward, scrutinizing my shoes poking along the brink of the cliff.

Nora dragged them away.

"Thank you." I puffed.

"It's alright," said Nora, stroking my tresses with her fingertips and around my ears. She leant forward and pecked my cheek.

Clarence strode through the round archway and abruptly stopped, judging if Nora had just kissed me on the lips or not. He was astonished at my pallid complexion and tilting his head, he strode towards me.

"*Are you alright?*" exclaimed Clarence, expelling a breath from his lips.

"No, he's not," answered Nora.

Clarence averted his glare to her. "What happened to his eyes?" he asked.

"Gharkoll absorbed the acid from the rock," I blurted. "It turned into disturbing poison and blinded me."

"Then you need Alkaline water," said Nora. "It will neutralize the acid in your body."

"How?" I blurted, weakly, lying on the floor. "We don't even have a bandage for wounds."

"We can make it," said Nora.

Clarence glared at her. "Make alkaline water?" he asked.

"Yes," she said, opening her pouch and rummaged through the equipment. "I can use the small vial of baking powder from the ship's scullery," She pulled out one lemon, one teaspoon, a bowl and a piece of dried coral she had found in the island. Nora poured a teaspoon of baking powder and tapped it on the rim of the bowl, using a wooden spatula and crushed the coral against the rock. The crushed mound showered into the bowl.

Nora lifted out a clump of sea-salt and she crushed a handful and lowered them into the other ingredients.

"How do you know?" asked Clarence.

Nora looked up and arched a brow.

"Boredom of long sailing hours on the ship and speaking to the cook," she said, with an exhale. "which unfortunately, he's now dead." She pulled out a small knife and sliced a piece of yellow lemon, lowering it into the bowl. We're going to need Spring Water, it has high alkaline levels, because it falls into the rocks minerals." She looked over her shoulder through the silhouetted arch. "It's a few miles from here, you're going to have to help support Douglas on one side of your shoulders."

Clarence knelt to the floor and helped me stand from the floor. He wrapped his arm across my shoulders and I groaned, from the pain.

"Your back..." he whispered, broad-eyed and gasped. "Douglas."

I couldn't imagine how my back appeared, after clamping the sticky, reddened and bloodied welts to the ground. I could feel debris clinging to the last remnants of green poison.

"Quick Clarence," urged Nora, lifting the pouch from the ground and swung it over her shoulder, carrying the bowl.

She bowed beneath my other arm and I slouched between both of them, as they guided me through the round arch. My eyes were still stinging, and the walls softly blurred with each weak and doddering footstep down the tight tunnel. It was after treading through several more chambers, the air became moist. We stepped through a broad, wide arc and stopped at the edge of the turquoise spring. The smell of the water was a relief. Nora hurriedly dropped her pouch to the floor, pulling the spoon out and dipped it into the surface. Clarence untightened the thick rope belonging to the shrouds from the ship and pulled out his own bowl, splashing it abruptly into the water, while I lay on the sharp ground, glaring at the ceiling. My breathing was slow and a tinge inside of my back, made me wince and I softly tilt my cheek onto the jagged edges on the ground and moaned. Clarence dripped a trail of water on the front of his shoes and clamped the bowl to my lips. The water splashed alongside my mouth and jaw. The long, pained thirst in my throat vanished. Nora neared us. I swallowed the last remnant of water and the last of the trickles still stained on my jaw and drenched my linen collar. Nora lowered her knees to the floor. She stroked my hair again. Somehow, even amongst this havoc and distress, I felt she liked touching my thick, brown hair and regardless of my injury was trying to calm me.

"When you're ready," she whispered, dabbing the linen cloth on the side of my jaw and lifted the bowl closer to my lower lip. "Drink."

"I'm ready," I mumbled, weakly and clamped the bowl to my lip and the cold water drizzled down my throat with the sour lemon.

The alkaline water, really wasn't that appetizing and I yearned to splutter it out of my mouth, preferring just natural spring water. However, I forced myself even amongst the silent growth of nausea in my throat to keep drinking to the last remnant and after I did, I struggled to breathe and was queasy. My cheeks burned with heat and I rocked my cheek to the ground.

"Douglas, you rest and sleep," she whispered, putting the bowl back into her pouch and pulled out the crumpled, torn piece from the foresail and covered my arms and legs. She tenderly fondled her warm fingers onto my cheek and traced my jawbone, with her thumb. "I'm worried about you, though, I hope you'll be alright." She looked at my back. "Oh, and your back needs some as well." Nora mixed another round of alkaline water and dipping the linen cloth into it, she softly dabbed the poison and blood away. Clarence's jealousy, overshadowed, as the silhouettes mirroring from the cragged ceiling and the spring, sensing her affection through her caring assistance.

"I'll do it," he stated, and the sudden tension raise in his voice, accentuated his manipulation. "He's my brother, after all,"

Clarence lingered his fingers in front of the cloth and he stopped Nora from dabbing anymore of the dried poison away.

Nora was bewildered with his urgency to do it and pausing, he snatched the cloth and dipped it into the water, shielding his back to her and over his shoulder, he said, "It's alright, you can rest now. You've done enough for him, it's my turn now."

I gnashed my teeth, frowning and bit my lower lip, annoyed. When would I have a quiet, affectionate and intimate moment with Nora? Why did he always have the yearn to want to compete with me? Maybe, Nora and I did really like each other, maybe, I had been wrong, all along, from my own insecurities of not feeling good enough for her. I didn't know if Clarence was just competing for the sake of it, because it was satisfactory to his ego, or, if he actually did like her. Either way, it still annoyed me, and he was acting kind and innocent, though, his hidden jealousy was reeking through his demeanour. All night, we lay beside the spring. I brusquely would revolve onto my arm and groan, as the alkaline water reduced the acidic properties of Gharkoll 's poison in my blood. On the first of August, I was still unwell and couldn't move- every inch of my muscle and body ached, and there wasn't a choice, though to lie there on the ground. Clarence and Nora sat together on the boulder, beneath a jutting cliff and with agony, I watched them sitting closely. It was with the charming smile and laugh my brother had, I knew he was attempting to be enticing and he hurled a soft, pebble into the water.

I watched him turn over his shoulder and echo, "Don't worry, he's going to survive. Just keep feeding him more of the alkaline water."

"I know," whispered Nora.

I gnashed my teeth, loathing his purposeful boasting. On the tenth of August, early in the morning, my brother left us alone, in search of more fire-wood to prevent the cold air, from causing an infection on my body and keep us warm in the flames comfort.

Nora didn't leave my side and leant her elbow on the rock.

"How are you feeling?" she asked.

I knew my hair was oily, my complexion was pallid and my lips were softly dry- it was at my worst appearance, though, she was still willing to be there.

"I'm better, the alkaline water has helped," I muttered, flicking my gaze at her. "Thank you."

"You're welcome," said Nora, stroking the tresses around my ear and loose-ly beamed. "Do you want some more?"

"I'm alright for the moment," I whispered. "Sorry about my brother, I know he's acting strange."

"Strange?" she asked.

Maybe, I shouldn't have said this observation, I thought.

"Never mind," I whispered, looking up at her.

Nora smiled, and I reached my fingers across the dust and rocky ground, stroking her hand, tenderly.

"You're holding my hand?" she asked.

"Why wouldn't I?" I muttered.

I heard my brother's footsteps wending through the archway in the oppo-site wall and rubbing my thumb across her knuckles, I pulled my clasp away to ensure he didn't see it. It was only for one reason-if he thought he didn't have competition; he wouldn't bother behaving in this manner. I felt patience wasn't an enemy to me. It was sooner or later, after I was feeling well, hope-fully, I could find the time to tell her how I felt, without Clarence or Gharkoll around. I suppose even if I felt they were the same as each other.

CHAPTER THIRTY-THREE

QUICKSANND

The following day and a few hours past midday on the twenty-seventh of July, every step was stridden with *fear* and *shaky breaths*. The cave felt as one endless labyrinth of intersected, winding tunnels and openings, never being able to be escaped. My thirst was irrevocable and my throat itched, despite swallowing a remnant of water from the flask and my lips parched in the dust falling from the ceiling and itched my cheeks. I thought of the ship, bobbing amidst the ocean and the bulwark teetering with each plashing wave to steer its direction to the north-east in the breeze. The slow steering wheel with burnt oak holders, creaking amongst the swinging, thick ropes and netted shrouds became a poignant memory with each pace. My freedom seemed to be gone forever. The doubt from my grumpy mood was clouding my thoughts- I hallucinated the debris was dotted seaweed and the white froth elongated on the denticulations in the rocky ground, scraped on the bottom of my leather shoe. I felt a piercing pain swindle in my head and exhaling a breath, I double-blinked and swayed, clutching the cragged limestone piece. The cacophony of Nora's and Clarence's footsteps striding on the floor, crunching the debris into bits and layers of dust and nudging the arid glow-worm shell fragments, intensified into my ears. The flashes of the fertile palm trees, the wild verdure, the rustling ferns and their oscillating green leaves in the island's tropical rainforest, taunted my entrapment. I felt each step was a struggle; the floor slanted, and the cries of the sailors leaping over the bulwark plashed ashore, and the rupture of tawny-yellow flames burning the masts, flickered in my perception. I double-blinked and the floor became more precise, the visions faded and after a heartbeat and the beige debris blurred. Clarence's dark-golden luminance flashed along the huddled debris piled against the walls and he stopped and turned, hearing Nora's rapid skid of her shoes on the floor.

Her hand tenderly embraced my shoulder and her silent yearn for fondness reeked in her demeanour, as she neared closer.

"Douglas, what's wrong?" she whispered.

"The poison," I murmured back. "It's still in my blood."

Nora loosened her clutch of the hessian pouch and the clattering of the gathered vials echoed in the silence. She opened the top, sinking her hand inside, pulling out her coconut and offered it to me. "There's one quarter of water left to drink if you need it."

"It's alright," I murmured, reluctant to concede to her and lowered my fingers onto the brown coir, flicking a few to her shoes and knew she would need the coconut water later. "Save it for yourself."

"No," refuted Nora, pulling the green stalk piece of cane from the hole and strode a few steps around the front of me. "Here, please, drink, you're going to collapse."

"Nora," I whispered, and the subtle waft of the moist water drifted out of the hole into my nose, as she lifted it closer to my lips.

My cheeks burned with a combination from a growing fever, my attraction and the heat looming in the passage.

Nora scowled. "Stop being stubborn and strenuous." she snapped, holding my cheek and tilted my head against the wall. The mild warm water with the sour taste of kept coconut water trickled down my throat.

Clarence eyed her fingers spread on my cheek and after a few swallows, she pulled the coconut away from my moistened lips. I perceived the sharp twinkle in his dark, emerald eyes- the bronze flecks were gone and his jealousy was there, the kind that prickled like Gharkoll 's venom from his picket teeth. Nora stroked a few of my hairs over my right ear and they nudged into the rocky ground.

"That's enough, he doesn't need anymore," said Clarence, coldly. "We still have hours more to be treading in the cave and he'll need some in one hour's time." He held his gaze one moment longer onto my ear, where her fingers had traced affectionately, and he softly exhaled through his nose and pressed his lips together. He shifted his back to us.

"He's right," I said, trying to remain appeasing amongst his mood.

Clarence sat down on a rock and sunk his shoulders against the wall. He stretched his legs. "It's nice to sit down. I think we should sleep and camp out here tonight." he said.

I walked towards the round archway. "I want to check Gharkoll isn't around here first, just to be sure," I said.

"I'll come with you," offered Nora.

We both walked down the passage. When we reached the end, I stepped forward expecting to tread on the hard ground, though my foot sunk into the floor, engulfing my ankle. Nora squealed as she drastically sunk beside me. She dropped the oil-lamp and quickly lifted the ringlet, hurling it to the side. The small, bronze door loosely opened, and the shrunken candle rolled onto the ground, leaking wax. I flickered my firelight forward, revealing the round pile of quicksand.

"Quicksand!" she shrieked.

"Clarence!" she squealed. "Help us!"

"Clarence!" I called out, looking down the passage. "Hello!"

"Oh see, this is your fault again!" she exclaimed.

"Stop blaming me!" I said, holding her stretched arms. "I didn't see it coming, okay? You decided to follow me, that was your choice."

Nora frowned. *"You always bring us into trouble,"* she said.

"Really?" I retorted. "You're still arguing that claim?"

"Yes," she said, and her voice lowered to a serious tone. *"Really."*

"Well, I can assure you, we will find a way out of here, especially, after finding we are heading in the Southern direction and we'll be out soon." I said, trying to sound as convincing as possible. "I don't want to die in here anyway."

"This is what you *always* say," said Nora. "How long has it been we've been stuck in here?"

I groaned rolling my eyes and retorted, "Do you always have to argue with me?"

"Yes," she said.

"Why?"

"You make bad decisions," snapped Nora.

"*I do not*," I disputed.

"You do," said Nora. "Why won't you admit your faults?"

I felt the quicksand rising further on my waist and exhaling, I panicked and looked at the nearest archway, wondering *why* my brother hadn't heard us.

"We're just going to be dissolved in quicksand, now," pressed Nora. "Maybe, a ship would've found us on the island by now, *instead*."

I put a finger to her cherry lips, and she silenced. I smirked, somehow finding her even more attractive, when she was argumentative and fiery with her own opinion amidst being insulted, despite *I* felt it wasn't true.

"What is funny?" asked Nora.

"Just you," I said, broadening my cheeky smirk and I flicked a few her black hair strands on her shoulder.

"*Don't* do that," said Nora, annoyed.

I ignored her and flicked another strand of her hair again, swinging it onto her back.

I laughed.

"*Stop!*" she insisted.

I tried to grab her fingers, though, she waved them around airily and I missed a few times, until I caught her right hand. We sunk a notch further down in the quicksand and it levelled to our stomachs. Her annoyed scowl dissolved into a grin. Our hands and palms clamped closely together and were coated in muggy sweat. I didn't want to release her hand. We slowed their pace rotating in the air and our grins stretched in-between our cheeks, disappeared. We exchanged a glare of silent, softened emotion and became under a daze, forgetting we were sinking in quicksand. Our mouths were partially opened and inches away from each other. My cheeks flustered, the longer I gazed into her brown eyes. I wanted to look away to avoid revealing how I felt about her and the uncomfortable, ardent feeling of emotion pooling inside of me, burning as a flame, though I couldn't. I was entranced, and I emerged nearer towards her lips. We both seemed to ignore our hands weren't held in a playful manner, though, were loosened and touching affectionately. I pulled her closer towards me and suddenly, we snapped out of the daze and heard the rushing footfalls in the passage drift through the round archway. Clarence's shadow skimmed across the denticulate wall and emerging out of the passage, he stopped, noticing our hands were clutched. I moved them away and turned, realizing the quicksand had deepened to my chest and was nearing our necks.

"Clarence!" I exclaimed. "What took you this long?"

I was trying to determine whether he was upset or not. It seemed apparent he had tightened his grip around the rope in his right hand.

Nora turned, and she swayed her arms in the air, eyeing the rope coiled in his hand.

"Help us! Can't you see we're sinking?" she exclaimed.

Clarence exchanged an intense, sharp glare with me. I immediately sensed his prickling resentment and it shone in his emerald eyes. He tread around the brink of the quicksand and he unrolled the rope, throwing it into the quicksand.

"Are you sure you two were *only* just sinking?" asked Clarence, with a sting in his tone as a snake would hiss and rise from the ground.

Nora grabbed it quickly and climbed her hand on the rope, until she reached the rocky edge.

"What do you mean?" I asked, knowing exactly what he meant.

Clarence exchanged a glare of enmity with me, not looking anywhere else.

"I think you know exactly what I mean," he stated, bluntly and with a rush of impatience.

Nora clamped her arms and elbows on the rough surface, lifting herself out of the quicksand. Clarence glared at me for a moment longer, communicating to me in silence, he was going to elaborate when we were left alone. He diverted his attention to Nora and he wrapped an arm around her waist.

"*Here*, let me help you," boasted Clarence.

He lifted her out of the quicksand and I didn't like how he was holding her in his arms and looked at her intently in the eyes. I could've strangled him. I inhaled the air, trying to calm my burbling anger in the bottom of my stomach and reminded myself, I was relieved he had come to rescue both of us. I hauled myself across the rope and tugging it brashly, it yanked his left hand and he was distracted away from her.

Clarence dropped his arm around her waist and glared at her.

"I have to help my brother." he said.

"Thank you, for finally coming and hearing us," said Nora, pecking him on the cheek.

I stopped midway, watching her and I became confused at why she would do this to him and not quickly to me. Did she like Clarence? Is this why she hesitated to kiss me now? I thought. Or, were we both just too shy to make the move? I continued to haul myself up along the rope, wondering all of these confused questions and I was relieved to reach the crusted, rocky edge of the quicksand.

I lifted myself up out from the quicksand.

"Thanks," I said, clapping him on the shoulder, trying to break the tension between us, emerging out of thin air. "I really thought I was going to sink in there."

Clarence pulled the rope out of the quicksand and side-glanced at me.

"You're welcome," he said.

Nora shook the sand from her shirt and hurried through the narrow tunnel.

"Come on, let's eat. I'm starving." she said.

"We're coming," responded Clarence, waiting for her to disappear from sight and further down the tunnel.

The silence lingered between us.

I knew by the thoughtful concentration on his face and focusing his gaze on the floor, he thought something of his own.

"What's wrong?" I probed.

Clarence hesitated to answer straight away, and he flicked his glance from the floor.

"You like Nora, don't you?" he asked.

"She's *a friend*," I lied, glancing at him and hid how I truly felt to see what he was going to say first, before I admitted it.

Why do you care this much? I thought.

"You're lying," said Clarence. "I see the way you look at her all the time and what happened just here in the quicksand. Even when we were always on the ship's deck, you would glimpse at her coming out of the cabin. Also, near the island's campfire."

I elbowed him in the arm, urging him to stop.

"I think it's *you* who likes her and this is why you've asked me. The only reason would be to attain my permission." I teased.

"No, I'm not," denied Clarence, and he uneasily ruffled his brown hair covering his eyes, and he brushed it onto his forehead. "I'm not asking for anything."

"Why do you always interrupt us, when we're together?" I snapped, becoming agitated at his lies.

He frowned and stopped. "I do *not*."

"*You do*," I insisted, frowning more than him and I blurted uncontrollably, "Then, *why* are you asking from the beginning? Why do you care this much?"

"Why can't you just admit the truth?" he retorted.

"I care about her, *yes*," I snapped. "Satisfied?"

I strode further away from him, quickening my pace to avoid him seeing my exposed anger. I stopped further out in the tunnel and inhaled the musty air, releasing my anger and I slowly turned, listening to his footsteps hindering behind me in the distance. I balled my hands into fists, hearing his footsteps approach closer and becoming louder.

I turned and muttered in my lowest tone to avoid Nora overhearing me, "I don't want to concentrate on how I feel about her now, I have to focus on keeping us alive."

"Oh yeah, what if we never find a way out of here?" retorted Clarence, reaching me and stopped. "What if you never tell her? What if she dies or we do, and you'll never have the opportunity to see her again and to be with her?"

I swallowed. *Could he be this negative?* I had never doubted my ability and myself to venture out of the cave *alive*. It was even amongst being poisoned I thought I was being succumbed to die. However, now, such negatives were agitating me. I felt worried, she would unexpectedly die.

"Clarence, we *are* going to find a way out of here, don't think like that. It may take some time, though, if we're cautious enough and move correctly, we're going to be alright, I know it," I said, thumping a hand onto his shoulder and I added, "What if she only sees me as a friend, as well? This is the last thing I want is to feel rejected and be lost in here in this labyrinth!" I moved closer and muttered into his ear, "Which is why, I didn't kiss her a moment ago. I couldn't handle this kind of rejection amongst our situation."

"But she wouldn't," persisted Clarence, striding beside me. He shrugged his shoulder brashly and my hand was swung away.

I started to become annoyed. "She likes you too- I can see it, even though she acts like she doesn't. How she cares when you were poisoned and close to death? It's even how she argues with you and tells you to be-careful, meaning she worries for your safety and doesn't want you to encounter danger and have yourself at risk. She cares about your health and your life. Nora has never done this with me. However, be a *realist* Douglas. This cave is massive." He rolled up his sleeves and he sneered, "It's because of *you*, we're never going to find a way out of here. If you look at what happened to William-," he paused, gritting his teeth and his anger flustered inside of his reddened cheeks. "He's dead, because of *you*."

I felt a lump of guilt in my chest, thinking of his headless body, hanging amongst the stalactites and sorrow. *To think it was all because of my curiosity to wander in the cave...*

"I suppose with Nora?" he retorted, spitefully, "You might as well kiss her, before she *does* die, like him."

"Clarence, just *stop*," I pressed, halting my footsteps. "I would never let her die."

"Oh yeah?" retorted Clarence. "Can you predict the cave or Gharkoll ?" He frowned and stepped closer to me. "No, and what about Leighton ? Is he around here?" His cheeks were smeared with a thin layer of sweat. "Did you even consider yourself, before anybody else?"

"It was Leighton 's choice," I snapped, glancing at the end of the tunnel over my shoulder, worried Nora was overhearing us bicker. "He didn't have to come in here. He could've chosen differently."

"Leighton is too brave to want to stay on the island," declared Clarence. "William is too afraid to even *glimpse* a stalactite in here," He lifted a finger. "However, admit it, you're selfish and we're all going to die." He shoved me in the chest.

"Chee," I said, feeling infuriation inside of me and lowered my crinkled shirt, covered in diluted streams, over my trousers and added, sourly, "Thanks, *Clarence*." I followed after him and we walked into the small cavern with a low, declined and rugged ceiling. "*Thanks* for having the confidence in me."

"Confidence in you?" said Clarence, swinging around. "From the moment, I followed you in here, of course I trusted you!"

"*Just calm down*," I said, while we circled each other and I reminded, "And *you* threw the chlorine on Gharkoll ."

"You went looking for it!" burst Clarence. "It was going to kill you!"

"I told you for the hundredth time," I said. "It was innocent and curious of me, as I was of him. You caused the metamorphosis!"

"I don't care anymore," stormed Clarence, "*About your interest in Gharkoll* . All I want to do is to find a way out of here and go home! Yet, home is very, very far away- even if we do make it to the island."

I gnashed my teeth together, loathing his negative practicality.

"All of this triggered because of Nora and I were stuck in the quicksand together?" I asked.

He returned me a bitter glance, clamping and tightening his lips.

"I know you like her too, Clarence." I said, slowly, "If it makes you feel any better, she was the daughter of the captain. I am a beginner *rigger* and sleep in the storeroom under the ship. It's *never* going to work."

"Her father is *dead*," insisted Clarence, bitterly. "Remember? The societal expectations won't exist."

"What if when we come out of the cave and leave the island, it will still be the same?" I asked.

"There isn't a ship, we're going to be here on this island *not* for a while. Though-," paused Clarence, and his tone lifted a notch. "*forever!* You know it! *Neglected…*" He trailed away and sighed, kicking a pebble with the front of his shoe.

Nora reappeared at the arc in the passage. We both awkwardly stopped and turned at her presence. She held up the bowl of soup.

"What took you a long time? I have a tomato soup. Do you want some to eat?" asked Nora.

She lowered the bowl in the air, glancing back and forth between us. She observed our angered expressions. .

"What's wrong between you two?" asked Nora.

"Nothing is wrong," blurted Clarence, sounding stiff and obvious he lied.

Clarence eyed me and communicated in silence, *Don't say one thing we have discussed.* He walked away from me and glancing at the tomato soup held in her hand, he looked at her.

"It smells good," admitted Clarence.

I perceived he doubted himself to have a chance with her, because of me. Clarence continued down the passage and his footsteps echoed, until they sounded feeble in the distance and as dropping pebbles on the floor.

I sighed, sinking my hands into my pockets and pressed my shoe on a pebble.

"You had an argument, didn't you?" asked Nora, softly.

"We did," I said, bluntly, wondering why I was never a good liar. "I don't want to talk about it, I'm sorry Nora."

"It's alright, I understand," said Nora, putting a hand onto my arm and rubbed it with her thumb.

I loosely smiled and wrapped my arm around her shoulders, and we walked back down the passage in silence. The thought of this not lasting forever, became daunting and I didn't want to alter my poise. We walked through into the chamber and I dropped my arm away, catching the prickling glare from my brother again. I became uncomfortable and I sat down on the rock beside my hessian sack, not excited to eat coconuts again for dinner. I put my elbows on my knees and became under a daze and wondered, *Should I tell her how I feel? Clarence is right- maybe, I'm being too positive about finding a way out of here. Or, maybe he's wrong and I shouldn't say anything to her.*

We all ate in silence, until Clarence dropped his spoon in his tomato soup in the bowl. "Someone has to stay awake and keep watch," he announced.

"I will," I offered, with a firm nod, confirming the decision. *I knew he had meant me.*

"Good," he said

After we finished eating, we lay down on the callused ground, leaning our heads on our hessian sacks and knew the rocks would be twice as uncomfortable. I put my arm over my head and stared at the ceiling, while my brother rolled onto his arm and shifted his back to me, wanting his privacy and to avoid having me in his sight.

"Good night, Douglas," she murmured, sleepily beside my ear.

"Good night, Nora," I said, winking and lifted the corner of my lips.

Nora beamed and squeezed my tanned arm, turning her back and showed she was shy to sleep in front of me. I looked at her spread black hair on the floor. I remembered when I lay amongst the potato sacks, imbued with remnants of salty sea water from the storeroom, and I found it uncomfortable. It was only now I realized, I had taken it for granted and sleeping on the cave's floor was worse.

It was during the night, I stared at Nora, while she slept close to me and gently stroked her hair and leant my cheek on my palm, and I gazed at her ruddy lips. I felt comforted in her presence, yearning to wrap my arm around her waist and hold her close to me and have her cheek resting on my chest. *Urgh, what should I do?* I thought, frustrated and I shifted away from her, leaning on my shoulder and shifted onto my back. *Tell her? Don't tell her? Kiss her unexpectedly? Be more affectionate and show her how I feel, instead of telling her?*

I stared glumly at the short stalactite in the distance, unable to sleep. I was restless and anxious about everything. I listened to the ticking needle of the compass near my ear. *I'm too shy. I can't tell her anything. Sometimes I can't look at her, because if I look, I'm going to be unable to look anywhere else and it will be for too long.* I turned and glanced at my shadowed, round, bronze compass, eyeing the *N* and my heart sank at the thought of the cave's blocked entrance. I flicked my glance down to the *S* and it seemed far away, where I wanted to reach. I felt everything I had suffered to endure and to see it all be thrown and disappear, was my largest fear. I was different to my brother this way. I couldn't risk not knowing, *if* we could reach the South portion of the cave and escape back to the island. I couldn't think negatively and to suggest we all would suffer from the worst circumstances. I didn't want to fail them, as it seemed impossible. I was too determined and stubborn to attain what I want. I felt especially, if it involved Clarence and Nora- the two people I truly cared about. Nothing would be in my way, not even Gharkoll . *Staying alive* wasn't going to be an option, it was going to be *a necessity.* The *S* on my compass blurred in my drowsy eyesight and I fell into a deep slumber, dreaming of walking into the hollow opening with a shaft of shining golden daylight and the smell of the fresh, rained dew on the palm tree trunks, amongst the summer humidity. I wondered what happened to Leighton and if he was still on the island, catching fish and listening to the waves spreading along the shore. Or, if he truly was dead. The next day, we stepped into a neglected, impenetrable dolomite cavern, with scrawny, light brown speleothems and after stepping out, I couldn't find any trace of Nora anywhere, not even a piece of her belongings. I panicked and looked at the message scrawled in the dirt with a stick, '*It's best I find my own way out.*'

"Where did she go?" I said, frustrated and frowned. "*I can't believe it.*" I glanced at my brother. "She left because of you! If you hadn't said anything, maybe, she would've still stayed with us!" I tread closer to him. "You made her feel uncomfortable!"

"She has to be somewhere around here," snapped Clarence, flashing his lantern on the stalagmites, surrounded with mist whirling in his beam. "Don't worry, we're going to find her."

"Why it is I feel, we won't?" I asked. "I'm just becoming worried now."

"She should be here," said Clarence.

"The cave is too large," I said, frowning my eyebrows and tread on the burnt shards separated from our firewood.

CHAPTER THIRTY-FOUR

THE SPELEOLOGIST SKELETON

I wandered for hours in the cavern and stopped at the end of the narrow tunnel, noticing a few stones dropping from the precipice. In the wide cavern, there were two short ochre stalagmites with round peaks and another sharp jagged row, surrounded with soft-red puffy clouds of mist, festering from the round crevice. I felt dizzy after treading amongst the totem poles and splattermite pillars crusted with round, calcite plates.

"I can't recognize where we are now," I whispered. "The stalagmites all look the same to me."

"Oh no," said Clarence, stepping back from the pile of shredded fur and skin, in-between the gaps of the stalagmites.

The mist swished beside his body and legs before he stopped in the middle of the chamber in the shadows. He wobbled his lantern-light towards the cliff. *"He's here,"*

"I don't see him," I said, squinting and skimmed the jagged edge of the precipice.

The winds blew from the above hollow in the limestone ceiling. The neglected body dropped from the cliff. I hailed, ramming against the wall and the wispy hairs of the body wiped all over my cheek. A crowd of bats swept down from the ceiling and flapped over my brother and past me, knocking the lantern and the candle titled on the glass pane.

"Uh!" I gasped, wincing at the sight of the rotting, yellowed teeth, flecked with mildew lingering close to me.

I pushed the moldy, beige clothes covered with holes away. The skeleton clattered to the floor into a mound of bones, amongst the rotting clothes and dust. Clarence swiped around, trembling the light from the lantern on the dropped skeleton and he glanced back to me.

"Who is it?" he asked.

"I'm not sure," I said, treading closer to the skeleton.

A round, brown carpet bag fell from the edge of the cliff and collided on the floor. I bellowed, not expecting its appearance and a bat flew from the shadowed patch above the cliff. It screeched and whipped its membranous, ebony wings, through the fissure and disappeared into the passage. The bag was bulgy, with a few poking lumps and it rolled on the floor, echoing a feeble clatter noise towards the front of our shoes. My heart hammered and my brother, standing diagonally opposite me near the rock, glanced down at the bag. I waited for the whiff of white dust to linger in the air, before disappearing and I tread towards the bag, around the pile of bones, not wanting my shoe to nudge into the round knobs. I lifted it from the floor and I rummaged through it, discovering an inclinometer for measuring the ground. I found a rope harness, tallow candles, a matchbox and an old compass with a guidance needle that didn't swivel properly, and the corner was bitten from Gharkoll's gnawed teeth. It was covered with dried, saliva and drowned ants. My fingers sunk into sticky, black ink spilled from a broken bottle and a dappled, black quill. Clarence moved closer, awkwardly glancing down at the skeleton and watched me pull out a light brown, leather diary, with thick, crumpled yellowed parchment. I opened the cover and blew away the dust and the feeble strand of web, crammed to the front page. Clarence lowered the lantern light to the front page, bowing over my shoulder and his silhouette slanted on the ground.

"It belonged to someone," I whispered, pointing at the journal and the inked words.

"What?" blurted Clarence, snatching the diary from my clasp and lowered it into the candlelight. "Ernst Harford." He looked up and the candlelight silhouette flickered on his chin and cheek. He lowered his lip. "He was a Speleologist."

"He was killed by Gharkoll ." I said, breathlessly.

Tears moistened in my eyes.

I flicked through the pages and his notes of the cave formations and different tunnels inside, leading into other caverns. I stopped at one page and it had a drawing of Gharkoll and a written explanation. I squinted and read the sentences quietly, with the occasional drip of water tapping from the stalactite on the floor.

1843

This diary belongs to Ernst Harford, the speleologist.

Dear diary,
After much exploration on the seas and the island, I accidentally stumbled on a shrubbery bush, uncovering a round, hollow entrance leading into a shadowed tunnel and the Helictite chamber in the cave.

CAVE ORGANISM
TROGLOBITE

TROGLOBITE is the definition for 'CAVE DWELLERS', who are specimens that can complete a portion of their life cycle above ground, though, they can't survive their entire life without a cave environment. The others include: glowworms, flatworms and blowfish.

I strongly believe the unknown, cavernicolous creature lurking in the narrow, rough passages is a Troglobite, due to his footprints leading out to the Parahypogean Caverns, nearby the entrances in the limestone walls. However, after hiding behind the stalagmites, I observed within a few hours, Gharkoll hurried back into the opening with such fright in his glowing, yellow eyes. It seemed, he loathed the exterior environment and verdure.

It was afterward, he encountered a Troglomorphism- blindness and a loss of his eyes. When I stepped into the Hypogean lair; the darkest of stalactite caverns, my tallow candle shriveled a whiff of smoke. I was horrified to see he feeds primarily from the chemical energy in the limestone and the other minerals by chemoautotrophic bacteria. He hungers for it and consumes long remnants with his tentacles from his ears, just as the glow-worms nestled in the walls.

Also, I observed soon, while following him into the tunnels, he halted in the Hypogean Caverns, hibernating in the shadows. It's been known scientifically, Troglobites dwell there and it's even more convincing he is one himself.

However, his specimen category is bewilderment? What is he, other than an Earthly troglobite, that I am not sure of? Is he from Earth? Did he encounter a mutation? Or, another morphologic process? I can't determine the connection to another animal, especially with the shape of his three toes and the peculiar long ears, and lime tentacles. I do assume he's male, without other egg specimens found.

Additionally, due to being able to swallow fluids of lava, he is considered to be an Extremophile, as no other living specimen has the ability to consume such a liquid at a blistering temperature.

"He couldn't have been a mutant back in time," I said. "This was written three years ago.

He became a mutant now, after you threw the chemical at him and he became evil." I lowered the diary to my dark beige trousers with spread dusty patches and leant the parchment closer to the flickering flame in the oil lamp.

"He is a troglobite," insisted Clarence. "Ernst was right about it."

"Alright, we know- he's a Troglobite Mutant and an Extremophile," I stated. "However, the one question we have to answer- is he from Earth or not?"

"He doesn't look it," answered Clarence. "How would he be from here? Do you think any other animals would've encountered a mutation if we had thrown the chemical at them? I doubt it, especially with the combustion of Chloride and carbonic acid."

"I agree," I said. "A glow-worm wouldn't have had the same metamorphosis. He can't survive without being in a cave and would die if he were to live outside a dark habitat."

"Ernst already defined what Gharkoll was, which makes sense to what we were talking about before- him being very sensitive to the exterior elements."

"Wait," said Clarence, tracing his finger across the diary and moved it closer to the lantern's flared radiance. "He is prone to blindness and shredding skin?"

"Where?" I asked.

He tilted the diary and dabbed his fingertip to the page.

"There," said Clarence.

"Gharkoll killed him," I said, sighing. "Even he knew more about Gharkoll and didn't survive. I don't know how we are going to survive in here." I stood and reminded him, "Well, he didn't figure the water could definitely injure him. Maybe, we should try it. The water lacks the acidic properties compared to carbonic acid."

A groan echoed from the tunnel and we both turned, listening to it whirl into the air of our cavern. We followed and stopped at the archway and lifting my dimmed light, I swallowed. A few black strands of wispy hair flapped in the round, shadowed archway.

"Nora?" I whispered.

CHAPTER THIRTY-FIVE

NORA'S ATTACK

A gust of warm wind flew in the adjacent passage and the black strands swindled from the poking, jagged dents into the shadows. The gloom elongated in my stomach. I sighed and shone my glow from the oil lamp onto the floor, watching the dark hair strands flying in the opposite direction.

Clarence stopped beside me and flashed his light onto the floor, revealing a footprint and a blood driblet and he pointed, "*Look!*"

My heart leapt a nervous beat and without thinking too much, I followed in the south-western direction of the passage, knowing we were detouring from our needed destination.

It was meanwhile, at the hour of seven o' clock', Nora emerged out of the impenetrable tunnel, with her harried breaths echoing from her opened pout. Gharkoll roamed amongst the wall of boulders, fixating a malignant glare on her back. She swayed her lantern's dimmed, tawny beam around the neglected chamber. He sniffed her scent, observing it was sweeter, than the other masculine aroma he had smelt before.

"Douglas! Clarence!" yelled Nora. "*Where are you?*"

Gharkoll 's eardrums widened, and he twitched his long, pointed ear, elongating the lime tentacles. The blood runnels drenched on the side of his mouth had become arid. Nora shifted into an arcuate tunnel and the lantern's light skimmed on the wall and was engulfed in the dark. Gharkoll followed her, with an effervescing urge and his iridescent, yellow eyes shifted to his nocturnal vision, deepening to the shade of red and he lurked around the forest of uneven stalagmites with sharp peaks. Gharkoll lifted his gaze to the jagged speleothems hanging from the ceiling, and he pondered if he should crawl amongst them. However, he changed his mind and remembered the scrawling noise from his claws would frighten her. Gharkoll felt comforted from the warmth lurking over his fee and burning his toes in the ambiance. He inhaled the whiffs of drifting, orange fog. Gharkoll slowed his pace as he reached the end of the tunnel and hid behind the sarsen, camouflaging his dark, beige fur. The three-tentacles protruding from his ears, oozed green poison beside his enormous foot with thick, dark brown fur. He toyed a piece of debris with his singular, curved claw.

Nora stopped, hearing the feeble *plink* noise echoing in the silence. She swiped around and spotted the round, lime glow, behind the speleothems grown near the boulder.

Gharkoll stretched a sardonic beam in the dark, as she skimmed her lantern's radiance on the misty, clustered stalagmites. He hindered to move and he slouched his claw on the debris and his lime illuminance vanished.

Nora gasped, sensing his presence and slowing her presence closer to the speleothems, she believed his short, beige horns were a part of the clustered, jagged stalagmites. She perused the broadest, middle one, where he was hidden. Gharkoll lightly, twitched his right ear and listened to her heart-beat thumping in her chest. Nora hovered her beam onto his fawn-brown horns and tilted her head to the side, eyeing them with fascination.

"I never knew stalagmites had such a formation..." trailed Nora, reaching out to touch the left one with her fingertips, though refrained herself and flinched them back- there were loose lines across the horn.

Gharkoll heard her thudding heartbeat, quickening in her chest

"Wait a minute...it's not rock." murmured Nora, conceding to her curiosity, and she touched his thick, soft hair. "What could this be? A cave reed specimen or...is it...fur..."

Gharkoll slid his eyes upward and snarled, furrowing his thick, dark-brown eyebrows. He lowered his jaw and he hissed, and his upper lip curled into his slimy gum, loathing she was dwindling his hair and he scampered away. Nora squealed at the suddenness of his movement and she dropped her lantern, shattering the glass into a pile. The melted, tallow oozed into a solidified puddle, with a floating cloud of warm fog. The candle flame flickered beside her shoe. She huffed and fearfully glanced at the dimmed stalagmites, arisen in the shadows and lifted the candle from the floor, swishing the flame back and forth.

"*They're gone,*" whispered Nora. "I knew it."

Gharkoll lifted his short horns and dark furred cones and he lifted his gleaming, red eyes above the flowstone in-between the columns. He hid back down, before she turned to gaze in his direction.

Nora stared and her tight breaths blew from her softly, opened mouth and they echoed louder over her footsteps.

She strode closer.

"Are you there and what are you?" asked Nora.

Gharkoll leapt onto the flowstone, indenting miniature craters around his claws and he raved an ear-splitting yawp. Nora screamed, dropping the candle and tread backwards into the round, lime pool with floating clumps of moss. Gharkoll growled, infuriated she was attempting to escape him and jumping, he squashed the melted candle and smeared it into a layer of wax beneath his enormous, three-toed foot.

He pursued her around the edge of the pool.

Nora swiped around and screamed.

Gharkoll strode after her in long strides in the pale mist simmering from the surface of the pool and he ruptured an earsplitting screech. Nora covered her ears with her hands and she trampled down the tunnel, amongst the tawny clouds of fog and the cavern. A group of slender, soda streams descended from the ceiling. They quavered with Gharkoll's feet thudding on the ground. Nora glimpsed above and with his thudding stride, the ground waved a vibration through the walls and thin cracks splintered around the soda streams.

They fell, soaring towards her.

Nora squealed and ducked, dodging them as they clashed to the floor and spread into an array of chiseled bits. Her foot caught underneath a rock and she tripped, falling to the ground. Gharkoll arrived in the archway and sprinted towards her, with his broadening jaw. Nora swiped around and her pulse raced, and her heart hammered, as if it would lurch from her chest. She dragged her knee across the chipped bits of rock and panted.

Gharkoll thudded closer and raised his claw.

Nora eyed his silhouette looming on the floor in front of her shoes and the chipped bits of rock bounced on her dark hair. She turned over her shoulder and squealed- the claw swiped towards her nose, scraping the air and a whiff of air blew onto her cheeks, slicing a few black hair-strands to the floor. Nora threw a rock at the dark-beige, tufts of fur, and it crumbled into a fountain of rocky bits and they showered onto Gharkoll 's foot. He hissed, and poking his slender, dark-green forked tongue, he scraped his claws across her shirt and the fabric tore, forming three bloodied scratches onto her back. Nora screamed and her elbows clamped on the ground began to wobble and she collapsed onto the floor, sliding her fingers across a few, rolling soda-straw pieces. She retrieved one and jammed the sharp, slender calcite point into Gharkoll 's furry shoulder. He halted, dragging his right bent clawed foot and engraved three-lines into the rugged ground. Gharkoll released an ear-splitting, guttural screech from a rush of heated fury. Nora became fatigued and exhausted. She panted with a reddened complexion and crawled faintly, feeling the sharp dents in the rocky floor nipping into her knees and tiny stone bits sunk into her clammy palms. Her hair messily dangled on her shoulders and wispy strands smeared onto her cheeks. She stopped at the gigantic flowstone in the middle of the cavern and hid there, panting and blinked a tear from her eye. It streamed down her dirt-stained cheek and touching the fresh scratches, they stung underneath her brushing fingertips. She whimpered and gritted her teeth together, clutching another rock and skimmed the clustered long, elongate calcite carbonate, not having formed into stalactites. Their small silhouettes tilted and loomed on the uneven ground and she shifted her attention towards him. Gharkoll had driblets of green blood oozing on his furred shoulder. He nudged the poking chipped, soda-straw piece with his claw and he released an eddying growl from the bottom of his throat, annoyed it wasn't sliding out. Gharkoll puffed a whiff of warm breath and he pulled out the piece of calcite. He roared and the soda straws shook and stormed downward, smashing into bits on the ground. Gharkoll opened the crowd of eyes on his forehead, skimming the cavern and he spotted the movement of the black hair behind the flowstone. He scampered towards her. Nora ran, clutching a pile of rocks and threw them over her shoulder at Gharkoll , though, he whacked them with his claw and they clashed into the walls, disintegrating into a fountain of pebbles. Gharkoll increased his speed and he was close and could smell the sweat drizzling from her skin. They emerged into a tight tunnel and he lunged forward, scraping his claw into the bottom of her shirt. Nora halted, and the rocks fell from her clasp. She squealed and she turned, listening to the ripping noise echo in the tunnel-his claw scratched down the bottom of her shirt and frail, cotton strands dangled from the fabric. Nora tilted her head and screamed a notch louder and pushed forward, running down the tunnel.

Gharkoll growled, loathing he had been close to her and now she was running away from him. He whipped the piece of cotton caught in his claw and scrounged it in his palm. He hastened his pace and the ground and walls rumbled, showering stone bits onto her hair and shoulders.

"Douglas!" screamed Nora.

Nora stepped forward and she released her clutch from the rock and gritting her teeth, she tried to cope with the swelling in her back. Her throat ached from screaming and itched. Her mouth was dry of thirst and a sharp pain jabbed in her chest and her legs, strained with long streams of pain, pinching in her muscles. Nora slowed her footsteps and inhaled the stifled rocky air, before rising her speed again.

Gharkoll slobbered a slimy, dark green driblet of saliva from his picket fangs and his pupils dilated with a ravenous hunger, churning in his stomach, as he inhaled the scent of her fresh, bleeding blood. A heavy breath puffed from his jaw. *He would tear her blood-stained leg away, swallow half of her bone, crunch it into splinters and dissolve the warm blood, with her marrow. He licked the corner of his lips, and re-swallowing the clinging droplet of saliva, he deflected his gaze to her neck. He'd rip her neck, engulf a portion of her flabby skin and tear away her veins, until they were mushed in his jaws.*

Gharkoll could barely breathe, as he neared closer, and thudded his feet amongst the stalactite shadows. Her sweaty, sweet scent lofted into his nostrils. Gharkoll widened a golden glow around his pupils and his lime tentacles brightened, seeping yellow poison. One droplet trickled onto the front of her boot and dissolved a hole. Nora screamed and felt the burning sensation. She swiped over her shoulder, flicking her black hair onto her back. His luminance from his tentacles, and his horn and coned shadow skimmed on the wall, behind her own silhouette.

"*No*," she puffed, with panic.

Nora heard a crackle, echoing from the ceiling and she looked up and screamed.

PART THREE

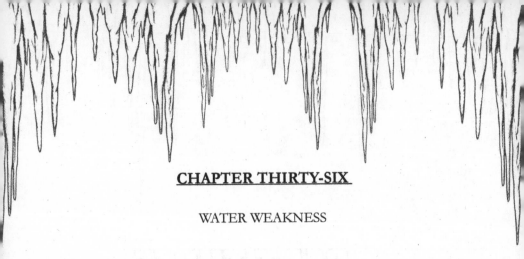

CHAPTER THIRTY-SIX

WATER WEAKNESS

I heard the scream distantly reverberating into a frail echo and silence. I paused, clutching the crinkled piece of the torn sail and slowly arose my short daze to the opening at the end of the tunnel.

"Did you hear it?" I asked, listening to the feminine scream.

Clarence slid his dirty stained hands onto his trousers and listened, slowly-moving his glare to the nearest arch.

"It sounds like Nora," I said, putting the sail into my pouch and strode towards the opening in the wall. "You don't think she came wondering in here looking for us?"

"Well, we did say we would come back to the campsite and we never did?" suggested Clarence. "Maybe, it *is* her."

"She's found *Gharkoll*," I said. "Come on," I sprinted down the passage, not caring if Gharkoll would appear at any moment, only I was concerned and worried of her safety. I skimmed the firelight scorching on the stick amongst the tight tunnel. *Was she hurt? Had Gharkoll killed her? Was she dead?*

"Nora!" I yelled, puffing a breath and beginning to panic. "Can you hear me?"

I waited to hear her response, but I only heard my vast footsteps crunching on the scattered debris. My pouch bounced on my back and I was worried, I would never see her again and my pulse raced.

I heard another shriek and yelled again, "Nora!"

"Douglas!" she yelled back. "Douglas, is that you?"

"Yeah!" I answered, increasing my pace and emerged into the cavern, stopping in the cluster of short and pointed, tawny stalagmites.

My heart thumped in my chest and sweat drizzled on my skin underneath my clothes. I panted, stepping closer to the warmth floating from the lake spread beyond the stalagmites. The stalactites surrounded her, exploding plumes of beige dust into the ceiling. Gharkoll stopped, skidding his claws on the floor. He hailed with an incessant fury and his jawbone was covered with reddened feeble veins, stretching from underneath his dark brown beard. I trampled out from behind the stalagmites and tugged her by the arm, hauling her away.

Nora shrieked, startled with my sudden appearance.

"You found me," she said, with her watery and distressed tone.

"I meant what I said before," I blurted, over my shoulder and guided her into another chamber. The walls were cragged obsidian and shrouded with shadows.

"Where are we going to hide?" she asked, looking back.

Gharkoll lurked closer.

"Down here," I said, noticing there was a hole beneath the cragged rock.

Nora followed me. We lay down on the floor beside the rocks, disguising our canvas pouches, as boulders underneath the rocky dais. Our bodies were huddled together, exchanging heat. Gharkoll roamed in the cavern, trickling saliva and inhaled our scent. He prowled towards us. I clutched Nora closely and our lips lingered near, as we sunk into each other's eyes, under a contradictive daze of attraction and fright. Gharkoll's snuffling intensified, and he clamped his cold, moistened foot onto my cheek. I widened my eyes, and my face sunk into the sharp, rocky floor. Slowly, crouching, he lowered his right-foot, onto Nora's moistened black locks. I inhaled her sweet perspiration, clammy on her jawbone and churning with the sour mosses, rotting in murky, carbonic acid water. She flicked her shiny, brown eyes up at the round, beige-skinned toe and sharp, black toenail, sinking into my disheveled tresses. Gharkoll's green mucus slivered from the corner of his mouth onto my cheek and slowly, crawled to my jawbone. I tried not to exhale, knowing one whiff of breath on his fur, he would discover us hidden beneath the sheltering rock. Her heart beat thudded wildly, sinking into my chest and mimicked the pace of my own. I saw my brother peeking from the opposite stalagmite and eyeing the closeness of our lips and bodies. His prickling disposition permeated in the silence and disapproved our closeness. The claws arched, sinking deeper into my cheek and slowly, slid reddened welts on my complexion to my jawbone. I bit mosses to avoid myself from screaming and my complexion reddened with agony. He snuffled, wriggling his moist nose and inhaled our humane scent, drifting from our collarbones.

Gharkoll echoed a soft, curling growl through his picket-teeth and it wended into my eardrums; a surge of infuriation, from not understanding, *why* he couldn't see us. Nora softly quivered and closed her eyes, clamping her pale-ruddy lips onto my neck. He was bewildered and strode around the debris, shifting his back to us. I nudged Nora and nodding my chin forward, I listened and she crawled out from beneath the rock, sneaking to the other side towards the opening in the wall. Gharkoll 's ear twitched backward, and he swiped around. He screeched and watched Nora and Clarence disappear back into the tunnel. Gharkoll rushed away, leaping from the rugged periphery and back into the tunnel.

I rolled back out onto my arm and grumbled to myself, "*Nice move, Douglas,*" I stood, wiping the dirt onto my shirt from my elbow and trampled after him. "Leave her alone!"

I ran through the archway, down the tunnel and skidded into the cavern. I glimpsed Gharkoll 's wavering tentacles, the points of his ears and his horns disappearing into the shadows looming in the passage.

"Hey!" I yelled, collecting a mound of debris and the gritted bits sunk in my fingernails.

Gharkoll ignored me. I dashed into the tunnel, watching the six, lime glows from his tentacles shining on the walls.

"Dammit," I puffed, hurrying through the dark and panicked, as the luminance dissolved into the antechamber's dimmed silhouettes. I hastened my pace, ignoring the gash prickle on my chest. I stampeded into the chamber and abruptly stopped, perusing the right wall. My bottom lip lowered in shock- the stalagmites flickered emerald flames on their rugged peaks. Gharkoll roamed around them, closer towards her. Nora stepped backwards in the levitating, yellow and green mists.

"*Leave her alone!*" I screamed, running and tossing the debris into his furred back.

My stomach clenched, as I watched the slimy tentacles, leaking yellow driblets splatter on the floor. Gharkoll halted and swiped around, snarling with a hiss. His fangs opened in the hovering mists and stretched a slender string of saliva. He threw the last of the debris into my shoulder and they bounced to the floor. I bellowed and rammed into his furry torso, knocking Gharkoll to the floor. We rolled on the cragged stones, near the brink of the black pool and I grappled his neck, as the forked, red tongue poked to my nose. His paired fangs and slender picket teeth hung above my nose and cheeks, with the crowd of eyes gleaming at me. Gharkoll 's tentacles whipped in the air and speckles of spit dabbed onto my sweaty forehead and cheeks. I yelled, as his picket teeth neared closer and screaming, I sunk my fingertips into the moist corners of his mouth. I inhaled a whiff of his sour breath and it smelt like decayed, hot fish. I recoiled and picked up a piece of stone and thrust it into his crowd of eyes. Gharkoll screeched and I was hauled backward into the stalagmites. My hand knocked onto the peak, hurling stone bits and my fingertips brushed across the warm fire. Gharkoll 's shadow loomed over my sweaty complexion. I felt a rush of courage, I never knew I had, as he lunged closer towards me and I grappled his neck. *I'd had enough of him*. His picket-toothed mouth gusted more warm breaths. I cringed and I scrunched my nose, feeling disgusted. My fears and terror shattered with the rupture of infuriation. I gritted my teeth and sunk my fingertips further into his thick-fur.

A soft-choking noise echoed.

"I'll kill you!" I yelled, squeezing his neck and his yellow eyes swelled with tears. "You killed William! And you won't kill her *or, my brother!*"

Gharkoll echoed a penetrating screech and the tentacles wrapped around my ruffled hair, covering my eyes with a moist mucus. The speleothems blurred in the gap between two, spread coiled tentacles, as another one wrapped around my neck. I stifled a breath and choking, my fingers sunk into his blistering fur and covered my whitened knuckles and hands.

"He's dying! He's dying!" shrieked Nora, standing on the boulder and she threw rocks at Gharkoll. "Stop it! Stop it! You're killing him!"

Gharkoll rolled on the floor and one of the tentacles whacked onto the slender stalagmites and they chipped a mound of rubble, tumbling beside me. My fingers swept over one sharp, torn peak of limestone. I lifted it and slammed it into Gharkoll 's neck. The dark green blood sputtered on his torso, drenching his fur and the tentacles loosened around my forehead and cheeks, sliding away and whipped the air. Gharkoll squinted and he screeched and looked up at the ceiling. I pulled out the jar of dynamite powder and poured a handful into the coconut and struck a match on the rock.

I threw it beside Gharkoll 's three-toed foot.

Boom!

The rubble flew everywhere. Gharkoll strode backward and hailed. I crawled vividly forward with flushed cheeks and my head throbbed. Clarence and Nora rushed downward and hopped on each boulder and the lower rocks. They offered their hands. I held them and bursting a cough, I sluggishly bowed and we disappeared down the tunnel. Gharkoll lowered his claw to his inflamed furry shoulder and shrunk the flames into smoky puffs of steam. He pursued us into a gigantic chamber with a widespread cluster of rim stone pools. Nora and Clarence descended the slope, sinking into a spring with stalactites and a waterfall. We tread carefully on the edge of the rim stone pools and splashed into them, until I reached back to the rocky ground. We splashed through the spring. I huffed and stopped, holding the tall, beige stalagmite beside my shoulder.

Gharkoll lifted his claw above Nora.

I remembered water lacked acidic properties, like carbonic acid water and kicking a wave, it flew onto Gharkoll's legs, drenching his fur. The steam wavered from them. He screeched, flurrying away from her and he leapt onto the wall, disappearing into the silhouetted stalactites. I stared astounded and glanced down at the stalagmite's reflection on the rippling surface.

"Water," I gasped, "This is what he hates."

I trampled after it, beneath the array of miniature stalactites in the ceiling.

"Douglas!" shrieked Nora. "*Stop!*"

I ignored her and the distant plashing of my brother and Nora.

"Douglas, are you crazy!" yelled out Clarence.

I roamed in between the misty stalagmites, dodging them and I became determined with every stride, and the beads of water flicking onto my thighs and drenched my legs. I spotted Gharkoll on the wall and I kicked another wave of water. It splashed on his foot and another puff of mist drifted from his three toes and tufts of fur. Gharkoll wailed, and the stalactites quivered from the ceiling, with the intensity of his cry. I stopped and covered my ears, not liking the earsplitting wail. Nora and Clarence stopped behind me in the distance, doing the same. Gharkoll crawled further up the wall, chafing the rock with his sharp claws and rubble flicked over my head. The stone bits descended the ceiling from his claws and dropped into the rim stone pools. He spewed yellow poison from his mouth, and it dropped onto the ground, steaming tendrils. I trampled away. Gharkoll followed us back over the pool and crawled on the ceiling.

We trampled into the pool, leaping on the rocks, until we were behind the waterfall and discovered a fissure.

"In here!" I yelled.

We tread inside. I watched from the side of the waterfall, Gharkoll stopped at the edge of the pool and he wailed, scraping his claw on the surface of the jagged ground.

Gharkoll trampled away back into the nearest passage.

"*Phew*," said Clarence. "That was close."

"I know, tell me about it," I said.

Nora sat down relieved and wiped the blood trickling from her scratch. I leant against the wall, catching my breath.

"I'm going to go see if I can find some firewood," said Nora, over her shoulder.

"Alright," I said, with a nod.

Nora disappeared through a cleft and I heard the pattering of her footsteps echoing distant in the tunnel. I sat down on the sedimentary boulder and gulped a long sip of water from my flask, before placing it down to the floor beside my shoe. The scratches on my arm burned and bloodied streaks dissolved my yellowed linen, contrasting against the dank, beige smudges of rock. My thoughts were racing endlessly. I was relieved we were safe in the cavern. I could see the blurred, turquoise pool spread behind the waterfall and froth with the stalactites. I tossed a stone between my hands. I couldn't understand *why* Gharkoll was allergic and vulnerable to water- it seemed he was vulnerable to anything not of a warm temperature. Clarence appeared in the fissure, bowing his head underneath the point in the sleek rock and he plashed in the puddles. He groaned, relieved and sat on the smaller boulder opposite me.

"Something is bothering me," I confessed, not able to keep my thoughts to myself anymore.

Clarence pulled out his own vial and rotated it around, eyeing the whirring water. He sighed and he admitted, "Me too, though, you say what's on your mind first."

I silenced, leaning my elbows onto my knees.

"Well, it's interesting Gharkoll is frightened of water and this means he's allergic and vulnerable to a particular chemical," I said.

Clarence nodded and after contemplating whether he should drink the last remnant of water, he unplugged the vial's top and he pressed it to his lips, taking a long swallow of water to quench his thirst.

"Well, if he hibernates inside of the cave all the time, he's vulnerable not only to the water, though, the Earth's atmosphere," he pointed out, putting the bottle back onto the boulder.

I quietened, clamping my chin on my knuckles, eyeing my reflection in the nearest pool and I gasped.

"It's oxygen," I said. "He can't handle too much quantities of oxygen. Otherwise, he'd be able to roam around in the island's forest properly, as any other animal. Oxygen is in both water and our atmosphere. It would be then, Nitrogen and Carbon Dioxide, as well."

"Yes, but the cave has those elements," said Clarence. "How has he been possibly immune?"

I concentrated my glare to the opposite wall. "Anything cavernicolous would prefer low remnants of oxygen, which is obviously the cave's atmosphere, and this is why he can survive in these tunnels. However, because he can swallow lava, he's immune to phosphorous elements. It must be the combination of low oxygen, nitrogen and carbon dioxide amongst high dosages of phosphorous smoke, blowing in the air and he can live." I realised. "Why does this all matter anyway?"

"It will help us injure him and then escape the cave." I said, deviating my glance from the puddle and lowered my vial into the pool and filled it with water.

"Injure him?" he retorted. "Is it such a good idea? His eye is too powerful and those tentacles from his ears could strangle us in less than a minute."

"I know, it's risky," I said, glancing from the water back to him. "Though, it's our only chance of surviving him."

"We don't have many vials," said Clarence. "You were infuriated before, how I caused the mutant metamorphosis to occur. What if it happens again?"

"I know," I said, shaking my head. "If only I could poison all of the acid in the rocks and water, and he can die. However, we don't have the liquid."

"Maybe, you're right this time and we can?" he asked, changing his perceptive.

"How?" I probed.

"The Chloride?" he suggested.

"Are you mad?" I asked. "The Chloride did the opposite of what it would do to an ordinary animal."

"But maybe, the *combination* of the acid and the chloride would kill him?" he asked. "Last time, it was just the chloride alone."

"I doubt it," I said, disagreeing. "It would most likely, put him asleep. He's immune to acids, not weakened by them. It's the same with the Chloride. I doubt he will be poisoned, because of his strengthened mutation."

"What if it *did* work?" he asked.

"It won't," I said, shaking my head. "Clarence, don't try it without my consent."

Clarence stood to leave and lifting his sack from the floor.

"I won't," he said, swinging it over his shoulder. "I'll fill more vials with water, just in case he finds us again."

CHAPTER THIRTY-SEVEN

ARGUEMENT

I led the way down, following the sloped floor and guided them with the last remnant of my withered, tallow candle, guttering and reflecting a dimmed, round glow on the denticulate walls.

"The air is stifling," I warned, over my shoulder. "I don't know if this is leading us in the correct, southward direction."

"You don't know that," argued Clarence, stamping on a worm.

"I can't smell not a whiff of air," I said. "Isn't it the same with you?"

"Well, it's southward," added Nora. "Maybe, it'll be stifled just for a moment."

"Yeah, Douglas," echoed Clarence.

"Well, I hope you're both right," I said, over my shoulder. "I wouldn't want the atmosphere to imply we're treading into an enclosed underground cavern, without any holes or openings to other tunnels, leading back to the island." I sniffed the aroma and was disappointed only to inhale stale, dusty rock. "I can't smell not even a whiff of the ocean."

"Me neither," agreed Nora, carefully, avoiding a steep depression and clutched the dank, sagging rope swing in-between us. "Worst case, we'll just climb back up here and without choice, return to go to the waterfall."

"We'll be completely doomed," echoed Clarence, sourly.

"*Clarence*," I sung, over my shoulder. "Don't worry, we're just going to be fine."

My shoe slipped on the dusty debris and a flock of screeching bats flapped past and their membranous wings whacked onto my hair and moist cheek. We

265

all bellowed and tried ducking beneath them. Clarence swung his pouch from his shoulder, hurling it into the wall and whiffs of dust hovered beneath their wings. I toppled to the floor, losing balance and I slid on the slope, halting beside the short, huddled stalagmites and grabbed one of them. I rocked my legs on the rolling debris and dust. I panted and gazed up, seeing Clarence and Nora striding back to the summit of the slope in the dark and around the side of the wall. I frowned, feeling confused and gnashed my teeth and grappled the other stalagmite peak, sinking my chin into my collarbone. Where were they going? I stood, clutching the poking rocks from the walls and my annoyance lifted with every footstep, ascending the slope.

"Why did you go back up there?" I echoed.

They didn't respond and somehow, as much as I denied it, because it was illogical. The feeling prickled in my chest and warned something was wrong. I reached the curved, rugged slope.

My hitched breaths echoed in the dark.

I tugged on the dusty rope and tried to warn them. I was still on the other side, though, all I dragged was a lonesome rope on the floor, sliding on the crushed, stone bits. They were *gone* and the longer I stared down the vacant tunnel surrounded with shadow and the faint golden, dimmed flicker of my oil lamp in-between my boots, I became perturbed and confused. *How was it possible?* I lifted the end closer to my eyes, seeing the torn tendrils of the rope and rubbed my thumb against them. *It looks like it's been torn.*

"Clarence? Nora?" I whispered, holding the rope dangling in mid-air and brought it closer to the lamp light, squinting at the wispy chords.

I pulled one away, with peril widening my eyes with terror and dropped the rope beside my thigh. *There has to be am explanation for this- the rope must've dragged against a sharp protrusion in the wall and snapped it. However, even if it did, Clarence and Nora would've continued in this direction?* It only seemed apparent to me, there was a fork somewhere in the distance and they had turned down another tunnel. Jealousy emerged, as I thought of Nora and Clarence, having purposely gone in another direction to be alone together. I frowned and rubbed my eyes with my palm covered with a patch of smudged dirt and thought, *No, they wouldn't do that after only just surviving Gharkoll ? Would they?* I ascended the steep slope, determined to find them. How was I going to return to the upper floor without a trace of their footsteps or my own in the limestone floor? They were nowhere to be found. I strode in the tunnel, leaping my hand on the wall, heading into another passage. I waved my hand in the impenetrable passage, searching for an odd stalagmite.

"Clarence! *Nora!*" I yelled out.

Only the sound of my echo, mocked me. *Where were they?*

I tread down, bouncing my hand on each of the protruding rocks in the wall and skimmed the floor, ensuring there weren't any unexpected fissures. My shoe nudged into a sack and the clattering noise chimed in the silence. I stopped and looked down, recognizing it to be Clarence's sack. I squatted, rummaging through the sack and found his knife and the coiled rope with a packet of matches. I dropped them, feeling astonished and found there were a few still left inside of the packet. He had lied to me. *Why?* I pressed the end of my own rope into the coils of his own and they formed into a perfect fit. I probed at the knife on the floor. *They rope was too thick to be torn on its own. The rocks weren't sharp enough in the tunnel, either. Would he really tear my rope? No, he's my brother. He would never betray me?* I lowered the rope back to the floor. *Or maybe, he would…*

"Clarence?" I called out, striking a match and the crackling, flame glowed on the floor, covered with crawling scorpions.

My stomach writhed at the sight of them and I pulled one away, with the side of my shoe and the scorpion scuttled away. He didn't answer me. I held the match close, treading slowly to the end and discovered a dimmed glow. I suspected he had used. I heard their voices echo and I slowed my footsteps, trying to hush the sound of them. I didn't want them to become aware of me eavesdropping.

"*Nora,*" Clarence's voice echoed. "*I have something to tell you,*"

My clutch tightened on the matchstick. I didn't approve of the emotion in his voice.

"Why are you close to me?" she echoed. "Please Clarence. It can't be."

I stopped at the opening of the tunnel, holding the edge of the wall and lowered my lip, astounded at what I could see. An inflamed stick leant against the wall beside them.

"*It can be,*" argued Clarence. "Nora…I like you."

"You do?" she asked. "Why?"

I felt anger flourish in my chest at the sight of his betrayal and disloyalty. *How could he do this to me? I knew it. My love for my brother, had veiled my perception of him and I had disregarded my suspicion too carelessly. He did like Nora and he had tried to convince me against her and revealing my affection to her personally. Of course, this was why he was always negative every time he saw us close together and liked intervening between us, because of his jealousy. Did he just like the competition with me, for the sake of the game of winning her, or did he actually mean what he said?* I gritted my teeth, narrowing my eyes on his hands clasped on her arms and sliding to her bare shoulders. He traced her skin with his fingertip along her collarbone. I fumed through my nose, clamping my lips, until they tightened dry. His palms and fingers lifted to her jawbone, holding her face tenderly, as he took another step closer to her and their lips lingered less than, an inch apart.

"You're everything to me," he continued, spreading his fingers across her cheek. "I've been waiting for the right moment to tell you, though we've had many interruptions and I never had a moment away from my brother," he paused. "Well, apart from when he fell in the chamber and the floor collapsed, but, I wasn't ready to tell you. I'm asking you, not to choose him, but me."

No, he does mean it. I thought.

My stomach knotted at the loathing in his voice, when he said, 'brother'.

"Clarence, I-," she began, though before she could finish, he plunged his lips into hers.

My cheeks heated, as if I knelt beside scorching, golden flames.

I gnashed my teeth. The temptation to punch his cheek undulated between the morality of right and wrong. Clarence slid his hand down her breast to her waist and the sound of their moving lips, echoed in the tunnel. My clutch of the sack, tightened, until it shrunk in my clammy sweat of my palm and fingers from the humidity in the tunnel. He pecked her jawbone, slowly down to her chin, while she tilted her head. I waited a moment longer, watching them, until I couldn't anymore.

I raided down the tunnel, careless if Gharkoll heard me.

"*Traitor!*" I yelled.

Clarence pulled his lips away from her and he slightly widened his eyes, astounded with my presence.

"You don't fool me, *brother,*" I lashed, throwing the bulgy sack to his shoes and pushed his shoulder. "You betrayed me! *Why?*" I stormed towards him, "After, all I cared about was to help you out of here alive! *After,* I trusted you with my confession!"

"The rope tore on its own!" he blurted, stepping backward and avoided my vast approach. "I lost you! We couldn't find you!"

"Don't lie!" I bellowed. "You had the knife in your sack! You purposely tore it!"

"I'm your brother!" he yelled. "I would never do it! How could you even say this about me?"

I could hear the manipulation in his voice, as a snake slivering in grasses and it infuriated me more, like a gnarled bough thrown in a campfire, flickering inside of my stomach.

"*Stop acting innocent,*" I snarled, stopping in the passage, half-a-meter away from him. "You wanted to be alone with Nora! You just said it yourself! You couldn't find the right moment to tell her how you felt, because of me!"

Clarence hesitated to respond, holding his mouth partially ajar, before he clamped his lips together and he held his hips.

Nora stood in-between us. "Stop it Douglas! Clarence would never tear the rope!" she exclaimed.

"He did!" I yelled, enraged. "The rope fits exactly! The cordage is thick, like the shrouds on the ship! It's *impossible* for the friction to occur instantly, as he claims it to be against the wall!" She stopped and glanced over her shoulder at Clarence, realizing my explanation was more sensical, than his claims.

Clarence lowered his chin, with shadows surrounding his cheeks. His hand balled into a fist and his voice became tremulous with anger, from my overpowering rationality and his lies, unable to be perceived as the truth.

"*I didn't lie, the rope tore on its own*," he snapped.

"You're only becoming angry, because I'm announcing the truth! Your manipulation and lies are obvious, you're not liking you can't win again!" I stated. "I pity you!"

Clarence stomped towards me. "I'm not lying!" he yelled.

"You are!" I roared back, shoving him in the chest and he steadied backward a few steps. "Stop denying it, you fool!"

"Fool!?" he blurted, grappling my collar, "*Who* is the one that led us into this cave from the beginning!"

"Clarence, I've always been there for you!" I yelled, brashly dropping his clutch from my collar and a wretched tearing noise echoed from his shirt and one brown button popped and fell beside my shoe. The shirt tightened underneath my arm and I shoved him into the wall. "Always! You've betrayed me and you don't respect me enough to leave Nora alone, do you!"

"Why should you have her? Just because, you're the eldest?!" he blurted. "I like her more, than you do!"

Nora gasped, looking at me. I felt awkward in her presence. My cheeks burned with embarrassment. I wondered if I preferred to be hiding near a stalagmite, with Gharkoll roaming around me, than be here and have my feelings exposed in front of the girl I like.

"Do you ever shut up!" I yelled, pushing him harder, with strength developed from my anger and he lurched, hitting back into a sharp, jutting rock.

Clarence grunted, rebounding from the edge of the rocky wall and his chin swung down to his shoulder, and his disheveled, dark-brown tresses covered his forehead. He tripped in a deep dent in the floor and clashed into the opposite wall. He surged his head into my chest. I clashed onto the ground. We wrestled and I gnashed my teeth.

"Stop!" shrieked Nora, hurrying towards us and tried pulling us apart, by holding Clarence's shoulder. "You're brothers! Everyone makes mistakes! Forgive each other! This is ridiculous! Stop it now!"

"It wasn't a mistake!" I bellowed. "He did it purposely! *This is why I'm furious!*"

I formed a fist and punched my brother in the cheek with a frail, bloodied scratch from Gharkoll 's claws. My fingers brushed against his nose. Clarence yelled, knocking into the wall and tumbled to the floor. He lay there for a moment, with his thick, dark brown hair messily hanging on the side of his cheek. He pressed his palms to the cavities and lifted onto his knees and he puffed a breath, revealing the trickling blood from his nose. The sight of him injured, made my heart sink into a pool of dread and somewhere, amongst the infuriation, I felt regret burdening my chest. I had never wanted to hurt my brother, though he had wanted to hurt me, which pained me more.

"This is enough!" exclaimed Nora, stepping in-between us. "You shouldn't be fighting each other, when our lives are at stake."

I couldn't look at her and instead, I gazed at her ankles smeared with dirt streaks. All I could feel were my cheeks warming with embarrassment. I decided to ignore her, and I held my gaze to the floor and stood, diverting my attention to my brother.

"Be gone out of my sight, traitor" I lashed. "I can't bare the sight of you!"

"With pleasure," he snapped, wiping the trickling blood with his crinkled sleeve. "It's not like I want to be with a brother, who leads me around the cave in circles and never finds a way out, with a stupid compass that doesn't even work properly."

I stopped treading down the tunnel and fumed through my nose. *Is this the gratitude I receive, after all I ever wanted was to help us all get out of here and care for him? And loving him?*

"*Clarence,*" hissed Nora, in the silence.

I turned over my shoulder and challenged, "Very well, Clarence. You can find your own way out of here-," I glanced at Nora. "-*with* Nora. The two of you, all *alone.*"

I loosely beamed, kicking his sack, and spread the rope, skidding the knife on the floor.

"I'll see you both at the last tunnel in the cave and that's *if* you can find it," I stated, smugly.

"You're not really leaving, are you?" scowled Nora, frowning, and clutched her hip. "How could you!"

"Why do you care?" I snapped. "You *have* my brother."

Nora strode towards me, pointing her finger at me and she yelled, "If you leave now, don't you come back! You shouldn't be leaving, that is a form of betrayal and disloyalty, neglecting us in the cave!"

"Well, he and I, then, I suppose are even, aren't we?" I retorted. "I *want* to be alone, anyway. I don't need anyone. I'll resort to injuring him, if I stay beside him now, which is very unnecessary. Excuse me," I turned, treading down the passage, with rage burbling inside of my chest.

"With Gharkoll roaming around!" shrieked Nora, following me. "You would risk *us* being injured! All for a stupid action done!"

I inhaled the stale air and I stopped, hearing the pain arisen in her voice.

"Why does it bother you this much?" I retorted, swinging around. "You're frightened my brother isn't strong enough to handle Gharkoll on his own, aren't you?" I flicked my glance to Clarence on the floor and he crawled towards me.

"*I too can kill Gharkoll*," blurted Clarence, with an egotistical demeanour.

I nodded at Nora and I snapped, "There you are, there's your reassurance,"

"I don't want you to leave," she blurted, with her eyes swelling with tears and held my arm. "Stop it,"

"Nora, release me," I stated, feeling angry she had *allowed* Clarence to kiss her. "Please."

"Never," she said, sniffing from her nose.

"I need time alone," I said. "Stay close to Clarence for the moment," I deviated my glare to my brother, "Clarence, I'm dissatisfied with you."

I brashly pulled my arm away from her clutch and I strode away from them, turning into the nearest tunnel. I sighed, watching the floor skimming beneath my footsteps.

CHAPTER THIRTY-EIGHT

LOST

I felt every speleothem was a blur, slanting sideways and frontward with the feeble echo of my footsteps dilapidating the limestone debris. My fingers slithered and knocked onto the serrated stalagmites, scraping on the side of my legs and waist. I could feel my shoes splattering through a puddle in the floor, flicking driblets onto my ankles and yet, when I looked down, I saw only the cragged floor.

Where was I? What chamber?

I strode into a round opening and trembled. I didn't know. I was somewhere, I had never been before; lost in deep darkness and every wobbling footstep, was out of my control. My fingertips brushed across the sharp walls and even though my palms swept on round formations, I couldn't clasp them. The tunnel lightly churned, and the dizziness rocked in my head, like I was lying on the ship's rocking deck, after tumbling from the foretop and being washed with seawater. It was even a dangling rope from the foresail, could be my savior from this fall. I strode another step and perceived wrongly an indent to be on the left, though it was actually on the right. My shoe slipped into a deep indent and I bellowed, falling frontward and clashed my chest to the sharp floor. The impact swept pain through my ribs and groaning, I shifted on the floor, until I sat up and indolently, slouched on the wall. A cold sweat swelled in my armpits and drizzled down my chest, soaking thin runnels on my crinkled shirt and accentuated the stained dirt streaks. I yearned to change into a pristine, clean shirt and smell fresh again. I was tired of smelling with a mixture of aromas; stale rock dirt, perspiration and sea water. I stared at the denticulate wall, deep within a reverie and clutching a stone, every arm and limb, ebbed with pain and the reddened welts prickled. My mouth and throat were dry without a remnant of water sipped within a few hours. The township afar haunted me, seemingly a blur of terracotta and fawn rooftops, beneath gleams of golden sunlight with the arrival of dawn. My mouth watered at the vague memory of the burning loaves of bread put in the oval stone oven from the bakery. I remembered the ocean ripple in the distance, with twinkling specks on the surface from the beam of sunlight and inhaling the pewter waft of salty water, lathering on rotting seaweed. I wondered how my mother was, soaking dingy clothes in the iron pot and swindling them with an oak spoon, in the simmering smoke. Without my father having left, I suppose I would never have found the cave; I would never have become a boatswain on the ship, sailing afar on the sea, encountering the stormy waves. It was with the pressures of my mother to stay in labor, against my preference, increased my will to assign myself aboard. Every hardship endured on the ship, being mistreated, as a boatswain and oiling the anchor, and smearing my fingers with greasy streaks, hadn't mattered now. It was within this moment, I had felt the difficulty overwhelming me and now, being neglected inside of the darkest depths of the cave, I realized it was simplicities such as catching fish near the deck was a joy. The survival in these obscured, shadowed tunnels had shifted in all directions. I felt without finding an ending to the tunnels was worse. I was forced to being succumbed to the dark without a trace of light and it was the greatest struggle, more than, a gigantic, stormy wave engorging the bowsprit of the ship. I felt I had been thrown everywhere, battered to my core; mistreated by the people on the ship, to being pursued almost to my death by Gharkoll and even betrayed by my own brother, after all of my hard work. It felt everyone, had been controlling me to different tunnels in the cave, I didn't particularly want to be in- the darkest ones. They were willing to push me there and gain satisfaction to see me struggle and try to change me for who I was.

"No…" I muttered. "…you won't…*see me to my last fall.*"

My clasp around the stone tightened. I bellowed with a rush of fury. I plummeted the rock onto the wall and it bounced onto the ground, crackling into two pieces. I panted, tilting my head into the wall and I closed my eyes, listening to the sound of my heartbeat. This was all that mattered- I was *alive*. I was breathing and although, I was in the hypogean tunnels, nothing could falter me from *surviving*. None of their influences couldn't shatter me, until I perished in these impenetrable shadows and became a skeleton and a pile of deteriorating bones, having reached the quintessence of difficulties. I *couldn't* die in here, even after being poisoned and felt it reeling through my veins, as it contorted my thoughts to a negative state. I gnashed my teeth and I leant my shoulders away from the wall and crawled on the ground, rolling the granules beneath my knees and legs. My breaths echoed in the darkness and very slowly, I shifted, following only what felt right to me. I naively ignored the possibility of encountering another mound of porosity. If I did, the floor, beneath me, would shatter and I would die, and everyone would conquest. I arrived closer to the end and the darkness slowly faded, and an array of light-green gleams shone through the end, reflecting onto the wall. I tread through the picket crevice, the radiance shifted over my cheeks smeared with beige-dust streaks and the irritated wound scarred on my jawbone. I knew I was somewhere I shouldn't be. The presence in the cavern reeked of threat, and was somewhere, hidden in the shadows. I slowly stepped down the winding tunnel and sliding my dirt-stained fingers across the rugged wall and reaching the end, I hesitated in the opening. The red light flickered on the wall, over the saw-toothed, long stalagmites arisen from the ground. I swallowed, roaming further in the tawny smoke flooding them. I heard a loud crackling noise from beneath my shoe and I looked down at the bones. Goosebumps swept down my shoulders and arms. My eyes dodged all over the floor, amongst the picket stalagmites and I couldn't think straight. The bones were everywhere; knobs, splinters, gnawed piles of marrow and dilapidated skulls. The plumes of tawny smoke simmered and hissed, from the limestone stumps with holes in the corner of the chamber. I swallowed, and I kept treading onward, loathing all of the picket stalagmites augmenting over my shoulders. Gharkoll's heavy-throated growl echoed through the passage ahead of me. I stopped beyond the stalagmites, glaring into the dark. I tread in the opposite direction, through the archway and with lime-light flickering on the rugged wall, infested with crawling ants. I inhaled a whiff of air and tread into a small cavern. I turned and screamed-the yellow mist puffed through the skull's round hollow eyes and opened mouth of rotting, black-mottled teeth. I panted, and shortly bellowed, feeling distressed. I stepped backward into the wall, feeling my shoulders scrape onto the sharp rocks. The goosebumps crawled on my spine as if maggots lurked beneath my dank linen shirt. *I was nowhere, where I wanted to be. I observed* skeletons nestled in gooey stalagmites, dangling their bony arms and their skeletal fingers sunk into the lime pools of poison. Their mouths were agape, stained with ash speckles and their chipped ribcages were smeared with droopy, green sticky-threads sinking into the porous, lime stalagmites. They were slivered with unordinary mucus and the yellow clouds revolved, exposing the three-toed footprints on the floor. I gulped and panted. Some of them, still had flesh and moist skin peeling from the marrow of their bones. It was another mound of maggots and ants crawled on them, dissolving into the lime mucus, drooping onto the porous formation.

I screamed.

Gharkoll's silhouette skimmed on the wall of the tunnel and snarling, he appeared beneath the archway. His crowd of crimson eyes flicked in my direction and he lowered his bottom jaw of fanged teeth, echoing a hiss. The tentacles were shortened and luminescent, poking from his ears, as the glow worms. He leapt with an incessant momentum onto the boulder and back down to the ground, trundling on the debris and he unrolled his forked tongue between his two, picket teeth, spitting a lime globule of poisonous mucus. The wavering warmth spread it across the floor. I bellowed, running away from the mist. It reached me and overlapped my shoes, growing up over my ankles, calves, legs and around my waist. I swayed forward and my stomach clenched, with my rumpled shirt smearing in the wall of mucus. It prickled, engulfing all of my buttons and threads of lime mucus splintered across my shirt, dissolving the linen. I screamed and wriggled in the moist mucus and poking bone knobs, slivering into porous lime droplets over my thighs. I couldn't move, I was stuck. Gharkoll lurked closer and the thick layer of lime mucus, sprouted over my stomach to my chest and began solidifying, with the rush of radiation beaming from The Eye. I screamed, clenching my fingers and wounds swelled on my skin around my collarbone, nestling near my neck. I was trapped in the stalagmite and my skin tingled and a rush of flooding warmth lifted to my waist. The stalagmite steamed. I tilted my head and *bellowed.*

It was at the beginning of eating my flesh- it was dissolving my pants.

I quivered.

I was going to become a skeleton in the stalagmite, with the others.

"No," I puffed, with agony.

Gharkoll leapt onto the stalagmite opposite me. I screamed, eyeing his tentacles extended from his ears and they stormed into the front of my shoulders. My harried scream echoed in the cavern and scratched my throat, as my blood and runnels of fluid gushed through them. A few purple bruises appeared on my withering skin. I sloppily drooped over the stalagmite's peak in the warm, levitating yellow mist. Gharkoll bowed and trickled yellow beads from his tentacle and they dribbled onto the floor, surrounding the bulbous stalagmites. The skeletons hanging in the stalactites blurred in the roaming mist and nausea swiveled in my throat. *He was suckling, everything out of me.*

I would die.

I would never leave the cave and I'd be condemned here forever. My skeleton would protrude in the stalagmite's rock. All of my bones will be infested with crawling ants. My blood pool would stain the conulites and become arid. Everyone, who had wanted to see me loom forever in the dark would be satisfied. It was such torment and agony, purged through my soul, with the thought. I noticed my fingers shifted from pallid to light green and the stretched veins to my knuckles, darkened to turquoise-green.

"AH!" I bellowed, feeling the prickle and pinch sensation in my chest from the poison being absorbed in my blood.

Gharkoll snarling in front of me contorted and his short horns swayed and the stalactites blurred, leaving a feeble beige streak. The burbling surge of my blood in his six-tentacles, hastened into my ear drums and the writhing of the ants on the slanted skulls in the rock, flurried. They withdrew from my skin, leaving six, small holes on my skin. I collapsed my arms onto the front of the stalagmites, sinking my fingers into the rough bumps and nudged them into the dust and the stone bits. I awoke on the floor, barely breathing. My vision was still contorted, and my eyes stung, burning along the rim. They shifted to the black holes of the skull, infested with a swarm of maggots. My pacing footsteps echoed. I closed my eyes and inhaled the suffocating tendrils of yellow mist and my breaths stifled. I was still infuriated with Clarence and Nora with their betrayal against me. Every time, I thought of my brother's face, my teeth gnashed, sorrow and jealousy stung in my chest, knowing they were probably kissing each other somewhere else in the cave, while I was dying. My head pounded, and sharp pain prickled in my wounds crusted with blood surrounding them. I panicked and gazed at the broad entrance of the cavern. I saw the pointed horns, and the three-tentacles' protruding from the long, pointed ears. I double-blinked and a moist tear slivered from the corner of my watery eye, blistering as the lava stream, gurgling in the canal of the Southern caverns. I only assumed they were in that direction from the phosphorous mists. Gharkoll 's horns shrunk, the lime tentacles, pointed ears, round head and shoulders vanished. I double blinked again, and a lime glow shone, covering my sight. I hailed, until my throat itched, believing I was going to die.

CHAPTER THIRTY-NINE

THE MAGNETISED STICK

"Lower it!" hissed a familiar voice. "He's horrified!"

The light dropped and a white patch of luminance shone for a moment, until I blinked again and my perception contorted to my brother standing in front of me.

"Clarence…" I trailed, lowering my gaze to the shriveled tallow candle held in his fingers, drenched with drizzling wax.

I felt my forehead lathered in trickles of sweat. Nora appeared behind him and she shrieked at the sight of me, clapping her hands to her ruddy lips.

"What are we going to do?" exclaimed Clarence. "He's stuck in the rock!"

"We'll-we'll-," stammered Nora, crunching the debris with her pacing footsteps and skimmed her lantern's glow on the bottom of the stalagmite. "Try hauling him out first." She stopped her glow on the oozing, green moist mucus lathering the brink. "I don't know if it's poisonous and it'll affect us, as well."

"I have water here," said Clarence, pulling out a coconut from his pouch and he poured water onto the green mucus.

The puffs of green smoke floated to the ceiling and a few coils of mist drifted over my nose. I inhaled the odor and shuddered, shifting my crammed legs and knees against the interior of the curved rock.

The green mucus rolled downwards in heavy rivulets, through the rock.

"This is the solution," murmured Clarence, watching the rubble slowly crumbling to the limestone ground. "The mucus and poison crumbles with nitrogen and oxygen." He pulled out another vial and poured more water onto the front of the stalagmite. An array of light-green threads sprouted from the base and the poisoned limestone collapsed into a steaming mound of debris in front of their shoes. I groaned, rocking forwards and collapsed onto the rubble, with mucus slimed all-over the bottom of my shirt, my trousers and shoes.

"Urgh," I echoed, rubbing my palms on my crinkled trousers, stained with light-green splotches. "It's all over me."

Nora leant over and hugged my body, raising me from the ground.

"It's alright, you're going to survive." she whispered.

"Thanks for rescuing me." I mumbled, leaning my cheek on her breasts.

"You're welcome," whispered back Nora, stroking a few hairs behind my ear and rubbed her thumb on a smudged streak of crumbed rock ash on my warm cheek. "I would never have left the cave, if I had never found you again."

Clarence side-glanced at us, observing our daze with each other. "Doug, same with me." he said.

The green mist heavily drifted from the hollow stump of the stalagmite and swindled over us.

"*Growl.*"

The relief dissolved into panic, tightening my chest.

We all turned to the opposite dark archway.

Crinch-crunch.

"*Growl.*"

Clarence and Nora looked at each other with fright and they hurriedly lunged downwards and snatched my spread arms. I moaned, as they dragged me on the debris, rolling the stone bits into the bottom of the stalagmites and left a slender trail in the ochre dirt from my sliding shoes. They hurried closer towards the wide-arc entrance and stopping behind the boulder, they ducked. I rocked my cheek onto Nora's shoulder and peeked from the edge of the rock.

Gharkoll prowled through the dark archway, hauling the limp body. His long, brown skinned hand with poking thickets of fur and pointed fingernails were wrapped around the pallid-white ankle.

I recognized the tousled hair and crinkled gown on the dirt.

"It's Henrietta," I whispered.

Nora recoiled and looked away for a moment.

"This is disgusting." she murmured.

"How did she even come into the cave?" whispered back Clarence.

Gharkoll stopped, ogling the crumbled stalagmite and he yowled, probing how this was possible.

"Oh no," whispered Clarence, seizing my chest. A thin bead of sweat dripped from his dark brown hair onto his forehead and temple. "He knows...*we have to find a way out of here.*" He side-glanced at Nora. "*Quick.*"

Clarence and Nora slouched behind the boulder, hauling me on the floor of the passage. My foot nudged into a piece of stone and the crackle winded down into the chamber.

Gharkoll flicked his ear back and turning, he glared at the wide arc of the passage.

My shoe slid on the corner edge of the arc.

His bright amber-golden eyes swelled with a rosined glow and narrowed downward.

My shoe slid in the dark and out of sight.

"*Hurry,*" hissed Clarence, his face covered with sweat.

"I'm doing the best I can," snapped Nora, feeling pressured and a few black strands of her hair clamped onto her flustered cheek.

"You're not fast enough!" he snapped, with impatience.

"Have I had a moment to stop?" she argued.

I groaned and listened to them.

"You guys..." I mumbled, with parched lips.

They trampled through the round archway into the long, winding passage.

Gharkoll roamed out of the opening with the limelight, flickering on his scrawny legs, covered with thick, dark brown fur and gazed in our direction. He screeched with rage. Nora and Clarence hastened their pace, turning to the left through into another passage and a crowd of flapping bats. I yelled, as their leathery-black wings spanned in membranes whacked onto my sticky face.

Gharkoll stormed towards us.

"Now what do we do!" shrieked Nora, feeling distressed.

She flicked her gaze to the end of the tunnel, as her black hair swished onto her cheek and neck, then looked back to Clarence.

"Any ideas?" asked Nora.

"Fire?" suggested Clarence.

I moaned, feeling nauseous from the hauling of my arms and the vivid movement. I glanced back over my shoulder.

"*Crea-ture...*" I mumbled.

They turned and yelled at Gharkoll screeching and curling his claws, with his tentacles, wavering as serpents in mid-air. Clarence and Nora hurried through the opening and both of them heavily panted, short of breath and with flustered cheeks.

I bounced on the floor.

Gharkoll's large eye in his forehead emitted dashes of grey-wind and the debris hurled at us in the tunnel. Nora and Clarence both yelled, bowing beneath the crashing rock on the walls and they disintegrated into mounds. They trampled into the nearest speleothem chamber and hauled me up a hewn, slender staircase poking from the wall and the limestone. I groggily moaned and coughed, as my shoulder rubbed on the layer of dust and they stopped. I lay there and Clarence opened his pouch, pulling his matchbox out and lifted a slender match. He swiped it on the side of the box, sparkling an iridescent, tawny flame.

"Is it going to stop him?" asked Nora.

"We have to try," implored Clarence. "We need sticks."

"Yes," agreed Nora, standing up from the ground. "Let's block the entrances by inflaming them."

They descended the stairwell and Clarence almost slipped on the bottom two stairs, swishing dust from his shoes and they gathered odd twigs as quickly, as they could. Nora rolled a pile in front of the North-West opening and inflamed them. Clarence wasn't quick enough, Gharkoll stormed through the opening.

I inhaled the musty, stale rock air and gathered the last of my breath and remnant of strength.

"Clarence! Behind you!" I yelled.

My head fell back down.

Clarence inflamed a twig and swiped around too late.

Gharkoll screeched with enmity, stretching saliva between his picket teeth and the warm tentacles' coiled around his wrist, oozing yellow driblets and reddened his skin.

"ARGH!" screamed Clarence, poking the fire into his furred torso.

Gharkoll 's screech lifted to a penetrating high notch, quivering the sta lactites and the hidden bats dropped from the ceiling and flew in a flock around them.

Clarence swiped the fire sputtering on the stick, back and fourth.

"Get away from me!" he exclaimed.

The bats screeched and soared through the archway. Nora screamed and trampled away, as they flew into the tunnel, whipping their wings on her hair, arms, back and cheeks.

I flicked my gaze back to my brother.

Clarence swiped the inflamed stick towards him and gnashed his teeth.

"Die! You monstrous vermin!" he yelled.

"*Growl!*" bellowed Gharkoll, swiping his claw through the golden yellow-tawny flames and his three tentacles poking from his ear, extended to the wall and pinched mounds of rock and threw it at him.

Clarence bowed, dodging them and the rubble showered onto the floor, exploding in whiffs of dust. He lifted the inflamed stick and side-stepped towards him.

"You poisoned my brother! Take this-," he yelled, stepping further and poked him.

Gharkoll echoed a high-notched scream, as his torso inflamed.

Nora scowled, trampling out of the tunnel back into the cavern and blurred behind the heat haze, as she neared my brother's pouch. She poured dynamite powder inside an empty coconut. Gharkoll noticed me lying at the summit of the staircase. Clarence leapt on the stairs, blowing whirls of dust from his shoes, swiping the fire and leaving a trail of tawny smoke.

"Stay away from my brother! Otherwise, I'll kill you!!" he bellowed.

Gharkoll echoed a louder growl, swiping his claw through the fire.

"I mean it!" yelled Clarence, barricading the stick in front of himself. "I've had enough of you!" He poked the fire into his eyes.

Gharkoll screeched, breezing silver-threads of wind from his One Eye and they flickered the flames away from the stick to the side wall. Clarence gasped, lifting the burnt stick puffing whiffs of steam to the ceiling. Nora climbed onto the nearest rock and hurled the inflamed coconut.

"That's for hurting me before!" she exclaimed.

Gharkoll recoiled, as the coconut bounced onto his furred shoulder and onto the ground, exploding rubble. The ground and walls quivered, as a large mound of dust soared across the cavern. I grunted, covering my arm across my face and leant on the rugged ground, tasting the rock dirt. Clarence wobbled and losing balance, he tumbled down the fleet of stairs and crouched against the wall. The stick tumbled to the floor. Gharkoll crouched and shrunk his tentacles, until they poked short from his ears. He wailed from the stinging of the crowded eyes on his beige wrinkled forehead and he trampled out of the opening, through the shadowed tunnel. I lowered my arm from my face and looked over my shoulder. Clarence echoed a loud cough and writhing on the floor, he stretched out his arm and clasped the stick. Clarence enraged, jumped from the staircase and lowering the flame to the mound of sticks, the fire erupted in front of the archway. He panted and wiped his hand onto his forehead, brushing sweat away, and his crinkled sleeve rolled to his elbow.

"I loathe him," he snapped, eyeing Gharkoll's short, beige horns and ears blurring in the simmering, tawny smoke to the rugged wall.

"Me too," said Nora, pacing towards him. "Let's help your brother."

Clarence turned, hearing her footsteps climbing the staircase. He shifted back to me. I heard him scavenging inside of their pouches. Nora clamped a coconut to my partially opened mouth and drained water rivulets into my throat. I swallowed them. Clarence pulled out a cap from a vial and tearing a piece of cotton from his sleeve, he scrunched it into a ball and dabbed it with the antidote, then onto my stomach and wiped away the mucus. I screamed at the pinching sensation and it reddened from the reaction.

"We need to seriously find a way out of here, from this cavern," said Clarence.

"I know," agreed Nora.

"Compass," I said, weakly.

"No," argued Clarence, looking down at me. "We're not having this argument again."

"Twig," I said.

"What twig?" he asked, confused.

"Just rest first," demanded Nora.

"He's not making any sense," said Clarence.

The drowsiness overwhelmed my eyes and they both blackened away, as I fell into a deep slumber with a twig in my thoughts. It was several days later, on the twenty-ninth of August, I awoke and I hadn't forgotten about the twig. I overheard my brother down below,

"We don't know which way South is from here. That's the problem, and I really do wish the compass was working properly."

I rubbed my eyes and sat up from the floor, clutching the wall and descended the staircase to the bottom of the cavern.

"I know a way," I said.

They both turned.

"You're awake!" said Nora, beaming and she hugged me.

I wrapped an arm around her shoulders and we tread across the cavern and I sat on the boulder.

I picked up a twig from the floor. "We can use this to help us," I explained.

Clarence groaned. "How?" he asked.

I smiled and elaborated, "We need the round metal knob from the leather diary,"

"We do?" he asked, slouching and lifting my bulgy, canvas bag. He dropped it to my shoes, blowing dust across my ankles.

"Yes," I said, pulling out the diary onto my lap and tugging on the round, aluminum piece, I put it in the iron pot and tread across the cavern to the flames.

Clarence and Nora exchanged a glance.

"What are you doing?" he blurted.

"Melting the aluminum," I said, watching it ooze into a silver pool. Clarence and Nora stood beside me and peered over my shoulder. "You see, naturally there's magnetism on the earth and in the winds. All we need is a needle to be a compass and guide us to the South. If I left the round knob to be the way it is, it's not going to float on water, it's going to obviously drop." I pulled the iron pot away from the flames and dipped the twig inside of the melted metal. "All we need is something small, like a sewing needle, though because we don't have one, this is the only option. It now can be magnetized and will float on water." I glanced at them. "Who has coconut water?"

"I do," said Nora, slowly and pulling out the coconut from her pouch, she gave it to me. "It's the last one."

"That's alright, don't worry, we're not going to need to refill them." I said.

I unplugged the green piece of bamboo, yellowed from the sun and treading around the cavern. Clarence and Nora followed behind me, wondering why I was perusing the floor, opposite the hollow opening. I lifted my hand and felt the breeze tingling my fingers.

"What are you looking for?" asked Clarence.

"Something to fill," I said, and stopped, spotting one in the middle of the cavern.

I knelt down and poured the water from the coconut into the deep curvature in the rocky floor. I rubbed the solidified aluminum around the twig, magnetizing it and dropped it into the puddle. Clarence and Nora crowded around me and we watched the magnetized needle twig, slowly whirring around on the rippling surface and align itself with the Earth's magnetic field. The needle stopped its revolving motion, with the North and South axis.

I pointed to the staircase protruding from the wall. "This is North," I explained, looking over my shoulder to the shadowed archway, "Meaning, in this direction, it's South."

"You were attentive to science, weren't you?" he asked.

"That's what I read at night by our fireplace," I explained, rising from the floor and slapping him in the back. "Let's get out of here."

"There must be lava in the southern caverns," I whispered, feeling my cheeks fluster from the blowing warmth in the cragged tunnel.

CHAPTER FOURTY

RED-TAWNY
MAGMA SMOKE

I stepped into the Southern magma chambers on the thirtieth day and observed they were different to the caverns in the upper story. The last wide walls of the tunnels shifted from limestone into scarlet rock and an enormous hall. I observed the golden light flickered onto the red rock and tawny-orange stalagmites with beige limestone patches on their dimples and ash-specked peaks. I knew time was running short; we had less than an hour before the volcano erupted and found the suspected crevice leading back to the island. The crimson and yellow magma pools in the craters burbled and sputtered driblets, flecking onto the walls and reflected a red luminance onto the sharp, slender stalagmites. The floor quivered. I looked down and watched the cracks spread and the whiffs of red and orange smoke soared out of the ground, billowing over my legs and mouth. I coughed beneath my hand and followed the glistening beam of tawny light spread on the rugged floor. We ventured through an archway and into a small, secluded cavern. Nora, Clarence and I, lowered our lips, as we gazed at the twinkling crystals with a lucid gleam molded in the denticulate walls.

I skimmed my fingers across them. My heart lightly pounded in my chest.

I glimpsed over my shoulder. "Clarence, we won't have to be poor anymore." I whispered.

"No, we won't," whispered Clarence, clutching a rotund crystal poking from the wall. He expelled a short breath and he traced the sharp contours with his finger. He squatted and opened his hessian sack and wriggled the small crystals on the lower level of the wall. "Can we call this The Crystal Cavern?"

"Yes," I answered, skimming the firelight on the long, slender selenite molded in the magma.

Nora knelt down beside him and slouched forward with a grin. She lifted the clusters of selenite crystal in-between her fingers and stared closely.

"I wonder how much they are worth," she whispered. "Nobody would have seen them."

"Definitely," I echoed, still under a daze and curiously tread onward beneath the crystalized, white dripstones in the ceiling.

I stretched out my inflamed stick, illuminating the narrow tunnel and the distance at the end of the passage. A faint gleam of emerald light shone onto the wall. I arrived at the round opening and I stopped, gaping at the tall, ochre stalagmite in the back of the cavern with a varnished, gleaming emerald protruding in the peak. It wasn't like every other stalagmite and had a regal presence, as if it had a hidden ecological, essence inside of the limestone. I heard the cacophony of rolling rubble, a swing of pouches and crunching debris behind me. I glimpsed over my shoulder. Clarence and Nora hindered behind me at the front entrance. I raised the wavering, tawny and golden firelight.

"What is it?" asked Clarence.

"I don't know," I said.

I tread closer to the stalagmite and stepped on the slanted mount of rock. I traced the sharp emerald and as I suspected, a whirring sensation tingled my fingers. The emerald flared a golden, lucid glow. I gasped, feeling startled and broadened my eyes. I swished my hand away and stepping backwards, I noticed there wasn't a crevice in the wall. A gust of wind burst from the emerald and swiveled, rolling the loose debris on the ground.

"What's happening?" whispered Nora, alarmed and tread backward, clutching my arm. "Let's find a way out of here."

"Wait," I said, flicking my gaze back to the emerald in the stalagmite and the light spread onto the back cragged wall.

A round archway dissolved and revealed a crimson terrain. We huddled together, open-mouthed and double-blinked our eyes. The orange fog blew across the stalagmite. I felt breathless and my heart throbbed. I looked back to my brother and Nora.

"I'll have a closer look." I whispered.

"No, what if it's dangerous?" asked Clarence, flicking his gaze to me and back to the archway.

"I have too," I said.

Nora loosened her clasp around my sleeve. "Be careful." she whispered.

"I will," I echoed, treading on the debris and shifted closer to the portal.

I tread closer to the glistening stalagmite. My shoes were engulfed with the flourished tawny smoke and a surge of carbon dioxide filled The Crystal Cavern. I looked out at the crimson terrain and the enormous, serrate speleothems.

"It's another planet." I realised.

"It can't be," said Clarence, treading across the floor and peered past the archway, gripping the edge of crusted rock and coughed, "No way."

"Didn't you ever remember reading the rock is red on Mars? The rocks in this section of the cave are the same. They have traces of iron oxide and this makes them appear red." I said. "The volcanic, basalt rock is also on Mars. We're in the *island's* volcano."

"What are you suggesting?" retorted Clarence. "Gharkoll is from Mars?"

"*Yes*," I said. "Didn't you ever notice he preferred to dwell in hot caverns, because he needs large clouds of carbon dioxide to survive? Why else did he dwell in here for years and became a troglobite? It's what I told you before, he loathes our atmosphere's nitrogen and oxygen, because Mars has different air and it's carbon dioxide. He's forced to survive by living in here and this is why he's The Cave Dweller."

"He hates water…anything cold…" trailed Clarence.

"This is *why*, he swallows lava and absorbs chemical energy from the rock. It seems crystals have the ability to open hidden portals." I probed.

"Well let's lure him here," stated Clarence. "And move him *out*,"

"*Oh no,*" said Nora, bossily. "We *aren't doing this suggestion,* we're continuing to the south and we're almost there."

The glow shining from the emerald shrunk into the stalagmite and with a swivel of tawny and grey mist, the crimson and volcanic, basalt plain of Mars vanished. I observed our cheeks reddened and our eyes moistened. We were barely able to breathe from the surge of carbon dioxide and we rushed out of The Crystal Cavern through the round archway. The further we tread to the end of the tunnel, we were relieved to inhale a whiff of oxygen and nitrogen.

"See and for us, it's the opposite," I said, with a grin. "We'd never survive there and that's how he feels, roaming on the island. Which is why now, I remember during the first night, I saw his shadow on our sail tents. Gharkoll too, must've heard the explosion of the ship and seen the golden flames from afar and us, rowing to the shoreline. He trampled back inside the cave, because he would've died." I looked to the opposite end of the tunnel. "We should keep heading South. I can smell traces of leafage amongst the lava."

An eruption of red-tawny magma smoke billowed through the opening and whirled into the cavern and the walls trembled. I coughed and screamed, as my cheeks flustered and my heart thrummed.

I heard a *crack* noise above me.

CHAPTER FOURTY-ONE

QUIVERING SPELEOTHEMS

The quivering speleothems dropped from the ceiling towards me. I bellowed, eyeing their points and one by one, they collided onto the floor, rupturing a surge of beige dust and it breezed over my legs. I screamed, gliding backwards and thudded to the dilapidated rubble on the ground. I looked watery-eyed over my shoulder and watched the rubble hurling into the walls. I knew there was only forty minutes left and all of us stood, trampling beneath the showering stone bits from the ceiling. It was after a cloud of beige dust cleared, we trampled through into another tunnel. The descent in the gallery was bumpy and we tread on the round, small conulites in the slanted, rocky ground and they pressed into our shoe soles. I observed the sunken sediments would eventually grow a crowd of stalagmites. I was satisfied I had finally found the tunnel leading South into the cave, rather than upwards and in the opposite direction. When we reached the bottom, we arrived into a large chamber and we all crowded at the edge of the doline, staring down into the long, dark funnel with a red glow flickering on the rocks at the bottom.

It felt like my heart leapt into my mouth.

The thick, whiffs of red smoke drifted upward and lurked across the chiseled stone bits on the floor. A wide hole was in the ceiling and a frail shaft of sunlight shone onto the wall. I sighed and thought of the sunken climbing equipment back in the quicksand pool.

"Are you sure, we want to go down there?" asked Clarence, peering down.

"Isn't there another way out of the cave?"

"No," I said. "The only way out is South."

Nora knelt and waved a hand through the red mist and glanced at me.

"It's going to be warm down there, I hope we survive the heat." she said.

I unrolled the rope ladders and they dropped into the long, dark funnel of the doline. I placed a copper nail inside of the loops and using a hatchet, I lowered them into the rocky floor, splintering cracks around my shoe.

"There," I said, wiping my hand on my forehead. "This should do it."

I exhaled and leant over, gazing down the doline. My arms stiffened and flecked with goosebumps at the sight of the vast darkness awaiting me. I softly recoiled and my fingers tingled, as my palms swelled a cold, clammy sweat from my inner fright. *I can't believe I suggested this*, I thought. *I, myself, am afraid of descending such a funnel.* The long, silhouetted vacuity forced my stomach to churn and the longer I stared, the more I felt dizzy and I was going to fall forward.

"Douglas!" exclaimed Nora, clutching my shoulders.

I fell onto the floor and my heart thudded palpitations in my chest. I felt sweat drizzle underneath my brown tresses and they matted to my forehead. Nora knelt beside me and held my hand.

I winced.

She looked at me offended.

I glimpsed at her hand, then at the hole.

"Are you alright?" asked Nora.

The dizziness didn't disappear and swindled.

I rubbed my head. "I don't know if I can," I admitted

"*You can.*" asserted Nora.

I rubbed her thumb. I wasn't showing any more of my fright in my stiffened cheeks and eyes. I gathered the last remnant of my courage and gazed up at her.

"You're right, I will." I said.

Clarence appeared beside me and gently nudged my shoulder. *How was I going to loosen it when we reached the bottom? What if we need the rope ladders again to leave the cave?* I wondered, eyeing the knots of rope.

I diverted my gaze to our belongings.

"Clarence, you take the water flasks and I'll carry my pouch." I decided, glancing at Nora, "You can hold the last of our provisions."

"No," she argued. "You were poisoned by Gharkoll and you can allow me carry the tools?"

"I won't allow you," I said, pressing my palms to the warm rocky floor and already, I could feel the lava's heat sinking and simmering from down below. "They're too heavy and it's for me to carry. I won't risk it."

"What about the ropes?" asked Clarence, eyeing them on the floor. "I'll carry those," he stepped around the brim of the doline. He slid the ropes up his arm and looped them onto his shoulder, tying a knot. "What's going to happen to the rope ladders after we reach the bottom?"

"I was thinking the same," I admitted. "We're going to have to leave them behind, or, maybe midway down the dark funnel, if there's a piece of jutting stone in the wall, we could tie a rope around it and then, I'll have to climb up and cut the rope ladder and then using the singular rope, I'll climb back down."

"It's a good idea," said Clarence, "Or, do you think we won't need it?"

"I can't presume anything, just yet," I said, avoiding the periphery of the doline.

I circled around it and inspected the inner, shadowed walls, trying to spot a jutting rock. I stopped midway, noticing one poking out near a jagged cleft.

I pointed downwards, "There, that one." I said.

I tread to our belongings and retrieved a coiled rope and the other rope ladder. I hammered it into the ground and after dropping it, I put the pack of tools onto my back. I clutched the rope ladder tightly and began to descend passively into the funnel. I glanced over my shoulder and ensured my foot didn't miss one of the slouching chords. Nora and Clarence began descending on the other ladder opposite mine. My hands had a subtle tingle and felt shaky, with every lowering step. *Don't look down,* I thought, concentrating on the shadowed, curved rock wall skimming downward. *You can do this, just don't look down…*the temptation prickled inside of me. I glimpsed over my shoulder again into the long, dark tunnel and my stomach revolved. I felt dizzy and I stopped, tightening my grasp around the rope ladder. I uncontrollably quivered and sweat drizzled on my back and stained my dirt-smeared, crinkled shirt. I squeezed my eyes closed and inhaled the warmth, gusting from the lower cavern.

"Douglas!" yelled Nora, from the opposite wall and over her shoulder. "What's wrong?"

"Nuh-*nothing*," I stammered, closing my eyes and I reopened them, inhaling a whiff of air.

I lowered myself to the next rope. *If I fall now, well this whole exploration inside of the cave and trying to survive Gharkoll , was a waste of time. I might as well have been bitten and engorged by Gharkoll himself. I have to concentrate and I have to make it to the bottom-,* I snapped out of my thoughts, noticing I had arrived at the jutting stone near the cleft. I was relieved and stopped, dragging the rope down my left arm with the rope ladder staying in-between my armpit. I tied a knot around the rock and the rope dropped whipping the curved wall. I continued descending into the shadows and my foot slipped.

"*Ah!*"

The sound of my cry reverberated up the funnel and my shoes dangled in mid-air in the dark. I loathed the worst of the situation was happening to me. I felt the fatigue pull in my arms and I was tempted to release my clutch and fall into the darkness, though, I gritted my teeth and reopened my eyes, glaring into the shaft of sunlight shining through the hole in the ceiling. A swivel of bats flapped upwards through the doline and screeched, soaring through the hole. I envied they could fly easily out of the cave without any struggle.

"Douglas!" shrieked Nora. "Are you alright?"

"No!" I confessed. "I'm not! However, we're going to make it-," I stopped abruptly, noticing Gharkoll 's head poking at the round brink of the doline. His bright, red eyes gleamed with an evil twinkle down at us.

I raised my voice, "*No!*"

Gharkoll 's head disappeared from sight. I heard the familiar scurrying footsteps around the doline, blowing dust over the outskirt into the funnel. I bowed my head, feeling the dust motes sink into my hair and shoulders. My heart thudded louder into my ears with the growth of fright inside of me.

"He's *here!*" I yelled.

Now it was a race of who could reach the bottom first before we all died from Gharkoll . My rope quivered and the right side of my ladder swung forward, leaning the other end into the wall. A long driblet of saliva dashed splatted onto my hair and shoulder, trickling onto my chest. I recoiled and loathed the trickling, sticky sensation and looked back up to see the rolling stones skid across from Gharkoll 's furry, clawed foot.

I heard moist biting noises echo from afar.

"He's *chewing* my rope…" I trailed, widening my eyes with fright.

The one side of my rope ladder dropped and rapidly swung forward. I hollered and my shoes knocked into the wall. I dangled in mid-air, holding the left side of the rope ladder, thwacking and skimming across the curved wall.

"Douglas!" yelled Clarence.

"Oh no!" echoed Nora, after him. "What should we do! Should I climb back up?"

"No!" I bellowed, feeling my heart race in my chest. "*Gharkoll -*," I stopped, as the rope ladder suddenly dropped. My voice lifted to the top of my throat, "*Ah!*" I fell into the dark and the driblet of saliva on my nose trickled into my mouth.

The sour taste of Gharkoll 's saliva dissolved into my tongue.

"*Urgh!*" I yelled.

"*Douglas!*" roared Clarence and Nora at once.

I felt my body falling and the rope tangled around my legs. I kicked the ladder and heard it flap to the ground. A thick explosion of fiery and golden smoke puffed up at the bottom of the funnel. I felt the flush of heat wave over my legs. I yelled a notch louder and my fingertips swiped on the other spare rope. I grabbed it, swinging in the air and my arm bumped into the wall and re-bounded. I wiped the layer of sweat from my forehead and the rope tangled around my right leg. I was relieved and holding the rope, I leant it against my cheek and hung there for a moment to catch my breath.

"He's alive!" I heard my brother's voice reverberating above me.

"I am!" I said.

Only just...

"Do you want us to climb down at the same time?" asked Nora.

"No," I said. "Just keep moving. Don't wait for me!"

I pressed my shoes onto the wall and resumed descending the tunnel and after a few more steps, I was shocked to see the terrain and a large, lava pool levitating orange and red mist.

"Be careful, when you reach down here!" I exclaimed, gazing over my shoulder. *"There's lava!"*

"This explains the explosion," echoed Nora's voice.

I waited patiently for them to climb down and reach the ground and wiped my sleeve across my forehead, dissolving the beads of sweat. We tread around the lava pool venturing into a molten-lava rock tunnel and stopped inside a cavern with three archways leading further into other passages.

"Not this again," groaned Clarence.

"The middle one," I said, pointing to the round opening with hovering red whiffs of smoke and inhaled the warm air. "I smell the salted scents from the ocean-water amongst the heat."

I tread inside and we observed the dried magma shawls and splintering cracks on the walls, provoking our terror- slender, golden lava spilled down-ward. At the end, the passage curved and there was a flicker of red light. The suffocating, mild warmth, arose into blistering heat, drenching streams of perspiration on our shoulders and back. We turned left and stepped out of the tunnel into a ginormous chamber. We gaped, not expecting to see what was down below. There were tall, gigantic, orange stalagmites circling the burbling, lava pools inside the craters, festering red steam and they were scattered on the scarlet, rocky ground. In front of us, was a pair of thick, splattermites towering to the ceiling on either side of the winding staircase. I descended the steps and it was only reaching midway, I saw the small, shadowed archway in the distance, leading back to the island.

"There it is!" I yelled, pointing to the other side. Clarence and Nora followed the direction of my finger. "We've finally made it!"

"Okay, everyone, be careful," announced Nora, anxiously, not liking how we had to move around the lava craters. "Stay close!"

Clarence and Nora passively stepped around them. The flickering, red shadows moved on our flushed cheeks and legs and reflected onto the bottom stair. It was midway across The Lava Pool Cavern, a growl echoed from above the staircase. We all swiped around to see Gharkoll emerging at the summit and he thumped down each stair, shifting his lime-tentacles through the red, orange and golden mists.

"Run!" I yelled, panicking, he would kill us, before we reached the other side.

Gharkoll stomped amongst the lava craters and prowled around the large, beige, stalagmites. It was halfway, my face was lathered in sweat. I peered over my shoulder and the plumes of scorching, red, golden and orange mists revolved and unveiled an empty, red terrain.

Gharkoll had disappeared.

"No," I muttered, looking to the opposite side and resumed trampling past another two lava craters. "Where is he?"

Clarence and Nora trampled to the end of the chamber and stopped in the middle of the last paired, lava craters. The Creature strode out of the golden mists in front of them. He blocked the arch and floated clouds of

dust around his three-toed feet. Nora hollered, and Clarence yelled, blocking his arm around her. They stepped backwards with their cheeks lathered in oily sweat and gashes of dried, crimson blood. I didn't feel afraid of Gharkoll anymore. I pulled out the chloride bottle from my pocket and I separated myself from them. I boldly strode towards him, mustering the last remnant of my courage inside of me. I frowned my brows and the welts on my cheeks burned and my body ached. I felt the dizziness swindle in my and head and the wavering flames blurred. I fiercely strode through the scorching plumes of mists. *I wouldn't be defeated, he had put me through too much. I had been poisoned close to death. I wouldn't die in here now from fear. It was his turn to encounter the Troglomorphism- anything from the dark could fester more darkness upon themselves.* I felt invincible, careless of dying or living with the only intention of defeating Gharkoll and what had caused such controversy in the cave after I hadn't bothered him. *I was going to escape the darkness, no matter how much pain he had given me. I decided it was with every inner and outer wound on my skin, they wouldn't be a scar of conceding to failures. They would be of strength where I obstinately conquered them.* I pulled the cork and hurled it to the ground and it bounced near my shoe. I lifted the bottle righteously and threw driblets onto the rocky ground. Gharkoll screeched, as the heated, thick smoke flourished in front of him. He winced and crouched, protruding the chestnut-brown fur from his back and the lime glow flickered on his tentacles. His crowd of eyes, squeezed closed and he curled his claws, sinking them into his palms. *I wanted to see him smolder in lava, hear him screech for a change with the same equivalent amount of pain, he had put me through in the cave amongst this cloud of infuriation.*
I remembered Clarence and Nora.

I turned and looked over my shoulder.

"Run!" I yelled, swiping my hand towards the arch. "Quick!"

"Are you crazy?" yelled Clarence.

"*Listen to me!*" I roared.

Clarence and Nora trampled around the right, small crater and they reached the archway. They waited, peeking from the side of the wall.

"*Douglas!*" called Clarence, swaying his hand airily. "What are you doing? *We have to leave!*"

I ignored him and pulled out the dynamite. I maneuvered Gharkoll slowly backwards by flicking more driblets of water into the puffs of red smoke levitating from the lava craters. Clarence's eyes broadened at the sight of the dynamite and he ushered Nora back inside of the tunnel.

I heard his voice echo, "*Stay here.*"

"I don't want too!" argued Nora. "I want to help!"

"You have too! He's going to blow up Gharkoll and the entire chamber!" exclaimed Clarence, peeking from the arch and cupped his hands around his mouth. "Douglas! *Stop!* Just leave Gharkoll !"

Gharkoll drooled poison from the corners of his mouth and they dripped to the floor, beside his furred feet. He lowered his bottom jaw, stretching threads of green poison in-between his glinting fangs and they drooped from his slimy gums. Gharkoll emerged closer towards me and his large, middle eye brightened to the shade of gold, infested with red veins from fury. I gnashed my teeth and clashed the chloroform to the ground and thick puffs of white, red, orange and yellow vapor surrounded his body and skinny, furred legs. He hollered and coiled his tentacles into his earlobes. His two, large, yellow eyes and the gleaming red crowd on his forehead, squeezed shut. Gharkoll thumped backward towards the lava pool and he curled his claws into fists.

"Douglas!" yelled Clarence, hindering at the arch. "Stop! It's dangerous!"

"*I know what I'm doing!*" I yelled, with the highest-notch possible and con-centrated my glare onto Gharkoll .

The wall beside me collapsed, blustering fire into the ceiling and rubble hurled towards me, undulating clouds of tawny smoke.

I screamed and raised my arms in the heat.

CHAPTER FOURTY-TWO

LAVA PITS

I leapt across the cleft in the magma rock and bellowed. The flames soared across the ground, burning the magma and the ash. A gust of warmth flapped my fringe on my forehead covered with trickled streams of sweat. I felt survival was impossible and time was thinning to less than half an hour. The ceiling rumbled; granules showered from the ceiling and dissolved into the lava craters, bursting steam. I lifted the red barreled dynamite into my mouth and struck a match, crackling golden sparks. My heart thudded with bouncing nerves inside of my stomach. I stepped backwards and threw the dynamite into the small crater. An explosion of lava soared into the air. I ran and hid behind the nearest quivering boulder and peeked from the edge.

Gharkoll stood amidst the crimson lava and peered up with his group of eyes. He rolled his glowing, lime tentacles out from his long ears. The thick, golden-red droplets of lava lathered onto his short fawn-brown horns and his brown thickets of fur. Gharkoll echoed a loud guttural screech and swayed his arms outward, curling his long fingers into his palms. A couple of frail streamlets of lava drizzled on his wrinkled forehead and splattered onto his furred body. Gharkoll double-blinked his eyes and coils of steam floated from them, as rivulets of yellow blood oozed down his crinkled nose. I dashed back to the archway with the debris falling from the ceiling and colliding onto my shoulders.

I bowed into the tunnel and abruptly stopped.

"*Are you this foolish?*" exclaimed Clarence.

"It had to be done!" I argued, turning back to see if Gharkoll was dead.

Gharkoll wailed, while his tentacles unrolled and jutted back out of his ears, widening yellow shields of light and they diminished the falling lava into smoky coils. I gaped. Gharkoll swayed and side-stepped around the lava pools. His crowd of eyes on his forehead, squeezed shut and his tongue loosely unrolled in-between his picket teeth. A remnant of lava burned into the side of Gharkoll 's torso and he burst a guttural screech, as the lava dissolved a tuft of fur and swelled a reddened welt. His lime tentacles leaked droplets of poison and it trickled from yellow to a gooey, dark green substance, denoting his injury and they pooled into the carbonate acid water. The lava dripped from the stalactites. They swelled and a dark-green, sticky stalagmite with stretching yellow threads sprouted from the ground. Gharkoll side-stepped inside, as it molded around him.

I gaped.

"Douglas!" yelled Clarence's voice from the arch. "Come on! What are you waiting for? *Hurry!*"

Boom

The wall rumbled and shook. The pool continued spreading on the ground. I watched, as another array of slimy stalagmites grew in the pools amongst the seething, whiffs of red and yellow mist, as the lava driblets flicked everywhere from the pits. I felt a hand tugging my shoulder and shirt, grappling me away and stones showered from the ceiling, falling onto my head. The walls and the floor rumbled, as we dodged falling rubble.

"What were you doing?" exclaimed Clarence. "Trying to get killed!?"

"Gharkoll !" I screamed. "It didn't work!"

"What do you mean?" he yelled.

I threw a thumb over my shoulder and explained, "He disappeared! He turned and hid himself into a stalagmite!"

Clarence returned me a doubtful glare. "You're kidding, right?" he yelled.

"*No!*" I exclaimed, dodging a portion of descended rock from the ceiling and a sheet of dust.

We passed beneath the vaulted archways formed in the long endless passage. "I don't know what he's done! All I know is the chloroform only poisons ordinary animals and only affected Gharkoll *a little bit*! I thought he'd encounter a troglomorphism!"

"*A what*?"

"Never-mind!" I yelled, over my shoulder. "I just read it in The Speleologist's diary!"

We reached the entrance of the tunnel. I almost fainted at the sight of the slender beam of afternoon, golden daylight shining through the hole. I smelt the familiar drifts of salted, sandy beach air and the canopy's lush, leafy scent, churning with the burning carbon dioxide and sulphate. We bowed out of the back onto the cliff, I panted and wiped the paste of sweat on my reddened cheeks with my palm.

"We're finally out of the cave!" I exclaimed, inhaling a large whiff of fresh air with the scents of the withered and verdant leaves and the salty ocean water.

"Wait, you're telling me, Gharkoll *isn't* dead?" exploited Clarence, in panic. I dismissed my sudden frustration of not killing him entirely, distracted with the beauty of the verdant canopy, the creaking boughs and the huddled coconuts clinging to the palm trees above.

"It doesn't matter, we're out of the cave!" I exclaimed.

"But-," stammered Clarence, skimming his fingers through his hair. "what-if-," he stopped, as the floor vibrated and a crack elongated in the rocky ground.

The volcano looming closely, puffed red smoke into the horizon and an explosive *boom* echoed. The thick, long, golden-red streams of lava drenched down the dark peak. Clarence, Nora and I, peered over our shoulders and hurried the descending slope, shuffling into the brittle weeds, dirt and grasses, as the plumes of smoke drifted above the palm trees. I coughed and my eyes stung, watering from the lofting heat. We trampled further on the steep hill, dashing underneath the branches and green leaves, swishing on our necks. My shoe sunk into the soil and although, I was pleased it wasn't rock, I teetered, swaying my arms and was ignorant of dropping my pouch of dynamite powder. Clarence and Nora trampled into a huckleberry bush and they stopped. I heard the rush of lava flooding the tree boles and burning the bark, sticks and leaves, emerging closer towards me. I wriggled my boot in the soil and I pulled it out. Clarence hauled my arm and I collided into him, stepping into the foliage.

"Thanks," I puffed, glancing back to the lava steaming the slope.

"No worries," he said, clapping my shoulder and smiled.

Boom!

The dynamite powder exploded a cloud of dirt in the air, covering the verdant leafy palm trees and over us. We screamed and rolled down the slope to the dried foliage. The scorching, golden yellow lava pooled closer and engorged all of the dropped shrubs and burned the tree boles, erupting smoke. Nora, Clarence and I stood from the ground, flicking the dirt from our crumpled clothes. The lava pooled down the slope. We dashed to the east, hurrying through the verdure and the lush leaves whacked across our legs and arms. I panted, choking on the smoke and emerged into the thinning, grove of palm trees. I stopped and heard a noise.

"Wait," I declared, spreading my arms.

Nora and Clarence halted from continuing to run further.

"Douglas, *but-*," began Clarence, preparing to argue and he quietened.

He heard the same noise and he diverted his glare to the southern grove of palm trees. I peered down the foothill and listened to the trickling water, hidden in the depths of the clustered bushes.

"Water?" he asked.

I nodded.

We all exchanged a glare and trampled downward, flinging dirt from our shoes and bowing under a branch, we stepped through paired ferns. The waterfall gushed from the streamlet into the wet boulders huddled in the pool with thick mist and white froth floating on the surface.

"A *waterfall!*" yelled Clarence, trampling into the soggy piles of mud and splashed into the stream amongst the separated puddles.

"*Water!*" shrieked Nora, leaping over the ledge and she splashed into the pool. She stood underneath the waterfall, wetting her dark hair and it clamped to her shoulders.

Clarence filled his empty flask and drank mouthfuls, until watery driblets trickled on the side of his lips. He dropped it to the grasses and scooping a pool of water into his hands, he splashed a heap onto his face and laughed. The sweat and dirt smudged on his cheeks washed away. I dived into the pool and arose from the surface, stretching a grin on my lips.

"How many hours without water?" I asked.

"Don't even think about it," said Clarence, splashing a wave of water into my waist.

We laughed.

I felt the gash sting after it was left behind from Gharkoll with the instant touch of water. I swam back to the edge of the stream and noticed the cliff jutting in the forest. I stood in the water, feeling curious to see the view and lifted myself onto the brittle grasses. I climbed up the hill and tread though the palm trees and emerged out onto the precipice of the cliff, inhaling the fresh air scented with the salty ocean and lush leaves grown on the branches, without the stale rock aroma from the cave. My wavy, brown hair rustled around my ears and tapped onto my jawbone. I observed in the distance, the tilted stern and solid-oak mast with the remainder of the deck and bowsprit from the ship, poking from the ripples on the surface of the turquoise-blue sea.

My heart sunk into dread.

We were finally free, yet, how would we ever leave the island?

CHAPTER FOURTY-THREE

BACK TO THE ISLAND

At four o'clock in the afternoon, the golden sun in the horizon lingered behind the puffy, white clouds and shone it's fading rays onto the eastern periphery of the dark brown volcano's peak. They illuminated the cragged contours, sheltered with tephra and volcanic ash. and whiffs of black smoke drifting in the distance. The thick, yellow lava streams, levitated smoky tendrils and had drizzled into a winding river, flooding at the bottom of the volcano and shifted into molten rock, reflecting a red glow. A light breeze stirred through the undergrowth, shrubberies and gusted the balmy aroma from the blossomed flowers, through the verdant palm trees' leaves. I finally strode through the abundance of greenery and the wondrous exploration I had once yearned was now dissipated into exhaustion. It was on the seventeenth of September, we finally trudged through the mire clamped alongside the thickets, near the waterfall. Clarence, Nora and I trudged on the sticks and soggy leaves with a slowed pace. I stopped nearby a palm tree and inhaled the drifting, salty and sour seaweed engulfing the leafy scent of the forest. We strode through the bushes, bowing under the branches with the green ferns sweeping on our shoulders. We stopped at the periphery of the forest, treading on the dried dirt spread on the rocky precipice, overlooking the ocean. The sunlight warmed our cheeks and stung the lightly reddened welts, scratches and the small toothed bite holes on my arm, beneath my toiled linen shirt. I plummeted the pouch to the ground and smelt longer whiffs of the wind. I stared down at the enormity of the tropical rainforest; the huddled palm trees, ferns, coconuts and grasses, and the brook gurgling to the cascade spilling to the north-west province of the island. At nightfall, the palm trees slouched in the breeze, gliding the wilted, lush leaves and burning smoke from the volcano further out the sky above the ocean.

I still felt fatigued and weakened from escaping the cave.

Was Gharkoll alive? Had he temporarily escaped? Or, is he dead? I felt a presence standing behind me. I turned to see Nora.

"Oh," I began, "Hello, how long have you been standing there for Nora?"

"Not long," she said, descending the slope and moved closer towards me. "Are you alright?"

"I'm out of the cave," I said, with a simper on my lips. "I couldn't be better. How about you?"

Nora sat beside me.

"I'm the same. I thought I was never going to escape, though, I have something to ask you…" she trailed away, as if hinting it wasn't relative to the cave, Gharkoll and managing an escape.

I suddenly felt shy and my emotion flooded in the bottom of my chest.

"You can ask me." I answered.

Nora looked away from the sea.

"Why didn't you tell me how you felt?" she asked.

Nora traced her fingertips onto my hand resting on the leaves. I avoided her eye contact, watching the froth and water. I mustered enough courage and looked up.

"I was trying to survive," I said. "I was afraid of you refusing me, however, we did almost kiss. I suppose it should've shown how I felt about you."

"Really?"

Nora neared closer to me. My heart leapt a beat in my chest with a tingling nerve in my fingers.

"Yes," she said.

"Even after you rescued me, inside the cave?" I asked.

"Well," I said, avoiding her eyes and felt coy. I glimpsed down to the Pacific Ocean. "You were the captain's daughter."

"It doesn't mean anything," said Nora.

"Or, I was unsure if you liked my brother." I confessed, looking back into her brown eyes illuminated with bronze flecks and my cheeks flooded with warmth.

I held her hand.

Nora smiled and she shook her head.

"He's much too young for me." she admitted.

I grinned back and caressing her cheek, I plunged my lips into her mouth. We kissed amongst the sunlight beam flaring from behind the clouds and her curls waved in the wind alongside her shoulder. I pulled my lips away and I saw Clarence stood in the distance. He watched us in-between the trees and he turned, disappearing back to the grove. I released my clutch of her cheeks and leant my palms away from her jawbone. I traced my fingers along her chin and leant my forehead into her own.

"Clarence just saw us," I said. "I think he's upset."

"What?" asked Nora, glancing back to the forest. "He's not there."

"He was thought, I don't care anymore." I said.

I pressed my lips onto her moist lips again and we indulged into a long-lasting kiss with the white froth and waves plashing on the shoreline.

"He'll be over it." I said.

"You really believe it?" asked Nora.

I nodded. "He already knew how I felt." I said.

"Well, I hope he can find someone else," said Nora, kissing me again.

I embraced her waist. I heard footsteps thudding on the slope and to avoid being caught kissing, I turned around feeling embarrassed. I pulled away and hugged her, leaning my cheek against her face. I felt our warmth was being shared and embraced into one. I shifted my attention back to the sea, still feeling the imprint of her clamped lips on my own. *Would my brother care? Would he hate me? Would it affect our closeness if I made Nora, my girl?* I wondered, gazing afar in the distance.

I wouldn't want it. I love my brother.

A shadow appeared on the ground. I looked over my shoulder.

"Oh, phew, it's you." I said.

Clarence slapped my shoulder. I observed he appeared healthier with his arm bandaged and a dried cut beneath his lip. His cheeks weren't sallow and were flushed bright pink from the breeze. I was surprised with his cheery disposition.

"You're not worried, are you?" asked Clarence. "About Gharkoll ?"

"No," I lied. "I'm just wondering what happened to him, when he went inside the stalagmite."

"Me too," admitted Clarence, glancing out at the sea. "Do you think he's definitely still alive? Or, he suffocated himself in the stalagmite?"
We both grinned at the possibility and looked down to the ocean.

"I hope he did," I said, fading my smile and I straightened my lips with seriousness. "No, Clarence," I glanced back to him. "He's still alive."

"What did you see?" he asked.

"He dribbled liquid from his tentacles. I'm assuming he's going to be in the cave for a very long time." I said. "For how long? I don't know."

Did I ever want to return back to California, as a poor-rigger boy? No, I didn't, I had changed embarking on my adventure. The island was my free-dom. I stared at the cave in the distance, feeling satisfied I had escaped its shadowed entrapment with the belief of following the light amongst the darkness.

ABOUT THE AUTHOR

Bettina Victoria enjoys developing characters and stories. She wrote a few manuscripts, before she graduated with her creative writing degree with a double minor in literary studies and children's literature. A couple of these were *The Witch Haunting* and *The Cave Dweller*.